Private Dancers or Responsible Women

A Novel of Intrigue

by
Andrew Parkin

Strategic Book Publishing and Rights Co.
12620 FM 1960, Suite A4-507
Houston, TX 77065
www.sbpra.com

ISBN: 978-1-62857-431-9

Design: Dedicated Book Services (www.netdbs.com)

For Françoise

ACKNOWLEDGMENT:

I am indebted to Jack Stewart who read with great attention an earlier version of this book and to my editors and proof readers who saved me from a number of errors.

This is a work of fiction and any resemblance of its characters to real people is coincidental.

CHAPTER ONE

"It was such a gentle landing that there was a round of applause for the pilot. After a few minutes of taxiing, we were able to deplane. I stepped from the jet into that elephant's trunk tunnel reaching into the terminal building. It took only thirty-five minutes to go through immigration, find my suitcase on the baggage belt, and walk through Nothing to Declare. Straight to the car rental counter in the main concourse at Gatwick."

Paul took another gulp of very cold beer. "I was one of the weary bunches of red-eyed travelers in the terminal building," he continued. "Outside, the fresh air hit me and I was wide-awake, walking fast, and excited to be in the United Kingdom again."

Paul Wills, fair-haired, looked at his friend, Graham, as if challenging him to find England exciting. He raised his eyebrows above his dark blue eyes. They were having beers in a waterside pub near the small fishing town of Steveston in British Columbia. Flower baskets overflowed with green trailing foliage, fringing small red, blue, and white flowers outside the windows.

"That's pretty good going for exiting the airport hassle," said Graham Curtis, looking at his friend expectantly. He pushed his mop of dark hair back from his forehead.

"And I rented a category *B* car from their list. I drove to Cheltenham, where I stopped for a snack in a stale, smoke-smelling lounge of an old AA hotel. After that, I drove on to Malvern and checked into an old coaching inn called The Abbey."

"Sounds very British. Automobile Association, not Alcoholics Anonymous! I know the scene. Dusty drapes and worn carpets. Go on," commented Graham.

"It was quite good, actually. I settled in and wasn't hungry, so I went for a walk outside and then wandered into the bar for a drink and a few nibbles before turning in. Jet lag was catching up on me." Paul took a gulp of his beer.

"Cheers," said Graham and took another dose of the cold bitter he was drinking.

"Each cluster of events sprang without warning and in a particular place," Paul continued, lowering his voice. "They seemed at the time totally unanticipated and isolated from one another, until I associated them with an extraordinary woman."

"Ah, now we're getting there." Graham smiled, showing perfect front teeth.

"Seriously! I'm convinced that these events influenced my major decisions, the ones, I mean, that I took later. Did the events cause or bring about these decisions? Frankly, I don't know. Decisions that turned out to be lucky for me followed the events. Causes? Results? These remain . . . mysterious. Looking back, though, I feel that I was helped, perhaps guided, in ways I cannot understand, by a force that seems perfectly natural, yet in some ways totally unreal. I cannot explain, or explain away, what I experienced in Malvern and later."

" 'There's a divinity that shapes our ends, rough hew them how we may,' says the Bard. Was she good in bed?" Graham's pleasant Canadian accent added an edge to both remarks.

"There you go again. You married men! It wasn't like that." Paul laughed.

"You disappoint me. I thought this was going to be the beginning of a glorious new *something* after that unfortunate live-in affair you barely survived . . . what, a year ago?"

Paul raised his eyebrows, grinned, and then ignored Graham's remarks. "How many people encounter beings or forces who have helped them—or led them astray—forces that they cannot rationally assess?" Paul asked.

Not waiting for an answer, Paul added, quite suddenly, and in French, " '*Qui peut donc refuser à ces célestes lumières de les croire et de les adorer?*' Pascal's *Pensées*. In other words, 'Who could thus deny to these celestial luminaries belief and worship?' Now, after what has happened to me, I won't deny them."

"Nice translation, Paul. And who indeed would deny them anything, these extraordinary women!"

"Thanks, professor. A year after the Malvern episode, I had changed my life completely." After another sup of his beer, Paul cleared his upper lip of suds with a paper napkin and went on, "They simply happened, these events. I didn't plan them."

"Yes, but what events? Get on with it, man!"

"Why do visitors go to old churches and graveyards, Graham? Before going into the bar for my nightcap, I wandered out and unerringly homed in on the abbey's graves. My hotel overlooks the old abbey. The real one. I'm always intrigued by the ages of people at death. I deciphered some of the inscriptions on the flaking stones and felt the sadness of the deaths of the very young, while awarding a good innings to old codgers of eighty or more."

"I do that, too—a lot of people do that."

"I was too tired for sweaty discos, even if they exist in Malvern. I expect they do. So I went back to the hotel bar for a Chivas Regal served by a blousy barmaid, a ragged blonde with a Yorkshire accent. Her remarks to passing waiters usually ended with a "what?" rendered more as a statement than a question. A small jug of water came with my Chivas. The peanuts and raisins were enough to stay my stomach before I toddled off to bed at almost ten o'clock. Yes, that night in May . . . another life ago, because after that time in Malvern everything changed."

"Did the barmaid creep in for a goodnight roll in the sack?"

"She did not. In fact, I took a bath in the old tub with little curved feet—chic once more—and marveled at an Edwardian WC designed with a sort of shelf, so that whatever one deposited in the toilet could be inspected, presumably for any irregularities, before being flushed away."

"I'm not surprised that design went out," observed Graham, pushing his dark hair back from his forehead.

"Don't worry. Some smart designer will bring them back at double the price of a normal one! They'll turn up on eBay, if not already there, you mark my words. Anyway, the abbey clock struck ten. The bliss of being horizontal in a real bed, however old fashioned, flooded through me, though the hiss of aircraft air-conditioning still seemed to be with me."

"I know the scene all too well."

"Sleep! And then suddenly I was awake. The abbey clock struck and I counted seven chimes. I turned on the bedside light. My watch was showing 6:00 a.m. And I'd already changed it to local time, GMT, and all that." Paul leaned forward.

"Maybe you never learned to count properly. No, you probably missed out one or two circles of the old watch face," smiled Graham. Paul sat back and looked at his friend intently. Their eyes met, and they both smiled. They were old friends.

"No, Graham, I don't think so. The bedroom was now enormous. In fact, I appeared to be no longer in bed, but in a vast hangar-like building. I found myself walking rapidly towards the far wall, when a couple of swing doors were flung open and a hospital bed on wheels appeared, pushed by a bald, portly man in a white coat."

"Portly! Haven't heard that for a while."

"Yeah, well, he was an orderly, not a doctor, though his natural tonsure suggested some kind of monk. On the trolley-bed, a white sheet totally covered a person—newly dead? As I came up to him, the monk-like chap turned, indicating the trolley, and said in a South London accent, as barefaced as you like, 'Here you are, mate, wheel this into that room. I need a smoke break!' He just nodded his head in the direction of another pair of swing doors a few yards to my left. It never occurred to me to remonstrate or even to speak. I obediently, as one does in dreams I suppose, wheeled the corpse through the other swing doors, nudging them open with the end of the trolley."

"Always obey orders from barrow boys, Sunshine!" remarked Graham, taking another sup of bitter.

"If there are any barrow boys still barking around in London. I was in a small, clinic-type room with white tiles from floor to ceiling and a canister of liquid soap and a roller towel fixed to the wall. There was a sink and a cupboard with glass doors. Medical supplies were stacked on its shelves. I don't think there was a smell of disinfectant. Hospital smell! Not a sniff of one. Are there smells in dreams?"

"Search me," remarked Graham, smiling again at his friend.

"I was suddenly shocked to notice that a dusty brown lizard about seven inches long was standing in the sink, motionless. The tip of its tail was in the plug hole. Did this indicate that it had got in through the drains? Before I could speculate further, the corpse under the sheet sat up."

"No kidding!"

"The sheet slipped down, revealing a woman of extraordinary physical beauty."

"There you go!"

"She stepped from the trolley, perfectly alive and smiling," said Paul, as if he had not heard Graham. "She was naked. Her slender body was a milky coffee color. Her dark eyes were large and shone with attractive intelligence. Her breasts, perfectly formed, were beautifully finished by the darker nipples and aureoles."

"Aha!"

"Shut up, Graham. Do you want to hear this or not?"

"Okay, okay, carry on."

"Her hair was long and shiny black. She was so lovely that I felt no fear. Was she a vision? Was she a ghost? Was she a nurse playing a trick?"

Paul sounded serious, perhaps intense. Paul saw Graham smother an impulse to laugh.

"She approached me, holding her arms out slightly to the side so that she could hug me, and hug me she did. As she came closer, I looked into the velvet depths of her eyes and felt warmth and energy flooding into me. As she held me, I put one arm around her, feeling her soft curves, and, as I closed my eyes, felt the warm imprint of her lips on mine.

My left hand reached down and stroked her pubic hair. It was not silky, but tightly curled and scratchy— like a Brillo pan scourer!"

Graham let out a guffaw.

"No kidding. When you want to glow, get Brillo!" Paul gave Graham a do-me-a-favour look with a dismissive shake of the head.

Graham looked serious again. He wanted to hear the rest.

"I'm sorry, but that was the exact texture. I held her now in both arms, but it seemed that she held me in a stronger grip. My hands felt her back's silken flesh and then the unmistakable overlapping of feathers as on a great wing. She retreated from me, smiling, and turned to climb back on her trolley. Her arms had grown tawny, speckled feathers, like the ones on a thrush's breast, but edged with gold, and these framed her slender back, the wonderful buttocks, and the lean backs of her thighs and calves. She settled back on the trolley and closed her eyes. I walked to her, feeling immense longing and loss as I realized she was certainly dead."

"Dead, resurrected, dead. We sleep, wake, sleep. I get the picture." Graham smiled. He felt that he had gone too far. This was not a ribald barroom story. It was obviously important to Paul.

"Her nose was slightly more prominent now, her lips drawn back a little from her teeth, and her feathers were thick with dust, as though from spending millennia in some desert tomb. I covered her with the simple sheet, taking one last look at her altered face, rigid with its calm repose, as it confronted death. As I let the sheet fall over her, I hoped that if there's a God, her spirit would be blessed."

"I'm glad to hear that, Paul," said Graham, again keeping a straight face.

"You can laugh all you want, but I felt a sharp pang of loss once more. My eyes even filled with tears. I wiped them on my sleeves. Somewhat irrelevantly, I noticed that the lizard was no longer in the sink. I wondered whether I should wheel the trolley back or simply leave her in the room. In fact, I turned, still undecided, to find that I was miraculously outside the building and in a great sloping meadow of wild flowers."

"What did you do next?"

"I ran, holding up my left hand high in the air with my thumb extended. With this hand I had touched that lovely girl so intimately and instinctively. Now I seemed like a sort of priest, blessing the people coming up the slope towards me. I bounded along in that beautiful field, blessing everyone."

"Bless 'em all!"

"Oh God!"

"What? Go on. Honestly. You know me."

"Behind me I heard the abbey bell. I counted and, as it reached seven and stopped, I was sitting cross-legged like Buddha on my bed in the hotel bedroom."

"Seven again! Must be your lucky number. You're at a real crossroads, Paul. Seriously! Malvern's British camp, ancient Egypt, Buddha—that's heavy stuff."

"I *am* serious. The events of that dawn are as real and vivid to me now as they were then. I can't explain it, that hour, or non-hour, or where I had been, or whom I had met. Did I sleep or was I awake? Was it a dream or a vision? I know I was awake. Was it an out of body experience? The touch of that girl was very much an in body experience. Poets have spoken of waking dreams. Was this a waking dream? It seemed more substantial than a dream. I was aware of the abbey clock or bell striking seven when my watch showed six, and then it seemed it struck seven again. One hour or not of unaccountable, inexplicable vision, of dream-like reality or a realistic dream that I cannot explain took hold of me that dawn and seduced me. Yet, I was left with a greater sense of freedom, of limitless possibilities, of the welcoming mystery of life itself! I now felt no loss or sadness. This was a visit. I was privileged in some way I didn't really understand. And these words came to me out of somewhere, but from where I cannot say:

"Malvern Abbey's bells swing metal tongues across soft evening air. The weathered headstones imperceptibly subside above commemorated dust. Some tawny girl awaits me here at dawn. Fine high fashion bones grow living flesh again and worms have left intact that silken skin. Four thousand years focus on an image here. No breath, no sounds, come from her smiling mouth."

"Hey, that's okay. Not bad, Paul. Is it another quote?"

"I don't know. As they came tumbling into my head from somewhere dark and obscure, I scribbled the words down on a pad with a pencil I found on the little table next to the bed—the kind of night table that has a Bible in the drawer. But the words come back to me anyway. A few days later in a book I picked up in a library, I read, 'Our real tomb is the memory of the living; we are truly dead when they have forgotten us.' It was in a book by a couple of French writers, the Tadiés, called *Le sens de la mémoire*. Otherwise known as *The Meaning of Memory*."

"Well, you're a lucky man. Everything drops into place, without the drop of a hat."

"What was it, Graham? A dream? It all seemed real."

"Well, I think it was what used to be called a waking dream, just as you thought it was. You mingled Egyptian images with Gray's *Elegy* and Langland's long poem, "Piers Plowman," which begins in the Malvern Hills with a fair field full of folk."

"Hmm. I never thought of that. But what does it mean?"

Graham finished his beer. "I think it means that you were at a crisis point after your last love, and you need another one. You are also more creative. You're in touch with your Jungian anima, the sensitive, female part of yourself. That's what I think. You want another beer?"

CHAPTER TWO

The neat but tiny semi-detached house had door and window frames painted light blue and white. Mary parked her Volvo outside. She'd had an emergency earlier, but arrived in time to check that all was going normally during Nurse Reynolds' delivery of the baby.

There were no abnormalities evident during Mrs. Baxter's pregnancy and, as labour had already started, the midwife had assured Mary there were no complications so far. Mary had no objections to another home delivery by this midwife. The next tiny Baxter to arrive would be Nurse Reynolds' five thousandth delivery and counting, with another month to go before she retired.

Nelly Baxter was following the breathing exercises of the natural childbirth group Mary had recommended. She was sweating as she panted and pushed. The birth, it turned out, took less than four hours. It was Nelly's second baby. Nelly's husband, Ted, a blonde, prematurely balding young man with a frank smile and dimples, had opened the door, before Mary rang the bell. Alison, Nelly's slightly freckled, younger, and unmarried sister, was hovering on the stairs behind Ted. Mary swept a stray wisp of her black hair over one ear as she followed Ted Baxter and Alison up the narrow stairs, carpeted with an oatmeal-colored matting, like woven sisal. She loved Alison's auburn ponytail. Mary guessed that the girl had a boyfriend. The bedroom was not large, yet it was spacious enough for a double bed, built-in wardrobe, small kidney-shaped dressing table, two chairs, probably from a dining set, and a small cupboard near the little white cot waiting for the new baby. There was a bright yellow and rose-pink flower design on the curtains, a dash of color contrasting with the off-white matte paint of the walls. Mary gave cheery greetings to the pale young mother and elderly, rosy-cheeked midwife. Ted had arrived a few days earlier, back from work abroad.

"Tea anyone?" asked Ted. "I'll make it," he added, going to the kitchen, followed by Alison. It was just 11:15 a.m. when, after Nelly Baxter's final efforts of pushing and panting, her new baby came into the world in Sutton Coldfield and yelled with brand new lungs.

"It's a boy!" exclaimed Nurse Reynolds, beaming.

"Oh my, we wanted a boy this time," gasped Nelly. Ted ran in from the kitchen, leaned towards Nelly, and kissed her hair and hands. They had not urged their doctor to let them know the sex of the new baby. They wanted a surprise.

"Well, nurse, he's got a big sister as well as Mum and Dad to look after him," said Mary. She had looked after Nelly Baxter three years ago when Patricia—Patty as she was known—was born. They quickly wrapped the baby and put him into his mother's arms.

"Isn't he just grand?" asked Nurse Reynolds of the world in general.

"He's a lovely baby, Mrs. Baxter. You've done a wonderful job. Worth all that hard work, eh?"

"Ooh, yes, Doctor Rao. I'm glad I did that natural method. Thank you, nurse, and thank you, doctor." She smiled at her new baby and stroked his pink, slightly crinkled cheek. She thought, *He's got a look of Ted's grandpa.*

After Mary had checked mother and baby, and had seen there was no need for any stitches, Nurse Reynolds dealt with the placenta and recorded the baby's weight: 7 lbs. 2 oz. She measured him with her tape, which flopped, like a tongue, out of the mouth of a plastic Scottie dog.

"It looks like he'll be as tall as or taller than his father," said the midwife.

"Didn't you say he'd be a William or a girl would be a Karen?" asked Mary.

"John it is, after his granddad," said Ted.

"He's as pleased as Punch is Mr. Baxter! Just look!" Nurse Reynolds observed. "Yes. Who's a little scamp, then?" Ted, grinning broadly, stroked his son's head.

"Hairy little chap, isn't he? Not a lot of the Winston Churchill about this one, so far as hair is concerned."

Mary had heard her English mother say that although there was a song about Lloyd George's supposed promiscuity, all new babies nevertheless looked more like old Winnie. Mary glanced at the watch pinned at the midwife's ample bosom and checked her own wristwatch.

"Ted's got quite a few days before he has to be back at work?" she asked.

"Yes, little John took us all by surprise coming a day or two early," Ted grinned. He was very much a proud father. "He's a little eager beaver!" he announced, as he held out his little finger, hoping the baby would grasp it.

"But it works out all right, Doctor Rao, because Ted has two weeks of leave to be with us," said Nelly, once again a proud mother. Nurse Reynolds dabbed Nelly's forehead with a cool, dampened facecloth.

"That's good," nodded Mary, asking if Ted would be going abroad again.

"Yes, but not permanently. He goes back to Bahrain for a month, we're not sure when, and then he's posted back here for the next few years," Nelly informed her, as Ted held out a thick forefinger and stroked his baby's little puckered brow.

"Well, that's good. He'll be glad to see the children growing, when he gets back home. Well, I must be off. Surgery won't wait," said Mary, picking up her bag of tricks, as she called it.

"I'll call by tomorrow to see Master John and his mum. By the way, where's Patty?"

"She's out with Granny choosing a pair of white bootees for baby and a pair of sandals for herself. They'll be back any minute." Mary was about to leave, assuring Mrs. Baxter that she could telephone any time, if she needed help.

Alison, grinning and still sipping tea, suddenly said, "I can see you out, doctor."

"Oh, I'll let myself out, Alison, you finish your cuppa. Call me if you need me. But I'll look in tomorrow in any case."

"Thank you for everything, Nurse Reynolds and you, doctor," said Ted. Mary smiled, nodded, and went down stairs to a chorus of bye-byes.

Her cell phone rang as she got into the Volvo. It was Liz, her receptionist, who told her there was a confused old lady at the surgery with her daughter. It seemed quite urgent.

"I'll be five to ten minutes," said Mary.

She drove carefully, but quite fast through the housing estate, slowed as she passed the Elmsway Junior School, and then turned into the main road leading to her High Street surgery. It was raining and the streets were dismally wet. Sutton Coldfield, on a day when the sky was a huge wet blanket, was definitely not tourist brochure material. Mary was already thinking of taking her annual holiday in Goa. She parked at the back of the building and went into her premises by the rear door.

"I'm back, Liz," she said over the intercom system and pressed the green light button. The door opened and Liz, a confidant nurse-receptionist in her late twenties, showed a Mrs. Amphlett and her frail old mother into the office, announcing that she had already taken down the relevant details. Liz, glancing at her watch, went back to her desk at reception. There were no other patients as yet. One appointment had cancelled.

"We're not your regular patients, doctor, on account of we've not long moved here. But my mother got lost and ended up at the news agent's shop round the corner."

"I see. Well, let's check your mother's blood pressure. How are you feeling, Mrs. er . . .?"

"I'm Mrs. Horton, doctor. I've been a widow for twenty years," she added, with a note of pride in her quavering voice.

"Is that so? Well, Mrs. Horton, let's see now. It's Mrs. Amphlett, isn't it," said Mary, turning to the daughter.

"Who's Mrs. Amphlett?" demanded the old lady, looking from one to the other.

"I am, Mother. I'm Mrs. Amphlett. Tessa, your daughter."

"I know Tessa's my daughter," snapped the old lady. Tessa Amphlett looked at Mary with raised eyebrows. She sighed. Mary realized that Mrs. Horton had had a slight stroke. She discovered from the daughter that the old lady had been lost once before, just after they moved to the new neighbourhood.

"Not surprising, really, doctor. A move to a new place is a bit of a strain, especially for Mum. Besides, what else could you expect with identical houses and identical streets everywhere?"

Mary nodded and made a couple of notes. But this was a different, deeper confusion in the old girl. "Where's your new place?" asked Mary, jotting down the blood pressure figures.

The daughter gave her the address and then said, "The road from home to the paper shop, it's dead straight. It's only a five-minute walk. Luckily the girl in the shop had our address and telephone number, because we're now regulars and have papers delivered." Mary listened and then said she would get Mrs. Horton into hospital for observation. The daughter was a bit alarmed.

"Oh, it's better to be safe. They'll make sure she's comfortable and she'll probably be fit enough to be home again in a few days. Her own doctor and I can get her a bed in there."

"Well, doctor, if that's best, we'll do that; it's Dr. Anderson, only he's now a bit far away from the new place. He's on Handsworth Wood Road," said Mrs. Amphlett.

Old Mrs. Horton, peering from watery blue eyes, stated, "But I haven't been near a hospital or a doctor since Fred died. He always said they'd not get him under the knife." She lapsed into silence and stared ahead of her, perhaps into the past.

"You'll need a nightie and your toilet things. Glasses, books, or favourite magazines. There'll be TV, too," advised Mary.

"Well, when can she go in?" asked Mrs. Amphlett.

"Oh, straight away, after you've collected her things in an overnight bag. Don't worry. We'll phone Dr. Anderson. And the hospital. They'll be expecting you and your mother. You're lucky, Mrs. Amphlett. I know that just now there are some spare beds for a change."

"Who's Mrs. Amphlett?" asked the old lady.

Mary looked at the daughter who raised her eyebrows higher, as much as to say, There she goes again. The daughter had been undoing and then fastening again the little bone toggles on her light grey duffel coat throughout the consultation.

"I'm Mrs. Amphlett, Mum. It's me, Tessa!"

"Oh, yes, that's a good girl." She looked at Mary before continuing, "She's a good girl is Tess. Always has been. Always will be. She was brought up that way you know."

"Tessa, Mum. Tessa."

"I'm sure she was, Mrs. Horton," said Mary.

Since it was almost lunchtime, Mary suggested they take something with them to the hospital, perhaps sandwiches, because by the time all the formalities were completed, they might be hungry and lunch for patients would have finished.

Mary saw another patient (tummy trouble) and then asked Liz to ensure that Mrs. Horton and her daughter were coping with the admission to hospital. Frankly, Mary felt that the daughter was feeling better, even if Mrs. Horton herself were suffering from the inescapable effects of "anno Domini" as a colleague called it. The daughter looked tired and a little sheepish, as if she could be held responsible for her mother's condition and lapses of memory. She would appreciate having professionals take care of her mother for a few days. She certainly needed a break. Mary would phone Dr. Anderson for him to see Tessa Amphlett again later to convince her she was not in any way responsible for what was happening. It was nature showing her hand.

That afternoon Mary saw a procession of people with colds, then an adolescent with a fury of acne, another case of tummy trouble, and a frightened teenage girl who turned out to be pregnant. By the time she had finished for the day, she was exhausted. Liz appeared at the door, ready to go home, with make-up refreshed, and her streaky, highlighted, urchin cut teased up a bit.

"Doctor, this came for you. Anything else before I go?"

"Thanks, Liz. No, see you tomorrow."

Mary took the fat envelope Liz held out for her. Papers of some sort. Bedtime reading. More medical reports? No! It was from Paul Wills of all people. A brief note and a wad of papers.

CHAPTER THREE

Mary had almost decided to go to a chamber music concert that evening, but she didn't feel like venturing out in the rain after dinner. Instead, she went home where she checked the contents of Paul's thick envelope and found that it was a story of some sort. That could wait. But she could picture Paul as he was when she had last seen him. They got on well together. Always had done. Good friends. Or was there something more? She sighed. Then she added a little more to her fund of knowledge by reading a journal article about some of the latest developments in the treatment of Alzheimer's disease. Then she made a pot of Chinese tea. When it was ready, she settled down with a cup of the pale, yellowish-green tea and began to read what Paul had sent. Had it simply been a letter, she would have read it before leaving the office. There was, in fact, a very brief note and a wad of A4 typing paper. As she read, she felt that she needed to see him again. Did he need her? His packet occupied what was left of her evening. When she had finished reading, she knew she must see Paul and get a little closer to him.

Mary wondered what had really taken Paul, her good English friend, to Paris. She had, she remembered, felt at the time that he had been at a crucial point in his life. She wondered if he had made a decision to try to resolve a perhaps subliminal problem, or at least one that he did not want to discuss. Why did he now send her this account of some psychic turbulence? Did he seek her professional advice, no fees attached? She thought not. It was more a statement about himself. Perhaps, she decided, it was a revelation of himself that he was now intent on sharing with her. It was not a cry for help. It was more: this is what has happened; bear with me; I hope you will still be close, even though I am irrational and superstitious. It was almost, but not directly, a question: Could you want this person as more than a friend? A close friend? She let the matter rest at that.

Most people are superstitious and irrational, and Mary, despite her medical education, or perhaps partly because of it, knew she was, at times, capable of irrational lapses. She put the packet on the coffee table and went over to a bookcase. She took out a photograph album. Yes, there she was with some other students on the day she finished her internship. Paul was laughing, but looking away from the camera, distracted by someone, or boyishly shy. Ah, he had been a boy, really, even in his early twenties. Paul, she recalled, had been in town for a story. "A Crooked Alderman"? No, that was another article. In any case, the "gang" had gone for an Indian meal after the photograph. She had written to her father that she was keen on a young journalist. English. He had sent her a telegram saying, 'Nothing against them, now we're independent. Don't do it. Practise medicine before taking it!' Typical! It had arrived not very long before his death in a train accident in Uganda. He had been a good father, but was too often away on business. On the other hand, the deals he had done had left Mummy very well off. Mummy had liked Paul, though she had not seen much of him, and she had occasionally asked after him. Mary's most recent snap of Paul showed him with one arm over her shoulder. He was a man in this one. She would write to him when she had time.

***

About a week later, Mary received another package. It contained more autobiography and a postcard of an image of the disturbing statue in the Luxembourg Gardens of the giant Polyphemus surprising the lovers, Acis and Galatea. Mary had remained fairly close to Paul in her thoughts, even though actual meetings had of late been infrequent. Neither he nor she had proposed living together, and she didn't know what she would do if he were actually to suggest marriage.

It seemed clear from his papers, as she thought of them, that he was searching for a true mate. Both of them were still unmarried. He no longer had a significant other. *What a phrase*, she thought. He had lived with someone, but he had been alone for about a year now. She had better read the sheets and then write to him. She opened the second packet he had sent and read the contents at a sitting.

Events in Vancouver, British Columbia

The adventure was not finished and, I am sure, will continue until the end, whatever and wherever that may be. I am sure of this because of the events that followed the strange interlude in Malvern. On the flight back to Canada, my next stop, I read a little, drank a little, ate a little, and slept a very little. I planned my article on the Gold Rush Theatre in the Yukon and British Columbia. From time to time, my mind and my heightened senses felt again the presence of that angelic girl. I decided to give her a name. It was not easy. Nothing came to mind with that instant recognition of rightness. The letter *K* was as far as I got. I thought of her as someone beginning with *K*—but certainly not Kafka nor Kierkegaard! What I realized, as the plane touched down in Vancouver, was that I would attempt to write more prose poetry as well as verse. I was vaguely aware that one part of me was telling the rest of myself what to do. I knew also that now I would in some sense always be British as well as Canadian. The Pacific coast was like a vast mirror, its frame embossed with islands and mountains. I had come as far West as one can go from England. To go further was to go to the Far East. Perhaps that was also a portion of my destiny. Yet, I was now further from Egypt, the land that I knew unmistakably to be the origin of my Malvern angel. Was the vision a parting gift to one who must leave

Malvern, passing that iron bridge that cradled the Industrial Revolution, and choose the modern, the new world, the immense promise of Canada itself?

Mary broke off to get an atlas. She looked at the Pacific coast of Canada and the United States. It was remote! The Canadian cities seemed like small clearings in a vast forest. They probably were. It was the back of beyond. But California was there, too. Why did she not think of California as the back of beyond? *He gets around,* she thought. *Journalism,* she supposed, *involved travel and dislocation. The land mass was huge.* She settled down again to read.

Not long after I got to my digs, I made my way through the Vancouver suburbs to West Point Grey and went to look up some Celtic literature in the university library. Down in the stacks, I followed the usual path towards Irish literature. Suddenly, irresistibly, and irrationally, I turned down a different alleyway of books leading to another section. There was a T-junction ahead, and on the shelves blocking my way, a book commanded my attention. It seemed placed deliberately in my path. The book was by Flaubert. I took it down and opened it at random. I read, "Effect of her necklace between my teeth." I found an account of Flaubert and a friend taking a boat to a river town in Egypt. They had heard enticing accounts of a famous *almeh* or dancer, an expensive prostitute, called Kuchuk Hanem. Led to her house by a maid who pulled along with her a sheep, its wool dyed yellow, as a sort of advertisement for her employer, the two men encountered their object of desire. They paid her and, after a few customary preliminaries, they mounted her, one after the other. Kuchuk Hanem speaks to Flaubert with words I do not invent, but which come from my Saxon throat, on my Norman tongue, between my Yorkshire teeth, in a mid-Atlantic accent: "You call me 'star among almehs.' Does that mean you pay –Yes, I'll settle— more than the others? And I'll be your pet lamb, my fleece golden with henna! I'll use merely this tongue to repay indignities, this tongue you made a fetish. My kisses smack of luxury; your tongue is agile with foreign words. You seek your image in the mirror of my race. In the scent of roses warm from my breasts. I can see you still, my necklace of gold coins between your teeth. You stare into my eyes. As you spend, you growl like a tiger."

What impulse had sent me this outburst? Was it the ancient beauty I knew only as *K*? Was it the ghost of Kuchuk Hanem? Did my scarcely articulated *K* signify Kuchuk? I could not answer. I recognized, all the same, a heightened awareness in myself induced by the waking dream in Malvern and then by my chance encounter with Flaubert's Egypt! I felt the excitement of coincidence, coincidence that can be interpreted as a signal, a nod in the direction of some overall plan. I felt that I was involved with forces using me, doubtless for some purpose of their own. Yet, I was not the loser by this contact. I sensed benevolence and beauty of a strange order, rather than mischief or evil. This new consciousness of contact with a mysterious, liberating, yet demanding force, gradually faded, though, as the days of routine work swung me this way and that, caught in their momentum.

Mary stopped. She thought of Paul, wondering about forces. It seemed obvious to her that he was a man of his age. He was sweet. He was shocked by Flaubert's typical male escapade of certain nineteenth century artists. Paul had a sensitivity to the female that Mary found attractive. She felt sure that he respected her work. Hmm. Was he actually sublimating his desire for a good, satisfying, sexual relationship? Perhaps even a readiness for marriage? She looked at the page she was reading:

> Then one morning over breakfast, I opened the local paper to find that an exhibition of Egyptian antiquities from the time of Ramesses II was to open in Vancouver. Immediately I thought of drafting a popular piece, "Egypt, the Mystery and the Magic." And then I favoured rather an essay on this exhibition linking the Romantic poets, the early copiers of Egyptian hieroglyphics and tomb pictures, with Napoleon and his project for the description of Egypt, the discovery of the Rosetta Stone, the early interest by British amateurs, including Byron's friend, Bankes of Kingston Lacy House, the seminal John Wilkinson, the most professional of early explorers, and, of course, Shelley's response in "Ozymandias"— all these could wonderfully enrich the study of the period. So could a lively account of the decoding rivalry of the English and French scholars. That would sell a translated version to French editors. And this rivalry between French and British and others trying to decode the Egyptian hieroglyphics could actually be very exciting. All this came boiling up in my head. What an essay I would write! It would be scholarly, yet not stuffed with jargon. It would be lavishly illustrated and I'd sell it to an extremely glossy magazine. It could reveal how the Egyptian sources wound their way into the rich flood plain of nineteenth century European decadence, symbolism, and beyond—finding their way to Gustave Moreau and to Epstein's flying sphinx on the tomb of Oscar Wilde. The greater Vancouver public, and the tourists of course, would enjoy the exhibition, because of the stunning beauty of the artifacts as well as popular ideas of ancient Egypt, the curse of the Pharaohs, strange picture writing,

tombs with treasure, and bandaged mummies that resurrect to go on a rampage.

Mary's phone was ringing. She put down Paul's papers and answered. It was Nellie Baxter. She was agitated.

"Yes, I can be there in about ten minutes. Give him some water in his bottle. Don't worry." She rang off, got her bag of tricks, and rushed off to see what was wrong with Master John Baxter. On the way to the house, her thoughts kept coming back to Paul. His articles were selling. He was freelancing rather successfully now. Maybe she would invite him over to see her. She remembered her father's remark and smiled. Parents never quite realized just how worldly wise their children could be. "Don't worry, Daddy, I'm a big girl now and I know what I'm doing!" she said to herself and smiled as she parked. The front door of the Baxter's house opened as she was picking up her bag. Mary followed Alison who held hands with Patty Baxter, a chubby, auburn-haired, three-year-old with a friendly little face.

"Mum's upstairs and doesn't know what to do. Dad's out. It's something to do with going back to Oman," Alison informed her. Mary could hear the infant. Hiccups! There it was again. Nellie was nursing her little son and looked worried.

"I know it's only hiccups, but he just won't stop, doctor! It's on and on!"

"How long has it been going on, Nellie?"

"Over an hour. What can we do?"

"Let's see." Mary took the baby and rubbed his back and his tummy. He hiccupped again. "Do you have a bottle with a little warmish water and rose hip syrup?"

"Yes, I'll go and make it," volunteered Alison.

Mary examined the baby. No real problem. Perfectly healthy. He hiccupped. She picked him up and burped him again, patting his back.

"Here, doctor, here's that bottle."

"Thanks, Alison. Good. That's the ticket." Mary tested to make sure the syrupy water was warm, but not hot. There was a sound of contented sucking. Mary removed the bottle. The little brow puckered. Hiccup! She gave him the bottle again. He finished the drink. She removed the bottle. No more hiccups.

"Here, you take him again, Nellie."

A sudden, pungent smell filled the little room.

"Oh, he needs changing."

"That's nothing new," said Alison and grinned.

"That's nothing new!" said Patty and chuckled.

"Thank goodness for disposables!" exclaimed Nellie with a sigh as she undid the little plastic pants.

"Stinky poohs!" said Patty.

A sudden stirring and a jet of urine arced into the air before the new nappy was in place.

"Well, well, well!" said Mary, "What goes in must come out!" They all laughed. "He's more comfortable now. No hiccups."

"I'm sorry I troubled you, doctor, I was that worried when it kept on and on."

"Better safe than sorry. A boy of ten once had hiccups day and night for eight days—or perhaps eight weeks! Nothing much happened, it seems. He got back to normal. It's a little spasm of the diaphragm. But don't hesitate to call me."

CHAPTER FOUR

Mary was soon back home. She drank a glass of water and then poured herself a small glass of sherry with which to settle down again to Paul's papers. Where had she got to? Oh yes, here it was.

> I wanted to go alone to the exhibition to make some notes before getting down to the library for my article. Accordingly, a day after the opening, I went along to get my ticket. I was hoping for a reduction or even a free ticket by showing my press card. There were hordes of people milling around, all with the same idea, all eager to goggle at ancient Egypt. The lucky ones, already armed with tickets, stood patient as cows, in a long queue marshaled by attendants who let a group of people inside, only when word came that enough had left, so that there would be room for more. I thought the situation hopeless and resolved to return later in the week.

Mary sipped her sherry. This seemed an honest, but strange revelation of Paul to her, a trusted friend. Was it because she was a doctor? Was it that he needed her help? Her expertise? She read on:

> Suddenly a middle-aged woman brandishing a ticket was asking, "Would anyone like a ticket for Ramesses?" Before I could even turn towards her, an arm had shot past my chest, and another woman had snatched the ticket.
> "How much is it?" she asked.
> "Oh, give me ten dollars. That'll be okay."
> I realized how slow I had been, and I began walking past the head of the queue towards a ticket office. A

tall, emaciated man with no visible facial hair, not even eyebrows, approached me, his cheekbones almost like rods from which hung the concave, pallid flesh of his gaunt face. He wore a Stetson hat and a long, heavy-duty raincoat called in Australia a "dryasabone." It was not the usual rusty brown. It was black.

"Hey, pal, do you want this ticket?" His voice was a not unpleasant bass with a hint of a European accent.

"You bet. Thanks. How much do I owe you?"

"Zilch. I'm beat and can't take any more exhibits for today."

"Well, thanks, that's really kind."

An official standing near the entrance walked over to me and took my arm. "You can go in with the next lot, sir."

I was now at the head of the queue under a grey autumn sky with rain approaching. It was my lucky day. Luckily, too, we began to move into the tunnel-like entrance as the rain started. It was as if we were walking into a chamber in a great pyramid or maybe a lost temple. I heard the dull rumble of thunder from outside. We emerged into a room lit as if by torches in an Egyptian tomb. There was a close, sombre atmosphere from the subdued light. I lingered at a turn in the far wall to let the crowd go ahead. I wanted a bit of space. I would start with cases of exhibits where there were the fewest people. I turned a corner to go into the main exhibition room. It was then that I saw her, majestically larger than life. It was the girl of my Malvern vision—fashioned in gold. Her winged arms were held out to me. On her perfect features was all the serene grace of the goddess she must be. The beauty of the statue was overwhelming. My eyes swam with tears. I was unsteady, my knees trembling. I could not stand. I sank onto my knees;

one hand trying to steady myself on the metal legs of what I saw later was a glass-topped case. The golden statue seemed larger now. I could hardly breathe. It was as if some spirit were holding me tight enough to squeeze my heart and lungs.

"You, you are here," I gasped.

"Are you okay, sir? A glass of water?" The attendant looked at me anxiously.

"No, no, I mean I'm fine, thanks," I said, glancing at the young man. I was dabbing my eyes. I got up, steadied myself, and just stood there, I don't know how long, looking at the golden figure whose beauty was like a physical as well as emotional encounter. A sensation of total aesthetic pleasure had taken me and held me without letting go. Was it religious awe as well as beauty that had me in its power? Then I brushed the question aside. I decided I had to see other exhibits. Glancing at the case beside me, I saw an assortment of small objects—the bibelots of a king. The smallest of these objects caught my attention and I kept looking at it again and again. After wandering among the other exhibits, I returned to the glass-topped case for one last look at this smallest piece of carved loveliness.

It was a bit of wood, about four centimetres long, fashioned into the naked form of a young woman swimming, her arms and hands pointing straight ahead, and her slender legs stretched straight out behind her. This simple wooden figure was an inconspicuous, four-thousand-year-old masterpiece. It caught and held me in its force field. It was a sort of compass needle, maybe pointing out directions. I was drawn to it—or her. I loved that swimmer. And I loved the artist who had fashioned her. The figure was so arranged in the case that its arms pointed straight towards the golden goddess. Again, fragmentary words came to me out of some other level of being: 'You cleave the river's flood with grain-breasts seal-smooth. I will not let you drown under waves of indifference. Slide, little swimmer, slide like a splinter through my soul.'

It had stopped raining when I got outside. There was even some sun. It was like coming out of a film in the mid-afternoon.

That evening I was sitting at home reading Flaubert's *Salammbô* when the phone rang. It was my friend, Graham, calling from a colleague's place near London. He told me he would be back in Vancouver in a few days' time. I said to hurry so that he could go to the Egyptian exhibition. And then I told him a little rhyme that came into my head from childhood, but was wrenched into another dimension by something involuntary in me, something that came out of me as he was talking and which was beyond my control:

Hey diddle diddle
The cat had a riddle:
Queen Nût jumped over the moon.
The dark hound god laughed
To see such sport
And the fish
Swam out of the tomb.

I laughed. "I'm sorry, Graham, I didn't mean to say that."

"Well, I'm glad you did," he replied, "See you in Vancouver."

Mary loved the little swimmer. Paul was making too much of coincidence. It was, she surmised, his way of finding order in chaotic experience. Order made to measure, yes. The supernatural—no. It was the way his subconscious was ordering things that would become part of his writing of essays, poetry, stories. She tidied the papers she had read and then decided to write to Paul there and then. She glanced at the clock. It was past eleven and she was tired. She'd write in the morning.

Sutton Coldfield

Dearest Paul,

I'm using Sunday morning to jot down my impressions of the bundles you sent to me. Are those extraordinary events autobiography or fiction? You claim it all happened as you describe it. If so, I'm intrigued. If it's fiction you are pretending is autobiography, then I'm a bit lost. Of course, I'm not a literary critic, but I cannot really identify with anyone mentioned in the events. I am just giving you my honest reactions. Like a true friend. I don't see much connection between the events either, except for the idea that you have had a paranormal experience with a phantom who, you think, returns again and again. It's shards of ceramic as if a pot has been smashed and you cannot see the whole design. Or a mosaic. Crazy paving, you said. As writing, it intrigues me. Your ideas for articles seem fine.

If it all really happened, though, I cannot give you expert guidance as a mere GP. My advice is that you see your own doctor and get referred to a specialist in counseling, if you think it might help. How you do that in France I haven't a clue. You might be better advised to do it when you're in the United Kingdom.

Now I'll talk as a good friend, though a bit of me, the medic, might show up. But please don't treat it as what I would say to a patient. That would simply be, as I said just now, to get some counseling. I've read a bit of Freud in my time and some Jung, but neither really helps me much in practical ways. I think frankly that you are working too hard, or have been, that you're very tired, and that you're suffering from stress. After all, yours is a pretty stressful job—deadlines, editors breathing down your neck, uncertain income. I don't need to tell you.

When you arrived in Malvern, you were really tired from a long-haul flight. I think you were dreaming in a special way. What might be dream or even vision can be explained like this: you dream and something wakes you, but you are so tired that your mind is still in dream mode, though you think you are normally awake. In fact, you were only partly awake.

The other events are different in kind. Your sensitivity to Egyptian art provoked the dream in Malvern and encouraged you to connect it later on with Flaubert and the exhibition in Vancouver. But that's not supernatural. Turning off your path and going down a file of books and finding one you weren't looking for is normal library experience. I think you actually met the people you describe at the exhibition and you were lucky. They were not phantoms or spirit guides.

When you have got time to rest and you are on an even keel, or back to normal, you will meet someone you want to live with. She will not be a phantom, but a person who is loving, companionable, and friendly. She will be mysterious, because we all have our mystery. We are not mere chemistry. You'll marry, I hope, and it might all work out well.

By the way, when are you going to propose to me? Don't worry; we have the channel between us. Actually, I'd be a hopeless wife. It's as much as I can do to try to be a good GP.

Look, I must close now, but you know where I am, if you need me. I'm serious about the holiday. Your life is full of news stories or investigations that are mainly traumatic and depressing. Drop everything, Paul, even for a few days, and give editors the rejection slip! When you feel ready, come to Sutton. I can put you up for a few days. I have a room for guests. You know my routine. You'll see me in the evening. Thanks for letting me in on your inner life through this writing. You know I'm scientific and practical. It's brave to show it to me. I do respect your own sense of the extraordinary, even though I'm not into paranormal experience. It reveals more about you than about the other world. And that's why I

Love you, sceptically,
Mary

CHAPTER FIVE

A few days later, in his Paris apartment, Paul read and reread her rather untidy scrawl in the purple ink she always used He saw her pretty face framed by tendrils of hair breaking away from the French pleat she had when he had last seen her. He saw her writing on a letter pad, balanced on her knee, one leg crossed over the other, a shoe hanging free of her heel, and held only by her toes. She was smiling and her dark eyes twinkled as she wrote. She frowned a little when she was sincere and serious in what she was writing. All she said made sense. But he didn't believe it. Okay, she could explain a waking dream. But the deaths and resurrections of *K* had all been one woman's. He must send her the Kalitza sheets.

Paul looked out of his window at the old, ivy-covered wall opposite across the inner courtyard of his building. Sutton Coldfield! God, she had been writing the letter only three days ago. How many prescriptions had she doled out since then? Perhaps he should do as she advised and rest for a few days. Did she do that? Did it keep her sane in the face of the idiotic, bureaucratic, necessity of the penny-pinching National Health Service? Maybe a few days in a picturesque village in *la France profonde* would be just what the doctor ordered. He didn't like the idea of a health farm, even in a chateau. All those flabby people sweating it out on muscle machines, health drinks, and boxes in which you were steamed like a fish, massage. Massage! But not by lissom beauties. By hard-bitten men and women slapping you around to earn a tough living. Now wait a minute, massage wasn't a bad idea at all! Maybe he should go to Sutton Coldfield and get massage on the National Health. He didn't want a shrink as some Americans and Canadians so wisely call them. He didn't need to be shrunk. Not at his age. In fact, his ego needed a boost. "I need to grow and spread my wings," he murmured.

A bird flew out of the ivy and perched on a nearby silver birch tree. *Well, fancy that*, he thought. The bird looked warily around. A pigeon appeared and landed near the top of the same tree.

Paul looked at his watch. Almost time for lunch. He could write another paragraph or two just to show willing to his editor before breaking again. He did not write, but sat gazing at the spine of Brewer's *Dictionary of Phrase and Fable*. He would telephone Mary tonight. He had known her so long as a friend, that he had forgotten she was a . . . desirable woman! No. He could picture her very clearly. She was an attractive woman all right. She seemed very adult. If he went to see her, perhaps he would be helped by her common sense. Perhaps that's what he needed. 'The Mixture: Common Sense. Take three times a day with or without dreams.' Immediately he felt happy. Yes. He would go to Sutton Coldfield of all places.

***

The sun went behind a cloud, the courtyard darkened, and Paul suddenly felt cold. An idea came to him. It was grim and unrelenting. It could not be dismissed. It came back to him each time he vainly tried to think a different thought. *If he saw Mary and became closer to her, perhaps even proposed to her, she would surely die. She would not come back to him. She did not believe in such things. He must not see her. He was doomed to lose any woman he loved. It was better to stay away. Live alone. Never be involved again.* He felt a great gloom spread through him. He got up and paced the room. This was a terrible thought. He must shake it off. He was under a sort of spell that was bent on binding him now instead of liberating him. Looking out into the street below, he saw an old man labouring along with a stick in one hand. The man stopped. A woman stopped also and chatted to him. *The old people of the neighbourhood. They laboured on until the end. Life is too short. No, it's too long. No, it is short and not to be wasted by indecision and dread.* He decided to post to Graham and Mary his adventure in Hong Kong. He then resolved to telephone Mary that evening; there was no point in disturbing her at the surgery. Meanwhile, after the post office, he would go to that bistro which presented sangria and olives on the house to customers staying for lunch.

Paul locked up and went down the winding wooden stairs—late nineteenth century—to the entry hall with its mosaic tiled floor. He walked across the bluish dolphin picked out of green wavelets and the orange circle that framed it all. At the row of mailboxes, he found nothing but a publicity sheet from a locksmith who could also supply bulletproof sheet metal doors. *Handy*, thought Paul, *but what a pity there's no advertisement for bulletproof vests to go with the doors.* Smiling to himself, he stepped out of the hallway into the paved courtyard. Nothing was stirring. He strolled to the large doors that let onto his street, pressed the button to unlock them, and went out into the usual traffic noises of the neighbourhood.

***

After the habitual queue of the resigned and the glum in the post office, it was a relief to walk among the bustling people on the street as he made his way to the bistro. The sangria was in a large jug on the bar's counter. Paul made for Mme. Laborde and shook hands. He felt he was now a bit of a regular.

"Bonjour, messieurs, dames!"

"Comment allez-vous, ça va, Monsieur?" Mme. Laborde asked, looking at him with her large blue eyes and flashing a bit of gold as she smiled.

"Oh, ça marche, et vous, madame?" Paul replied. He looked around for a suitable table in the cramped little dining area. There was one near the window, well enough away from the would-be smoker at the counter, a beefy, unshaven

man with a large dog, a German shepherd crossed with another less distinctive breed, perhaps a retriever.

"*Je m'installe ici, madame?*"

"*Où vous voulez, monsieur. Vous vous installez. Voilà.*" Paul sat on the bentwood chair and unwrapped his place setting from its napkin. Mme. Laborde appeared with sangria in a small earthenware jug and with a glass dish containing plump black olives, gleaming like wet pebbles from a riverbed.

"*Voilà. Vous commandez quand vous voulez, monsieur.*"

"*Très bien, merci. Ah merci.*" Paul thanked her twice, because she had also brought a morning newspaper with her to the table. *She is thoughtful and she deserves to make a go of this business*, he thought. He opened the paper as he took a sip of sangria. The newspaper was much concerned with rumours about the latest political scandal. *Precious few facts*, he thought, scanning the articles with a professional eye. *Lazy. Not probing investigation. Rhetoric and a bit of hearsay about the inevitable Swiss bank accounts.* He looked at the wall, where the blackboard listed the lunch choices. He'd take the steak and fries followed by plum tart. He started the crossword puzzle and finished his glass of wine. He poured himself another from the little jug. He ordered his meal and then reread Mary's letter.

He realized that she cared about him. Seriously. Did he care enough about her? Yes, yes. Enough! Enough for what? The church bells started ringing loud and clear from the direction of the crossroads. Marriage? Why had that come into his head? What a hope! As he listened to the bells clanging a hundred yards away, Paul realized he could not ignore the fact that he himself was at a crossroads. Was it Dostoyevsky who had asked himself why he always found digs near a crossroads with a church on the corner? Or was it Kafka? No, Dostoyevsky. The *Notebooks*. Paul decided to see Mary as soon as possible. Her letter had mentioned marriage, but then rejected it as a sort of joke. But was it? For her, perhaps. *For me*, he thought, it's . . . *a new responsibility*. Mary and

Kalitza in all her incarnations had brought him to this turning point. Mary was waiting. Was she waiting for *him*? Had she made scales fall from his eyes? He felt a surge of energy. *Free energy.*

CHAPTER SIX

Graham Curtis sat in the kitchen having a coughing fit. He had given up smoking some time ago and was now, he hoped, helping his lungs to recover. The coughing had diminished considerably and Graham looked forward to breakfasts without any coughing at all. He selected a couple of slices of multigrain bread and dropped them into the parallel slots in the toaster. The paper he was writing for a conference was at a standstill, because he had to finish a stack of student papers he was grading. All the news in the front-page headlines of his morning paper was bad. He sighed and sat scanning the paper until the kettle whistled. He made of a pot of tea. There was some of a neighbour's homemade marmalade left in a recycled jam jar. The toast abruptly popped up and sat peering at him over the chrome edges of the toaster slots. Graham buttered his toast, a paltry two slices rather than a Dickensian haystack, and put a spoonful of the marmalade on his plate. The jar bore a handwritten label of the sort that come in a long roll suitable for computer address book printouts. It proclaimed: 'Donna's Very Own Vintage Marmalade.'

As he tasted this morning's dose of Donna's expertise, Graham said aloud, to the world in general, "Donna, you're a genius!"

Oh, one more piece, why not? He pushed another slice of bread into the toaster which immediately popped it up again. Graham looked at the toaster belligerently. He pressed its little black handle down again. This time the toaster glowed and went to work. "Don't try any funny stuff on me, you little twit," he muttered to the toaster. His hair was flopping forward as usual. He swept it away to the side with his hand. He, as a professional person and a mature human being, was determined to get the better of inanimate objects, whenever possible. He also liked to lecture them, as if they were perverse slaves who needed reprimands. He counted himself, however, as a latter-day Aristotelian, a scientific humanist, rather than a primitive animist. When he read ghost stories, usually in preparation for some junior undergraduate course, he found them neither mysterious nor frightening, but irresistibly humorous, even if the humour happened to be largely unconscious. Indeed, when he taught "The Ancient Mariner" even, he revealed its sly humour rather than dwelling on supernatural dimensions. He reveled, as did some of his students, in his reading aloud, in a supposed Coleridge-type Devonshire accent, the passage about all manner of slimy sea creatures. Of course, the famous "Kubla Khan" was a veritable treat in a real Devonshire accent or even the BBC's "Loamshire."

Graham spread his third piece of toast with butter and Donna's marmalade. He proclaimed to all their friends and to Donna in particular that the special homemade breakfast fare was at once as luscious and tangy as Donna herself. The net result was that Donna gave Graham and Jacqueline two pots every year without fail.

After breakfast, he went to retrieve the mail from a row of mailboxes further down the street. The system speeded up delivery, it was said. Back home again, he walked up the half dozen stone steps to his Oxford blue front door and let himself in while reading a postcard from Corsica. *Heinz and Gill do get around*, he thought, making the following mental note: Memo to self from self: Take Jacqueline to Corsica for a holiday. He opened the large packet from Paris. It was a bunch of typed pages from his good friend, Paul Wills. Graham thought it must be a novella or even a novel. Memo to self from self: Go to Corsica via Paris.

Graham read the package at a sitting. It was the rigmarole about a dream in Malvern and some other stuff about Paul in Canada. *To hell with grading and to hell with conference papers! Paul deserved a reading.* And so the morning passed. He was thinking over Paul's narrative as he quickly prepared his lunch. It was a black pudding sliced down the middle "from the nave to the chaps," its semicircles of blood and fat making a circular space he filled with coleslaw to make a homely, if somewhat savage, edible design on the plate.

"Ah," murmured Graham, when he had devoured one half of the blood sausage, "the new moon wi' the auld moon in her arms!" He then repeated this in a Devonshire accent. While tucking into this lunar concoction, he decided there and then to write a letter to his old friend and fellow-me-lad, Paul.

5864 Macrae St.
Wednesday

Dear Paul,
    You will be amazed to get so rapid a reply from the likes of me, but I am myself amazed that you are living through an adventure part surreal, part paranormal, and part entangled in some sort of secret self-shemozzle. Do you really believe in the supernatural or have you been to Ireland on holiday and frequented the village shebeen? I predict that the whole goddamn shebang will continue and get out of hand unless something is done to keep you in order. In fact, as soon as we can get away, I plan to take you on holiday with us to Corsica, God and Jacqueline willing. As a formative influence on no less a person than Bonaparte, Corsica would, I think, encourage you to brace yourself for an injection of realism into your system. Your professional pals have perhaps made you prone to accept the fantasies that nowadays pass themselves off as celebrity journalism. Is Elvis still alive? Will Princess Diana resurrect, etc. And if you're a secret agent with journalism as a cover, you should drop it all and run for safer cover—what better place than Corsica?

The letter then changed tone as Graham mentally donned his academic cap and gown. As he thought things over when he had finished, Graham told himself that he had written Paul a long, friendly, and thoughtful letter. After the jocular beginning that was always necessary in their letters to each other, he had picked up on the obvious, but probably unconscious mythological aspect of Paul's largely—as he deemed it—irresponsible imagination. Graham was firmly convinced that the *K* woman was certainly not a goddess, nor an angel. She was not even a mummy. Paul's separate encounters were with different parts of his Jungian anima. They had looked alike because Paul wanted them to look alike, and, believing *K* to be supernatural, Paul would think the women were identical because, in mythological terms, they probably were, the same goddess in different incarnations. There were some thirty of them, Graham suggested in his letter, all born to the same woman, a very beautiful Greek. Whether they all had the same father was a question Graham left unresolved for Paul's journalistic mind and its imagination to grapple with. It was clear, though, that in each case the father had been either Egyptian or Asian. That there were thirty of these tall, very beautiful, winged sisters was, as far as Graham was concerned, a given of the situation Paul had stumbled into. Graham had advised, too, that if Paul were in future to encounter any of these sisters, he had best act with extreme caution, preferably beating a hasty retreat. He should beware of any tall, emaciated stranger bearing gifts. He was clearly from a kind of underworld, a modern Hades. Proserpina and Dis?

On the historical as well as mythological level, these sisters were matriarchal. They were, he warned, as murderous as they were enticing. A postscript advised Paul to look at the painting "Wounded Angel." He wondered, as he was sealing the letter, how a modern journalist could get into such a frame of mind, a sort of psychological scrape.

In fact, he would telephone Paul right now. He'd probably catch him just getting ready for bed. He rang the number and heard the single tone repeated several times. He thought,

I'll get the answering machine, when suddenly Paul said, "Wills. *Allô. Je vous écoute.*"

"Ah, Paul, it's Graham. You're not already half asleep? I hope I'm not disturbing you?"

"No. Just reading . . ."

"Good. I got your packet of this ongoing story of the *K* woman/Egyptian goddess, et cetera. I've written some reactions that I hope will help you to clarify these experiences. You'll get them in a day or two, if there isn't a Canadian postal strike . . ."

"Or a French one!"

"Or both! But I suddenly got the urge to speak to you without delay. This *K* woman has a particular project. She defies not only reason, but all male authority. As an intelligent modern man, a confirmed reader, and one who takes a keen interest in contemporary politics, I feel that women deserve all the support they can get to pursue education to the highest levels and to embark on any career for which they show the potential to acquire a competence."

"Well, yes," said Paul, sounding slightly puzzled.

"I believe, too, that equal pay for equal work is self-evidently just. At the same time, there have to be controls, in order to ensure the equality with men, not the superiority of women over men."

"Well, yes, okay," said Paul. "So where do we go from here?"

"Paul, I just want you to realize that your encounters show a deep mental rift between the *K* women and modern civil society. I'm thinking of taking Jacqueline to Corsica for a holiday, calling on you in Paris en route in order to chat about this *K* thing."

"Great. It will be fun to see you and Jacqueline again."

"Perhaps we might all go on to Corsica together. In any case, Paul, I think the *K* woman or women are agents at once of the liberated libido and of some dark, essentially illiberal, and irrational spirit. This ambivalent role is part and parcel of your psyche, Paul, of your distinctive vision. I think you see *K* as a sort of Persephone."

"You don't say! Well, I'm sending you my adventure in Hong Kong. See what you make of that."

"Hong Kong, eh? Can't wait. These women are in some sense more powerful than you imagine. You are in touch with what Yeats might have called the great world eagle spirit, had he lived among the Pacific coast Indians, Musqueam Indians in the 1870s."

"But he didn't."

"Just as well!"

"Ah, you assume that visionary experience has its origins in the psychology of the seer and his culture."

Graham considered this for a second or two and then continued, "Well, let's say I prefer Jung and Claude Lévi-Strauss to Freud, with specific reference to sociological and anthropological ideas. Oh, I admire Freud as a writer rather than a shrink."

"I thought Levi-Strauss made blue jeans . . . just kidding. But I suppose you consider Freud more experimental than clinically useful, more literary than scientific, more speculative than rational, more improbable than provable."

"Absolutely! Couldn't have put it better myself. Freud's best read as a late nineteenth century writer as distinguished for his biographies of patients as for his fictional brand of science. The Frenchman, Lacan, would have been well advised to take this into account in his own deliberations. Though they, of course were usually centered on Lacan himself and his ever fatter pay checks. I would always temper psychological explication with some very welcome, let's say—scepticism. Even someone as slippery as Lacan can be gullible in his use of Freud. He probably went too far as well with Saussure's linguistic theories."

As he spoke, Graham remembered an occasion when he had once mentioned this view, frowned upon in the English departments he had known and done without, at a smart cocktail party in London. A certain Professor Eskobar? No . . . He could not pin it down. But a distinguished professorial guest had smiled and nodded at him, but had made no comment. Others had turned away as if he were suffering from some terrible contagion of which they were afraid. Graham preferred walking in his own mental groves to running along the tracks (or grooves) of other men's systems and jumping onto passing bandwagons.

"Great fun, Graham, but what is it I have been through?"

"Yes, well, I wonder whether I have the complete picture. What I have read makes me think that these events are best thought of as a series of advances along a new path of thought, or perhaps a very old way of thinking, that you have embarked upon, without realizing the fuller implications of the events. You seem to be thrashing about in the thickets of theory without realizing it."

"There's more. I'll fill you in when we meet. Or I'll send another package when I get another chance to write things down."

"Does it kind of help to get it down with pen and ink? Sorry, ink jet or laser."

"Yes, it does. It makes a welcome break from my bread and butter writing. It's almost as if I'm writing fiction about somebody else."

"Paul, my friend, you've arrived at what we, in the groves of academe, would call a post-Marxist vision appropriate to a post-culture."

"Wow! You don't say! Did you explain this in your letter? I'm not really with you."

"Exactly. I thought it best to talk about this straight away. Hence, this call."

"Is it a sort of new/old mode of thinking you've pinpointed?"

"You're getting there, Paul, but we should talk post-modernist ideas of post-culture over a drink, face-to-face. Better still over a few drinks. My letter, you'll see, has a few things to say on a theoretical level. I don't know whether you've looked into theory very much, but your encounters always leave something unsaid. You write not so much about events as about absences. This is commonplace. It's true of almost everything we say or write; it's true of my own very dissimilar experience of life."

"Well, every writer or speaker knows it's impossible to cover everything. You have word limits. There isn't a book of everything."

"I wish students realized that."

"That sure comes from the heart, you know."

"You bet. For one thing, I'm a believer in what I call 'cautiously enlightened rationalism.' I don't believe in noble savages or noble students for that matter. In both cases, their existence was posited by irresponsibly optimistic do-gooders. That's obvious. I don't remember myself as noble during my days as a student."

"You can say that again!"

"I'll ignore that. And my quarrel with the Eden myth is that neither Adam nor Eve nor Pinch Me had ever been innocent or blameless. In fact, evil existed from the origins of human experience. God himself, if he existed, had envisioned evil and incorporated it as an element in his plan. Adam and Eve—or humanity—evolved or was created, please yourself, to be innately capable of evil and goodness, rather than eternally young and innocent."

"When do you think you'll be coming this way?" Paul yawned, covering the phone's mouthpiece and wondering how to extricate himself from Graham's flight of philosophical folderol. He hadn't realized that the experiences were so real to his friend as well as to himself.

"As soon as we can get away. I'll e-mail. Okay?"

"That'll be good. Nice of you to ring, Graham. It's good that you don't just ignore these weird things."

"What are friends for? Be seeing you. Take care."

"So long."

CHAPTER SEVEN

Graham sucked on a choc-ice and then contemplated the creamy-brown, tongue-shaped mass still adhering to its flat little stick. This was the last of the supply he kept in the freezer compartment of the refrigerator. He picked from the side of the ice cream an oblong fragment of chocolate which he then savored as it melted in his mouth. Paul, he felt, was adopting a subaltern posture with the *K* woman who, in colonial times, would have been playing subaltern roles. Paul was as subaltern as he was nostalgic, as nostalgic as he was stubborn, and as stubborn as he was lovelorn. He had probably read too deviously that fashionable, influential, stimulating but flawed book, *Orientalism.*

From a theoretical point of view again, the number of sisters could be any multiple of three. The three weird and wicked sisters of *Macbeth* (Graham touched wood at this point) could well turn up in Paul's phantasmagoria, just as easily as might the sacred Nine. Theoretically, Paul would have further encounters with the sisters; all these subsequent meetings would be just as inexplicable, logically, as were the previous ones. But they would be more dangerous, even to life and limb, unless Paul could resolve the curious work his mind was engaged in. *And,* thought Graham, *the last encounter will either be a triumph or a disaster.* As soon as he had expressed this proviso, however, Graham promptly modified it. After all, he had reasoned in his letter, was it not a mere sentimentality to suppose that any encounter, any event, any person, was explicable? A journalist, like Paul, should at least know that people were ultimately inexplicable. Or were they? This additional insight and uncertainty—or was it ambivalence?— led Graham to the level of literary interpretation. Reading over Paul's essentially inexplicable events, Graham had realized that their inexplicability was not sentimental, in the way that even the toughest, most nightmarish crime fiction sometimes was. At the heart of all explained characterization and, indeed, crime, there existed a neat mechanism too much like an engine whose parts were greased with gooeyness of feeling. Of course, Shakespeare, in a masterly stroke, avoided this modern sentimentality by making Iago refuse to explain himself and his actions to the authorities, or to express remorse, or even to elaborate, even in the most oblique way, on what he had done to Othello and Desdemona, to Roderigo, to Cassio, and to his own wife, Emilia. Iago! Santiago! Santiago de Compostella, the ultimate pilgrimage. Various routes led to Santiago, as they no doubt did to Iago. The ironic phrase, "honest Iago" summed up the profane wretch who seemed a good fellow. There was a pilgrimage of mankind towards grace or Santiago and another towards damnation, or Iago himself. The Moorish empire had been overthrown and the colonial masters driven back to Africa. The Empire had fought back. Paul had felt a sudden grace and liberty at Malvern. Wasn't that the Brits' last stand in the face of Roman colonialism? But Graham feared that what now awaited Paul was a pilgrimage to the icy kingdom of evil. The man in the dryasabone, emaciated, skull-like of visage, in fact, in the ticket incident, was he a lord of darkness, a freezing of the spirit? Paul had better be careful.

Graham had thought fairly deeply about the possible religious and moral level of Paul's experience. He had decided he could not comment on those particularities. It would be impertinent, indeed intolerable, to do so. Yet, he asked himself if Paul's dreamed up experience had in the end been religious. From a moral point of view, he decided that Paul was, for an unmarried man, a very decent fellow. And was he, Graham, a married man, a very decent fellow? It suddenly struck him as strange that their friendship, over the many years they had known each other, had not once led him to think of Paul, or indeed himself, as a moral being. Moral choices and crises that could have made morality a crucial crossroads in the relationship had never occurred.

Everything had been . . . what? . . . comfortable? No. Empirical, if anything. He was an empiricist and had always been one. But what was Paul?

Graham thought that moral choices appeared only when human beings were not struggling simply to find the next meal, to support mere life. When people had enough to eat then they could afford to have moral scruples. At this stage, though, the issues were often so complex that they were beyond the reasoning powers of a majority of human beings; they were resolved sometimes only by instinctive action. He had not put this idea, though, into his letter. Better let it *simmer*, he thought, *a while longer*. He really had to see Paul in person. The Corsican jaunt was the answer. Or maybe somewhere in North Africa. Morocco? He would have a stopover in Paris or the United Kingdom. Graham finished his choc-ice, put some water on to boil, warmed a pot for tea, and at the same time, warmed to the idea of travel.

The phone rang.

"Graham? It's me. I'm calling at Food Giant on my way home. Is there anything you fancy?"

"Only you, my love, but give the Food Giant my regards. It pays to keep on the right side of giants, don't you find?"

"Absolutely. I'll tell him you smell his blood and will eat him if he's not careful. Crumpets?"

"Ah, Jacqueline, you are a woman to be conjured with. Crumpets it is!"

"Gotta go, honey. Kiss, kiss." There was a click. The phone resumed the dial tone.

***

A cup of afternoon tea is in order, thought Graham, most of his grading of papers finished for the academic year. *I'll nip to the post first, though, with the letter to Paul and then I'll put the kettle on again, when I get back. And I'll get on with that grading I have piled up. By the time the tea's made, Jacqueline will be back with crumpets. And crumpets!*

About twenty minutes later, just as the kettle whistled, the phone rang. Graham answered it with the kettle whistling. A male voice asked if he was Mr. Graham Curtis.

"Yes, but hang on a sec, the kettle's boiling." He dashed to the stove and poured hot water over the tea. "Yes, I'm with you," he said to the man on the other end of the line.

"I'm afraid there's been an accident. Your wife is in Queen Charlotte Hospital. Could you come quickly? Do you have transport?"

"Oh, Christ, Christ! What happened? Tell me. Tell me, damn it!"

"It's serious. Get here fast." The man asked again, "Do you have transport?"

"Yes, I'll be there—"

"Go to reception. Give them your name. Go to the head of the queue."

"Yes. I understand. Bye." Graham put the phone down and then picked it up and phoned for a taxi.

Jacqueline had taken the car that morning. His hands were shaking. He took his jacket from a peg in the hall and went out to stand in the drive, waiting for the cab to appear. He felt cold and he was shivering. *What in God's name had happened to her? Why the hell wasn't the cab there? Was she taken ill? Was it an accident? Yes, the man had said it was an accident. She could be a hopeless cripple. My God, she could die!* The taxi arrived. He fumbled with the door handle and then got the door open.

CHAPTER EIGHT

Paul looked at the telephone. Should he call her? Or would that be a mere complication at this stage? He wanted to hear her voice, bright, alert, and clear, as if she were speaking from his hallway, with the door to his room open. Paul dialed her number, but there was only the machine ready to take a message.

"Paul here. I'll call another time. I just wanted to hear your voice."

So, she was out. She would have interrupted the recording otherwise. He decided to work again on the article, but it was impossible. He could not settle and concentrate. After twenty minutes of messing about and scribbling odd words and phrases on a scratch pad, he decided to go out. He'd mailed the Hong Kong pages and would mail more of his Kalitza papers to Mary and Graham. Now he had started, he might as well continue.

The rue de la Collègiale was empty of people and full of parked cars, half on and half off the pavement. He made his way to the boulevard and headed for the Place d'Italie. Headlights and some sidelights were showing on trucks and cars. In the doorway of a closed shop, a young couple, probably students, were nibbling each other's lips with the delight of lovers seemingly besotted with one another. Paul passed a lamp shop where some vandal had scored an illegible gang slogan across the glass door. This kind of vandalism as well as the paint spray variety that defaced some of the finest doorways and stonework irritated him to the point of exasperation. One of the most beautiful cities on earth was thus being turned into a place that was unworthy of the artists and craftsmen who had made it so fine. There were alcoholics and beggars sleeping rough and defiling the pavement with urine and even excrement at times. Hooligans set fire to cars at the slightest excuse. Doctors, nurses, firemen and even police were attacked from time to time. Drug gangs proclaimed buildings and neighbourhoods as their territory, sometimes terrorizing old, retired inhabitants. And when you went on the RER trains deep underground and *banlieue* bound, you were depressingly back in a place often more infernal than the Third World. *In the Third World or developing countries,* Paul mused, *there was squalor, poverty and yet, often, a pride of place. There were tribal customs and codes of behaviour based on community and caring for the village.* Paul remembered finding on the door of a shack in a tropical shanty town of refugees a superb drawing in white chalk of a galloping horse. *Underneath his feet,* Paul thought, *there's a labyrinth of wonderful technology, helping people get to and from the city stations, all defaced and messed up for no good reason.* Whenever he took certain RER trains, he felt depressed. *Why should some people have to destroy what was supposed to be a pleasant, quick, and relatively cheap way of getting about? Don't think about it. There isn't a saleable article here. Most editors had other things on their minds as they drove their Saabs and BMWs and Jags.* In any case, trendy intellectuals, sociologists, and art critics seemed to agree that the graffito was a form of urban pop-art. It deserved reverent lip-service, not articles condemning some of it as vandalism, however mindless it might be. Paul knew when a graffito was art and when it was not. *Ah, there in a narrow side street was Chez Auguste.* Paul headed for it, glancing at his watch. Auguste's wife would be opening the little restaurant.

It was a modest, clean neighbourhood restaurant, despite its rather grand name. In fact, the Auguste who had founded it was now concocting heavenly desserts. His widow, in partnership with his son by a first wife, ran the place and had spruced it up a bit, making it livelier. The food was just as good. It was honest and was good quality for the price. All that. *Un bon petit restaurant du quartier,* thought Paul.

He then considered the modernity and the museum quality of the city. The drained Paris marsh was now like a huge

Gruyère cheese, the land eaten away by sewers and metro tunnels. He remembered that in the limestone regions of some wine growing districts, the land was eroded by natural forces. One famous wine village was collapsing and there was subsidence in some of the vineyards. That could make a good article if brought up to the minute and it would be enjoyable to visit the threatened areas because of the wines they were still making. He took a small table for two and ordered a half bottle of red Sancerre. The waiter returned very quickly with the wine. It was light, good fruit, delicious. He was ready to order his meal: terrine of rabbit followed by a veal cutlet. The waiter nodded and retreated with the order through a door leading to the kitchen. Paul's cell phone vibrated in his pocket. As he took out the mobile, he glanced across the almost empty room and watched an old woman taking a sip of her kir. She had heavy, unsuitably crimson lips.

"*Allô*," he said. There was a slight pause and then Mary's voice came to him clear and precise.

"Is that Paul? I'd recognize your 'allô' anywhere."

"Yes, it is, and it's Mary? It's sweet of you to call back so soon. It's lovely to hear your voice. Did you get my parcel?"

"I did. I've read it. Did you get my letter? I want to see you. Can you get over here for a few days?"

"Well, I'm working on something I'll finish in a day or two. Why don't you nip over to Paris? If I were in Sutton Coldfield and someone invited me to Paris, I know what I would do."

"Yes, but you see I'm not you. Besides I'm inviting you to Scotland." She laughed. "Are you on?"

"I'm on! And thanks for your letter. It helped."

"Good. I have to go. Can you call me back in a couple of hours, at home? We can talk details. I'm still in the surgery just now. But I'm intrigued by this Kalitza. That was her name?"

"Yes. I'll call you when I get in later. Exciting!"

"Bye, et cetera."

Paul smiled with pleasurable anticipation. He noticed that the old lady was eyeing him with a glare of disapproval. No matter. The waiter placed the terrine on the table, with a small basket of bread. The terrine was garnished with crisp lettuce leaves and some small gherkins. Perfect. He took another sip of wine before starting on the food. The old lady was now studiously watching three young women who were motioned to another table against a wall, where there was a blackboard on which the day's specials were written in a meticulously neat hand. Her wrinkled face expressed an intensity of interest, sharp-eyed appraisal, and sour, pursed-lip disapproval. Paul was alarmed by the ferocity of her stare. The male gaze of brief dismissal or lingering approval of women seemed mild in comparison. He made a hasty note: article on "The Female Stare." It might sell. He knew an editor who might take it. She had read the male gaze stuff ad lib. And might well be looking for a shift of vision. *Are all women hated rivals? Are men? Are all humans rivals as well as rivals of the animals and insects and fish? Fish, flesh, and fowl,* he remembered, *and it led to slaughter.* He finished the terrine. *Excellent. More wine.*

***

When he was back home, Paul realized it would take two days to finish off what was in the journalistic pressure cooker. Things on the back burner could wait. His pocket notebook would be ever ready for ideas to be noted He sent an e-mail to the editor who might take "The Female Stare" idea. He tidied his desk and then rang Mary's home number. She had returned from surgery. Swapping ideas with a lot of laughter, they decided to take the train together from Birmingham to Edinburgh, traveling with a minimum of luggage—an overnight bag each would be enough for the four days they planned to be together. They excitedly confirmed the arrangement, Mary booking the train, and Paul planning to arrive at Mary's home in the evening before their departure for Edinburgh. She explained to him that he could sleep on the hideaway bed. It was very comfortable. He told her more of his pages were in the mail.

CHAPTER NINE

Three evenings later, Paul had finished the pressure cooker work and sent it off. He was in Sutton Coldfield, having traveled by rail and taxi, and was now ringing Mary's door bell. He was excited. He was alive again. Truly alive.

That's Paul. She glanced at herself as she walked past the mirror in the hall near the front door. She felt full of energy and smiled a broad smile as she opened the door.

"God, it's good to see you, Mary."

He took in her brilliant smile, the regular, very white teeth framed by a rose-brown lip gloss, her wonderfully fine, regular features, the deep brown eyes, and a small, jeweled teardrop in the centre of her forehead just above the dark lines of her eyebrows. Her sari was brown and white with gold embroidery. He kissed her twice on both cheeks. She took his hand.

"Come in, come in, you handsome rogue!" she laughed.

In the hall, he put down his bag and slipped the smaller bag containing his laptop from his shoulder.

"Is that what I think it is?" She looked him in the eyes.

He raised his hands in a defensive gesture. "Yes it is. I was working on the train. I'll work on the way back to Paris. But don't worry. I'll not be taking it to Scotland."

"Oh, I see. You want to come back here after Scotland?"

"Ah. I thought that it would be okay. Even if I just pick it up and go on my way."

"Waste of time. You might want to go straight on to London and then Paris. Why not bring it along and then if you go straight back, it's no problem. If you don't and your return to Paris is not too urgent, well, it's not heavy for taking on the train with us there and back."

"Okay, that's settled then. I won't work in Scotland. I certainly wasn't planning to anyway. Scout's honour."

"Come and have a drink. It's not that I want to stop your work. It's that . . . when I get away . . . I just have so little time that I want to relax and just 'work' (she made the sign with double fingers so favoured by Aldous Huxley and Californians) at enjoyment, pleasure, luxury. You know the sort of thing? Before the surgery and the postpartum mums claim me again." She looked at him and smiled again.

"I get the picture. I understand. What shall we drink to?"

"Medicinal compound? Brave beginnings?"

Mary took hold of his hand and led him into the sitting room. "White or red wine? Sherry? Scotch?"

"I'll take red wine, please. I've heard that men who drink it have less cholesterol than those who don't."

She smiled and took a bottle from her silver drinks tray. It was already opened and breathing. She poured two glasses. "I've prepared a few nibbles. Then I thought we'd have a steak and salad."

"Sounds wonderful."

She gave him a glass of wine. There were beaded bubbles and they were definitely winking, but definitely below the rim.

"So . . . to medicinal compound and brave beginnings!"

"Yes, well, and here's to you, Mary. Thanks for asking me to come over here and go with you to Scotland. But why Scotland?"

"Here's to you, Paul, and thanks for being so ready to come when I needed the break. Paul, I've missed you. I'm glad you are not rushing off to Hong Kong in search of Kalitza."

"No . . . no. Look, now that we've got this mutual toast over and done with, to Scotland!"

"To Scotland! Mmm. That's good. No, I mean what I say."

"I know, I've noticed. And I count myself lucky to be one of your friends. Why Scotland? Have you ever been there before? Do you know, I thought you'd want something like the Scilly Isles or the Channel Islands. We could be in for bad weather. Or at least very capricious meteo. But I have not been up north since I was a kid. At least not that far."

"Actually one of my locums is a Scot. St. Andrews educated. He's working in England, but he goes back quite often and always seems to have had a very good holiday. He says the countryside is the most beautiful in the world."

"He's a real Scot all right. But it is lovely. Even the French like to visit Scotland, though France really is the most beautiful country in the world. Not a patch on Goa, though!"

They laughed and she took his hand again. She led him into a sort of study-cum-office-cum-guest-room. This was where she was putting him for the night, for she reached up to a handle on what appeared to be a tall cupboard and pulled a bed, ready made-up, down from the wall.

"Pillows are there," she said, pointing to a cupboard under a window. "Ready for nibbles and another glass?"

"Well, I never!" Paul replied in a cockney voice. "Yes, I'm ready for another. I'm ready for anything." She smiled.

They settled down with the olives and a spicy dip for raw celery and carrot sticks.

"You said you got my letter. I got your adventure in Hong Kong."

"I did get your letter. It was very good for me when I read it. I realized you're not only lovely, but you're wise. And you care deeply. I think I must face the reality of loss. The fact I sent you a bundle of what I now think of as Kalitza papers means, I think, that I am working something out that's rather odd. There are further encounters with this strange Egyptian. I found she was called Kalitza in Hong Kong."

"Kalitza. Odd name. If you want to tell me more about this Kalitza, or just talk, please do."

"I need to . . . I need to. Just read the Kalitza papers when you can get back to them. Perhaps you'll know what's happening better than I do. But, Mary, I . . . I already feel more *myself*. And alive."

"In fact, the Hong Kong adventure arrived in time for me to read it all. I'm sorry you had to go through that. But you seem to have coped. After all, you're here."

Paul looked at her and smiled, but said nothing.

"How's your work going? Tell me what you are writing. Oh, let's eat, you can tell me then."

Over dinner, Paul explained something of the articles he had recently sold and told Mary his idea for an article on the female stare. She thought anthropology, sociology, literature, and psychology could all provide rich material for the article. Yet more useful, she told him, was the observation of real women in the real streets of busy cities.

"Could you photograph different female stares?" Mary asked.

"I'll certainly do that as surreptitiously as possible. Tricky. Another use for the cell phone."

Over dinner, they caught up on things each had done since last seeing each other and mentioned a couple of mutual friends. Paul told her about a trip to Vancouver, where he had seen Graham and his lively and practical Canadian wife.

"Hmm. Practical. Just what he needs." Mary had known he was married, but had not yet met Graham's wife.

After they had washed up and cleared everything away, they looked at maps and decided to plan their days together while they were on the train. They had to be up at six if they were to get ready and be in Birmingham in time to catch an express train. Mary turned to him and kissed him on the lips.

"Paul, you really are at a milestone. You need to make some serious decisions. Sleep, rest, and an escapade will help, I'm sure. Good night." She smiled again. "It's really good to see you. Early start. You can use the bathroom next to the guest room. I have my own bathroom en suite with my bedroom."

He watched her walk away with her natural elegance and a faint perfume that he could not name. He picked up his bags from the hall and settled into the guest room. Later, in bed, he thought it was wonderful actually to be in Mary's home, trusted. A friend. He wondered if she had actually slept in this bed. Had she tried it out? Had another male friend slept here in this bed? Probably. He hoped so. He hoped that some other man had not shared her main bedroom. Why was he thinking like this? They were adults. She had a full and busy professional life. But had she a personal, intimate one with some man he didn't know? Not just at the moment, because she had invited him here and she was honest. She knew he would not try to force the issue. No, he felt privileged to be in this flat, in this room painted white, with a block of light yellow from the curtains and the warm, brown, grainy wood of the desk and the cupboards. He was happy. Really happy, he realized, happier than he had been for a long time. He started reading a fat textbook on clinical medicine. Diseases, symptoms, chances of cure, treatments. He was asleep almost as soon as he had drowsily switched off the light.

CHAPTER TEN

The old lady who had been brought to see Mary had been observed briefly and then suddenly died in her sleep in hospital. The daughter's own doctor had informed Mary as a matter of courtesy between colleagues. Mary thought it was probably for the best. The old woman would have drifted into the darkest night. The daughter would have less worry and stress.

On the other hand, the new baby boy was now thriving. In the midst of life, we are in death. In the midst of death, we are in life.

***

The woman who had called herself Kalitza, unknown to the great public, was back in Paris in a secret section of the French government. She was alive and well and living in Paris! She had been debriefed about the Hong Kong mission. She had moved on. She was known as Kim to her associates, who all had code names, often simple forenames. She had no elaborate code name like the British agent who had been called White Rabbit and whose house in Guilford Street now had a memorial plaque. When he had been operational many years ago, there had been no such plaque. He had been simply a senior officer in the Royal Air Force. If she survived and retired, Kim wanted no blue plaque on any building. She supposed White Rabbit had felt much the same.

CHAPTER ELEVEN

They were lucky. The express train was on time at both the start and finish of the journey. They had planned enough to know that they were going to spend perhaps a day or two in Edinburgh and then motor to St. Andrews and onwards. Mary remained vague on the next bit of the trip. Play it by ear. Then they would return to Edinburgh for the train back to Birmingham. As Mary told Paul and Paul told Mary, it was not a plan chiseled in stone. It could be swerved away from. Flexibility was always the name of their game, they realized. But they had to be in Birmingham again on the right day, because of surgery. They also spoke briefly of Kalitza.

"She's not a phantom, Paul. You made love with her. But she's given you the slip."

"She always slips away. I've come to the conclusion that I am an embarrassment to her."

"You're right. Try to live your own life. You're single, you're independent. You're an adult."

"After my parents died, I felt very lonely . . . perhaps I wanted desperately to get them back."

"You certainly think or thought that the soul continues after death."

"Do you think Kalitza is a sort of substitute for my parents?"

"I shouldn't think so, but you might be right. I don't know. I *do* know that you have lost her, whoever she is and wherever she is. And she is or was a real person."

"Yes. I have. But I've still got you and other friends. I have found you again. I feel we're on a sort of wavelength we never were on before. I mean, since we were first friends."

"I know. It's good."

"It's wonderful, Mary. I feel sort of . . . adult?"

Mary smiled and put her finger on the end of his nose. Then she stroked his face. They relapsed into silence.

59

"And instead of giving me the slip, you've invited me over for a real break." She took his hand in hers and they watched the land flash by. Moors were now stretching beyond the train. There was an occasional house or cottage or a small village. There were low hills and patches of heather. A few windswept trees.

***

Mary had booked them into a large Georgian house, now a hotel in a quiet Edinburgh street not far from the antiquarian book shops her locum had recommended. At the desk, Paul watched her concentrating on the plastic key and times of breakfast—things like that. He smiled as she pushed back a strand of hair that was falling across her cheek. In the lift, which had been fitted ingeniously into the generous stairwell, by modern standards, of the capacious house, Paul and Mary hugged and, as they did so, chuckled together. Their bags arrived almost as soon as they had looked around their room.

The room was of noble proportions, with a pair of tall, well-proportioned windows in between which stood a Pembroke table against the wall. It had a large white porcelain vase full of dahlias. The bed was king-size and backed by a paneled headboard with recessed lighting and bedside tables for breakfast trays, or books, or hotel Bibles. The apple-green bedspread went well with the light tan of the fitted carpet, a combination of colors repeated in the heavy curtains and in the shade of a table lamp on an elegant wooden desk. There was a telephone, a bowl of fresh fruit, a small fridge full of expensive beverages, and a sleek TV set, doubtless hooked up to a dish on the roof of the hotel. The ceiling had beautiful plaster work that was probably the original. The elegant and intricate plaster molding, Paul guessed, was Italian. Migrant plasterers had probably worked in Edinburgh, as in Dublin, two centuries ago and later. Mary was running water in the bathroom. Paul looked in and saw gleaming marble tiles, a huge, freestanding bathtub with a heavy chrome shower attachment and heaps of fluffy white towels. In the midst of it all, Mary stood testing the temperature of the water. They undressed hastily and got under the shower, soaping each other and laughing.

"I needed this, Mary, how did you guess?"

"Guessing what you want, and what you need, is great fun, Paul."

They rubbed each other down and donned huge toweling robes, only to slip them off with great deliberation on the big bed. Then they made love. Mary knew exactly what excited him, even though they had never made love to each other before. The simple contact of their skin and the tenderness and intimacy each gave to the other was something so natural and so satisfying that thoughts or words were unnecessary. Their eyes and their hands and their excited bodies were what mattered on that late, late afternoon, or was it early evening? They didn't care. They were free—at least for a few days.

They dressed again in casual clothes and wandered into the town for dinner. Paul was amused by some of the surreptitious looks they got from other people. Mary's striking Anglo-Indian beauty was the major reason, of course, and not mere curiosity about this white man with a colored woman. That kind of curiosity had become increasingly rare in Britain. He was also amused and, to be honest, a little embarrassed by the way the girl on reception had discreetly taken an impression of Mary's gold credit card, when they had checked in, and then had hastily smiled and looked away from him when he smiled at her.

***

They were back in their room after a light meal and were almost lost in the centre of the huge bed; Mary's head was on his shoulder. He loved this perfume discovered again, but of which he still did not know the name. French? Indian? American? She seemed to be studying his neck and chin.

"What's the name of your perfume, darling?"

"Like it?"

"Adore it."

"It's called 'Stately Home'! And it's made in Wales. Don't laugh!"

"Sorry. It's wonderful. Makes me go wobbly at the knees."

"It's not well-known, but I like it. It seems to be perfect for the chemistry of my skin. Some other perfumes don't wear as well on me."

"You wear nothing but this and I'm in a heaven all of our own. Don't laugh. Are you glad to be in bed with me?"

Mary laughed again. "I'm very glad to be in bed with you, Paul. If I weren't, I wouldn't be here, or at least, you wouldn't be here with me."

"Aha. You little wretch. Anyway, I'm excited to be in bed with you and, you know what?"

"What?"

"I can't believe my luck. I'm excited by the way you make love to me. You know exactly what to do. I love your coffee color."

"Yes, I gathered that," she laughed, caressing him very lightly with her slender fingers.

"More Kama Sutra?"

"Shut up. This is nothing to do with books, *How To* . . . or *Joy* . . . or otherwise. It's just us." She kissed him on the mouth, climbing onto him. "It's to do with us," she insisted, "and not doctors and nurses!"

"So, they didn't teach you this when you were a houseman, er . . . housewoman?"

"Shh. It's what women know, or get to know, if they're in their right senses."

They held each other tight. They belonged together, didn't they? Both of them thought so. They savored this moment of happiness.

CHAPTER TWELVE

When Paul awoke, a grey morning light filtered through a slight gap in the curtains. Mary was still sleeping soundly, her face turned away and framed by the wavering spread of her long hair, contrasting with the delicate apricot hue of the pillow. This dark sun seemed to him to radiate life and beauty in a tropical morning sky, in the middle of Edinburgh. He thought he would need nothing more than to wake each morning to this wonderful, fragrant abundance of her hair on the pillow. For all the daily news of the perfidies of human beings, life could still be magnificent. Yes! One must never forget that. It was worth hanging onto that. He went to the bathroom, but when he emerged into the bedroom there was a knock on the door. Room service? Breakfast!

He opened the door and a stocky Scottish maid came in with a laden tray. Life could be, was, good, and should be so, there was no denying it. He poured the tea. Mary was sitting up and yawning and stretching. He was enchanted. She vanished into the bathroom.

When they were contemplating the porridge and wondering whether to put a little salt on it or to eat it with sugar and milk, Mary surprised him.

"You eat your porridge, laddie!" she said with a Scottish accent not exaggerated as in comedies.

"Hey, that's very good."

"Oh, I've known a few Scottish medical people in my time!"

Paul looked at her and found himself smiling, though his innermost being was gripped by a sudden jealousy for the past that she had lived and he had not known. The feeling lasted all through breakfast, though he concealed the effect her few words had had on him. As they were looking at the map to see which route to take, she suddenly said, "It's good

63

that we have our separate lives and that we do not know all there is to know about one another. After all, do we know everything, even, about ourselves?"

"Well, we can deliver a few surprises now and again!" Paul replied. He knew she was right. It was as if she had picked up his feelings and thought about them. Paul was surprised by the sudden jealousy he had felt. It was foolish, he knew, and normally he was never what one could call a jealous or possessive person.

"Just then, I felt a pang of jealousy," he confessed. "I know it's ridiculous. After all I've told you about my one-time fixation on . . . Kalitza."

"It's important that we are ourselves and keep on being ourselves, even if we are . . . close," she said.

"I love being with you and I don't want anything to change you," he said. He kissed her lips lightly. She looked into his eyes and they smiled at one another.

"Are you sure you have recovered from the Kalitza experiences?" Mary asked.

"I'm sure," said Paul. "The name Kalitza now seems to me contrived, artificial, rather than full of her allure. I am certain I'm back in the real world. And the real world is now wonderful, because we're together."

"When you said you love being with me, I feel the same way," she said, as she took out her lipstick to complete her make-up.

To watch Mary getting dressed, ready to go out with him, and to watch the details of her make-up, while ostensibly he was scanning the morning paper, added immensely to the excitement of being alone with her on holiday, for however brief a time. *We have so little time*, he thought, *but that makes everything more vivid, more exciting.* She powdered the slight, thin curve of her delicate nose. She put on a little more lipstick.

"I thought you had finished your make-up."

"So did I," she replied. "But I noticed I needed a little more." She winked at him and laughed, shy suddenly. He picked up the shyness. She had seen him spying on her make-up procedure and it had made her self-conscious.

Their day in Edinburgh was as thoroughly fascinating as it was tiring. The castle was a must and equally the National Gallery of Scotland, where the range of work surprised them both. They climbed to the top of the Scott monument and watched the crowds below, each person or each group walking along the paths of different lives: good or not so good, or even evil; idling or purposeful; in sound or ill health; happy or blighted by ill chance; caring, improving the little world in which they walked, or indifferent to most of it. They looked for a place for lunch and found a wine bar that appealed to them both. It was furnished rather as if it was a male club and the dark-green walls were hung with old sporting prints.

"I think this place is late eighteenth century and has flourished ever since," remarked Paul as they sat down on a settle-type seat and took in more of their surroundings.

"I bet Surtees came here. Surtees was here!' said Paul, feeling very much at home in the place.

"Surtees?"

"Nineteenth century. He created John Jorrocks, 'a great city grocer of the old school.' A sportsman."

"Ah, a novelist with characters who could have been modeled on the denizens of places like this?"

"Mary, if you ever tire of medicine, take up English literature or comparative lit."

"I'll make a note of it. No. I prefer just to read for pleasure in my spare moments. P. G. Wodehouse, for instance. A master of revels."

Paul said, "Ah yes. A master at what he does. Comedy is a very difficult and exhausting business. I suppose his wartime stupidity is now forgiven by readers who relish his comedy of clubmen and silly ass Englishmen."

Over a glass of Chinon and some cheese straws that were probably homemade, Paul suddenly asked, "Have you ever lived with anyone, Mary?"

"No. I never have. I've had my adventures, as the actress said to the bishop, but I've always kept my own place just for me; it was like that in digs of course, landladies being what they are! And now my own flat is sacred to me alone. It's a good feeling, having a place of one's own. I don't know if I could cope with my job and a live-in man at the same time. Have you lived with anybody—I mean since . . . Vanessa, wasn't it?"

"Yes, Vanessa was a big mistake. You met her, once or twice?"

"I also met her papa, the architect. Tall, jovial, and had a moustache."

"Yes. He wanted me to rush into marriage. But it was not going that way."

"Well, now all that's a thing of the past, how many years? I was in my final year of medicine. You know, Vanessa's papa tried to get me to be his mistress."

"Good grief. The old bugger."

"Buggery wasn't on his mind! He wanted to whisk me off my feet. He fancied himself as what was called 'a sugar daddy'! A flat in London. Sex after the office, his office, or some weekends in pink satin sheets. I was too bogged down with work to do anything but laugh and give him the brush off. I didn't mention it to anyone. He had no idea of how hard medics work!"

CHAPTER THIRTEEN

Their Edinburgh sojourn continued with exploring the old town and its bookstores. They then went into a couple of little galleries and ended by taking a light dinner that evening with a good half bottle of white Sancerre, all delivered impeccably by room service.

Next day, they decided to motor in a hired car over the spectacular Forth Road Bridge. They might spend a last day of their little escapade in Edinburgh on their way back to England. Mary wanted now to explore more of the country. Once over the bridge, they left the motorway for the A 92, which took them to Glenrothes, where they left it, heading for Kirkton of Largo, because they liked the intriguing name, and because they wanted to take the coast road through Pittenweem, Anstruther, and Crail. At Pittenweem, they wandered around the old fishing port and afterwards found a charming place for tea and oatmeal biscuits. From Crail, they took narrow roads across country so that their next views of the sea would be when they neared St. Andrews. Long and slender fingers of weed-gloved rock stretched into the sea. Paul and Mary walked around the ruins of the cathedral, holding hands, their fingers interlaced.

"They built many a house with stone from the castle and possibly even the cathedral," Paul remarked. "Did they want to possess some of the holy magic in their houses and walls? Or were they just stealing to save money?"

"A bit of each. Come on," Mary said, "Let's look at the university. It's the oldest in Scotland."

They thought it was suitably solid and medieval looking. They were astounded by how young the red-gowned students looked. Mary explained that the insignia of St. Mary's College was a superb image, with its fleur-de-lys and heart; now she had seen the place, she would love to have been an undergraduate there. Quite a few of the rich, yet-to-be-famous had been students there.

"Are we old?" Paul demanded.

"Yes, but not very old. Not old old. We can keep fit by playing golf. This is the hidden agenda. Though golf shoes and a couple of clubs are difficult to hide. We'll have a round on the famous links."

"Seriously?"

"Of course."

"But I'm no good. I'm a pitch and putt rabbit."

Mary laughed and explained that they would do a quick round together. She would teach him a few shots. In fact, he made many shots with her hands guiding his. He loved her standing close behind him, her arms encircling him, her hands warm on his.

"Relax. Keep your eye on the ball!" The better he managed to do this, the better his strokes became.

"Your strokes are improving!"

"As the actress said to the bishop," Paul replied quickly. "Got you that time. Later on, I want to show you a few more strokes."

"Aha. Good idea. What else have you got up your sleeve?"

"Up my sleeve? That's a funny place for it!"

"As the actress said to the bishop."

Jokes seemed funnier to them because they were discovering their love and complicity. Their hilarity on the course did not bother other golfers, of which there were only a few, since it was time for drinks and lunch. They walked fast, did not bother with some of the holes, but thoroughly enjoyed themselves.

Getting back into the car, they motored on, instead of staying in St. Andrews for lunch. At Dundee, they admired the famous ships and had Arbroath smokies for lunch. They shared a piece of Dundee cake.

It was Mary's turn to drive and they had not gone far when she saw a shop with colorful bolts of cloth festooned in the window. She stopped, declaring, "I want some Paisley pattern cloth. It's just what I want." They went into the shop, where a woman, at once motherly and business-like, was smiling and nodding. Her dark brown hair was piled up high on her head, with a few loose tendrils around her ears. She watched them enter and start looking at the stock.

"I've to go now, Helen. I'll see you tomorrow. In the forenoon. Bye." Putting down the telephone, she asked if she could help.

"Yes, please!" Mary had already found a striking bolt of cloth, a silk mix, in the paisley design; it was in red, orange, yellow, and black, all the colors and shapes wonderfully harmonized one with another.

"How much will you require, madam?"

"Can I wrap it around me?"

"Of course. Here, I'll hold this and you unfold as much as you need."

Mary wrapped herself in the cloth and looked across enquiringly at Paul.

"Mary, it's wonderful on you. Brilliant!"

"This is what I'll need for a sari," Mary explained, holding out a bunched length of the cloth.

The shopkeeper measured out the cloth and wrapped it carefully in tissue paper sheets before putting it into a stiff, glossy white bag printed with the shop's name in red. As she made out a bill and Mary paid, Paul wondered if there were any other Paisley pattern saris. Mary was excited with the purchase and, in fact, so was Paul. He wanted to see how a sari was made. The saleswoman told Mary the material had come in from Dubai.

They drove on out of town and into the countryside. Mary explained that she could make a simple sari herself, but she might give this rather fine cloth to an Indian tailor she knew who would add certain trimmings to make something rather special. Paul asked when she had learned how to make a sari. Mary started talking about her youth and, as she drove on, Paul wished he could have lived that youth with her. They talked naturally and intimately, as they had never previously talked when they knew each other as students. They were reaching a newer level of friendship and it was companionable, honest, and privileged. They were lovers, but there was something else. They were both adults. *I'm a real adult*, thought Paul, *and so is Mary. We're real adults driving along together.* Paul knew, with an elation he had never felt before in anybody's company, that he loved this woman. She was smiling as they talked, and driving so smoothly, so confidently, through the beauty of the Scottish lowland countryside. *Would this feeling last? Could such feelings last?* He doubted it. Yet, he realized, yes, he was in love. Would he love her always? *Yes, always*, he promised himself. He did not actually explain these feelings to Mary just then, nor could he have done. He needed a bit more time. They needed to be in each other's arms.

Mary slowed down and turned into a smaller road leading from the major one.

"I've a surprise for you," she said.

"Love in a haystack?" asked Paul.

"Not quite. But I think you'll like it."

She turned off the road into a drive leading to a small airfield. There was an office, a hangar, and a solid-looking, weather-beaten man sitting in a rattan chair outside the office. Mary stopped near him. He got to his feet, grinning, and held out his arms. Mary ran to him, and they hugged, and looked at each other again and laughed before they spoke.

"You're here then, lass!" he said. He looked at Paul and held out his hand.

"Jack Moffat. I'm Mary's pilot."

"Hello, Jack! Paul Wills." The two men shook hands. Jack's grip, Paul noted, was firm and warm. Jack looked at Paul searchingly. Paul smiled, hoping he passed muster with this old friend of Mary's. Jack was somebody she had certainly known for some time.

"Is everything ready, Jack?" asked Mary.

"It is, my love. We're ready to go."

"Where?" Paul asked.

"This is my surprise," said Mary.

Jack put his arms around each of them and all three sauntered over to a twin-engine aircraft, painted red and white. They climbed in, buckled their seat belts, and it was only a few minutes before they were taxiing along the runway preparing for take-off. Mary and Paul sat on a bench seat, like the back seat of a car, behind Jack. Each had a small window. They held hands and kissed.

"Marvelous," Paul murmured. And then they were climbing away from the tarmac and flying over the green countryside. Jack circled and they saw the rented car, like a toy, parked between the office and the hangar. Then Jack climbed higher and they were on course for somewhere mysterious. It was a fairly clear day with some cloud, but no rain and so there were wonderful views of the Scottish countryside spread richly and sometimes ruggedly below them. A river, small lochs, and heather-covered rocky moorland passed beneath in a brilliant show. Paul had flown many times for his various assignments, but this was altogether different. There was something infinitely magical and satisfying about the unexpected quality of the experience. No airport delays and hassles. Mary had thought of this, arranged it all, and now it was happening! What a woman!

"I'm a very lucky man!" Paul said, loudly enough, he thought, over the engine noise, for Mary to have heard.

"What did you say?" she shouted.

"He said he's a very lucky man," yelled Jack, without turning away from the controls. They all laughed. There was no more talk. They were too busy looking at clouds and brilliant blue sky and bonny Scotland passing in and out of shadows from the clouds. The journey was fairly short. They were descending. Jack was talking into his microphone. As the wing dipped and they circled the toy aerodrome below them, Mary smiled. She had spotted the large car parked near the little runway.

When they had landed and rolled to a stop, Jack turned and said he would collect them the next day at five in the afternoon unless they telephoned with a different plan in the forenoon. He was finished for the day now and was going back home. Mary and Paul waved him off. A driver was standing by the large navy blue Daimler. Mary and Paul, hand in hand, approached the car.

"We're the couple for the Black Barony," she said.

"Right, madam, we're all set then. Shall I put the bags in the boot?"

They nodded and he picked up their bags. They were soon on their way through leafy countryside. They saw what appeared to be a forest in front of them. The road skirted a beautiful old stone wall. The car slowed down and then swung into a gateway with a lodge, *Victorian by the look of it*, thought Paul, *with a bit of the Hansel and Gretel about it*. They rolled steadily along an avenue of trees. The drive curved and then, across a field, they saw a handsome eighteenth century country house, with a Palladian façade and broad, shallow steps leading to the double front doors. As they stopped in the drive near the steps, a hotel porter, a lad of about seventeen, came out of the house and took care of their bags. They followed him into the hall that seemed to occupy the entire ground floor except for the reception desk, a baggage holding area, porter's cubby hole, and the stately staircase.

"Mary, what a lovely surprise. How clever of you to know about all this!" Paul looked around at antlered heads, tapestries of hunting scenes, and some nineteenth century landscapes on the walls as they went to the reception area.

"I'm Dr. Rao," Mary said to a pert, smilingly efficient young woman at the desk.

"Yes, madam. I've put you in the garden suite overlooking the terrace."

"Wonderful."

"Breakfast is served between seven and ten in the morning. What time will you need breakfast?"

"We don't know, but if we want it by room service, should we give you a time before we turn in for the night?"

"As you wish. Or phone down when you wake up. But we don't do breakfast after ten a.m. Last orders in by nine thirty a.m. Dinner is served between seven p.m. and ten thirty in the evening."

"Sounds good," said Paul.

They completed the formalities and made their way through the enormous hall which, they noticed, had open, plate glass doors at one side. Through the doorway, they glimpsed a bar serving drinks, coffee, and snacks. There were comfortable sofas, armchairs, and low, spacious tables placed strategically around the room which seemed to occupy part of the ground floor, left-hand wing of the manor.

Hotel guests, dressed mainly in expensive casual clothes, sat talking in small groups, while some waited silently for a partner to come down from their room. Paul and Mary followed a girl from the front desk up the broad staircase of beautifully crafted and polished massive oak, dark and gleaming. The thick blue carpet led up to a landing where the stairs divided into two, doubling back to reach the first floor corridors. A brass sign directed guests to the various rooms. At the end of a brightly lit passage, they saw ahead of them a solid-looking mahogany door. Beside the door was another brass plate proclaiming, The Garden Suite. The girl inserted a plastic card into a slot near the handle and smartly took it out again. A dot of red light went green and she opened the door.

"I hope everything will be to your satisfaction, Dr. Rao. If you need anything, just call us at reception. Your bags should be inside already."

They both thanked her and Paul followed Mary into the suite. The apple-green carpet stretched into a sitting room furnished with thickly cushioned rattan furniture, designed for a sumptuous conservatory. The walls were covered in an expensive paper that recalled a sunny conservatory atmosphere. Two large windows were hung with delicate, white, net curtains and heavy brocade ones, depicting giant green and blue irises, the motif repeated on the immaculate pelmets. They walked in, enjoying the room. Its atmosphere was immediately agreeable. They both made for a table between the two elegantly proportioned windows.

"What a wonderful flower arrangement!" Mary walked ahead to take in the scent of the flowers on the table.

"Are they real?" asked Paul.

"Course they are, in a joint like this!" They laughed at her attempt at the know-how voice of a worldly American from New York. Paul reached out and felt the bottle of champagne in an ice bucket beside the flowers.

"Great. It's nicely chilled," he remarked.

"Course it is, in a joint like this!" said Mary.

"Want some?" he asked.

"Please."

"What?"

"Champagne, of course."

"Okay, I'll open the old Veuve Clicquot."

"And then?"

"Admire the view."

He handed her a flute and then poured another for himself.

"And what a view!" Mary was looking out the window. Paul joined her.

"Mary, I am paying for our sojourn here."

"No, you are not," she said. "Don't bring money into it."

"Look. Frankly, I'm a bit uncomfortable. We'll go Dutch on it all. I'll make my contribution when we get back."

"No."

"There's no reason for you to treat me to all this luxury, Mary."

"There's every reason." She put her forefinger on his lips. "First, I want to do it and second, I can afford it once in a while, and third you need a rest and a complete change. Besides, I have to do it."

"Why?"

"You chump! I . . . I love you." They embraced.

"I love you, too, Mary." After a few moments he added, "Well, okay. You have to promise to come to Paris soon and I'll treat you to luxurious outings."

"Agreed. It's a deal!"

They looked out on an elegant, stone-paved terrace, bedecked with enormous planters, their flowers giving splashes of vivid color against the greyish stone. The balustrade stretched out from central steps, which were marked at each side by a balled finial. The steps were shallow and generously broad, leading down to graveled paths bordering the lawn. The lawn stretched towards the darker green skirts of the old trees at its further edges. Rhododendron bushes and longer grass filled in the spaces between the trees, giving the impression that here was the beginning of a dense, enchanted forest. "It's as if we were in the middle of an enchanted forest," Paul observed.

There seemed to be no path in or out of the forest. He opened the window near him and looked out. The air was clear and sweet. Suddenly, a burly young man in the white working tunic and black and white check trousers of kitchen staff appeared below them, crossed the terrace, made his way down the steps, and ventured several yards across the lawn, where, at an edge near the trees, he scattered some vegetable leaves and peelings. He looked around briefly and then retraced his steps. Calm returned. A wood pigeon hooted in the distance. There was a shaking of the leaves at one edge of the lawn. An animal nosed out from behind the lower branches of a tree and then came onto the lawn, its head slightly raised.

"It's a deer," whispered Mary. "Isn't that a surprise?"

"Yes, but why are we whispering?" whispered Paul.

"We're whispering because it seems right, like whispering in empty churches," whispered Mary.

The deer ventured towards the peelings and the few leaves left out for it. Satisfied that it was safe, it started to eat. A speckled fawn came onto the lawn and was soon next to the doe. Paul put his arms around Mary's waist, standing close behind her. The scent of her hair, the slanted light and shadow across the lawn, the apparition of these gentle animals, the total contentment of being free of work, here, with Mary, and his love for her—was it all real and true? Yes. It was real. It was true. It was happiness.

"This is a perfect moment," Mary whispered.

"Perfect and lovely," whispered Paul.

The deer and the fawn looked up, gazing at the terrace. A couple with a boy of about ten came onto the terrace. The boy was pointing at the animals. The father said something, putting his fingers to his lips. The boy moved very slowly down the steps and onto the grass. The deer watched intently his very slow progress across the lawn. The animals turned and ambled back to disappear into the foliage of the enchanted forest.

"Moments like this never last," Mary sighed.

"No. But it's given me an idea about Proust."

"Really? Is there a hotel like this in Proust?"

"I'm not sure, since I'm only on the third volume, *Le Côté de Guermantes.*"

"How long will it take to read all of them, if you ever do?"

"I'm not sure. It depends on how much time I can take out for that kind of reading."

"What's your idea?"

"I hope it's the same idea as yours."

"Later. I meant about Proust."

"Oh . . . yes . . . it was just that he lived in the age when everything began to zoom around faster than the old horse and carriage. Life, in fact, seems to flash by, once we get over childhood. I think Proust wanted to slow life down. He did it in his fiction by reviewing life in such detail that the reader is sure to feel the slow pace of the action such as it is. He takes life off the conveyor belt to examine it closely. It's mainly interior action. Quality control!"

"How old was he when he died?"

"Fifty, fifty-one. He was an asthmatic in childhood, an invalid for much of his adult life."

"I expect he saw life being lived around him and he was sort of left out?"

"Perhaps. Life was accelerating, that's for sure. I think by diving into his own memories and his inner life, he was able to present life at the pace he wished it could have. Time for feeling, sensibility, depth. Not life as waterskiing."

"Waterskiing?"

"Skimming the surface, only to sink at the end!" They laughed.

"Proust celebrated moments by prolonging them almost unbearably in his poetry masquerading as prose. Yet, he showed his society not as static, but gliding inexorably into changes. The Dreyfus affair and the Great War were the shocks, the catastrophes, and those who pretended changes could be ignored were simply wrong."

"Moments like this one we're in now shouldn't get lost."

They held onto each other, standing still, in the light of early evening. Paul wondered if he were to propose marriage, would she accept him?

He let the moment go by, but he thought perhaps there was a better time for a proposal. If she refused, this moment would be blemished. They sipped their champagne and walked around the rest of the suite, liking the bathroom with its green plants in a pink marble decor. The tub was huge and freestanding. There was a separate shower, also big enough for two.

"This is Scottish cleanliness with American plumbing guided by Italian ideas, no, Roman ones."

"Isn't it!" agreed Mary.

"We're very lucky people," said Paul. Mary looked at him and smiled. She kissed the hand in which he held his glass.

"We are—lucky to be born when we were, and where we were, and to the parents we had, and under democratic conditions. Don't forget that."

"I won't."

"And yet we had to make efforts. We had to persevere. We jumped through many a hoop and over many a hurdle and took and passed exams."

"And respected our abilities. We didn't waste a lot of time doing pointless stuff."

"You have talent, Paul. I like to see the results in print."

"God, Mary, you sound like an editor or an agent!"

"Maybe I am. Maybe I'm something more."

"I believe you are." They were silent for a while. Then Paul asked, "How far is the nearest town?"

"Oh, ten minutes or so by car. Why?"

"I just wondered if we have time to go there before dinner."

"No, we do not! We have time for this." Mary kissed him on the mouth. She took his free hand. She led him to the vast bed. "Let's undress and make love," she said.

"Mary, will you marry me?"

"I'll think about it." She smiled, wetting her lips with champagne. She unbuttoned his shirt. "Yes," she said, and kissed his chest. "I love you because you are kind, you're ready to follow me and do what I want. Yet, you do your own thing. You are stronger than you think, Paul. Yes, I want you. I'll marry you!"

They were half-naked as they clinked glasses.

"Here's to you, Mrs. Wills."

"Here's to you, Mr. Wills."

"Gretna Green? A quick marriage?"

"I canna stay in Scotland twenty-one days, laddie."

"Surgery calls?"

"Yes. Let's carry on from here!" said Mary, and they continued undressing. Naked, they stood holding each other in the comfort of their total trust.

CHAPTER FOURTEEN

When Graham arrived at the hospital, he got out of the taxi where it was waiting for cars in front of it to move along the narrow entry for visitors. He was some way away from the entrance and reception. He raced across the asphalt parking lot, passed a line of taxis waiting for customers coming from the hospital, leaped onto the paved forecourt. He stopped abruptly, panting heavily, when he reached the entrance door operated by an automatic electronic eye. He ran to the reception desk, aware only that there was a woman already there in front of him asking questions. Luckily, there was no long queue. The woman smiled, took her handbag off the counter and made to go. Then she thought of another query. Graham felt all his impatience attacking his stomach, like a blow from a knotted rope. The bored-looking, placid woman behind the counter nodded, looked down at some papers, and then checked her computer screen. Her half-lens spectacles were perched on the end of her nose, nestling small, fine nostrils.

"Take the elevator to the fourth floor, turn right, and follow the red arrows."

"Thank you."

"You're welcome. Yes, sir?" The receptionist let her spectacles hang by the cord that passed behind her neck.

"My wife is here in emergency. An accident. They told me to come here."

"Oh, that figures! What's your wife's name?"

"Curtis, Jacqueline."

"A moment. Yes. Address?" Graham gave the details and then the woman pushed her fingers through her hair, wiped the corners of her coral pink lips with thumb and forefinger, looked at him, and said that he should go straight to Professor Spurling's office to see the secretary there.

He obeyed her instructions to take the elevator to the fifth floor and follow the orange arrows. He had now become aware of the pervasive odour of the hospital. Disinfectant in the air conditioning system, he supposed. Or simply the cleaners' materials? He soon found the office. The brushed metal name plate on the wall next to the door had Professor B.S. L. Spurling in black lettering. Graham's stomach was now a knotted rope. He knocked on the door.

"Come in!"

"Hello. I'm Graham Curtis. They told me to come up here. My wife is Jacqueline Curtis. She's had an accident." Professor Spurling's secretary was sitting at a desk with a computer, a notice which thanked people for not smoking, a miniature koala fashioned of what looked like donkey fur, and a couple of files next to the telephone with its array of buttons. There was a name plate on the desk. She was Mrs. S. Gilmore. Her dark hair was done in a top knot with tendrils of dark curls falling down about her ears and neck. She was tanned, wore a light-pink lipstick and matching nail varnish. She smiled at Graham with bright, even teeth.

"Please have a seat, Mr. Curtis. Your wife's in theatre at the moment."

"They're operating right now?"

"Yes. Professor Spurling will come up to see you as soon as he can."

"They're operating then?"

"Yes. They are doing everything they can for her. If you'd like a coffee, there's a machine just down the hall. Or there's water over there."

Graham took a plastic beaker from the dispenser and helped himself to icy water from a huge, blue, inverted bottle that gurgled and miraculously conjured huge air bubbles that wriggled up through the water to vanish at the surface. There was a knock on the door.

Mrs. Gilmore already knew the next people to arrive. It was a Chinese family. An old man with his foot in a large stiff bandage of some sort of foam rather than plaster hobbled in, supported by a younger man, and was then eased down onto the sofa. His wife and perhaps a middle-aged son with a young wife sat on chairs so that he could stretch out on the sofa. Old Mr. So was hollow-cheeked. He looked fragile with the kind of emaciation that sometimes afflicts the very old. He cleared his throat, but did not speak.

"That's right, Mr. So. Make yourself comfortable," said Mrs. Gilmore. The son said something in Chinese and Mr. So nodded and smiled weakly.

Mrs. Gilmore got up and put the two files away in a sleek filing cabinet and then asked Graham if he could give her some details for the new file she was opening on his wife. This occupied but a few minutes and then he sat down again, waiting, waiting until whatever it might be— the news that would arrive with Professor Spurling. *If only*, Graham thought, *I had gone to the shops myself, this might never have happened.* He had been grading, reading Paul's missive, and working on jotting questions for an examination he was preparing for the PhD comprehensives. The graduate committee wanted it tomorrow. Luckily, he had finished it and e-mailed it to the chairman before he was called to the hospital. He should have dropped everything and gone to the Food Giant himself. But she had dashed off to the supermarket before setting out for home. So, what had happened?

"Was it a car accident?" he asked aloud, without realizing he had spoken. The middle-aged Chinese man looked at him and decided to answer.

"No, my father was struggling with a heavy tub of . . . a barrel . . . of beer at the back of the restaurant. He dropped it and it broke his foot."

"Oh, I'm sorry. That must have been painful. Big shock." They all nodded. They all looked concerned.

"Professor Spurling's very good with bones," offered Mrs. Gilmore.

"Is he a specialist in that?" asked Graham.

"One of the best," murmured Mrs. Gilmore, looking up from her files. Her phone made a buzzing noise. She pressed a button with a forefinger.

She spoke into the phone without lifting the handset off the machine. A brief reply came over her speaker.

"I'm ready now." A green light flashed above her desk. She walked over to Graham. "I'll take you in now, Mr. Curtis."

Graham got up and followed her. She knocked and then led him through into the professor's office.

"This is Mr. Curtis."

"How do you do?" The professor stood up, revealing that he was about six feet tall and slim. He shook hands with Graham and they both sat down. Graham looked into Spurling's face. He was impassive. He was not smiling. Spurling's hands were on his desk, their backs quite hairless, though dark hair showed at his wrists. They were strong hands. He wore no rings.

"I have bad news. We did all we could for her, but we could not revive her. We've lost her."

Graham sat looking at him. He could not speak. His mouth was dry. He had to clear his throat. There was silence. A clock ticked as if it had just started.

"I . . . I should have gone to the super market. I should have . . ."

"It is not your fault, Mr. Curtis; it's one of those terrible things that happen."

"Don't blame yourself," said Mrs. Gilmore. Graham felt her hand rest on his shoulder. He looked up at her. She was calm and very pretty. She had a chain of small golden leaves around her neck. She wore earrings with a pearl set in a disc of gold. He hadn't noticed this before.

"Would you like another beaker of water?"

"Please." She went out.

"What was the cause of her death, doctor?"

"Well, she came into emergency with head wounds and a gunshot wound."

"Gunshot!"

"She had lost a great deal of blood. We did all we could, but she died during the operation."

"A gunshot! That's too much! Terrible. Gunshot. My God! It's crazy. Where did it happen?"

"I don't know, Mr. Curtis. I expect the police will be in touch or you may want to contact them."

Graham was silent. He sat staring at the desk. There was a porcelain dish with a few green paper clips in it. He stared at them. Jacqueline dead. It was a violent physical shock. Mrs. Gilmore came in with a glass of water and a cup of tea on a tray. There was also a small plastic pack of pills.

"Here. Swallow one of these, just for the shock, you understand? That's it—with some water. Do you want some tea? That's it," said Mrs. Gilmore.

"Professor, I'd like to see my wife."

"I understand. Yes. But have your tea first and then we'll go down."

"Why was it impossible to save her, doctor?"

"Well, she had lost a good deal of blood. The wounds were large and she died quickly, almost as soon as we had started the operation."

"Would she have been crippled had she lived?"

"She would have been very handicapped, mentally and physically, I'm afraid. There's no way of knowing how much longer she would have lived on in that state. Her spine was damaged."

"Was she ever conscious when she arrived?"

"No. Do you have any children, Mr. Curtis?"

"No. Thank God. Thank God she died unconscious of it all."

A telephone was ringing in the waiting room. Mrs. Gilmore went out and came in again after a few moments.

"It's the police," she murmured. "Can you see them, Mr. Curtis?"

"Yes. I'll see them."

"Come with me then. We have a room across the corridor. It'll be empty just now. You can see them there. I'll send them in."

"But what about my wife? I'll see her, too?"

"Yes, don't you worry. I'll take you down to her when I get the word from my people," said Professor Spurling.

"Thank you, professor, and for what you did to try to save her."

"Thank you. Don't worry. Sam . . . er . . . Mrs. Gilmore will come to find you when it's time."

Graham followed Mrs. Gilmore through the waiting room and across the corridor into a small consulting room or office. There were half a dozen chairs and a large table. A large filing cabinet with a lock above the top drawer had a glass vase on top of it and there were some flowers that Graham could not identify. He sat in one of the chairs. He felt strangely empty and stupid. He could hardly believe this thing had happened. He could not remember the morning that was so ordinary. Just like any other morning—until this. After about five minutes Graham, lost in thoughts about Jackie and their life together, hardly registered a discreet knock at the door.

Mrs. Gilmore announced the arrival of the police and retreated, leaving him with a tall, lean man in civilian clothes and another, smaller man with a black moustache. He was in uniform. They shook hands. The tall man held out a visiting card, stating he was Detective Sergeant Burns. His companion was Detective Constable Spiers. Spiers gave Graham his card. They sat down. Burns began.

"We understand, sir, that you have just heard that your wife was shot and was brought here."

"Yes. She died. Some bastard shot her."

"Our condolences, sir. I'm very sorry to hear that bad news. Do you feel able to talk to us about how things were this morning, before all this happened?"

"Yes."

"Good. It will save time. We want to catch whoever's responsible. Speed counts in these cases."

"What do you want to know?"

"You both had breakfast as usual, I take it?"

"Yes."

"Then what?"

"Jacqueline wanted something mailed. I said I'd go yesterday, but I didn't. I'm working on something for the university and also an article. I said I'd go this morning. She said she'd call at the Giant, Food Giant, and I could have done that. And she brushed it off and told me to get on with my work. I wish I'd gone and she'd stayed in."

"So you stayed in and she went out—at about what time?"

"It was about nine-thirty. Our usual time for doing chores, shopping . . ."

"Did she drive?"

"Yes, she took the little car. She usually drives it."

"You didn't go out?"

"Only to collect the mail from the end of the street. Not really until I came here."

"Did you telephone her or did she telephone you?"

"No. Oh, yes, she called to say she'd shop."

"When was the last time you saw her?"

"When she went out."

"When did the hospital contact you?"

"I don't know. I just dropped everything and came here. And I've just learned she died in the operating theatre. The surgeon said I can see her."

"I see. Do you mind if we come with you?"

"Whatever for?"

"Well, sir, we need a formal identification. If we come with you, you will not have to make another journey to see her in the city premises where they do the autopsies. It will spare you more stress and worry."

"Oh, yes. Okay then. Can I ask what you know? How did it happen?"

"There was an armed robbery. Your wife happened to get out of her car in the parking lot in front of the row of shops near the bank. At that moment, we understand two men were running to a car waiting nearby. Your wife saw them shoot at the security guard and she cried out. One of the men then shot her. That's what we have from witnesses."

"She was in the wrong place . . . at the wrong time. A minute later and she'd be alive. Now. I still can't believe it."

"Yes, sir. It's hard."

Mrs. Gilmore came in. "The professor can take you to see your wife, Mr. Curtis," she said. They all stood up. Graham followed her out with the policemen. Professor Spurling came from a door leading straight from his office. Detective Burns explained that they would come down as well. Mr. Curtis had agreed. "Follow me, then," said the surgeon.

They took the lift to a floor marked one and emerged into a broad corridor. No one spoke. It was an uncomfortable, heavy silence. When they were almost at the end of the corridor, Spurling rang the bell at a plain, steel door. After a few moments, they were admitted. The room was cold. There were artificial lights and no windows. On a steel trolley and stretcher there was a form covered with a green sheet. The man who had let them in led them to the trolley. He gently pulled back the sheet at one end as if he were being careful not to disturb the deceased. Graham looked down at his wife's face. He bent down and kissed her forehead. She was cold.

"Yes," Graham said. "Oh Christ. Yes. That's Jacqueline. God in his mercy, keep her now."

Graham felt Spurling take hold of his arm. He heard him say to the detectives: "Actual cause of death was head injuries. Mr. Curtis, I'm so sorry." Graham thought it was not just that she had fallen; the bastard had kicked her head hard.

"We'll get them," said Burns.

The detectives shook hands and nodded to the mortuary attendant and the surgeon. The attendant let them out. They were obviously in a hurry. Graham looked at Jacqueline. Her make-up had been removed. *She was pale*, he thought. *Of course she was*. Tears welled up into his eyes. Professor Spurling took his arm.

"Shall we go, Mr. Curtis?"

"Oh, yes, of course." But Graham put his hand on the sheet where it covered Jackie's shoulder. It was hard to leave her. He turned to the attendant, "Thank you," he said.

Professor Spurling took Graham back to the lift, saying, "I'll let you out at the ground level if you are fit to drive home. If not, I'm sure Mrs. Gilmore will let you rest a while until you are ready."

"No, I'll go home as I came, by taxi. I'll be all right. Thank you, professor. You've been very thoughtful and kind. Please thank Mrs. Gilmore."

"I will. Good-bye then."

The lift stopped and the doors opened. Graham got out and waved as the doors closed again. He watched the lighted numbers as the lift went up, and then he abruptly turned and left to find a taxi. There was a line of cabs waiting. He was luckily behind just one couple. He opened the door of his cab, got in, and buckled his seat belt. He looked at the front passenger seat. The driver had a few oddments dumped there. Jacqueline would never sit in their passenger seat again, her mini skirt exposing a goodly amount of thigh. Or in one of her long skirts. Or one just riding up above her knees. The seat belt would never again divide her breasts covered by blouse or sweater or jacket. He sat quite still and then he wept. He dried his eyes, sobbed, and then wept again. He dried his eyes again. He sat staring at the cars creeping in and out of the area of the hospital. An ambulance arrived. Another left. *This is no good. I want to be home, now! I'm going home*, he thought, and sat back as the city slipped by outside. He was unaware of it. The driver asked for the number when they reached his street.

CHAPTER FIFTEEN

Their home was its usual comfortable self, but it was silent. There was no sound of a washing machine in action. There was no radio playing jazz from another room. His tea stood untouched and cold. Graham felt the desolation of a terrible, aching void. He wandered into the bathroom. Lying in disarray, waiting for her to get home and wash them, were a bra and a pair of lacy panties. One of his shirts lay with them, one sleeve across them. It seemed a gesture of protection. He had not been able to protect her, though.

She's gone, without a chance or any choice. She's gone forever. Stupidly, her clothes are still here. Her underclothes once seemed mysterious and exciting. Now they are just garments, waiting to be washed. All the urgency of life has vanished. Why, why? Graham found no answer. Where had she gone? There was no answer. There was no answer in the silence. Then the phone rang. It was the police. The car and some of his wife's things could be picked up when he was ready.

CHAPTER SIXTEEN

When Graham had collected the large envelope from the Canada Post outlet nearby, he settled down to read what Paul had sent. It was better than thinking about his own situation. He took a pill with his coffee. He had his favourite coffee mug in one hand, and the top sheet from Paul in the other. He read:

EVENTS IN HONG KONG

Pleased to have finished the Free Press business meeting and the dinner served afterwards as a reward for attendance, I emerged from the Kowloon YMCA building on Salisbury Road just before nine-thirty on a Saturday night. The traffic, piled up as usual, had stopped all the way along to the traffic lights at the T-junction, the end or beginning of Nathan Road. Vehicles seemed woven into a fabric of bright metallic threads. I turned to look at the colored, bouncing sprays of the fountain of the Peninsula Hotel. Resisting the temptation to drop in for a drink, I pressed on towards the Middle Road car park, where I had left my car. It had by now, I hoped, been cleaned and waxed.

I had reached Nathan Road and was waiting at the pedestrian crossing, when I saw her standing on the narrow island in the middle of the road, waiting, like me, for the walk sign to glow green. She was a tall, dark-skinned woman of supreme and compelling beauty. Her features were fine-boned and regular, her nose narrow and straight, her lips pleasingly full. Her dark, steady gaze had a force that allowed no escape. My eyes met hers and, perhaps from timidity or maybe good manners, I looked away. I felt compelled, though to catch her eyes again. I looked at her again. Her eyes met mine again. This time she was surely staring at me, unsmiling, intent, her eyes larger, opened wider. She raised her left hand and arm in front of her face and made a serpentine gesture, neither beckoning nor repelling, but simply sliding, snake-like, down in front of her neck and body. I was fascinated by this woman, enchanted by her dignity, her poise, her beauty, the elegance of her dark clothes, and, most of all, the strange gesture. She repeated it, still looking me in the eye, calm, unsmiling. It was a signal, but its meaning escaped me. I had never seen such a gesture before. It seemed natural to her and yet part of her mystery.

Her gravity and, yes, hieratic beauty, suggested some ancient ritual of a forgotten culture. Perhaps, too, she was a memory in me of the exalted female figures in Gustave Moreau's sketches and paintings. The small green light for pedestrians glowed in the crossing signal and I walked towards the little space left by the pedestrians coming towards me. The tall, dark woman stood still as a statue as I approached. I was now just a yard in front of her. She was not a Chinese, not a Philippina, not an African, not an Indian, nor a European. I detected neither race nor country in her, just the most exquisite mixture of genes that produced this human beauty, in perfect, sculptural repose. As I got level with her, she turned so that she was close beside me, facing the direction I was taking, and slipped her slender left arm through my right one, resting a slender hand on my right hand. I stopped and glanced down at her long, brown fingers, nails meticulously manicured and painted alternately silver and gold. She turned her head towards me and speaking gravely in a low voice asked, "Where are you going?"

She had no distinguishing accent. I didn't speak. My blood was racing. Again, she posed her question.

"Where are you going?"

I smiled, gazing into her deep brown eyes, almost animal in their beauty. "Where are you going?" I replied. Immediately, I felt my words were foolish and trivial. Her words, though the same, seemed to pose a real, and an urgent question, reaching into the secrets of my life and all its circumstances. She was startlingly different from any other human being I had met. Moreover, she spoke with the air of knowing me already.

Had we met before? No, we had not met before, unless in a previous life. Reincarnation? I'm a journalist. Articles on it come up from time to time. Belief in it? That's another matter. Yet, she reminded me of someone. I remembered the waking dream or vision I had had in Malvern, a year or so before. Was this the same woman I had met before, but in a dream? Was this the incarnation of a goddess I had seen in Vancouver? Was this my little swimmer alive again? Was she a traveler from the world beyond human and material life? I dismissed these thoughts at once. I've had some training in linguistics; I have to be rational and scientific in method and thinking. Is not linguistics, in a nutshell, the science of language? Yet . . . is not journalism the reporting of real events? Sometimes. What I report here is what happened. I was for a moment convinced that I was in contact with a phantom. Or was she just a very expensive call girl working the luxury hotels? This other extreme seemed the most likely explanation of her disturbing presence.

The busy junction seemed suddenly still, the roar and squeal of traffic distant. Time was at a standstill, yet we walked. I went towards the Sheraton Hotel and she towards the Peninsula. I looked back for her over my shoulder. She was nowhere in sight. She was either an extremely fast walker or she had vanished like a ghost suddenly repelled by the unheeding, careening bustle of modern life.

I did not want this to be the end of it. And as the crowds surrounded me, it was as if my desire had been a command, for she was at my side again, her hand again on mine, with a pressure I felt. It was she that was at the helm. We turned into the comparative quiet of Middle Road. Ignoring the car park, we climbed the steps near the Mariner's Club and pressed on into the angled streets leading from Minden Road. I recognized the names of streets as we walked, but could not recognize the streets themselves. I had known them well, I thought, until this evening. Most of it was now different, irretrievably lost were yesterday's realities. The glare of shop fronts, the smell of boiled rice, boiled offal, and pungent, spicy odours of restaurant kitchens, the press of late model cars, gleaming under the neon, were all different, and yet my mood was that of the excited young man I was when I first arrived, walking these very streets. I followed a mood-map in my confused, but finely etched heart. From fragments of sacred walls like old bones, street names I knew were whispered in words. These were her words in my ear as we walked. Suddenly my tongue unlocked and I heard myself say to her, "I step from glittering streets into the shadows of dank passages. Tourist in a new-found city, I clutch in my secret self the mood-map of the old."

Another example! I had noticed on several occasions since my experiences in Malvern that words came to me like an unsolicited gift; I would be doing some research for an article, or simply walking along a busy, congested street when a few lines of prose or even verse would become unblocked, like broken branches clustered at the edge of a river suddenly swinging out into the current.

The woman, not reacting to my musing, turned quickly into a narrow doorway. I followed her along a murky hall with metal alloy mailboxes on one wall. We took an old-fashioned elevator with latticed steel doors to the fifth floor. On the landing at either end were the identical doors of two flats. Each had a screen door behind which was a wooden door with a peephole.

"Which shall we take?" she asked. After the clatter of the lift doors, her low, solemn voice filled the silence like the first notes of a song.

"Do you know? You must know."

She smiled. "It's your choice." She smiled again.

"Let's take this one then," I said, moving towards the door to the left. On the wall were papers, colors fading, depicting chubby children and proclaiming double happiness, longevity, prosperity, for a Lunar Year, evidently many moons ago.

She stepped in front of me, already holding a key to the door, as if she had known my choice without even thinking about it. I followed her into a neat little hall. Through a half-open door ahead, I saw the red glow of a household shrine, as she took my hand, leading me into a small sitting room with a Danish-style couch and chairs in teak and light tan leather. In one corner was a round dining table, again teak, covered with an intricately worked beige tablecloth of Chinese design. In the other corner was an ancient TV set on a flimsy-looking stand. Outside the narrow window was an empty bamboo birdcage in the shape of a small pavilion.

"What's your name?" I asked.

"Is it important? I'm not an artist or a politician. They always want people to remember their names. I have been to an exhibition of oils and of pastels by Simone Poon. Do you know her work?"

"Not really. Well, not at all. I know her name. I've heard people say that she uses her European techniques to great advantage with Asian subjects. Where is she being shown?"

"She has a magnificent sense of color. She spies on the colors of the modern world. Oh, her exhibition is in a little gallery in Paris, in the *cinquième*."

I was about to state the obvious, with remarks like. Paris! Lucky you! Have you just got back? Did you have a good flight? But she spoke again.

"You'll need a drink," and so saying she went into a small kitchen off the sitting room. I noticed for the first time the slow propeller of an old ceiling fan. The night was warm, but not humid. From the kitchen came the agreeable sound of clinking ice cubes. On the wall near the table hung a large photograph of the Eiffel Tower glowing spectacularly against a night sky. On the wall near the window was an even larger photograph of a small portion of the Great Wall of China.

"What's your name?" she asked, leaning out of the kitchen doorway, head at an angle, smile dazzling and warm.

"Paul."

"Like a famous citizen of Rome. He wrote many epistles. Isn't he a saint?"

"Yes. But, I'm no saint. Yet in fact, I am a bit of a writer myself." She was out of sight in the kitchen again. "I'm a journalist; some might think they are the opposite of saints."

"A journalist?" she called.

"Yes, but I also have become a bit of a poet."

"You can't be a bit of a poet. You're either a poet or not," she rebuked me sharply, from the kitchen door, and added, "Are you a serious person or not?"

"Yes, I'm serious. It's just a habit of speech, 'a bit of,' I picked it up. It's an expression of modesty. Australians often use it of themselves to seem modest, though they may not be, and Yorkshire men use it of other people, sometimes to disparage. And what's your name? You haven't told me yet."

"Can you think of me as a Kalitza?"

"*K* for Kalitza. I certainly can, my love! I don't know any other women called that. It's a name to be conjured with!"

I looked at a bronze copy of an ancient urn. It stood on a small wooden stand with curved feet. After a few seconds, Kalitza came in from the kitchen. She was holding a glass in each hand. Her street clothes had gone. The long clean lines and color of apple-green pyjamas suited her light brown skin, the deeper brown of her eyes, and set off marvellously the black swathe of her hair. She was bare-footed and still very tall even without high heels. Whatever her several racial or ethnic origins, the blending was perfection itself. As I took the glass she offered, I noticed that gold rings adorned the second toe of each slender foot. Her toenails also were silver and gold alternating. At her neck there was the glint of a fine gold chain.

"What's the drink?"

She smiled her dazzling smile again and then explained that it was an old recipe handed down for generations, a kind of pomegranate brandy. The subtle pink of the liquor was beautiful, but the smooth warmth of the powerful old brandy was nectar. It was not sweet, like a liqueur, but more like a Poire William, fragrant and powerful.

"Don't warm it like brandy. Keep it ice-cold, like vodka; after all it's the fruit of Greek myth, the underworld, all that," she said, smiling again and that smile, bright, happy, amused, seemed to bring more light into the little room. We sipped our drinks for a moment without speaking. I thought of Proserpina. Was Kalitza telling me she was a sort of Proserpina? Was she telling me she would soon die? It was too fantastic, but I felt a moment of panic at a possible loss. I was conscious of the strength of the alcohol, the faint movement of air from the fan, the privilege of being the guest of such a woman, and at that moment traffic noises from the street seemed friendly, even comforting. She held out her hand. I took her cool, slightly damp fingers in my warm, dry hand. She led me through the little kitchen, a converted corridor I guessed, into a bedroom.

A warm, subdued glow came from a white marble lamp in the form of a winged horse. The prancing horse was topped by a Thai silk lampshade in a wonderful light green. The same green, flecked with red and gold thread was used in the silk bedspread. Above the bed, from a small golden crown, there hung a fine, white mosquito net. In a corner, near the foot of the bed, stood a portable fan, almost silent, that moved in a whispering arc of 180 degrees. The brown shine of the parquet was a good foil for a Persian rug with a rich blue and red design—a scene of warriors hunting deer. Next to the window with its set of narrow Venetian blinds stood a small oblong table, inlaid with different woods and pieces of mother-of-pearl. On the table was an oblong box of red carved lacquer, featuring on its lid a pair of nimble-looking dragons.

"What do you keep in it?" I asked, touching the deeply incised surface of the box.

"Take a look."

I lifted the lid and found inside on the smooth, black bottom, two, small circular packs of playing cards, white, with orange dragons decorating their backs. They looked new and unshuffled. They suggested order. A settled life.

"They can be shuffled and bring great fortune or bad luck, even death."

"Are they responsible? Or do they simply foretell what seems likely?"

"Neither. Who knows!"

She smiled. It was a statement not a question. Was she one of those astrologers, clairvoyants, or mediums who advertise in newspapers and TV magazines? Perhaps she did a daily horoscope for a Chinese language or Hindi newspaper. In other words, a journalist of sorts. I thought not. She seemed totally removed from commerce. Yet, her personal clothes and accessories suggested French luxury shops. A fashion model? That would fit. I'd never seen her on posters or in glossy magazines. If she were a model, I surmised, she must be at the beginning of her career. I suspected I knew her real trade. She was physically the most beautiful person I had ever seen in real life or on film or in photographs. Race seemed irrelevant to her, yet I was curious about the origins of such beauty.

"Could you be part Sri Lankan?"

"I could be, but I'm more Greek, I suppose. I'm hybrid, Eurasian."

"From India, from France, from England?"

"Perhaps. But definitely I'm Mediterranean."

"From Egypt, Greece, with a tad of England, too?"

"That's quite likely. Why do you ask? Race is an accident. We are born into a certain time and space by a succession of chance events. To some of the ancients, birth was an unlucky chance. Births happen again and again every second, all over the world. And yet, men think it is all planned beforehand in heaven. If so, God must have an enormous planning department full of civil servants. Men think it matters which tribe chance pulled them into, out of the womb.

"Well, they like to think they belong, I expect. They understand their culture's ways."

"Or think they do. They forget that we all learn our culture, it isn't born with us. Cultures change, like everything else. Change! Isn't it enough for them to be alive and to be human? They need to live the fully human life. Courageously! Intrepidly! I love brave men, men brave enough to work and marry and have families. That takes courage for a lifetime. I ignore moral cowards and avoid physical cowards as much as possible."

"Brave men are few; courage is admired wherever we go, because it is rare."

"Oh, the ordinary brave men are legion. When it comes to the showdown, in battle for instance, there are more than you might imagine. Isn't it the brave who deserve the beautiful?"

"I expect you're right, Kalitza. A man has to be brave to take on a beautiful woman!"

"Oh, so that's how you think. Why do you say that?" she smiled.

"In my experience, physical beauty presents problems and beautiful women are a handful for any mere man, even a brave one!" We both laughed.

"I expect, from my experience, that you might have a point. How do you write? I mean the process—pencil, pen, pads, typewriter, computer?

"The latter, but I'm thinking I must get a new and better laptop while I'm in Hong Kong."

"Soon every three-year-old will use them!"

"Yes, that's on the cards. I travel and it will be easier if I take a really fast laptop with me. What's your line?"

Pause. Smile.

"Who are you, Kalitza?"

"Oh, I'm a spy. One of God's spies, as Shakespeare has it."

"A spy! A real one? But you work for God. In other words, the president of the French Republic!" She laughed. I continued, "You must be a prisoner then, like Cordelia. I don't see you in prison, somehow."

"Ha! There are prisons and prisons." She looked suddenly older.

I smiled and took her in my arms. We stood cheek to cheek, as if dancing. I thought to myself, I must ask her how much she charges, before we go any further. She spoke before I could work out exactly how to phrase this indelicate question.

"This is my gift to you, Paul. You will serve me faithfully. We shall keep in touch until you do not need me and I don't need you. You will find your way."

"Will I? I'm not so certain. I have traveled. I've visited lots of countries. Yet, I have never known where I was going." I smiled, shaking my head, amused, I remember, by my own boundless, naïve sense of adventure.

"That's nothing new. Your name tells me that you always find the true way, even if you don't recognize it. Follow the true way. Scales will soon fall from your eyes."

"How will I recognize it, the true way?" I asked, somewhat impatiently.

"There is always a signaler and a signal." Smiling suddenly again, she pulled me to kneel beside her on the bed. We held each other and I felt perfect peace and a heightened awareness of my senses, yet without tension or brute desire. Was this nirvana?

We took off the bedspread and then made love on pale green sheets like a tropical sea in some calm lagoon. It was an intense, exquisite, prolonging of desire. Completely spent and exhausted at last, we slept.

After I don't know how long, I woke and looked at Kalitza lying next to me, magnificently naked, her strands of unpinned hair stretched across her pillow around her head, the rays of a dark sun in a pale-green sky. I had never contemplated such beauty before, never possessed it before, never before been possessed by it. I feared I might never find it again, after this one extraordinary night. I feared that I might lose, too, something of my own precarious being. I had already lost any idea of equilibrium, yet I had no regrets. I looked at her in repose, loving the mystery of this woman, a mystery that seemed total, even though she was lying next to me. Around her neck, the golden chain with the ankh symbol gleamed faintly in the shadowy bedroom. I stroked her pubic hair. Tightly curled, it seemed like moistened silk. I will not describe in any detail our love-making. All I can say, when I recall that night, is that now I know why the ancients insisted that from time to time mortals coupled with gods and goddesses.

Was Kalitza some supernatural being? I thought so then and, stupidly perhaps, as I write this account, I am still convinced of it, as I'm convinced by the theorem about the square on the hypotenuse. Yet the scent of roses from her warm skin and of violets in her hair was so immediate and seductive that I reveled in her bodily presence: QED. She was real, all right, totally, blissfully real. Now, as I write this, a few seconds later, I think she was no phantom, but really a spy, the agent not of God, but of some other country. In that case, though, why would she bother to pick up a person like me, seemingly at random? I had to accept now whatever destiny had in store for me. With this new experience giving me a strange sense of confidence, despite my confusion as to her real character and my total ignorance of her life, I must have dropped off to sleep.

I awoke at about nine in the morning. I was alone. I could sense the emptiness of the flat. The playing cards were on the table, next to their lacquer box. They were shuffled together. Inside the box there was now a small notebook, its cover bearing my name, Paul. I stood there naked, flicking over the pages. They were all blank. I looked everywhere for any note she might have left. Nothing. She had left the blank notebook for me. That much was clear, because on its light-green silk cover my name was printed in dark, racing green. I felt the anguish of loss and longing. I wanted to be with her forever, but she was gone. She could be anywhere. I felt certain she was not coming back. The bright enamel of flowers fades forever. 'The life I have lost meanders through a world half-hidden by rain.' Repeating those ancient words to myself over and over again, I showered and dressed and was about to leave, when there was a knock at the door. She was back! No—it was a male voice.

"Hello! Anyone there?"

"Hang on a moment," I called.

When I opened the door, I found a pair of Hong Kong policemen in uniform. One was solid-looking and had sergeant's stripes. He wore horn-rimmed spectacles. The other man was younger, a constable, very thin, fragile-looking. He seemed no more than a boy, too young to be pitted against criminals.

"May we come in, sir?"

"May I see your ID?"

They looked at each other. Then Sergeant Kenneth Lam Koon-fei and Constable Wong Yat-chuen as they turned out to be nodded and they produced their IDs. I ushered them into the sitting room.

"Now may we see your ID, sir?" asked the sergeant.

I found my wallet and showed them my passport. Luckily I had it with me. It had not occurred to me to check my wallet before, but I now noted that my credit cards and a few bank notes were still there. I felt a little shame that I had even for a split second doubted Kalitza. The policemen looked grim.

"What's it all about, sergeant? Is anything wrong? How can I help you?"

"Do you live here, in this flat?" the sergeant demanded.

"No. I'm just visiting. I'm a guest. My friend has gone out. I'm sure she'll be back soon." The policemen glanced at each other.

"Can you describe her for us, sir?"

"She's a tall, amazingly beautiful woman, late twenties or early thirties. Very early. Let's say twenties. Maybe she's only twenty-one. Difficult to be precise. I don't know the details of her life."

"Is she Caucasian?"

"Eurasian, sergeant. What's happened? Oh God, nothing has happened to her?"

"When did you last see her?"

"It was very late or very early, maybe about four thirty a.m. We were . . . just . . . sleeping together. I woke about nine this morning and she had already gone."

"A prostitute?"

"Heavens, no, sergeant. If anything, she's a goddess. Perhaps a top model. No, something less narcissistic. She has gravity and keen intelligence. I'm not sure if she has a job. She could be a millionaire's wife or mistress."

"Did you give her any money?"

"No, I did not!"

"How long have you known her?"

"We met yesterday evening."

Only yesterday! The sergeant noted a few things on a small pad. Yes, I thought, it seems we have always known each other, yet I know nothing about her in effect.

"Where did you meet her?"

"In Nathan Road, near the Sheraton."

"I see. When exactly?"

"It must have been ten, ten fifteen at night."

"Was she soliciting?"

"Heavens no, sergeant. I have already told you she is not that kind of woman. We met on the pedestrian crossing. A lightning flash passed between us and we talked and talked and then she brought me home with her. It was not a commercial transaction."

"You can make a statement at the police station now."

"Look, what is this? Has there been a crime of some sort?"

"A young Eurasian woman was found in the road near here at about seven twenty a.m. She is dead. She was wearing something green, judging by the sleeves. She was killed by a vehicle. A hit-and-run."

I was dizzy. My irritation with the sergeant's assumption about Kalitza had evaporated. Grief felt like a heavy stone inside my chest. I sat down on the sofa. I could not speak. I could not see. I held my head in my hands. My lips trembled and I wept, making no sound except for gasping for breath. Sobbing.

"Sir, sir!"

"Yes?" Looking up at them, I dried my eyes on a tissue.

"Will you come with us now?"

"Yes," I managed to say. I took a minute or two to control my voice before I asked, "How did you know she had been here?"

"She had this address on her person when we found her."

I got shakily to my feet and followed the policemen. I cannot remember how I arrived at the police station, cannot remember the statement I wrote, or how I got to the morgue. I do remember a trolley, a green sheet over a body, an attendant lifting one end of the sheet. Her face was calm. There was a slight smile on her lip. Her eyes were closed. Her beauty was as miraculous as ever. Yet remote. Remote from me now. Was the remainder of my life to be as empty and impersonal as this quiet little corner of a morgue?

"Was this the woman you met? Did she take you to the flat?"

I nodded. "Yes, that's her."

"Did she tell you her name, sir?"

"She told me to call her Kalitza."

"Please to spell." I spelled it out for him with a *z*, though I suppose she might equally have used an *s*.

"Forename or family name?"

"Just that. That was all she told me. I assumed it was her first name."

They took me to the car park and inspected my car before I was allowed to drive home. I realized that they wanted to see whether my vehicle had been the one that had run over Kalitza.

***

After a shower and shave at home, I put on fresh clothes and hung up my jacket. Emptying the pockets to transfer my wallet, keys, and other things, I found a small square object, about the size of my thumbnail. It was some sort of electronic component, perhaps a microchip. It was not mine. How had it got into my pocket? It seemed that Kalitza must have put it there, perhaps in Nathan Road when we had met, or maybe later, when I was asleep and she was slipping out of the flat. This small component proved to me her existence and it brought tears back into my eyes. Did it indicate that she was after all a spy? After a few minutes, I decided to call the police. As I walked to the phone, it started to ring. When I answered, I recognized the sergeant's voice.

"Good morning, sir. It's Sergeant Lam again. Do you own a notebook with the name Paul embossed on it?"

"Yes, well, not at the moment, no, but it was in the flat and I assumed it was a gift for me from Kalitza. I forgot to take it."

"So, you had met her previous to that night?"

"Not at all. But I assumed it was meant for me. It had my name on it."

"But how could she select a notebook with your name on it, when she did not know you until the night when you met and slept together?"

"I don't know. I just assume it's meant for me. It's blank and . . . er . . . and she knows, knew, I write."

"Write? What?"

"I am a freelance journalist."

"I see. Did you handle the notebook?"

"Yes, it was in a box on a small table. I picked it up, flicked its pages, and put it back on the table."

"I am at the flat now. We found the notebook on the floor."

"Well, when the enquiries are over, I would like the notebook as a keepsake, if at all possible. But I have something you might find more significant. I think Kalitza slipped it into my jacket pocket at some stage last night. It doesn't belong to me."

"What is it?"

"It's a microchip. Some sort of electronic device—what we journalists refer to as 'wizardry.'"

"Stay at home, sir, I'll bring a colleague to look at this chip. Don't open the door to anybody else."

Less than fifteen minutes later, there was a ring at the door. Peering through the peephole, I recognized Sergeant Lam. He had another, taller man in plainclothes with him. This man's warrant card, or whatever they call them in Hong Kong, proclaimed that he was a Chief Inspector Charles Merrick. He was sallow-skinned, thin, and had startlingly blue eyes. He asked the questions. I judged from his accent that he was Australian.

"So the young lady gave you a chip?" asked Merrick.

"I assume it was she who slipped it into my jacket without saying anything. It certainly isn't mine." I held it out on the palm of my hand. He picked it up, looked at it briefly, and slipped it into a small plastic Ziploc bag."

"What else did she give you, sir?"

What she had given me could not be discussed. It was beyond price. She had given me her exquisite beauty and had asked me life's key question. She had made me her follower and then had gone, irretrievably lost.

"I assume she gave me the blank notebook."

"We'll be keeping that for the moment. If any person should approach you," added Merrick, his face a little crumpled, like a brown paper bag, "somebody, anybody wanting to know anything, or threatening you, or wanting to give you money, try to make an accurate mental note of everything, everything, and phone me immediately with the details as soon as you are alone."

He gave me a small visiting card. I then suspected, and as I write, am sure, that Kalitza was some sort of secret agent.

"Do you think I am in danger, inspector?"

"I don't think so. But after you and the sergeant here left the flat this morning, someone went in and searched the place. Everything was turned upside down, even before we could get anyone there to give it the once over."

"They were looking for the chip?"

"Maybe. Maybe something else, and maybe they found it, and maybe they didn't! We just don't know. If anyone phones you, asking about that flat or the notebook or the woman Kalitza, let us know. If anyone follows you when you're out and about, let us know. Don't tackle anyone by yourself."

"Okay, I am in danger, then?"

"I very much doubt it, sir. But it pays to be careful. A young woman has been killed, perhaps deliberately or by chance. Her flat has been ransacked. You were with her for a while. Maybe you were seen together, maybe not. I believe whoever killed her was hoping to find that microchip and maybe something else."

I was uneasy, if not a little frightened. If I had been identified by hidden watchers and possibly Triad killers, they might assume I knew exactly what Kalitza had been up to, that we were even working together, that I was also a spy, and that I had in my possession what they had searched the flat to get. The chip could contain information on as yet secret industrial processes, or be a key component of some kind of machine or apparatus. There and then I resolved that if I were cornered by any thugs, I would tell them I had found a chip and given it to the police. I would perhaps be able, at the same time, to make a publishable investigative article from all this, if I lived to tell the tale.

Who was the lovely woman I had known for a few hours? What was she? Where had she come from? What was she doing with the microchip? How did she know my name was Paul before asking? I had known her only in the physical sense; it again came home to me that I had no inkling of her real life. Then I asked myself, did I really know anything about the real lives of all the people I knew? So much is founded on trust. My trust in people is first of all instinctive and then either fortified, confirmed, or eroded by the things I later learn. I approach the levels of hope and also of despair. Kalitza's elegant beauty came into my thoughts again like a bright apparition. What dangerous game had she been playing in Hong Kong, when she was murdered? I was convinced now that this had been no accident. Whatever her role may have been, I decided not to sit at home waiting for a possible encounter with killers.

I looked out of my window at the splendid view of the green mountains and then down below at the courtyard in front of the main entrance. Everything seemed normal and unshaken by the sudden, violent death of Kalitza. I would go back to my research in the city archive for an article I was preparing. It might help me to cope with my feelings. In any case, I had to meet a deadline. Afterwards, I might be able to find out more about Kalitza's mission.

My job was now largely a matter of combing the local English language press to track down a few items not dealt with in any detail by the books I had read. Some of the material was already on microfilm; some of it was still actual newsprint, collected in huge folders. I started that day by scrolling through *The South China Morning Post* for 1988. I had checked a number of items and skimmed over a large number of irrelevant pages when I was suddenly pulled up short by a photograph of a young woman of striking beauty. It was a photograph of Kalitza. She looked exactly as I had seen her the previous night. Not a day younger. But the article was from the SCMP of 25 October, 1988 and the photograph could have dated from a time previous to that. I was amazed by the accompanying article, a short piece of about six or seven column inches. It hit me like a sudden blow to the heart. The woman whom I thought looked like Kalitza was, according to the article, a Miss Ari Zagoudakis, twenty-two years old, a promising actress on the brink of stardom. She had been signed up for a big budget movie, had taken a flight from Hong Kong to Tokyo, and had vanished. The film people had expected her at a certain hotel for a meeting. She had never turned up. In December of that year, a short filler piece, again with the same photograph, reported that she was found dead in Ikeda on the northern island of Japan, Hokkaidô. The verdict was accident or misadventure. She had drowned when swimming. I had to believe, I suppose, that Ari was not Kalitza, yet instinctively I felt they were if not identical, at least relatives. But how strange that two people, perhaps sisters, should have looked identical and both have died so young in "accidents." Many people die young, I told myself.

Strange as it may seem, I could not believe in either of these deaths. I thought I would meet Kalitza or Ari again, alive, and more mysterious than ever. Is this one of the irrational aspects of behaviour when one loses someone very close, a relative, a loved one? Acting on a hunch, I went to the registry of births, marriages, and deaths. I also checked a register of equity members. Ari, but not Kalitza was in the registry of births. I thought with a sudden pang of sickness, she will, though, soon appear in the registry of deaths. From the equity register, I learned that Ari Zagoudakis was an actress experienced in musicals.

She was a dancer as well as a singer. If my Kalitza
and Ari were in fact the same person, how could she
have died twice? If they were sisters, why had they
not both been listed in the registry of births? Was Ari
Kalitza's mother? Possible. The simple explanation
was that Kalitza, if that was her real name, had been
born elsewhere. I was half inclined to suppose that
they were, in fact, one person, a supernatural being
who appeared in this life only to disappear, but who
always came back from some other kingdom, all her
beauty restored. I then dismissed this ridiculous idea,
unworthy of any journalist worth a pinch of sea salt.

When I got into the car I felt a compulsion to
whisper into my cell phone words I would jot down
later, words that sprang to my lips: 'All are ready
now for ancient dance, for naked foot to press the
echoing green, for the girl's sidelong glance as she
floats in robe of lawn where wild flowers curl: in her
grove the year is born.'

I suddenly realized that I had published these
words in a longer piece in the seventh year after Ari's
death in Japan. It was at this moment in the desolate
tarmac space of the government office car park that
I realized I had to get away, not just from that place,
but from my old life. I had learned while I was still a
very young man that there are no certainties but death.
Now, I imagined, not even death was a certainty.

I had not eaten since the morning. I drove to Tsim
Sha Tsui and walked to the ground floor cafeteria of
the YMCA. I had been to the Y the previous night,
just before Kalitza and I had met. Was I retracing
my steps in the hope of meeting her again? No, she
was dead. I saw the cold, remote beauty of the face
in the morgue. But could a person die twice? Could
Kalitza rise again, like the Egyptian girl, surely her

counterpart, in Malvern? In my pocket, something shuddered. It was my mobile phone.

"Kalitza," I murmured, alone at my table, staring at the food on my tray. "Kalitza, where am I going? What can I do, now that you have gone?" I decided to take the call. Maybe she would be alive again, talking to me as if nothing had happened to her. It was not Kalitza, however.

"Is this Mr. Paul Wills?"

"Speaking."

"Inspector Merrick on the line, sir. I'd like to clear up a thing or two. Can we meet?"

I agreed and was relieved when he said to stay put and he would come to the cafeteria. About five minutes later, I saw his tall, rather gaunt figure hovering at the door, scanning the tables. I waved him over.

"Sorry to trouble you again, Mr. Wills," he said, sitting opposite me.

"No trouble, inspector. In fact, I'm glad you're here."

He opened his coat, reached inside and, taking out the notebook, handed it to me. "It's an absolutely ordinary notebook. No mystery, no sweat. It isn't evidence. But we have three people in custody. We want to see if you can identify them. Or at least see whether you have noticed them before. We have no previous record of them."

"That was quick!"

"Yes, sir, we had a bit of luck. Two tried to break into your flat, but our boys jumped on them. Fast." He chuckled. "We also nabbed a fellow who was following you. Not a very matey type. He had an offensive weapon, as we say."

I felt anything but humorous. I had been observed. I had been followed. Someone thought I had the chip, or that I deserved to die. I had also been under police surveillance without knowing it. My decision to get away was obviously right. I put my hand on the notebook and felt as if I could weep. I didn't. I went with Merrick to see whether I could identify the men under arrest. I had never seen them before.

As soon as I could, I left Hong Kong for Bali. I realized I must leave a false trail. From Bali, I took a ferry to another Indonesian island and from there flew to Singapore. If unsavory types followed me there, I figured, they would probably be apprehended by the authorities. From Singapore, I flew to London. I then took the Eurostar to the Gare du Nord. In the notebook, I wrote jottings about these places and these journeys. I also sketched from memory the ageless face of the woman I had loved so briefly and lost so suddenly and irretrievably. At last, I was ready to begin a new life in the city that had lost none of the charm and excitement I had found there, when I had first visited, as a schoolboy.

CHAPTER SEVENTEEN

Paul and Mary emerged for dinner looking relaxed in casual clothes smart enough for their evening meal in the hotel. Mary chose a table near the window. There were only three other tables occupied. There was a threesome of middle-aged golf club types, Paul thought, then another couple, quite elderly with grey hair, and a family with a boy of about eight and a girl of about fourteen. People were looking at menus and discussing the choices in discreetly soft voices. There was occasional laughter.

Then the eight-year-old asked, quite loudly, "Can I have the chocolate mouse?"

"Not mouse, Kevin, mousse. Say mousse," ordered his father, nodding his head.

Kevin nodded his own head in exactly the same way and replied, "Mousse. Can I? Please, Dad!"

"We'll have to see how well you behave," said his sharp-featured, rather slim mother.

A waiter appeared and lit candles on all the occupied tables. He came back to Mary and Paul to hand them each a leather-bound menu. Another document of many more pages he handed to Paul. It was the wine list. He explained, before leaving them to read these weighty documents, that there were two special starters: homemade rabbit *paté* or fresh oysters. A special main dish was fresh trout caught on the property. Another was venison. Paul glanced across the table at Mary and felt a thrill of pleasure as he watched her looking at the menu, a cluster of gold bracelets on her wrist. These slid a little as she moved her hand to turn a page. She was wearing a very light-tan, knitted jacket with her red skirt. The gold earrings gleamed wonderfully in the soft light of the dining room. The curtains had not been drawn and the elegant eighteenth century windowpanes had darkened to become oblong mirrors, where from certain angles, the handsome room and some of the diners were reflected. Paul marveled at Mary's poise and natural grace. *It is a moment,* he thought, *when she is free of the responsibilities of her practice and the multiple demands of affliction, suffering, and the natural processes of birth and ageing and death.* He felt a surge of pride because he was the man sitting opposite her. A silver-haired waiter approached and asked if they would perhaps take an aperitif while considering the menu.

"Do you have virgin cocktails?" asked Mary.

"Certainly, madam. This page has a good selection."

"Ah, yes, wonderful. I'll have a Sunset in the Glen. It sounds good with raspberry and mint," said Mary.

"Make that two, please."

"Certainly, sir. Will you be needing the wine list for later?"

"Oh yes. Leave that with us."

The sommelier, for this was written on a highly polished brass badge pinned to the top pocket of his black jacket, then turned and walked to another table. He was listening carefully to the instructions of a man dressed in a light-grey and black hound's-tooth suit. Two ladies with grey hair, one blue-rinsed, were with him at the table. All were bronzed as if just returned from a holiday in Spain or Italy. The ladies wore diamonds and pearls. The man had a gold signet ring. He leaned towards them, said something, and they all laughed.

Paul suggested to Mary that they might share a dish for two if there was one they fancied.

"Yes. There's a sirloin for two, Paul. I don't see another. Wait, there's a seafood plate for two. I'd go for that, if you will."

"You're on! Sounds good. So, Riesling, Sancerre, Chablis? Hang on, there's a Chardonnay Latour here."

"That's delicious, all of it. But there's a half bottle of a very good Puilly Fumé here. What about that?"

"Sounds perfect. Why half?"

"I need only a glass. You can have the rest."

The sommelier reappeared and started decanting a red wine for the man and the two ladies. It was the full treatment with candle flame, great care, and the leaving of about an inch of very expensive red wine in the bottom of the bottle.

A young waiter came across to their table with their cocktails on a small silver tray. He wondered if they were ready to order. They were.

"I'll have the Scottish smoked salmon with brown toast."

"I'll have the rabbit paté, and then we'll have the seafood platter for two."

"Excellent choice. Wine?"

"We'll have a half bottle of the Puilly Fumé."

"Very good, sir, madam. I can recommend this Chateau Favray." He smiled and walked away to place their order.

"What are you thinking?" asked Mary.

"I was thinking of my old friend, Graham. Haven't seen him for some time. I expect he's working away in some seminar at the university. It's not the same as it was when we were students. Graham says it's more political, theoretical. Less attention to the pleasures of literature."

"Medicine has changed, too. There's more work than ever that takes account of statistics; home visits take up time that should be better spent on filling in government paper work!" Paul nodded acknowledgment at her irony. They held hands across the white cloth.

"I thought computers were going to render the world paperless."

"Some hopes," sighed Mary.

"Just look at that sirloin for two over there on the trolley. I think all three are going to share it."

"I'm glad," she replied, "You could feed five or six with that."

The man in hound's-tooth sniffed the wine. He raised his huge glass and looked at the wonderfully rich robe of the wine. He put his glass to his nose again and then took a sip. He rinsed his teeth, it seemed, and then swallowed. His head

nodded. He looked at the sommelier and smiled. The wine
was poured. The threesome raised their glasses in a ritual
toast and all nodded and smiled.

"Oh very palatable," they heard the blue-rinse lady say in
a "refeened" Yorkshire accent.

"Tell me more about Graham," said Mary.

"I've known him since we were undergrads. He teaches
and reads as if books were the most delicious food obtainable
and he had been starved for a week!"

"Well, books are the food of the intellect, aren't they?"

"Yes, if they are good books."

"What's your definition of a good book?"

The first course for the threesome had been delivered. The
man looked at the sirloin on the trolley. He was obviously
hungry. He was starting his meal before the ladies had even
picked up their cutlery.

"A good book should be informative and readable.
Another thing . . ."

There was a clatter from across the room and they both
looked to see what it was. The man in the hound's-tooth
suit was standing up. His chair was pushed back. He was
looking at them in surprise, his mouth open, his face red.
He sank down to his knees. He was clutching his throat with
one hand.

"Hey, look!" exclaimed the boy. His mother put her finger
to her lips. His father said, "Mousse."

"What's the matter, Harry?" the blue-rinse woman was
asking.

Mary ran across the room and pushed the man's chair
further away so she could get behind him. The chair knocked
over a stand containing an ice bucket at another table. Water
and ice cubes and a bottle rolled across the carpet. The man
was down on his knees. Mary was now kneeling behind the
man, her arms around him. Gripping her hands together,
she squeezed him sharply and forcefully. Paul was still
at the table, gaping at her speed and the force with which
she performed the manoeuvre. The waiters were crowding

round, one went to get towels for the carpet, and Harry's hitherto silent silver-haired companion looked at blue-rinse and said, "Well, I never!"

Harry gasped and gulped down air. Mary asked a waiter to help Harry back in his chair. She put her arm round Harry's shoulder and asked him how he was feeling.

"You saved my life! I thought I was going to die. I couldn't breathe at all."

"I'm glad to see your decanter of red is still on the table," said Mary. "Tell me how it happened."

"You saved my life!" He gasped out a further, "Thanks. Did you do first aid?"

"In a way. I'm a GP."

"Oh, I see. I was lucky you were here."

"What happened?" Mary persisted.

"Yes. I was talking to my wife and our friend here. I took a mouthful of my meat and she asked me a question. I started to answer and tried to swallow the meat so I could answer properly. It wasn't chewed enough or small enough and it stuck and I couldn't breathe. I thought I'd die."

Paul had meanwhile been listening.

"You certainly could have done if my . . . Mary had not seen you and realized your predicament. Did you know Shakespeare probably died through choking on a surfeit of sirloin?"

"Well, I never!" said the woman yet again.

"We're having sirloin," said the boy. His mother frowned at him, her finger to her lips.

"How are you feeling now?" asked Mary.

"Normal," said Harry.

"Good. Now drink a glass of water. And then go on with your meal as usual, but take smaller mouthfuls, chew thoroughly, and slow down your reactions to conversation!"

"How can we repay you, doctor?" asked the blue-rinse lady.

"Oh, there's no need. But if you wish, you could make a modest donation to your local hospital. There's probably a benevolent fund or something for medical research, things like that. We'll get back to our table now."

"Thank you," resounded from all three of Harry's party.

By this time, the waiters had mopped up and restored the room to its usual elegant order. Mary and Paul sat down to find that a waiter had appeared with their seafood platter. He poured the wine for them to approve. The verdict was "delicious!" Mary and Paul took their time over their meal.

"Do you know, I almost called you my wife just then!"

"I noticed you hesitated a bit. I thought you'd forgotten my name!"

"Now that's not nice, Gertrude." Paul replied. Mary punched his arm lightly.

Paul was thinking, *so that incident revealed her to me as a doctor, a professional in action who knows exactly what to do*. He realized this was a new context. He had not seen that side of her before. They talked about their plans for getting married. Mary, whose mother was now a widow, wanted a small, almost secret wedding. Paul wanted just the two of them, but realized they would have a small, select group on the day. When would it be? They didn't know. It hardly mattered, as long as it was fairly soon. Mary's father had been back in India and traveled a good deal to Africa, where he also had business interests before his sudden death. Her mother was in Tiverton in Devon. Paul suggested they marry in Paris, but Mary favoured Tiverton or Sutton Coldfield. If it were to be near Mary's practice, Paul asked why not Lichfield, with its rather beautiful cathedral?

"Do you want to marry me in church, Paul, and in a cathedral to boot?"

"Well, yes, why not? Oh, are you Hindu and not Anglican? Or Sikh temples for you? Or do you favour that god with an elephant's head?"

"Ganesh. Not really. I wouldn't approve of such spare parts surgery, I must say," laughed Mary. "Actually," she continued, "I'm nominally Anglican. Mother's doing, I expect. Or was it that they sent me to the best school they could find and it happened to be Anglican? Probably that was it."

"It's not a big issue, then, religion? Do you believe in reincarnation? How about a Buddhist ceremony in Japan? We would probably be left to ourselves and could honeymoon in Japan."

"Reincarnation? I suppose it could be possible if there's such a thing as the survival of the soul. But what's the soul? Mind/body! I have enough to deal with in the here and now, trying to keep people alive. Do you know Russell's rhyme on that? 'What's matter? Never mind. What's mind? No matter!'" They both chuckled. Paul had an image in his mind of Russell's bird-like head.

"Yes, it's neat. But I think you are right to concentrate on the here and now of patients' lives," remarked Paul, "and you are not delivering babies wondering what they did in their previous life, or caring for the terminally ill and thinking, never mind, they could do better next time around!"

"Absolutely." She squeezed his hand. They were both laughing. "The here and now is fine for me and I love you as you are. I'm not thinking, how did a pirate king get to be reborn as a journalist, or how did a pussy cat get to reappear as a man?"

He touched her hair now and lightly placed his hand on her arm.

"I'm glad you are not thinking such thoughts. Actually, I think our energy, free energy, all that's left over from coping with our material bodies, surges around the brain, is responsible for mind, thought, perhaps the soul! So you think I'm a pussy cat, do you? Maybe I was a man once, and now I'm a pussy cat, and you are the only one who can detect it."

"What would you have been in a previous life? Think carefully, Paul."

"Mmm. Let me see." He closed his eyes for a moment. Her hand closed over his. "I know. I was an eighteenth century gentleman of private means with a good Queen Anne house in a small cathedral town—Lichfield? Yes, I think that I was interested in everything. I read David Hume and enjoyed George Farquhar's plays. I was a friend of Dr. Samuel Johnson and met Oliver Goldsmith on several occasions. In fact, I once lent him five pounds, but he died before repaying me."

"Good heavens! Well, I'm glad you weren't Anne's great captain. That might have left you to be reborn differently from what you in fact are, at the present moment. But you'll see a lot of changes in Lichfield when you go there I bet."

"What am I at the present moment? You tell me."

"You're a man who seems to be eternally young and whom, for some strange reason, I happen to love."

"And thank God for us lovers. I love you. YOU. But you never existed before this present life, I suppose?"

"I hate to admit it, but I was Prester John."

"Prester John! Who's Prester John when he's at home?"

"Did he have a home? And if he did, was he ever there?"

"But that was a man!"

"So what? If we can slip out of one body and into another, we can surely slip from one sex to another?"

"So, I could have been Casanova reborn as Virginia Woolf. Hmm. Well, if so, do we choose, or is it a sort of hiccup of nature that sends these souls scuttling into various bodies over the years?"

"To answer that, Paul, I'd need a very fat research grant. But let's leave hiccups out of it."

"Ah. You've dealt with hiccuppy patients at the most inconvenient times, I bet." Mary nodded and they held hands across the table. "I love you, Mary. But not Prester John."

"I love you, Paul, gentleman or no. But I am not taking on Virginia Woolf as well And do you really want to marry in Lichfield?"

"Lichfield! Lichfield. Mm. Well, that's a pretty good idea. Maybe we should think about it. We could even live in Litchfield. Would you mind living there and working in Sutton?"

"Not if I kept the apartment in Sutton, so that if at any time I had to be near in a crisis I could sleep there."

"I see what you mean. Sounds good—if we can afford two residences."

"We'll have to do our sums."

"Mind you, maybe we should just live in Sutton and visit Lichfield when the urge to wander out for a noggin or a sung service in the cathedral or a concert takes us by the ears and pulls us there."

"Then perhaps we could get another place in France. Perhaps in Trouville or Boulogne-sur-Mer. I mean, when we can afford it."

"Great idea. Or in London?"

"Yes. But I hear the price of flats in London rises every time you say 'Bob's your uncle.'"

"I hardly ever say that, but just the same they keep rising, as in Paris. It's the ever-rising middle-class. Like yeast!"

"Are you middle-class, Paul?"

"Yes. They try to keep us down, but they can't, as the bishop said to the actress. We are caned by Marx and Co. and by governments in many parts of Europe. You see, we're freer than most. We are not hidebound by aristocratic traditions, we're not in the clutch of an entourage like the super-rich, we're not tied to business expansion and global obligations like the big captains of industry, and we're not shackled by poverty. They try to herd us to pay for everything, because we are so many, as if we're cows supplying milk money for all and sundry. We're TTs. Yet we've still got get-up-and-go. To use a quaint expression."

"Well, quaint or not, I, at least, am not prejudiced against you, because I'm middle-class, too. But surely you aren't suggesting the middle-classes are teetotallers?"

"No. They are tax teats. Governments suck on them. But I thought you were an Indian of superior caste. Don't you wear a red spot sometimes?"

"Yes, but that's merely a beauty spot. It's cosmetic if you like."

"I do like. So why aren't you one of the aristocracy?"

"Well, for starters, I'm of mixed blood."

"But that's a racist or at least 'classist' objection."

"I know it is. Asia and Africa are full of racists as well as classists and they're not all white!"

"You can say that again."

"No. Once is enough. All this kind of talk is fine; it's as much as I can do to keep up with medical developments."

"Yes. Let's return to our sheep."

"I bet that's a translation of something French."

"It is. Let's talk turkey!"

"Actually, Paul, I've had enough of Islam, too, for the time being."

"Couldn't agree more. I was using an American phrase to say, 'let's talk seriously.' I mean about our future together."

"I know. I was joking. But our future together! It's exciting!"

They had finished their shellfish platter and a waiter appeared to clear the table. They wanted dessert, but no coffee. Both decided on gazpacho of fruit.

"We're getting married!" whispered Paul.

"We're getting married," responded Mary. They held hands and grinned at each other.

"Aren't we smug?" said Mary.

"Yes, but so are all lovers. I'm a teenager again," said Paul.

"I know what you mean," said Mary. "I suppose we can be smug for a while." The waiter appeared, and they both exclaimed with pleasure at the dishes of red fruit coulis with morsels of strawberry, peach, and fig scattered into it as if it had been poured from a cornucopia. After they had eaten, exclaiming to each other at the taste sensations, and both had declined coffee again, the waiter offered brandy or single malt whisky of impeccable pedigree, or a liqueur, such as Drambuie, Cointreau, or whatever they would like. They both had a single-malt, aged eighteen years. They decided they could be smug at least for the duration of their escapade as they left the dining room, waving to Harry and his two companions, before going up to bed, thoroughly contented and happy. The boy, Paul noticed, had eaten a generous helping of chocolate mousse.

CHAPTER EIGHTEEN

Mary stirred. She was dreaming of running to catch a Midlands country bus, just managing to climb aboard, before it lurched on its way towards Stourbridge. She woke with a start and a flush of relief. Why? Anxiety! Why? She drove always nowadays in her own car. She had not been on many buses since she was a houseman. And soon she'd be a housewife as well as a doctor! But she would continue her medical practice, even if they had children. She was not yet too old for that. Was she worried that it was all too much too soon? Or too much too late? No, there was still time to start a family. Ample time by modern standards. Paul was sleeping soundly. She smiled in the dark as she heard his regular breathing. Getting out of bed quietly, she slipped into her toweling robe. It was a luxurious, creamy yellow. She walked over to the window and peered through the curtains. Black night with stars everywhere, bright, and twinkling. Almost wow, Walt Disney wonderful! *Not that*, she thought, because the night was so much grander: real and remote, cold and inhuman. Yet a vast mirror full of humanity's longing for revelation. Useful, too. You could navigate by the stars. Of course they outdid both Hollywood and Bollywood rolled together. Mary decided to go out to get the night air and that countryside starlight, none of it enfeebled or even obscured by thousands of city street lamps. It was a bit chilly, so she decided to dress, getting into her day clothes. Paul sat up in bed.

"Mary?"

"Don't worry. I'm just going down to look at the stars. It's a wonderful night."

"Do you mind if I come?"

"No, of course not. But I didn't mean to wake you."

Paul was out of bed and already pulling on his clothes. He didn't bother with socks. They crept out of the room and almost forgot the key card. The hotel was silent. They assumed they were the only ones awake. They were wrong. At the foot of the grand, ornamental staircase, they saw that the night porter was at the reception counter reading a local newspaper.

"Can I help you?" he queried, looking up from a photograph of a theatrically jubilant soccer player.

"We're just going out to look at the stars. It's such a lovely night."

"Aye, it is. It's God's own country!"

They went out of the big house and walked around it to the terrace and the lawn.

"They say that in the United States and in Canada," Paul remarked.

"What?"

"It's God's own country."

"Well, it's true of every country. It's certainly true of the sky tonight. It's God's own universe," Mary asserted and added, "If you believe in God. And actually it's still God's universe, even if you don't believe in him."

"I do," said Paul, "despite the daily mess the world is in. Give us this day our daily mess, except that it isn't God's fault, it's ours."

Mary gave him a little glance of surprise, but said nothing. She took his hand in hers. They fell silent, looking up into the jeweled cloth of the sky. They were motionless on the lawn near the terrace. There was a slight rustling of foliage. Five deer strayed into the garden from the surrounding trees. In the distance, there was a sound repeated at long intervals. Was it a barking dog? Not quite. Was it the cough of a horse? Not quite. The deer turned their heads. One of them made the same sound. Paul put his arm around Mary's shoulders. The deer saw them, then, as if for the first time. The animals backed slightly towards the trees as they watched the two interlopers. They turned and suddenly rushed into the woods.

"I expect herds have been here for centuries," Mary observed. "It's their place."

"And the stars for a much longer time," added Paul, attempting to match her mood with the right words. Mary was, however, more precise.

"Since the big bang."

"The big bang started all that contagion of the stars. Is it still spreading across the face of the universe? Like chicken pox?"

She didn't deign to reply to this sally. Paul realized his words were silly and redundant. He had allowed a journalistic vulgarity to cloud a moment of rare beauty. He was rueful and embarrassed. They looked across the lawns in silence. There was a slight mistiness, rising from the grass it seemed, in the night air.

"That was a bit pretentious. Sorry."

"Look!" She was now pointing at the sky.

They saw a shooting star. Then there was another. Then all was still as if shooting stars had never crossed the darkness above them. Nor could ever again. She looked at him.

"Every person says something silly or pretentious at times. But only the honest ones admit it. We can't be clever all the time. It's enough to be clever when we really must be smart," she said. Then she smiled. She linked her arm through his, putting her hand on his. She kissed him on the cheek. "Let's go in now. Let's have a big bang of our own!"

They walked in and held hands as they walked slowly up the stairs. The night porter looked back at his sporting pages, moving his false teeth with his tongue, and was thinking that newlyweds had it cushy nowadays. Some lassie that.

"You are a very special woman, Mary. Did you know that?" Paul murmured. At the top of the stairs, he savored her gracefulness as they entered the corridor leading to their room. He knew that she was not only clever and professionally very competent, but sexually—well, she was wonderful and unstintingly generous. It was as if she had read his thoughts.

"I need you close. I need you again. I haven't had intimacy like this before. I've been too busy!" she said, looking at him over her shoulder.

"You mean you could have had others just like me, but you were too busy?"

"No. There might have been others, if I'd had time—after all, I don't want you to get too cocky! No, but seriously, I mean—but not like this. You're very special, too. I might have missed the bus!"

She led him into the haven of their suite, where they shed their clothes and climbed onto their king-size bed.

"Mary, will you marry me?"

"You've already asked me!"

"I know, but I want to hear you say 'Yes' again."

"YES!"

"I'm a very lucky man," said Paul. "Do you think those stars were a good omen?"

"Yes, I do and you are a very, very lucky man, and never forget that!" She rolled him onto his back and knelt above him, letting her hair fall like a sleek curtain across his chest.

CHAPTER NINETEEN

The psychiatrist sat back in his shiny leather chair and said nothing. This last patient was an intelligent and articulate man full of a sense of missed opportunities. The poor man was pretty desperate. The silence was broken by a half-repressed sob from the man on the comfortable sofa.

"I failed her in many ways," Graham said at last, gazing out of the window.

The psychiatrist, a stocky man with badger hair of shiny black mixed with a lot of grey, took a quick glance at the clock. There were a few minutes left for this consultation.

"Maybe," he replied. "But you must also remember, Dr. Curtis, all the good things you did for her. You have to see that this senseless crime is nothing to do with the relationship. You cannot be held responsible in any way."

Graham could not stop himself from weeping. "I'm sorry," he mumbled.

"Don't be." The doctor picked up a box of tissues from his desk. "Here."

Graham dried his eyes. The tears started again. It was a few minutes before he could control himself. He looked at the man the hospital had recommended that he see. "I'd like to see you again, doctor. When will you be free over the next few days?"

I think we can fit you in." The man smiled.

"Thursday, Dr. Poynter?"

"Yes. Perfect. See my receptionist and make an appointment for Thursday. This is enough for now."

As if it were an afterthought, he took a small packet from the desk. "I suggest you take one of these about half-an-hour before you go to bed each night. If you need more, let me know. See you on Thursday."

He got up, smiled, and held out his hand. Graham shook hands and, thanking him, left the room.

***

There was a knock at their door. From the corridor outside a brisk voice informed them that here was morning tea with a newspaper. Paul rolled out of bed and donned his toweling robe. He opened the door and a dark-haired maid—Spanish? Portuguese? Italian?— was standing outside holding a large silver breakfast tray. Paul took the tray and thanked her. She smiled and walked off, pushing a trolley to deliver the next tray, as required on her list.

"Bliss!" said Mary.

"Beatitude indeed," agreed Paul. "Here, you can have the newspaper."

"That's generous. I suppose your day usually begins with scanning all the news. I never do. It's all depressing, anyway."

Mary looked at him, pulled him towards her, and kissed one of his nipples. She then started to look through the paper. Paul poured the tea.

"No milk, no sugar?"

"Correct."

They settled down comfortably on the plump duvet, their backs propped by capacious pillows. Paul sipped his tea.

"They always select the worst, never the truly representative; their trade is ruined marriages and lives," said Mary, handing him the paper.

"And the sports wars. Mustn't forget to keep nationalism on the boil." He sipped his tea. "That's why I'm a freelancer, not a journalistic hack. I don't want a politically loaded pay packet. And those TV people with powerful images carefully selected and edited to show a lying reality! I avoid them. I prefer to be a nobody."

"Nobody's a nobody, Paul. Some celebrities might think they are somebody and the others are little people, not important. That's an illusion. We're all frail. And we all have an extraordinary power and resilience. I like to help the sick, but I know I'm not famous and never will be," Mary responded, taking a sip of tea, and then continued, "I'm not a discoverer of wonder drugs or almost magic potions. Nor do I demonstrate to students. Nor do I demonstrate on the streets! I didn't even join in protests when I was a student, and it wasn't raining or snowing. But I can help. You can help, too, to improve the way the world looks at itself. You're not a nobody, Paul. Nobody's a nobody."

They kissed without spilling any of the tea.

"You're right. Everybody's a somebody. Everyone has a story," Paul went on. "I'm glad I'm out of the party propaganda racket, the ideologue racket. No more TV or radio except for quality programming—did you know I was in *The News Show* for a while? Now I pick and choose. I can afford it."

"Glad to hear it. You've earned enough. You are rich enough, I suppose? I'm quite rich in a middle-class way."

"You are? Mary, you really are a poppet of the first water. If poppets can have a water, first or not. I must confess, I do like a rich lady."

"Quite rich, not rich rich."

"Quite. I see. Same here. Shall we do the crossword?"

"What do you think?" asked Mary.

"When life seems sweet, love is an exaltation," said Paul.

Mary looked at him. "That's good, Paul. You're a remarkable man."

"I'll confess," he replied. "It's not mine. It's John A. MacDonald in *A Purple Place for Dying*. He wrote good crime novels."

"Hm. You are an honest chap. That's as good as being clever. Let's not think of death though."

***

Graham's hand shook as he lifted the glass to take a sip of water to swill down one of the three, small white pills. It was already releasing bitterness into his mouth. If he took all three, he would not die. *That's why he gave me just the three*, he surmised. Jacqueline had been dead for two days. 9:30 p.m. now. An early night. He'd go to the university tomorrow. He would see students. He would go to the library. He would see some friends.

He would try to escape into activity. The phone rang. He left the bathroom and picked up the receiver on his bedside table. It was Detective Burns.

"Sorry to call you so late, Dr. Curtis, but I wanted you to know, before you see tomorrow's papers, that we have arrested two individuals in relation to your wife's murder."

"Amazing. That was quick. Great news, sergeant. Congratulations."

"I know it's a terrible thing for you, sir, what has happened, but at least we were able to catch them before the trail went cold." Graham yawned.

"I'm sorry, sir. Did I wake you?"

"No, but I've just taken a sleeping pill."

"Well, I won't keep you. Take care now."

"Thanks, I will. Thanks for ringing."

Graham slipped off his robe and stretched out in bed, naked. The cool sheets felt good. He yawned again. Thank God they had nobbled the bastards. Maybe he'd ring Paul tomorrow as well. His eyes filled with tears. He wiped them with a bit of the sheet. Yet in a few minutes, he was asleep.

CHAPTER TWENTY

The little aircraft suddenly dropped fifty feet. Mary gasped and thought, *This is it*. The windows were covered by rain and visibility was negligible. At least she was with the man she loved. Loved! If it had to be, it had to be. Paul squeezed her hand.

"Sorry about that, people. Turbulence. Should be okay soon," said Jack. Suddenly, they were out of the rain and clouds into a clear patch of sky. Paul could see the green land below looking very safe and inviting.

***

He was running through a dense wood, so dense that although it was during daylight hours, he could see only a few yards into the trees. The rest was darkness. There was no birdsong. He stopped to catch his breath. There was a sound of someone else thrashing about not far away and approaching slowly and with much cursing. Graham stood still and listened. There were two of them. He stopped and picked up a weighty broken bough. He shifted it from his right hand to his left. He put his right hand in his pocket and gripped the pistol. He heard a voice just to his right. Graham turned to find there were two men emerging from the trees about three yards away.

"Drop that stick." It was a stocky fellow with stubble all over his ugly face.

A slighter man with a loose-lipped mouth laughed. "Now we've got him, shall we waste him like we did his wife?"

"Drop that stick!"

Graham dropped the stick and drew the pistol, shooting each man in turn. As they dropped, they seemed to be wearing red carnations in the middle of their chests. Graham was walking up the path to his parents' house. Jacqueline stood at the open door, smiling.

"Will you be my wife, Jacqueline?"

A buzzer was disturbing him. Graham opened his eyes in the familiar bedroom, and realized he was alone. The bed seemed too big. He thought he'd been dreaming, but remembered only Jacqueline smiling at him from his parents' front door. He switched off the alarm to silence the buzzer. Was it a dream or was it a memory of her as she had been before they were engaged? It was both, he decided. Memories returned in dreams in a time that was always the present . . . was time a sort of eternal present? Was everything simultaneous, synchronic? History was in an eternal present? This memory or dream of her was not disturbing. He felt stronger today. He would pull himself together. He'd find out more, if he could, about the arrests. Jacqueline would return only in his mental life, in the tantalizing torture of memory. It was a real step forward, though, and very pleasing that those probably responsible for the crime had been caught so quickly and would have to go to trial and to prison. He wanted them executed. He wanted them wiped off the face of the earth. He didn't agree now with this abolition-of-the-death-penalty nonsense. His friends and colleagues had been dismayed when the death penalty was upheld or reintroduced in certain states in the United States, though they were not vocal about its use in the People's Republic of China. *On the whole*, Graham thought, *progressive intellectuals and politicians always thought they knew best what was best for other members of the human race. But they were wrong. People wanted revenge for certain crimes.* He wanted revenge. Revenge was a very human feeling. There were probably as many—no, more— revenge cultures than rule of law cultures. Yet . . . Graham realized that in the end, revenge was a senseless cycle of bloodshed. Look at the Middle East, he said to himself aloud. *Hell, now I'm talking to myself*, he thought. *Hell, why think about it? And I'd rather not look at the Middle East.* It did no good, going over and over the same ground. He knew it was unsound. But he could not suddenly switch to other things.

***

Paul waited for Mary to open her front door. He carried their bags into the hall.

"Welcome home," she said. They hugged and then Mary closed the door. "A cup of tea?"

"Yes, let's. I'll make it. Yes, it *is* home, our home," Paul replied, going into the kitchen. Mary took her case to unpack. She had to start work early the next day and everything had to be organized accordingly. *Paul will stay the night*, she thought. *He can sleep with me.* She smiled at the sudden breathless feeling of excitement inside. *I'm going to miss him.*

CHAPTER TWENTY-ONE

Graham was in a supermarket. It was a different one from their usual. He no longer went near where Jacqueline had been gunned down so brutally. He had already found most of what he wanted and now needed only a few apples and some lemons. He had finished another of his sessions with Dr. Poynter. He was feeling much better, although he was troubled by the intensity of silence, whenever he went back to the house. Would the house ever seem like home again? Could he ever get used to being alone again? He kept reminding himself it was all a matter of time. But was not that another way of saying that our most deeply felt relationships with other people could simply take a back seat in our consciousness? Time was not the only cure. There was survival. One had to start living all over again. But when? When was that possible? How was that possible? It was a matter of time and of strength, the desire to survive, to carry on. So, he was on a sort of mill wheel plunging into the waters of grief and memory and the past and then coming up for air. Could he ever jump off? Would selling the house and getting another place help?

He was mechanically filling an opaque plastic bag with Granny Smith apples when he heard a woman standing near the oranges say to the man she was with, "Yes, she won a little windfall at the races."

The man laughed and Graham's eyes suddenly filled with tears. He put the basket down and fumbled in his pocket for a tissue. He had remembered Jacqueline jumping up and down with excitement on the one occasion they had gone to the races with a friend. Jacqueline had bet on a horse called Summer Lightning and her winnings had covered the cost of their little jaunt. He wiped his eyes, picked up the basket, and went to the checkout. Jacqueline's luck, their luck, had suddenly run out.

Back home in the silent house, he prepared a ham and salad sandwich and poured out a can of beer. He would go to the office and work as long as he could. But first he needed to talk to his closest friend. After lunch, he dialed Paul's number. He heard the familiar single tone of his friend's Paris phone. He got the answering machine. He didn't bother this time to leave a message. Then he thought how silly he was and rang again. This time he said, "It's Graham. Call me at the office between nine a.m. and ten p.m. as soon as you can or at home after eleven p.m. and before eight thirty a.m. I must talk. Please. As soon as possible."

He drove to the campus and walked up the stairs in the arts building to the department's general office. Clara, the graduate committee secretary, was photocopying a file. She smiled at him with high-gloss lips.

"Hi, Dr. Curtis. A Mrs. Gilmore wants you to call her. The number's in your mailbox."

Graham thanked Clara and took the bundle of mail along the corridor to his office. He put a piece of paper with the name and number of Mrs. Gilmore near the phone. Sorting through the other items, he found a couple of catalogues from publishers with lists of the latest publications of possible interest to him. There was a letter from a friend in Alberta. Would he be the external examiner of a doctoral dissertation that would be finished in January? Why not? Yes, he'd do it, but not if he had to go to Alberta in January. A bit later, yes, that would be okay. He sighed. He looked at the bookshelves. Shakespeare's sonnets. He got up and took the volume down. Then he opened at random this book that had been with him since he was at school.

> Those lines that I before have writ do lie,
> Even those that said I could not love you dearer;
> Yet then my judgement knew no reason why
> My most full flame should afterwards burn clearer.
> But reckoning Time, whose millioned accidents
> Creep in 'twixt vows, and change decrees of kings,
> Tan sacred beauty . . .

Graham could not continue. He dried his eyes and turned to look out of the window. He could see a group of students sitting under a tree, chatting. He read on, "Tan sacred beauty, blunt the sharp'st intents . . ." And what were his intents, now that she was dead and her murderers caught? He could only await what the trial brought. There would be the usual arguments about intent and accident. The little criminals might be shown to be as unfortunate as their victim. It would be seen no doubt as an accident, but it was rather an unforeseen murder, one with the same consequences as premeditated murder. He'd get revenge. One way or another he wanted revenge and was determined to have it. He knew now why so many revenge movies had come out of Hollywood. The human response was tearing at his heart. The justice system was so careful to protect the rights of those who destroyed their victims' rights. To hell with it! To hell with legal technicalities! What were victims, in real terms? The irreparably damaged? These criminals are not frightened by the power of the state, only by the rule of their gang bosses. Then he would ensure they would be afraid of him, before they themselves died. When he killed them. But how? How? He realized his love for Jacqueline was now stronger than ever. His actions would be a proof of that love.

There was a knock at the door. He said nothing. Again someone knocked. Blast it! Some busybody knew he was in.

"Come in." No response. Another knock.

"I said, 'Come in'!" he shouted.

The door opened and a skinny youth in torn blue jeans, Che Guevara tee-shirt, and frizzy dark brown hair swept back in a ponytail, said he was sorry to be a nuisance.

"Sit down, Bill. It's Bill, isn't it?"

"Yeah, that's right, Dr. Curtis."

"Well?"

"I don't want to trouble you, but I was wondering if there'll be a memorial service and can students attend?"

"Yes, there will, and yes they may. The department will announce details. Anything else?"

"I was wondering if our papers were ready to be collected."

"As a matter of fact they are. Almost. They'll be in the department office for pick up, when grades have been recorded. Drop by for your paper in the morning. We'll talk about it then. It was very good. I gave it A-."

"Oh, yeah, wow, well, thanks, Dr. Curtis. Bye."

Graham got up and closed the door behind the retreating student. This was normalcy again. *How tedious it is*, he thought. He picked up the note near the telephone. *What,* he wondered, *did Mrs. Gilmore want?*

"Professor Spurling's office. How can I help you?"

"Hello, Mrs. Gilmore, I have a message to call you. It's Dr. . . ."

"Dr. Curtis, isn't it? I recognized your voice. Thank you for calling."

"Is there anything wrong? Is there a problem?"

"No, nothing like that, just a bit more paperwork, I'm afraid. I need another signature. Old John Henry is always in demand."

"I'll drop around at the hospital on my way home."

"I can mail the form to you."

"No, I'll drop by. When do you close the office again?"

"At five p.m. I'll see you before then?"

"Sure. I'll be there. Bye-bye."

Graham replaced the handset, swept a few remaining papers into his briefcase, and put a note on his door saying papers would be available in the office next day. This was a handy notice he used whenever students began to wonder when papers were to be returned. He always tried to return them within ten days of their due date. Going in person to the hospital would give him something to do, use up some more of his day.

At the hospital, he found Professor Spurling's reception room and knocked before entering. Spurling's inner office door was closing and he was announcing without looking back as he left, "I don't want to hear any more about it, Samantha." His tone was angry and, Graham thought, *offensive.* Mrs. Gilmore looked at Graham and gave him a brief smile. The atmosphere was unpleasant. *They've just had a lovers' row*, he thought.

"Hi, you need my signature."

She smiled again. "Yes. How are you feeling today?"

"Terrible. You don't want to know. I'm angry."

"You're not the only one. Well, I am truly sorry to have to bother you again with paperwork. It's for the release of your wife's . . . the body, for a police autopsy."

"I thought that was already underway?"

"Yes, it is, but we need your signature right here. We didn't do it before, when you agreed verbally to the autopsy." She took a pink form from a grey folder. Graham looked through the form and signed on the line she had marked with a small penciled cross. She wore a gold ring on one of her forefingers.

"That's it then," she said.

She smiled again as Graham left. He looked at his watch. Well, that had dispelled a little loneliness and used up some time. So that was how officialdom kept track of dead bodies. His car started reluctantly. He must get the battery charged. It was one damned thing after another. A sleek red sports car, low slung, a Lotus probably, emerged from the staff parking area and suddenly stopped. A door opened and Mrs. Gilmore climbed out of the car, inevitably showing a lot of tanned leg, sleek leg, because of the low seat. Tanned! She straightened her coat, and walked briskly towards the main road. The Lotus passed her and turned into the street. Graham slowed as he caught up with her.

"Hi again! Can I give you a ride?"

She stooped and looked in at him. She had remarkable eyes.

"That's kind of you. I'm in a hurry. Got to get to the shopping complex on Yew."

"Hop in! I'll take you there. Was that a Lotus I saw you ejecting from?"

"Ferrari. George Spurling's seduction wagon. 'Ejecting'— Perfect. He's obsessed by beautiful cars. Thinks he's an airline pilot."

She got in and Graham turned to her.

"And always hires beautiful assistants?" asked Graham.

She looked grim and did not reply.

"I'm sorry. That was indiscreet. I was not trying to pry. It was just a clumsy compliment. I think you're great."

"I can stand any amount of flattery!"

"Your husband's a lucky guy."

"I'm divorced, and I don't even know where my ex-husband is. He skipped the province."

They lapsed into silence while Graham concentrated on getting them to the Yew Street shopping complex, where they pulled into one of the parking spaces.

"Why don't I buy you a coffee?" she asked. "I know you're having a rough time. So am I. Let's splurge on a Starbucks." A few minutes later, they were ensconced in the coffee shop with beakers of coffee and sharing a huge bran muffin.

"I noticed a funny atmosphere when I got to your office."

"That! That man is a very good surgeon, but he thinks he's God's gift to females. I've had it with him. I'm going to take the leave I've accumulated and go to Europe. I'll also apply for a change of duties in the hospital."

"I bet there are plenty of doctors who'd like to work with you."

"Do you mean what I think you mean?" she asked and both laughed aloud.

"Do you know, that's the first time I've laughed since it happened."

"Well, healing takes time. You lost both of them. It's hard."

"Both?"

"Oh dear. I'm sorry, didn't you know? She was pregnant. I thought you must have known."

"Christ! Dear Christ!" he whispered. He suddenly felt drained of all energy.

"Oh dear. I'm so sorry. Look, I'd better leave you and get my shopping done."

"I'll wait here for you. Please let me drop you off at home."

She smiled, touched his arm, and left him, saying she'd be quick. Graham got up to find a newspaper on the rack. He looked at it without reading. He suddenly knew what he wanted to do. He took out his mobile and rang Detective Sergeant Burns. Burns answered and confirmed that the autopsy report had been filed. The body could be released for the funeral service. And yes, his wife had been pregnant. Six weeks. He assumed Graham had known. Graham thanked him and rang off. The child had not been his. He was certain, because he'd been away for a week at a conference and his wife had been away for three weeks visiting her parents around that time. She'd been unfaithful. Would he have known, if she'd lived and given birth? Their marriage had seemed to him very good, very trusting. They had made love before he left. He would have to double check. Why hadn't she told him? Had she been about to do so? No, it was not an error. Wretched questions and distressing doubt crowded into his mind. There was no escape.

CHAPTER TWENTY-TWO

Paul had left early, as had Mary, who was going to a meeting at the local hospital. En route, she had dropped him off at the bus stop for Birmingham. From New Street Station, he went to London, where he took the Eurostar to Paris. He was in a good window seat on the train. He had charged both batteries before leaving and so worked with his laptop, having no fear of a sudden necessity to close down. He wrote for a good two hours. This enabled him to get a head start on ideas for "The Female Stare" and to jot down other ideas he'd been mulling over. He also kept writing and then deleting the name Mary, followed by a few lines of free verse. He would send her a valentine of his own composition. It would have to be of high quality, not the roses are red variety of doggerel. Or maybe it should be roses are red, but with a quirky surprise in it. He would also check his bank account. He wanted to buy her an engagement ring. They had forgotten to talk about rings!

After a brief metro ride and a short walk, Paul arrived back at his apartment in the Rue de la Collégiale. He immediately noticed that the message light was winking on his telephone-cum-fax machine. Listening to the messages, he found that Mary had rung and said simply, "I love you. I miss you already." The next was an editor who liked the idea of the female stare and wanted to buy the article. In addition, there were two messages from Graham.

Paul rang Mary's private number and left a message, "I love you, too. Where do you want to go for our honeymoon? If you want to choose an engagement ring with me, come to Paris, Place Vendôme. Or do you want a surprise on both counts?" He then called the editor and arranged the deadline, word number, and fee for "The Female Stare." Good. Then he looked at his watch again. If he called in about half an hour, Graham would probably be awake. He put the kettle on, unpacked, and made a cup of tea. He had a few biscuits in the tin. He bit into one of the Hobnobs he had brought with him from Mary's. Delicious. This was a mistake. One Hobnob tended to lead to another. He put the tin away in the cupboard. Then he settled down with a cup of tea and half a biscuit, all ready to telephone his friend.

"Curtis." He had expected a sleepy voice. Graham sounded wide-awake and grim.

"Graham. It's Paul. I just got back from the United Kingdom and heard your messages. What's so urgent in the groves of academe?"

"I'm in a mess. Jacqueline is dead. Murdered."

"Good God! No! Oh Christ . . ."

"She was pregnant by another guy."

"No. I don't believe that. Not really?"

"It's true. She didn't tell me she was pregnant."

"Graham, don't tell me you've done something very foolish."

"No, Paul, I didn't kill her, though cynics might think I did. I didn't even know she was pregnant. Luckily, the police have got two suspects in custody. It was the autopsy that showed she was pregnant."

"But how do you know it wasn't your child?"

"She'd been away. I'll explain it all when I see you. I was hoping to come to stay with you, or if an assignment brought you over here, you could stay with me. I need to be with a friend like you."

"Will the police let you come on a trip? There'll be a trial presumably."

"It's good to talk to you, Paul. I'm in a terrible state here."

"It's good to hear you. Look, I'll try to rearrange things. Of course, you're welcome here. Your term's finished when?"

"Classes are finished and my grades are almost in. I could get over to you in a couple of days I think."

"Good. Let's try for that and firm everything up by e-mail?"

"Sure. Thanks for calling back."

"You take care. I'll see you soon, either here or there. See you."

Paul heard the tone. Graham had rung off. He put down the phone. It was unbelievable. He found it hard to accept the surprises life could deal, like a bad hand at cards. But you played with the cards that were dealt. You made the best of it. And then, when all the chips were down, fate shuffled. We shuffled to the grave. We all lost. Or did we? Where was Jackie now? He had always thought of her as Jackie, though he knew Graham insisted on the full version of her name. He respected Graham's wishes when they were together. But for Paul's inner voice she was just Jackie. He had known them since they were students.

Adultery! Why? Poor Graham. Poor Jackie. Why would two men want to murder her? He assumed they were men. Paul poured a second cup. He rang his travel agent. He wanted to know the best prices and flight times. The agent wanted him to book there and then, but Paul wanted to check out the Internet before he made any moves. He poured himself another cup of tea and then went to his desk and started searching the Internet. The phone rang. Damn. He cut off his connection and picked up the handset.

"Darling, I got your message. You're sweet."

"Darling! I'm so glad you rang . . ."

"Goa. Let's have our honeymoon in Goa. It's full of wonderful places. I'll show you my Goan secrets."

"Now that's an offer I cannot refuse. I want to know all your secrets except for just a few."

"I'm glad you said that. Why did you?"

"Well, if I ever got to know all your secrets, there would be less mystery. You're a truly mysterious woman. I like it that way. I like you that way."

"Tell me your secrets! What are you doing now?"

"Actually, I'm worried, very worried—about Graham. I think I should try to get over to see him."

"What's happened?"

"Jackie's been murdered, and Graham has found that she was pregnant—and it was someone else's baby."

"Oh, the poor, poor, man. But was Jackie . . .? But how does he know it was another man's child?"

"I think he's going on the timing. She'd been on a trip somewhere."

After a slight pause, Mary asked him what his arrangements were for the trip to see Graham. "When do you go?"

"Well, I'm not certain about it. He said he could be here in a few days because he's finished work over there."

"That might be best, if he made the journey. It would take him away from it all for a while."

"Absolutely. But there's to be a trial and he might not be able to get away."

"Yes, I see. Well, be sure to advise him to have medical tests to see whether the child was his. That would be best, I think."

Then they talked about their own plans for seeing each other as much as possible in the next few weeks. They kissed each other over the phone before ringing off.

***

Graham answered his phone. It was Detective Burns. He wanted to come by to talk on a routine matter. After about twenty minutes, the two policemen were at Graham's door. They wasted no time on tea, coffee, or orange juice. They came straight to the point.

"When did you first learn that your wife was pregnant, sir?" asked Burns.

"Yesterday. I saw Mrs. Gilmore, you know, from the surgeon's office, and she mentioned it."

"So, your wife never mentioned it before, before her death?"

"No. It was a bit of a shock, I can tell you. And it was even more of a shock when I found out the age of the fœtus."

"The fœtus?"

"Yes, I realized then that she must have cheated on me. She was away for several days at the crucial time. It must have been the result of some affair she was having. Or a one night stand."

"Mmm. So you had no idea? You thought everything was . . . normal?"

"Exactly. I feel thoroughly cheated. I wanted to kill those guys you arrested. Now I just feel cynical and bitter, eh? Sorry for myself, I guess. But I've got to snap out of it. Get on with my work. Any idea when the trial will be?"

"Not yet. There's a queue of trials. But you can get on with arrangements for the funeral as from now. You know, in your place, sir, I'd have a DNA test to check out whether that baby was yours or not. Time isn't necessarily a totally reliable guide. Have a test, eh?"

"Oh, yes. I suppose so. I'll do it. Oh, can I travel? I mean, will I be needed when those two creatures come to court?"

"I don't think so, sir, but I'll check with my superiors about whether you can travel. Where to, by the way, and for how long?"

"I was thinking of France. I have a friend there; he lives in Paris. I feel I need to talk about all this to an old and trusted friend as well as to a shrink."

"I can understand that, Mr. Curtis. I'll get back to you on that one as soon as I can."

Graham's next task was the funeral. Jacqueline's parents were out at Fort Langley. They'd surely want it to be there. It would be easier for them to visit and tend the grave, poor things. She'd been their only child. Graham had, of course, been in touch with them, but could offer little that could comfort them. And all the time, images and conversations from the past came back. He could not really believe Jacqueline had had a lover or even a fling. But he had to be sure. Burns was right. Burns was a realist. Facts, not suppositions, were important.

Within the next twenty-four hours, Graham had his DNA test. Burns had telephoned to say he could go to France, but for no more than three weeks and he had to leave an address, telephone numbers, etc. so that he could be informed of any "sudden necessity for his presence." Fair enough. The funeral would be the next day, with just close family. There could be a department memorial service later. He had to get away, though, and talk to Paul. There had been an "urgent" on his test. Graham learned within a few hours that he was, after all, the father of the child Jacqueline had been carrying. He felt a wave of horror and guilt. How could he have doubted her? And then grief struck him again, harder than ever. He looked at his watch. He figured that Paul would be still awake. Graham picked up his phone and tapped in Paul's number.

"*Allô. Paul Wills àl'appareil. J'écoute.*"

"It's Graham. I'm coming to Paris. In a couple of days. May I stay with you?"

"Course. Goes without saying. Send me details by *courriel.*"

"Courriel?"

"Mail. Here that means e-mail, not the post."

"Got you. I won't talk now, Paul, but I need to get away."

"I understand. But have a test to see about that baby."

"I did. It was mine."

"Oh. Good. Oh, I'm so sorry Graham. Christ. It's . . . what a mess. But it . . ."

"Yeah, well, we'll talk when I arrive. Got to go."

CHAPTER TWENTY-THREE

Next day Paul received Graham's mail with the flight details. He'd be arriving at Charles de Gaulle, Roissy, on a morning flight from London in a couple of days' time.

Paul got down to stints of intensive and rapid writing. He made a call to Mary each morning and evening. On the day Graham was due to arrive, Paul took the RER train to meet the flight and then found the plane was arriving five minutes early. He went to the meeting point and had a coffee, waiting until he estimated Graham would emerge from the controlled area. He strolled about near the exit and suddenly there was Graham with just a cabin bag. They grinned at each other and hugged. Graham seemed leaner and taller than before. He had a very tired, world-weary look about his brown eyes. Jet lag. His hair seemed thinner. Paul thought he would try to keep Graham awake at least until nine that evening. Maybe he would then sleep right through until morning.

They took a taxi to Paul's place. It was the familiar cluttered, narrow Left Bank street, where cars were parked on both sides, some half on, half off the pavement. Paul walked over to a large wooden door, punched in his code and, on hearing the click, pushed open the heavy portal, allowing Graham to step into the short, covered area that led into a paved, inner courtyard. There were tubs containing an assortment of shrubs. An ancient stone trough harboured a vine that almost covered the high wall above it. Every window had window boxes or planters balanced, it seemed, precariously, from which flowers sprouted in many shades of red and blue and white.

Graham was impressed by the quiet of the courtyard, the lived-in prettiness of it, and the winding wooden staircase with its bottom step of stone, worn into a curve like a glossy smiling lip. It was similar to the plan of a college at one of the ancient universities, but it housed families, old people, young couples, and singles in studios or the smaller flats. He was also impressed by the elegant interior of Paul's flat.

"Wonderful," he said, as he looked round, and then asked, "How much rent?"

"Nothing! My father left it to me when he died."

"Wonderful. Thoughtful. You must be pleased."

"I'm very happy, Graham. And I want to tell you my news: I'm getting married. Mary and I. You may have met her? She's a GP in Sutton Coldfield."

"Is this her photograph?" asked Graham, picking up a large wooden frame with a girl on a beach, looking up from her book and smiling at the camera. "God, she's beautiful. Really beautiful. Is she Indian?"

"I think she's a knockout. She's Eurasian. Indian dad, English mum. Her father's dead, but her mother's alive and sprightly. Mary and I were in Scotland when you called and left your message. We've known each other a long time, since student days, that's why I thought you might have met her."

"Congratulations and all that. No, I'd remember her, had I met her even once. You're a lucky devil. Mary, did you say?"

"Yes. Not Kalitza, if that's what you were thinking. Enough about Mary and me, Graham. What's happening over there? When's . . . you've had the funeral?"

Graham sank into the sofa and looked out the window. He was struggling with himself to regain enough control to speak without breaking into a quavering voice or giving way to sobs. The funeral. That had been yesterday? No, the day before. It had rained. That figured.

"I'm sorry. It was abrupt. Stupid of me. Let me get you a drink."

Graham looked at him. But was silent, still fighting back the grief.

"Beer? Scotch? Gin and tonic? Vodka and orange? Pineau des Charentes? Kir?"

"Vodka and orange with no vodka."

"Yes! Hold the vodka. I'll get it. Hang on a mo."

Paul returned with a beer and a glass of orange juice to find that Graham was standing and looking out of the window. The sun had come out and a great shaft of light slanted in, making him partly silhouetted. He turned and held out a hand for his drink.

"I'm okay now. I've been giving in to self-pity and self-recriminations. It's not good. Getting on that plane and coming to see you are just what I needed. Life goes on. Even though Jacqueline's gone, gone forever. My father once told me that self-pity was a ruinous and treacherous emotion. He said it was a natural thing to feel, but it had to be rejected. It had to be mastered. The old man didn't let it all hang out."

"Was he happy, your father?"

"I think he was very unhappy in his youth before he married. Then his marriage deteriorated—my parents had terrible rows. But they stuck it out. They stuck to it until the end. When he'd retired, I once heard my old man tell one of his cronies at a barbeque with a bunch of neighbours that he'd had 'seven good years.' Seven!"

"How old was he?"

"Seventy-one."

"Sixty-four horrible years. Poor chap."

"Well, he lived about four years longer after his remark in the pub. So, let's say he had a total of eleven good years. I look back on it and think I have had happy years ever since I got into the sixth form at school until the day Jacqueline was gunned down. I've been luckier than my old man. Can you pity someone who didn't indulge in self-pity?"

"Yes. It's always relative. Pity, I mean," remarked Paul. "There's always someone worse off than oneself. And you might find some happiness again. Later on."

"Can you imagine anybody who's happier when you are happy—as you are now that you are getting married?"

"No. Now you ask, Graham, I can't. If I'm happy, I'm the happiest man in the world. But that's enough."

"You're right. Jacqueline was not cheating, you know."

"Good. Yes. I didn't think she would."

"I had a DNA test and it showed that the child was mine after all. The police advised the test as well. I wanted to be really certain."

"I don't blame you," said Paul, going for another drink. From the fridge he called, "More juice?"

Graham assented. When Paul reappeared, Graham seemed reluctant to continue with any further explanation. Then it seemed, after a short silence, that he changed his mind.

"No, we had the funeral a couple of days ago. It was with her parents and just close family friends. There'll be a memorial service later, arranged by the department."

Paul noticed that Graham's dark, thinning hair was now flecked with grey.

"Of course, I felt such a fool and so base when I realized I'd doubted her wrongly. And now I've lost them both. Now I know myself more than I did before."

"Self-knowledge is what is needed. Self-pity can bugger off. But not compassion," added Paul.

"Self-pity is another form of self-love, the easiest form of love. I didn't love *her* enough."

"Graham, self-flagellation's no good, either. You know that."

"The shrink told me that. It's true. It's what ridiculous religious fanatics do, in public. It's caddish behaviour . . . Caddish!" Graham laughed. "I suppose I am a bit of a cad, anyway."

"Graham, you've just laughed. Caddish, kiddish, kurdish, cod fish, that's a declension. What the hell!"

They both grinned. They hugged.

"Lunch? Dinner? We'll go by your inner clock, Andrágathos."

"Who's that?"

"Oh, a friend. I picked it up somewhere and it's stuck in my mind. But now I'd have to Google or Wikipedia it to find out what I once knew."

"That's my real Graham! Let's go out and buy stuff and I'll cook dinner."

It seemed a good idea. They would stretch their legs and take the late afternoon air. The two friends went out into the noise and bustle of the neighbourhood. They soon returned with a bottle of ready-cooled champagne, Bruno Paillard to be exact, a bottle of Château Landereau, red, a bottle of Sancerre, red, a baguette tradition, a box of Camembert, ready for dinner that day, a piece of old Mimolette, and a slice of Brie about to overflow. They bought a salad for good measure, some fresh vegetables, and a small leg of lamb. In a patisserie, they saw some savory *petits fours*. These were not to be resisted. They would go down well with the Paillard.

Back at the flat, they put the champagne in the fridge and opened and tasted both the reds. They were both excellent for the moderate price. Graham prepared the lamb and made the salad while Paul prepared the vegetables. They were chatting normally. Both, of course, were fully conscious of death. Paul was disturbed by the fact that death had brushed past them both, snatching Jacqueline away forever and had knocked Graham over and stamped his face into the mud. Kalitza was a loss, but he had hardly known her and she was, yes, still alive. Her life and death and resurrection were a mystery. But Mary eclipsed all that.

Graham, though, felt much better now that he was in a different country, with a true friend, and away from the scenes of so much happiness that had suddenly reversed at top speed into instant misery.

"We have to ride with the punches," said Paul.

Graham didn't reply. Ride with the punches. He must cling to the ropes of normalcy. He must get up and stagger on and then find his form again.

"Let's have a drink," said Graham. They both got up and took out the champagne and *petit fours* to settle down and enjoy their aperitif. Graham said they should drink a toast to the impending marriage. Paul said they should also drink to the memory of Jacqueline. Graham was subdued at first, but soon he began to recover some of his old *élan*. Yet, there was always a cloud, a tension, as if a rainstorm was about to burst. They talked as they drank and ate. Then Paul noticed Graham's eyelids beginning to droop. He looked at his watch. It was nine-thirty. They decided Graham would turn in. They made up a sofa bed in a few minutes and Paul left Graham to sink into oblivion, fortified by a tot of single malt, and a bottle of water in case he was thirsty in the night.

Paul took some reading (a book by Vladimir Fodorovski) and a glass of the Scotch into his bedroom. At least Graham had eaten something. And they had some champagne left and some of the reds still for tomorrow. He had not talked about Kalitza. That was the least of Graham's concerns just now. And she seemed less and less important to Paul. And the microchip was just a detail. Paul picked up the phone and was soon chatting to Mary. He told her Graham was going to be fine.

"It might take a year or two, even several years, but people never really forget that kind of loss. It marks them, like a physical scar," she said.

"You're probably right. I've known him for years—since we were students. I think I told you that."

"Probably. Sounds as if you had a good meal."

"Wonderful. Very simple. All good ingredients."

"So you can cook?"

"Graham did it. But, yes, I try. Do you know, I really love listening to your voice."

Mary laughed. "I'm glad you do. And Paul, I love your voice, too. And your brand of English."

"My brand of English? But I *am* English."

"Yes, but there are many Englishes now."

"Ah yes. Heinz—fifty-seven varieties. Where did that pop up from?"

Mary laughed. "I want to get you over here again, and over me," she said, and added, "All over."

"I'll be over. Very soon. In a few days. What's best for you?"

"Lots of cuddling, lots of kissing, lots of loving. You know what I like."

"Yes, but I meant when shall I come?"

"Why, when you can't hold back any longer!"

"Oh God, Mary, this is a refined form of torture. You wait 'til I get you to myself in Sutton Coldfield."

"Sutton Coldfield. I didn't know it was the sexiest little town on earth!"

They both grinned into their respective telephones. They decided that it was a remarkable discovery and a secret that must be kept to themselves. Otherwise everybody would be moving to Sutton Coldfield. They also made more plans for the wedding and the honeymoon. They reassured one another with "I love you" before ringing off.

It was gone ten-thirty when Paul put down the phone. He got ready for bed and then read Fodorovski for another half-hour before he dropped asleep, feeling secure, feeling loved, feeling lucky, feeling sorry about Jackie and Graham, and feeling as happy as any man could be, given the circumstances, and given the state of the world in general.

CHAPTER TWENTY-FOUR

Over breakfast next morning, Graham said he had read the Kalitza papers twice.

"That Kalitza woman is either dead or she's a special policewoman, still alive, or she's a very dead secret agent, Paul. In any case, don't let her come between you and Mary."

"I know. I won't. Mary thinks she's still alive. So do I. Kalitza was special, that's beyond dispute for me. But now I know what it is to love Mary. And she loves me. Kalitza has no power over me now."

"Good. All in all, she's like a modern Petrarch invention. She's a *femme fatale,* but she's also a *femme céleste.* You haven't been reading Balzac by any chance?"

"Graham, I know you're a critic, but I'm not writing fiction. The Kalitza papers are simply descriptions of what happened. I'm a journalist, remember. There's more actually. You can read it when you get back. I show it to you and Mary. Nobody else. Not for publication. At least, not yet. Too personal. Besides, if she's an agent, I don't want to publish for obvious reasons. And she doesn't need me. She used me for a specific job, I think. And if she's not human, if she's an imagined angel, then I think a space of seven years or so will allow the dust on her wings to settle!"

"Okay, I must say, I wish I'd met her. And I'm glad you can now be frivolous about . . . you know . . . her appearances as Isis or someone." Graham looked at his friend with renewed curiosity. How could this usually level-headed guy have thought all this supernatural stuff?

"You might meet her. One never knows."

They let it rest at that. Graham nevertheless realized that people confronted with death often began believing in the world beyond, some kind of survival. Or else they became totally atheist and believed only in the harshness of this life on earth. Graham realized too that he believed in some kind of survival. Yes. Survival. But how could that be?

The two friends discussed what they would do that day and the next. It was an opportunity for Graham to visit some old haunts. He managed not to weep in front of Paul. They talked again about the past, about Jacqueline, and about Paul's new life with Mary. Neither commented on the coincidence that Paul's accounts of death had arrived when Jacqueline was murdered. Graham assured Paul the trip had been good, but he was dreading seeing his relatives. Perhaps friends were better than relatives at times like this. He didn't really know. It all depended on the friends, on the relatives, the ones you had. He did know that the visit had been just what he needed. Life continued. A door closed, banged shut in fact. And then light stole back through a gap in the curtains. He could not think beyond that. Paul looked at Graham and noticed the pain in his eyes. He hugged him.

"I'm glad you could get over here," he said.

***

"Are there gradations of happiness, Mary?"

"Of course there are; it's obvious."

They were in Paul's apartment in Paris and within the apartment, they were in his bedroom, and within the bedroom, they were in his bed. To cap it all, they were between his sheets. These were new ones, bought at the Bazaar de l'Hôtel de Ville specially to mark the occasion of Mary's visit.

"Is it? How can I be happier than I am now?"

"Are you saying that there's nothing to add to this happiness, Paul? Are you a pessimist after all? Don't you think all this lovemaking just continues without consequences?"

"A family?"

"Aha!"

"Dear octopus! We never escape its tentacles! Or testicles, I suppose."

"But I know the end of that quotation: We never want to escape them."

"Which? The tentacles?"

Mary threw a pillow at him and covered his head with it, tickling him with a free hand. When Paul had extricated himself, he kissed her and said, "We're politically incorrect, you know that? All this talk of families is *dépassé*."

"Really, well, I don't want to sound medical . . ."

"But?"

"But studies show that kids who grow up with one parent are more prone than others to earn low incomes, be out of work, or have some kind of instability."

"So, good old mum and dad may fuck you up, but those who stay married fuck you up less. Footnote to famous lines by Philip Larkin. Yet people from stable marriages also have their problems."

"Yes. Most parents seem to try to do their best, even if they make a hash of it. There are so many pressures on adults and children now. But the studies show those from fatherless homes are *more* prone to these problems. Of course, there are strong women who can cope with the errant male, but there are others who cannot. Governments may soon be propagandizing again for hetero-marriages, whatever happens on the same-sex marriage front."

"How would you deal with errant males, Mary?"

"I'd smother them at birth! Then I'd hand them over to Kalitza. She'd teach them a lesson!" and with this she put a pillow over his head again.

"Have you seen her again? I bet you haven't."

"I have, but don't worry. You will get the rest of the stuff I wrote down as it happened."

"So you think she's resurrected?"

"Yep."

"Did you touch her in the morgue?"

"No. I just identified her. Why?"

"I think, young man, as I said before, she wasn't dead. If you've seen her since, that is."

"I'll send you more."

"Are you going to publish these papers?"

"No. It's a part of my experience, but it's for you and Graham only."

"Good. You still want to marry me? After seeing her again?"

"Yes. Yes. Do you still want me?"

"Yes, I do, Paul. I'm glad you let me in on this secret and I'm even more pleased that it's not keeping you under a spell."

"I'm not an errant male then? You still haven't said what you'd really do to them."

"I'd legislate so that the state could prosecute people for marital violence against each other or their children, whether or not the victims pressed charges."

Paul was not in a position to agree or disagree or modify this point of view in his own thinking. He could sense, however, that he might be able to write an article on "Family Matters" and sell it either to *The New Statesman* or *The Spectator*, depending on his slant (*You Can't Beat the Family*) and findings.

"I'd also ensure parents' incomes were garnered at source to pay for family upkeep, so that irresponsible men—or women—could not refuse to pay for their children and have to be taken to court."

Paul made a mental note to write himself a note on it later that morning. Perhaps he could find out medical journal information for "Family Matters." Family law would also be an important source. What was the legislation on marriage? He was getting married, yet in fact, he knew very little about it, apart from growing up at home with his parents. Amazing.

"It comes back to happiness," said Mary. "The pursuit of happiness is a complicated matter. Like taking an opportunity to get here from Sutton Coldfield at a moment's notice."

"That's true. And I'm grateful for it. Let's add an increment to our sum, coffee and butter croissants," Paul replied.

"Yes, you can get a lot of happiness from little things," added Mary, feeling virtuous suddenly as she got out of bed.

After breakfast, they showered together and prepared to go out. Paul wrote a note to himself on "Family Matters." *There was always something to do—and well worth doing,* he thought, *in Paris, as in London, or New York, or Madrid, or Berlin, or Rome or . . . how many other capitals had he visited? It was true of Tokyo and also Beijing. What about Mexico City? He had never visited Mexico. Maybe one day. Maybe not.*

"Mary," he asked, "is there always something worthwhile to do in Delhi?"

"Of course. But only when I'm there," she answered.

"Now you're here in Paris, I think we need to explore the Place Vendôme."

"One of my favourite squares. But why?"

"We might find an engagement ring there."

Mary flung her arms around him and planted a big kiss on his lips.

CHAPTER TWENTY-FIVE

Graham was back home. He had spent only three nights in Paris before going to London to see relatives. He had spent a couple of days there, before flying back to Canada. Arrangements were well under way for the memorial service. He and Jacqueline's parents had chosen music together. He had not argued with them. Their taste was more popular than his and they clearly wanted "Amazing Grace." He put up with it and they put up with some Vivaldi and Byrd. They were pleased when he also suggested Elton John. They wanted the Lord's Prayer. Graham would say "a few words" and so would some of his and Jacqueline's friends, but her parents didn't feel up to it.

They sat together at the ceremony, and when Graham rose to address the assembled friends and relatives, colleagues and others who had come from the university, he felt her father's hand patting his arm. Graham disliked the whole idea of funeral oratory and encomia. He remembered that Samuel Johnson had quoted Pope:

A vile encomium doubly ridicules;
There's nothing blackens like the ink of fools.

You can say that again, and it should be memorized by all orators when composing speeches for sundry occasions, thought Graham, as he walked to the light oak lectern with its microphone. He began:

"It is a sign of our affection and respect for Jacqueline that we are all here for this service today. I loved her dearly . . . I shall miss her, I am missing her, more than I could imagine before . . . this . . . and we all miss her. It was a cruel fate that plucked her from us, while she was still so young . . . and before we could raise the family . . . as we had hoped to do. Wherever she is, she's still the same humorous, even-tempered Jacqueline for me. I am certain that some of her abundant energy and life remains with us in all our minds.

Her kindness and her wonderful . . . sense of fun . . . are planted in our hearts. Once she was dabbing some perfume behind her ears. Then she dabbed some behind her knees. I asked why she did that. She told me it was in case we met any midgets."

Graham laughed and the congregation laughed and also wept. They all recognized Jacqueline in this little memory. There was silence again. Graham continued, "I hope we can all, in the quiet of our homes, as well as here, pray for her."

Graham went back to his seat and then a number of friends, going up to the microphone, recalled incidents and jokes which gave a sort of mosaic of Jacqueline's presence, her effect. A senior colleague got to the microphone and read Tennyson's "Crossing the Bar."

Graham mounted the few steps to the lectern. "Thank you all for taking time to be here with the family and, as I think, with Jacqueline."

After the service, about a dozen went back to Jacqueline's favourite Chinese restaurant for dinner. In bed that night, Graham felt immense relief. Jacqueline had not in fact been blackened with the ink of fools; she had been conjured up in memory and imagination by different people with obvious affection and genuine respect for her as a person—not just Graham's wife. He had noticed her parents dabbing their eyes with their handkerchiefs all through the speeches. Their mouths moved, but neither they nor Graham joined the others in singing the hymns. But they all prayed. He was thankful that it was all over. Sharon Olds was a poet Jacqueline and he admired. Her poem, "Ecstasy," meant a great deal to them both. It was a favourite. It kept coming to mind in fragments. Getting out of bed, he found the book and read the poem again. He climbed back into bed. Eventually he slept.

But now he had to deal with the possessions, will, and the bureaucracy that follows a death. This stretched over a period of weeks during which he knew Jacqueline's parents better than he had known them before and realized how genuinely kind and thoughtful they were.

He had thought deeply about the baby and whether or not he should tell them Jacqueline had been pregnant. If he were to inform them, the fact that they had lost a grandchild as well as a daughter would cause even more pain. If they were to be told by someone else, discovering their daughter's pregnancy by chance, they might be distressed that he had not let them know. Or perhaps she had told them, but not him? That was unlikely, though not impossible. In the end, Graham told them in as gentle a way as he could. Jacqueline's mother wept. They had not known. Jacqueline's father put his arm around Graham's shoulders and held him for a moment. Then he turned away.

"I'll make some tea," he said, going abruptly into the kitchen.

They heard the water coming to the boil with the old man sobbing quietly to himself. Graham remembered the kettle had suddenly started to whistle.

Thinking about the ceremony, he realized how kind his colleagues, friends, and acquaintances were. They all rallied round in helpful ways. It made him, he realized, a better person. He was grateful to them all. He noticed other people more than he had ever done previously. He was not smug any more. That had been one of his faults. He had thought he was a clever intellectual. Now he realized he knew very little. But he did know just how fragile we all are. He valued his friends even more than he had ever done. When he had his life back on track, or as far as it ever would be, the trial came along to revive all his misery. The two men were tried, found guilty of a cowardly murder, and duly sentenced to long jail terms. The gunman who had pulled the trigger received a longer term than his accomplice, who had "merely" kicked and stamped on Jacqueline as they ran past where she lay dying.

Graham was numbed by it all. He was so angry when he thought about the crime that he found it impossible to speak about it. His distress was tempered with relief, however, now that the whole thing was over. It was a social ritual, necessary as a part of healing, just as the funeral had been. There was, he discovered, a very good reason why trials of this kind were a kind of ritual in a public space. He no longer thought of revenge. The rule of law was an improvement on the old revenge culture. He decided that he'd go to France again, in the spring, after the teaching term. Perhaps he could persuade Paul to take him in again, at least for a few days, before pushing on to take a holiday. Alone. Being single again was a novelty he had to get accustomed to. He had spells of loneliness that were hard to bear.

He was walking in the shiny new mall in search of food from the supermarket, when he met Mrs. Gilmore again.

"Hi, there, Mrs. Gilmore!"

"Professor . . . Curtis?"

"You remember my name!"

"Yes, I do. And I remember we had a Starbucks coffee together some time ago."

"Look, why don't we have a coffee together again, my treat."

"That's not what I meant. But yes, let's."

They fell into step side by side. She said she was going to the new Market in the Mall to do some food shopping, but it would be good to have a coffee first. They soon found a coffee shop and were installed with their drinks.

"Look, why don't you call me Sam," she offered, "Everybody else does."

"Okay, Sam. I'm Graham. But don't call me Gray!"

"No, I'll remember to call you Graham, Graham." She laughed and her hazel eyes seemed to glow.

"Why Sam, Sam?" he responded, smiling.

"Short for Samantha. But Sam stuck."

"Weren't you going to get away from work by taking leave? Where did you go?"

"I didn't. We had a crisis and I felt I had to be there, even though Spurling is not an easy man. No, I'll be going somewhere in the spring. But I may be transferred to another service in the hospital in a few days."

"Well, that's something to look forward to. Are you used to living alone?"

"How do you know I live alone?"

"Oh, I'm sorry, I just assumed it, because you said you were divorced."

"That's correct. But I have a son."

"Silly of me. So, what's your son's name?"

"Sam."

"Sam? You're kidding."

"Yes. Actually he's a twelve-year-old called Greg."

"Is that Gregory, Greg or Greg, Greg?"

"Greg, Greg." They both laughed and looked down at their milky foam. They began stirring it into the coffee.

"Why don't I take you to lunch one day? When you have nothing on."

Sam laughed and then looked at him.

"You mean when it's convenient for me?"

"Yes." For a second or two, Graham looked at her and then put his hand in front of his eyes and then they both laughed.

"Yes, I mean when you want to."

"Okay. My best days are a Tuesday or a Thursday."

"Great. Next Tuesday? If that's free?"

"Let me look in my little social secretary book."

She opened her handbag and fished about inside its capacious interior. It was of soft brown leather with a long handle that she could hitch over her shoulder. She found a small, brown diary and after a moment, "Fine. Tuesday's good. I can be away for about an hour and a half."

"Great. I'll pick you up when?"

"Oh, noon. At the car park near the staff cars. That way you're near to the door I'll come out from and you won't have ambulances and taxis bearing down on you."

They both noted the lunch, Graham borrowing her rather elegant Cross ballpoint pen. They finished the coffee and then made their way to the Market in the Mall.

"I'll just rush round," she said. "See you."

"Okay, Tuesday, then."

"Tuesday it is."

Graham watched her walking away, pushing her cart towards the vegetables. He combed the aisles with tinned soups. He was already looking forward to Tuesday. It was Saturday morning. *Only three days*, he thought.

When he got back home, he settled down to a dull Saturday of committee reports he had to read before Monday morning. *Waffle*, he thought. *Well, most of it.*

On Monday, when he arrived at his office a few minutes before he was due in committee, Graham could not resist ringing the hospital.

"Professor Spurling's office." It was a different voice from the one he remembered.

"Mrs. Gilmore?"

"She's no longer in this office. May I transfer your call?"

"Yes, thank you."

There was a version of "Greensleeves" played by a bland combo of some sort with a guitar. Suddenly a voice came on the phone, breaking the music loop.

"Hello, Professor Tandy's office."

"Mrs. Gilmore? Sorry to bother you at work, but it's Graham Curtis. Do you have any dislikes or preferences, so far as food is concerned?"

"No. I'll eat all kinds of cuisine. Especially if it's a treat."

"Good. See you tomorrow then."

"Thanks for calling. Until tomorrow, Graham." There was a click and she was gone.

Graham realized he had wanted to hear her voice. That was all. Her voice. *But Jacqueline was only just buried. What was happening?* He walked into the committee meeting thinking that he must be careful. *This was a call for help? This was loneliness? This was disloyalty. Were his feelings for Jacqueline so shallow? No. But I must not get involved,* he reminded himself.

CHAPTER TWENTY-SIX

After they had looked briefly at the newspapers, *Le Monde* and *The Financial Times,* Paul and Mary went out and took the metro to Havre Caumartin, where they emerged near Printemps, the department store. They walked through the perfume concessions, where Mary bought some cosmetics and the saleswoman gave her a smart little bag in stiff, glossy paper for her purchases and also a present of a narrow tubular vial of toilet water and a sample of skin cream in a miniature pot. The air was laden with scent and Paul sprayed himself with aftershave testers as they walked along. Sales people held out little bits of perfumed paper for them to sniff, hoping to tempt them to buy something. Back on the boulevard, they made for the Galeries Lafayette. Mary wanted to see the great decorated roof again. It had been years since she had seen it. The store had recently been redecorated and cleaned, so the rich fantasy of the interior did not disappoint her.

"When I first saw this, Paul, I was a school girl. I thought it was the most beautiful place in the entire world. I thought it must be like the interior of the Taj Mahal! Now I know it isn't, but it's still wonderful."

"Yes. It's a triumph. Business and decorative arts combined. Like Maxim's."

"Have you eaten there?"

"No. Out of my range I'm afraid, but it's famed for all the art nouveau décor. This magnificent roof like a dome of many colored glass above our heads adds a Shelleyan thrill to shopping. I love it. I want some socks, actually."

"And I want some underwear."

"Oh really? I'll come with you." They made their way to lingerie. Paul found this an agreeable department to walk through, and today was even more agreeable because it was exciting; he knew she would be trying things and choosing her underwear with not just herself in mind.

"I'll go off on the socks hunt and see you back here?"

"Fine. Off you go."

When Paul returned with his socks, dark-blue, grey, and dark-green, Mary was nowhere in sight. He looked around and wandered through the racks of slips and bras and strings. He then saw her emerging from a corner near a cashier. She was putting the smaller bag with her cosmetics into a medium-size carrier bag.

"So, what did you buy?"

"You'll have to wait to see it when we get home. I'll model it if you like."

"I like."

"But first, let's have lunch."

"Not just yet." Paul led her into the street and made for the Avenue de l'Opéra. Then they cut across down another street to emerge in the Place Vendôme. They looked in several famous windows in the elegant square that had housed a radio link between Paris and London in World War II, and where Princess Diana had eaten her last meal. They looked at rings, necklaces, earrings, and brooches. *Everything that was to their taste was*, Mary thought, *far too expensive*. In a little side street Paul had heard about, there was a small artisan's workshop-cum-boutique. The young craftsman showed them a ring he had recently made. Mary was immediately delighted with it. Paul could just about afford it. They both loved the delicacy of the white gold setting for the two diamonds, each of them just over one carat. The young jeweler was pleased with their appreciation of his work.

"Is it your own design?"

"All my work is made to my own designs, madam, unless someone has a specific request. Your ring is my variant on a ring I saw in a painting at the Jacquemart André Museum."

"Great," said Paul, "That's where we're going for lunch!"

Paul and Mary walked back to the square and took a taxi to the Musée Jacquemart André. *What a wonderful house it is*, Paul thought, but he said nothing, simply leading the way around the curved drive up the front steps and into the restaurant. They were lucky to get a table, because the elegant, but unpretentious dining room was a favourite place for visitors and locals alike. When they were seated Paul said, "Look up at the ceiling."

Mary looked up and smiled. "It's wonderful!"

"Tiepolo."

"Do you know I have never been here before, Paul. It's amazing."

"The lunch is good, too."

A waitress soon appeared and they ordered a glass of champagne each, with a salmon quiche and salad lunch. When the champagne arrived, Paul took out the ring and slipped it onto Mary's ring finger.

"To a lovely woman and future happiness!" said Paul.

"To the man of my life and the one love of my life," said Mary.

They talked and held hands in between sips of champagne. They decided to come back for a museum visit another time. It was now more pressing that today they go straight home after lunch. As they ate their meal, they planned their wedding and the Goan honeymoon. The wedding would be in May and they would take a brief few days in France for a mini honeymoon. But Goa would be the real one, in the following November, after all the rains had gone, and the weather would be perfect, and a locum would be available to look after Mary's practice. After lunch, they walked through the museum shop, tempted to buy several books and some costume jewelry, but resisted the impulse. It would be a great place to come to find small gifts a little out of the ordinary.

*** *

Back in Paul's apartment they took a bath together, and then, wearing some new perfume, Mary donned a succession of very pretty and artfully made bras, panties, and a couple of strings. She made a superb model for the underwear. When she was clad in the last items of her new underwear, Paul took her to the bed and they made love with a renewed urgency and passion. And then they lay in one another's arms for an hour of closeness, of warm intimacy. In the half-light of the bedroom, the diamonds on the engagement ring gleamed. Paul kissed her fingers and the ring. Then he made a pot of Chinese tea and took it back to bed with some exquisite bone china cups. They sipped their tea in his big bed.

"Good Lord, it's almost six," Paul said, glancing at his alarm clock radio.

"What shall we do before dinner?" Mary asked.

"This," he said.

They did.

***

Sam walked out into the car park where Graham was already waiting in his car. He sounded the horn and she changed direction, walked towards him, and waved. He got out, leaving the engine running, and opened the passenger door. She was wearing a light-beige pant suit and gold discs as earrings. She had a wonderful light, but effective eye make-up.

"I'm glad I managed to get to you yesterday," said Graham. "I rang Spurling's office, not realizing you'd already moved. They put me through."

"Yes, it was a sudden move. Spurling doesn't mess about when he wants something. And he wanted this new secretary he'd interviewed."

"Well, I thought we'd nip over the bridge and go to a little Italian place I know. Does that sound good?"

"Sure does."

They drove through the lunch hour traffic, but were soon over the bridge. She pulled a small mirror from her handbag and retouched her lipstick with an ice-pink gloss. Graham was looking for a parking space and noticed there were about four in the lot at the side of the restaurant. He parked by reversing into one of the spaces. This way he could get straight out with no trouble and drive her back to the hospital very neatly on time.

They had a table for two next to a window and away from the entrance to kitchens or toilets. It would be quiet. He was pleased. There was a pleasant hum of conversation and the air in the restaurant was full of enticing aromas. Sam sat down as he held her chair. They smiled at each other across the table. Her smile was sudden, always, and brilliant. *He wanted to call her Samantha. Would she allow that?*

"Look, I know everyone calls you Sam, but do you think I could call you Samantha? Would you mind?" asked Graham.

"Go ahead. I like it, and when I hear Samantha, I'll know it's you."

At this point a young waitress in a black miniskirt came to their table with a jug of iced water. Graham noticed that her nails were short and painted with clear nail varnish.

"Hi folks, I'm Sheryl, your server this afternoon? I'll just tell you our specials? They're also on the blackboard over the far side?" She rattled off a series of dishes as if they were all questions. In a statement of plain fact, she then said, "Will you folks be needing any drinks today."

"Samantha?"

"I'll have a glass of Pinot Grigio," Sam decided.

"I'll have a glass of red, the Chianti Classico," added Graham.

"I'll be right back to take your orders?" stated the waitress.

Graham noticed how perfectly shapely her legs were and also how, behind her back, an order pad was stuck into the belt of her skirt.

"That girl's delightful," observed Sam, "but why do girls now make most of what they say into a question?"

"It's an epidemic in the university," said Graham. "I have a theory about it."

Sheryl came back with their wine and Sam asked for a green house salad with veal cutlet to follow. Graham remembered that they were not having a leisurely lunch and he rapidly ordered the antipasto cold cuts plate followed by hunter's chicken. Sheryl repeated their orders accurately, with aplomb, and with an inappropriate interrogative expression whenever she made a statement. Graham marveled at her wonderful figure as she walked away to announce their order to the kitchen. He decided to come back for lunch here another day.

"What's your theory, Graham?"

"I think some young person in the United States was a sort of leader of the pack, in her set, at high school, yet was not as sure of herself as she might have been. She developed this interrogative statement as a way of sounding not pushy or dogmatic. But because she was a leader, probably she was a teeny bopper school goddess in looks, and all the football jocks were falling over themselves to woo her, the other girls imitated her interrogative intonation. This then became a craze and spread like a forest fire to other high schools and then into the universities. It even leapt across the Atlantic, probably by means of television sitcom and lo and behold, half the females in the English-speaking world are asking statements instead of questions!"

"Including the lovely Sheryl," laughed Sam.

"I'll probably find she's a sophomore who will turn up in one of my classes. It's the grade ten plus syndrome writ large!"

"What classes do you teach? I've never asked. And how would you prove your theory?"

"I wouldn't dream of trying to prove my theory. I'm not a linguist, nor am I a sociologist. It would be a joint research project for interdisciplinary study and might merit a modest grant, but my field is pre-Shakespearean English literature. I used to be a medievalist, but then middle English became too hard for youngsters—as they existed in the minds of those who know what's what—and in order to keep my feet running on the spot, I teach anything leading reasonably and easily up to old Willy the Bard, as well as children's literature."

"Otherwise you'd lose your job?"

"Not really, because I have tenure, and I always manage to get a loyal band of rebels against 'korrekt-think' as I call it. It's now subversive in some places to be a medievalist. And soon, the same may be said of people who want to study Shakespeare."

"Shakespeare? But he's the one writer even taxi drivers have heard about."

"Don't knock taxi drivers, Samantha, many of them have a PhD in their hip pockets next to their driving licences!"

"But how could you be an English major without studying Shakespeare? I couldn't claim to be a nurse without knowing muscles and skeletons."

"Well, Shakespeare's certainly the skeleton in the 'korrekt-think' closet."

At this point Sheryl appeared with their first course. She put the dishes down carefully, remembering perfectly their respective orders. She then returned brandishing an enormous pepper grinder she took from a small table nearby.

"Pepper," she asked, as if stating the obvious.

"Please," they chorused. Sheryl ground with a flourish.

"Enjoy!" she said, as if gloating over something. Graham wondered if this girl would say, "Enjoy" in just that way if she were in bed with a boyfriend? And then he thought, *What's happening? Am I just nasty?*

"Would you like some of my salad?" asked Sam.

"Yes, but only if you take some cold cuts. We could share?"

"Was that a question or are you copying our server?"

"How can you ask. It was a question?" he replied. Samantha laughed. Graham smiled as they traded a little of their food. Sheryl reappeared with a huge salt grinder, a litre bottle of olive oil, and a basket of small, crusty slices of bread.

"Enjoy!" They did. By the time their main dish arrived, they had finished the wine, but declined second glasses.

"So, where did you do your training to be a nurse?"

"I was in Hamilton. I studied at McMaster for a while and then went to Ottawa and then came out West."

"Go West, young woman!"

"I followed a man. Then he upped and left. So I finally ended up working in British Columbia."

"But you are a nurse as well as a secretary?"

"Basically yes. I never wanted to be a theatre sister or a matron. I like what I do. My doctors appreciate me and I appreciate working with them, as long as they don't expect me to be a mistress."

"Wife, but not mistress?"

"You got it, buddy!" and she flashed him one of her perfect smiles.

"So, how's the new office?"

"Good."

"When are you going to take that leave you promised yourself?"

"That can wait a while, until I know my way in the new section and Greg's out of school for the Easter vacation. Do you have plans?"

"I need to get away. At Easter, I've decided to visit a pal in Paris."

"Paris! How wonderful. Do you speak French?"

"I get along. My buddy lives there and speaks it very fluently. I usually stay with him. I need a change of scene. I'll go to London as well."

"Sounds wonderful."

"Why don't you come over with Greg, while I'm there? My friend knows little neighbourhood hotels that don't cost an arm and a leg."

"Would you mind?"

"I wouldn't have suggested it if I thought that it would be a problem."

"I really like the idea. Let me work on it."

When they had finished and paid the bill, Sam insisting that they would go Dutch, Graham drove her back to the hospital. As she got out of his car, she leaned back in and kissed him on the cheek.

"I'll be in touch," she said and walked in through the side door.

CHAPTER TWENTY-SEVEN

Graham decided Samantha was a good woman and probably a good mother, too. He drove to the university and got back to some of his pressing memoranda, papers, and preparation. He even managed to read for an hour without thinking constantly of Jacqueline and the gaping hole in his life. There was a sound of people laughing and chatting outside his room. It was the end of classes and there was a changeover time gap before the next classes would begin. There was a knock at the door. Graham looked at his watch. He had posted office hours for this hour of the day, so students would be along to see him.

"Come in," he called.

The door opened and a young woman came in. She wore blue jeans that appeared to be worn so much that the color was washed out in a long stripe of white down each leg. This, Graham had noticed, was a current fashion gimmick. She wore a sort of tasseled blouse as a top and on her head was a capacious woolly hat. She had a flawless complexion and large brown eyes.

"May I see you about my paper, Professor Curtis?"

"Of course. Please sit down. How can I help?"

"Do we have to bring in new historicism for the Gammer Gurton essay?"

This is a young adult, Graham thought, *who's worried in the way a schoolgirl might worry and phrases the question in just the same way.*

"You write an approach to the Gammer Gurton text according to your critical insights and arguments. You use whatever scholarly ideas seem relevant to the text you are studying and to your thinking about it. If new historicism seems to you helpful, then you might think about that. If it doesn't illuminate anything, do not use it. That's my advice."

"But in another course we *have* to use it or we don't get good grades."

"I'm talking about my course. You're writing an essay for me."

"Thank you, professor."

"University is about learning to think and argue about the knowledge you acquire. You have to try to make it yours. You are a person, not a parrot!"

The young woman smiled and stood up, thanking Graham again.

"It's Ms. Harper, isn't it," Graham asked as she was leaving.

"No. I'm Melissa Hooper."

Clang! thought Graham. *I must go over my class list again, fixing the faces to it.* "Oh, I'm sorry. See you in class."

There were two other students waiting in the corridor to see him. He was glad he did not have to go home just yet.

CHAPTER TWENTY-EIGHT

She was sitting in an operations room studying her orders, committing paper to memory—they never referred to learning by heart. She had the orders well implanted now. No need for paper. She shredded the papers, watching sheets disappear into the machine. There was not much heart, she had always known, in this particular *métier.* The heart was in the original motivation for working: the notion that someone had to confront and defeat the wantonly cruel, or the ruthless criminal mentality that demanded every civil right work for *it,* while trampling over the civil rights of every one of its victims, direct and indirect. Crimes, she had discovered when she was a child, not only affected an immediate victim, but also those connected with the victim, such as, of course, family and friends. As an adult, she expanded the list of indirect victims to include colleagues and the unwary public at large. Each crime destroyed a portion, small or large, of civil society. She never talked like this to colleagues. She was simply there, on the side of the angels, working to combat evil and its crimes. There was such a thing as evil even if some goody-goodies denied it. She'd seen it in action and worked among its catastrophic results. There was, however, no cure for evil or quick cure for crime. Highly educated and privileged people, as well as the uneducated and underprivileged, turned to crime. It seemed an easier route than slogging away at a normal job. Her job was such that she was often lonely; it was very often also a dangerous slog.

She was ready to go back into the corridor. Bruno was walking towards her. He was abnormally thin. Well, what was normal? Normalcy for most people, she reflected, required persistence, courage, and the ingenuity to find work and either keep it, or find more work. It also preserved the deepest, intimate expressions of human nature, such as love, sexual or platonic. It was all this normalcy and decency of the majority of good citizens and their families that her outfit and the police were protecting. The state had to be reasonably safe so that life could flourish. These views were now part of her inner core of feeling, rather than an intellectual position. It was her nature to fight back against bullies. She did not like Hollywood movies showing secret agents as executioners tracking down and silencing or killing citizens to prevent the exposure of a sordid crime committed by some high-ranking politician. Kalitza was well aware of the crimes and corruption of politicians, but she fortunately had never known an operation, let alone been part of one, aimed at law-abiding citizens in order to protect a criminal bigwig.

"How's my favourite person?" grinned Bruno.

"This person is very well, thank you, Bruno. And how's my favourite cuddly skeleton today?"

"Not very hungry, but if you are feeling cuddly for once, I can always fall in with your mood."

Bruno was looking at some papers. He was . . . self-contained.

She had rarely offered her own intimacy to anyone else. She had to be careful while seeming spontaneous. She had used sex occasionally. That man in Hong Kong. He was a godsend and she had been grateful for his just being there when she had needed him as an unwitting courier and a means of winding down. Relaxing . . . but he'd become a nuisance. Why did he have to be a journalist? Why did he have to live in Paris? It could mean a silly error one day, if he were to see her during an operation and stumble along, getting in the way, unwittingly alerting an enemy to her presence.

"Are you going to the gym by any chance?" she asked, before the cuddly thing could get into second gear.

"I need to," said Bruno. "I have time, just. I will, Kim, if you will."

"Well, why not?"

After her pre-recruitment tests, grueling and exacting as they had been, she had undergone intensive training that was very thorough indeed. This gave her great reserves of confidence, strength, and energy. She had learned to control the desire to offer intimacy; she had learned to control fear. She had learned to ignore pain as much as possible. A certain amount of fear was useful; it kept her effective, alert, careful, and alive. False intimacy was useful. It was a sort of shield. In Section CG, she was known to Bruno and others as Kim. Outside, she worked under assumed names, all of them false.

Without more ado they walked along another corridor and took an elevator to another floor. The gym was well-equipped. She and Bruno went to their respective lockers. Bruno was pleased with the military equipment he had been practising with recently. *It's always excellent*, he thought, and very often it was astonishing.

She kept up her level of fitness and physical strength by frequent routine exercises and some that were more arcane. She was very pleased with today's orders and the new equipment she and Bruno had used. She was on the mats just before Bruno emerged.

"A warm up and then a combat bout?" she asked as he walked to join her. He nodded. They warmed up for about ten minutes before circling each other warily. Suddenly, Bruno made his move, but his height worked against him, slowing him a little. She avoided his long reach, one of his advantages, and moved inside his arms, turning as she did so and kicking back with her left heel. Bruno had anticipated that one, and he tried to grab her foot, but her right elbow crashed into his lower ribs. She was already bent over and pulled his legs upward from behind his knees. Her moves were so fast that Bruno was on his back, rubbing his ribs when she turned again to face him. She could have kicked him where it hurts most.

"Good one!" said Bruno. "You could have killed me."

She had, in fact, killed a few nasties, when killing was unavoidable. Afterwards she felt regret . . . and not exactly culpability . . . but a sense that if she had been just a little faster, a little better prepared, she might have been able to avoid the killing. Put them out of action. Interrogate. Imprison. She preferred that and so did Control.

"Don't worry. I'm on your side, Bruno."

She reached down to help him to his feet. But Bruno pulled her down, so that she was suddenly on the mat beside him. They then sprang up and continued their workout until they needed a breather.

"I hope we'll soon be working together again," panted Bruno, "making the world a safer place for mamas and papas and me and you."

"Yes. I'm sure Control will need us to work together again pretty soon."

"Why can't all teachers be good, all countries have a benign rule of law, free, clean elections with genuinely secret ballots, modern medicine, and a healthy economy, and no crazy or greedy dictators? In short, beatitude?" asked Bruno.

"Would that they would or could. And we could probably retire. Without crippling taxation and with peace, order, and good government."

"Agreed. As I was saying, many problems can be solved. But the ideologues and the religious fanatics spring up like the serpents in the garden."

"Serpents? I thought there was only one?"

"There is only one God, but there are many devils."

"What about goddesses?"

"Oh, there are lots of those, Bruno."

"You're most certainly one of them, Kim."

"I try." Kalitza smiled her dazzling smile and began another exercise routine.

"Well, terrorists and other problems always occur, but they can be contained as Control might say."

"Our society took hundreds of years to get where we are. It's always a struggle against powerful interest groups. Maintaining free societies means we can't just retire and go home. Or can we go home?"

"Wherever that may be," said Bruno. "No. We have no choice, really. And we always have to watch our backs."

"Agreed," she said, and panted, "Let's work the machines for a few more minutes."

Psychological struggle, she thought, *goes hand-in-glove with technological solutions and superior weapons.* They were both hot and getting tired. She felt good. When they were back in the machine room, they continued their putting the world to rights exchanges.

"People can get on with living productive, reasonably happy lives, as Control always tells me, only if our society is protected," Bruno said, as he sat on a pedaling machine and pretended he was in the Tour de France.

"If not, it easily deteriorates into the rule of fanatics . . ."

"Or criminal bosses," she said, as she started skipping next to his machine.

She did not skip in her apartment for fear of disturbing neighbours in the flat below. *How did Bruno have so much energy when he was mere bones and sinewy muscle? In the history of human beings*, she thought, *fanatics, religious and political, have a lot to answer for.* She did not commit intellectual suicide by believing in party lines or the gurus in the political or religious landscape. She felt fully justified, even privileged in her job. But the dirty tricks of politicians jolted her from time to time. Some colleagues were thoroughly jaded. Bruno was always delivering his ideas with a light irony behind them. Perhaps it was only a matter of time, of the duration of calumnies, before Bruno would find disaffection implanting itself in him, like a virus.

"Got new orders?" panted Bruno.

"Yes. You?"

"Yeah. And I always obey orders, Kim," he grinned as he puffed.

They all obeyed the orders of people they usually didn't even see. And for this, faith, and hope, and teamwork, and yes, caution, followed by surprise and intrepid action—these were essential, as they were for life itself.

Bruno stopped pedaling. He mopped himself with the towel he had to hand. She continued skipping.

"Do you ever do something just for you, when you're on leave?"

She considered it as if giving it serious thought. "Never," she said.

"Liar."

"Agreed. Everyone deserves a bit of fun. I take posh afternoon teas and go to galleries and theatres for the latest musicals. You?"

"I go to Blackpool and walk the pier and watch the waves. Bracing."

"Liar!"

"It's safer to be unreachable."

In the secret world, though, personal fulfillment was a passion for the job in hand; a desire to win, against whatever odds your opponents had going for them. If there could be a bit of agreeable diversion as well, so much the better. She thought of Hong Kong. Then of Bruno. This name suited him. His weak point, as she fully realized, was his personal appearance, so striking that it was hard to mistake him for anyone else. It was also her weak point, her physical beauty. If she had to work with him, she always suggested they use disguises. Bruno always rejected the idea. She trusted him as far as possible, but never totally. She was amused that he knew her as Kim. Code names were a delight.

Bruno was a code name, like all their names. Personnel files in a secure environment listed the names they had used in their normal lives, when they were first recruited. The *nomenclator*, perhaps *nomenclatress,* who dished out the agents' code names for various operations, was naturally unknown to the recipients of these code names. The naming of warriors and the keeping secret of their names was an ancient tradition, perhaps one as old as war itself.

She went back to concentrating on the skipping, slowing gradually until she stopped.

They warmed down for several minutes.

"Showers?" Bruno asked pointlessly.

They soon emerged from the locker rooms. She was relaxed now and let her speculations continue. *Not one of my colleagues*, she thought, *had ever used in her hearing anything but the section code names*. Nor had she. Yet she had heard that at least one of their number had succeeded in being recruited, using an already false identity established long enough before the screening procedure to be accepted as genuine. Thus, it was reasonable to assume, this person's real identity was nowhere in official files. Nobody in the outfit knew the origins of this mystery man or woman.

It had occurred to Kim, her section code name, and one that she particularly liked, because it could refer to a male or female, thus offering confusion and perhaps a shade more protection, that this must be a particularly brilliant, farsighted agent who had an excellent chance of staying alive long enough to retire. To retire with a pension or preferably a lump sum and to vanish into a real life with an ordinary family or live under the anonymity of yet another false identity—that was appealing. She also realized that this agent could be, in fact, a mole bent on undermining the outfit and even killing people as well as selling information to willing buyers. She was prepared, of course, to be ruthless, if it ever became a life or death situation. *I'll get her before she gets me,* she vowed to herself, whenever she thought about this rumour. Kim thought that the mole was most likely female. Women changed their names by marriage and it might seem that a false identity could be assumed even more easily by women than by men. She smiled to herself as she remembered the shredded paper she had been studying. After all, she herself had been recruited when she was using a false identity—the one in her personnel file—as far as she knew. Of course, the background check could have been far more thorough than anyone imagined. The rumour, she reasoned, could be about her! Furthermore, it could easily have been planted by Monsieur Martin. He was the shadowy section head, as Bruno usually said, echoing popular newsprint and TV journalism.

Shadowy was a favourite word trotted out when a secret intelligence scandal broke, or even if a government committee heard evidence from one of the bosses. The shadowy section head could have planted the rumour in order to keep them all on their toes. If so, the problem was that the rumour nibbled away at the trust they had to rely upon sometimes, when working together in pairs or in a larger team. But in any group of people, rumours circulated from time to time. There was always some sort of threat hanging over you. *There's no security*, she thought. But she came back to that nagging thought: perhaps *she* was the rumoured agent. If so, she had nothing to fear from a mole. But the source of this rumour might have an inkling that she was the one. Yes, there was always an element of doubt. They were like animals or birds, always looking around them in case of predators.

"Penny for them," said Bruno as they walked the corridor.

She did not reply. She just looked at him, raised her eyebrows, and smiled. He shrugged and then waved a hand vaguely. *Is Bruno a mole? Why did he ask questions of her?* This question nagged at her before she dismissed it. She had to concentrate on what came next.

"Don't forget the London rendezvous we decided on. It might be handy one day," said Bruno.

Kim knew the place he referred to; it was safe. *Or was it? Bruno was a colleague she could perhaps trust.*

CHAPTER TWENTY-NINE

Paul watched Mary's progress up through the passenger tube. Her visit had been another opportunity for deepening their knowledge of each other and of themselves. But it had been too short. They really did have to start living together. It was a matter of coordinating their affairs and, of course, his moving in with Mary, but only when she felt she could take the plunge and invite him. He felt total trust. There was no question of jealousy. But was she jealous of his contact with Kalitza? Younger, when he had first been dating girlfriends, he had often felt the sharp stab of jealousy. He had disliked the tendency of many girls to find safety in being one of a crowd with several young men in tow, all jealous of each other. This youthful jealousy now seemed very callow and the behaviour of the young women as working their suitors in pairs or in group outings seemed a very reasonable precaution against the erratic, romantic habits of the young male recently let into a sixth form or a college, or out of school altogether. *He was now mature,* he thought, *and confident. What was all that stuff about the mysterious Kalitza? What had been going on in his mind?* It seemed a hell of a long time ago. Easter was fairly soon. Graham might visit. Then in May, there was the wedding to look forward to.

He took a new, non-defaced RER train back to the Gare de Lyon. From there he was going to the Quai de la Gare at Bercy and would do some badly needed reading in the Bibliothèque Nationale. He disliked its grandiose empty platform with the "open book" towers. He was appalled by the way readers had to climb up to this windy eyesore, as if on a pilgrimage to Mitterrand's sacred mountain, and then find the escalator to descend into the bibliographic underworld. Once inside the library, Paul had, however, found it was orderly, comfortable, and reasonably user friendly. Nevertheless, he preferred the old premises in the rue de Richelieu. In London, he preferred the famous old British Museum reading room to the new premises, yet he preferred the new British library to the new French one. But when all was said and done, as people once used to say, it was largely academic, this question of preferences, for he most often found himself of necessity using the Internet or, when in London, working at the Colindale newspaper library or in some specific archive. The New York Public Library, though, he had to admit, was his favourite place for the kind of research he often wanted to do. Just as an environment, however, the library he loved to relax in was the one in the Oxford and Cambridge Club in Pall Mall. There he could mull over the newspapers and periodicals in a comfortable club chair, reasonably confident that nobody would join him. Furthermore, the London Library, haven for many a writer, was just a short walk away and was affiliated with that of the club.

Paul worked for about three hours and then decided he had enough facts and figures and arguments and references. He packed up his notes and headed for the cloakroom in the large open foyer area. As he went to collect his coat at the counter, he noticed an emaciated man, quite tall, dressed in light-grey slacks and a chocolate-brown polo neck sweater. He was flicking through a book in the shop area. Paul looked at him again, more closely. He was certain it was the same man he had seen in Vancouver at the Egyptian exhibition. Having retrieved his coat, Paul looked again and saw the man going out of the library. He followed the tall, almost ghostly figure out of the library and down the steps from the complex into the streets that led to the metro. Paul caught up with the man who turned to look at him while still maintaining his stride.

"Why are you following me?" the man asked in English.

"Following you? Yes, I suppose I was. I wanted to ask if it was you who I saw in Vancouver? And did you by any chance jump into the Seine one day?"

"Now, why would I want to do that? I'm too thin, I know, but I'm not crazy."

"Oh, I could have sworn it was you. I'm sorry."

"No problem. I'll be on my way. I'm here for only another day before I fly back home."

"Sorry. When did you get to Paris?"

"Two days ago. I'd like to stay longer, but I managed to do my research and now I have to get back."

"Where? Vancouver, British Columbia?"

"No. Tampa, Florida."

"Well, bon voyage!" said Paul.

The man waved and went to the platform opposite to the direction Paul was intending to take. A train clattered and rumbled and ground into the station. Doors opened. The warning note sounded a few seconds later. The train pulled out. The man smiled at him through a carriage window before vanishing into the dark tunnel, another life, a different realm. Bruno thought, *this chap was right. I was in Vancouver. So what? Is he with the Brits?*

Paul's train arrived a few seconds later. On the brief journey back to the left bank, as he thought things over, he realized the man had known he was being followed, though he had never looked back and had given no sign. He had spoken first and had spoken English. How had he known that Paul would speak English? Kalitza had told the man about her dealings with Paul. That must be it. Then Paul reflected that if the man was not Kalitza's friend or accomplice, he could have been merely an English speaker with not enough French to launch into a situation like that in French. He probably assumed that if Paul were French and was using the Bibliothèque Nationale for study or research, he would most probably also speak English. Yet the questions would not go away. How had he known he was being followed? Strangely enough, Paul had not made a very determined decision to follow the man. It was almost accidental. In fact, it was quite natural that readers leaving the library to catch the metro would walk in the same direction. They would be following one another, but not consciously, in the sense the man had meant. So why had he spoken at all?

***

She had not realized that at home in the evenings she would miss Paul so much. She had not realized, either, that she would miss him even at moments when she was seeing patients in the surgery. Was it so urgent, though, that they must marry in May? He could move in with her for a few days or a week, or maybe two, or perhaps a few months, while they hunted for a suitable place in Lichfield. She was not exactly disturbed or alarmed by his fanciful encounters with the angelic woman—or supernatural creature—he called Kalitza. She could not be sure, though, what exactly the Kalitza phenomenon, as she thought of it now, represented in Paul's psyche. Her first explanation was Kalitza as creative self. Paul seemed very alive and creative when he was with Mary. He seemed now adult, rather than the boy she had first met. He seemed to be exactly what he was: a successful freelance journalist with a steady writing income, as well as one from a legacy held in trust. Perhaps his artistic temperament as a writer gave him the idea that this Kalitza was special, even supernatural. That was curious. But Paul, so far as she knew, had no real problems. Paul had needed Kalitza. Now he needed her, Mary, instead. And Mary realized that she needed Paul. She also surmised that Kalitza had needed Paul just for a specific purpose, surely nothing enduring.

His friend, Graham, though, was in a terrible state, poor man. They had talked of Graham's impending visit. It occurred to her that Graham might want to spend time with Paul, but also be left to himself in Paris for a few days at a time. Or both of them might come over to visit her. She telephoned Paul that evening to hear his voice and also discuss these ideas.

Paul liked the notion of visiting her to go home-hunting in Lichfield. He would bring his laptop and continue working as well. As for bringing Graham with him, he was very enthusiastic. He wanted his old friend to meet Mary and to like her. It would be a very agreeable visit.

***

Bruno came into the secure, soundproof room. "Kim! What a surprise. I thought you had orders and that you'd already gone."

Kim looked at him, but did not show any surprise. "Correct, Bruno, and in fact, I'm on the road again in a few minutes. But I thought you'd gone as well."

"Yes, but I was advised to go to the Bib. Mitt. at the last minute. And you remember when we jumped into the Seine together?"

"Splash, splash."

"Yeah, well one of the crowd who saw the event followed me out of the library today."

"You mean the national one, not our section library?" They both grinned.

"Yeah, well he's not an agent, unless he's exceptional. I photographed him—covertly, as they say. I've just run a check on him. He's a journalist, freelance, of a certain standing; he gets around. Paul Wills. He was in Hong Kong for a while and got mixed up in an affair with a microchip and a female agent."

"Now fancy that. Is he tall and handsome?"

"He is. In fact, in Hong Kong the police almost caught him in bed."

"Really? With the agent or the microchip?"

"Both, according to the file. He gave the chip to the police and that's precisely what the agent intended him to do. It worked out well."

"Bully for the agent."

"But although that episode is closed, I wonder," added Bruno, "whether this Paul Wills is really a journalist."

"What makes you doubt it?"

"Nothing really. It's just a hunch."

"If you're suspicious, track down his editors, publishers, magazines, et cetera"

"Don't have time."

"Nor I. Perhaps M. Martin can get a neophyte onto it for you, my pet."

"Section," said Bruno, "is satisfied with the check made at the time by Hong Kong, and London, and Paris."

"That's okay by me. I have to be away for a few days in any case."

Bruno smiled, making his skeletal features even more into a death's head. He got up from his chair and went to the door. "Take care, Kim," he said.

They hugged briefly. "Yes. You, too, Bruno," she said, releasing him and turning to pick up a neat little shoulder bag.

"See you in a few days?"

Bruno did not answer. He had already gone. She felt suddenly that his mission was probably dangerous or difficult. He had dropped his ironic tone. Was that it? Her intuition was quite strong. Was it simply that nowadays missions were all getting increasingly dangerous? Or was it simply that *she* was a bit older, a bit wiser? Bruno was a tad slower, too. Would she see him again? Yes. She had faith in his determination to survive. But why had he told her about the journalist? Was Bruno angling to see if she had been on the Hong Kong operation? Was Bruno a bit too interested in her actions? Why had he reminded her of the London rendezvous point? Dismissing this for the moment, she concentrated on her next assignment. Kim took out of a special locker a piece of intriguing equipment, examined it carefully, put it into its carrying case again, and then left the secure room with her shoulder bag and the small case.

CHAPTER THIRTY

Paul Wills sat in the book-lined rear room of the café known as Le Fumoir. Over his coffee, he was scanning the English language newspapers and was just about finished. He put them back on the table near the front bar and ordered another coffee. He noticed that the only other person in this part of the café was still writing in a thick exercise book, smoking a cigarillo, and never drinking his coffee. Paul went back to the inner room, took out some scrap paper, and began making a list of jobs he had to do. He had to discuss a firm date for the Graham visit; there was a date to fix for the wedding; there was the optimum timing of the trip to Goa; the question of whether he would be able to meet Mary again before Graham's possible visit; and the other, professional business. But that was in a separate file in the computer. He thought he could smell Mary's perfume, Stately Home. He realized it lingered on his handkerchief. He had just wiped his lips with it.

Now, yes, "Family Matters" would be a challenge. It had to be real. It had to be gritty. How reviewers and editors loved gritty! It had to be compassionate. Not sentimental. The real emotions in families were too strong to be sentimentalized and made false. Yet, that was what often happened. That play, *The Homecoming*, had to be kept in mind. He looked out of the window and caught his breath. Kalitza! Surely not . . . yes, she was walking past, purposeful, alert. She was at the bus stop and crossing the road. *Let her be, let her be,* he thought. *Why follow?*

Paul hesitated for a moment and then put enough money on the table to pay for his order and leave a small tip. He hurried onto the street and went around the side of Le Fumoir. This put him outside the window near which he had been sitting. Kalitza was still in sight. Hang it all, he would not talk, but would see what he could find out about where she was going. She was walking fast and turned left, parallel to the right bank of the river. Paul started to run. He was afraid that he might see her plunge from a bridge into the now icy Seine. As he turned the corner, she was just about fifteen meters ahead of him. She was wearing a charcoal-grey slouch hat and a fawn overcoat with raglan sleeves. She had a small shoulder bag and a small case. Her long legs were concealed by slightly flared trousers matching her hat, but with a thin white stripe. She wore flat heeled, black leather shoes that made no noise as she walked. She turned left into a small side street. Paul was just in time to round the corner to see her go through a heavy wooden door painted a glossy dark blue. It was on a spring that closed it automatically, but slowly. Paul managed to push it open just before it closed. He stepped into a short, unlit entryway leading to an inner courtyard. On the wall near the great blue door was a switch labeled *Porte*. He could use this to get out to the street again, if he let the door swing back to close behind him. He walked into the sunlit courtyard.

Ahead of him, across the flagstones of the yard, was the classical façade of an eighteenth century gentleman's house, framed by trees with a dark network of leafless branches. There were stone steps leading to the entrance. Beside the front door a brass plate was engraved with the name of a business: *PRIVATE DANCERS CORPORATION.* Paul rang the bell. He suddenly remembered the beginning of a Hardy poem, *Come again to the place/where your presence was as a leaf that skims* . . . After a few moments a large, dark-skinned man—an Algerian or a Tunisian perhaps—opened the door. He was immaculately dressed in a discreet lightweight wool suit, mid-grey with a thin chalk stripe. He wore a dark-grey silk shirt with a silk tie of exactly the same color. A narrow, red, serpent-like line went down the middle of the tie. He asked in equally silky French if Monsieur had an appointment and if so with whom and at what time? Paul said he had no appointment. The man regretted that there was no unauthorized entry. The company worked only by appointments. Paul asked how one made appointments. The reply was that one wrote or telephoned for appointments with specific members of the company. How did one get to know who was a member? One was always referred to the firm and to specific members of it by other people, who already had dealings with the firm. The business depended on highly confidential private referral. Paul thanked the man and turned to go, but then asked him if he knew a lady who had just now entered. The man smiled and said that he had not admitted a lady, because he had only that moment taken over from a colleague who had gone to lunch. He was sorry he could not be more helpful. Paul thanked him again and walked to the street door, pressed the switch, heard a click, and pulled the door open. He felt foolish. Why in heaven's name had he followed the woman? A journalist's curiosity? Like an answer, more lines from Hardy's poem came into his thoughts, *Through the dark corridors/Your walk was so soundless I did not know/Your form from a phantom's of long ago . . .*

He went on towards the river. He stopped and looked up, alerted by the engine and the fluttering noise of rotors. A helicopter was climbing in a circle above the rooftops. It had evidently just taken off from atop a modern building that he judged to be a little way behind the eighteenth century house he had just so disappointingly and foolishly visited. The aircraft banked and, still climbing, headed east.

Paul felt certain that Kalitza was aboard that chopper. It was seemingly a commercial helicopter. A tour of Paris from the air? A quick trip to the airport? So what? He had to concentrate on work and also get in touch with Mary. Kalitza could go and jump in the Seine again with her ugly thin man. And not resurface. Yet his journalist's habits and the mystery of events in Hong Kong still prompted a certain need to find out more about her. Then he decided finally to give up worrying about Kalitza. There were, rather luckily for Paul, certain other, more pressing assignments. Family Matters, for example, involved going south on the TGV as far as Avignon, there to meet with Madame la Marquise de Crevennes, who would give an interview about the domestic strife in aristocratic families. This he considered to be a bit of a scoop. He was hoping for an abundance of credible details rather than mere scandal sheet sensationalism.

Divorced, Madame la Marquise, he had discovered, had never remarried. From an old aristocratic family, and married briefly to another aristocrat, she would appear in his article as merely one anonymous source for aristocratic family matters in the nineteenth and twentieth centuries, yet a very special witness, since she was, in fact, a noted historian. She wrote history under a pseudonym derived from an amalgam of her maiden name with that of a distant cousin. Paul had read some of her work, but had never met her before. She was a fairly frequent contributor of essays in French and in English to noted history journals. He was eager to meet her and also looking forward to being in Avignon again. She would talk as well about the violence she personally had suffered.

His appointment with Mme. de Crevennes was for the next day, mid-afternoon. He went to the Gare de Lyon by metro and bought his ticket for an early morning TGV. Then he went home, buying half a baguette from his favourite bakery near the flat. He prepared himself a sumptuous sandwich of ham, shavings of parmesan cheese, and thin slices of cucumber. He had also some cold leek for which he made a delicate salad dressing. Then he poured himself a modest measure of white Sancerre and phoned Mary's surgery.

The phone rang just as she was packing up her papers before heading for home.

"Dr. Rao's surgery. Hello?"

"Mary? I'm glad I caught you. But are you still working?"

"Just about to go home, darling."

"Can we chat for a bit?"

"Why not? What is it?"

"I love you."

"I love you, too. And?"

"I have to go to Avignon tomorrow, but if you need to catch me, ring my cell phone. You still have the number?"

"Does the Pope celebrate mass? It's the one with zero six, not zero one, at the beginning."

"Right. I may be a day or two down there. But I'm wondering if you have any more thoughts on fixing a date for the wedding? Mid-May?"

"I was thinking of May 25, darling. Does that sound good? It suits me and I can grab a few days of leave. My locum will be available."

"Terrific. My angel, guess what?"

"What?"

"It means that from now on May twenty-fifth will be our anniversary! Flowers. Champagne!"

"Paul, that's a wonderful thought. So it suits?"

"You bet. Perfect. I'll make sure I attend."

"That's a good thought, too. Make a note in your diary, darling."

"You're wearing saffron yellow underwear. Very lacy."

"You monkey! How did you know that?"

"You really are! Well, I'll be jiggered."

"Don't be so jiggered you fall off that bridge in Avignon. And get over here as soon as you can. I fancy a weekend in bed."

"Oh God, so do I, darling. I don't think I can wait until May, never mind the twenty-fifth."

"I know I can't. Look, I must lock up and go home. I'll call you when I get in. Okay?"

"Okay. Love you! Bye."

"Kisses. Hugs. Bye."

Mary still held the phone and then slowly put it down. She was smiling. The line had been so clear it was as if they had simply been speaking face-to-face. The twenty-fifth of May. So that was it. *That's the most important date in my life*, she thought. She hurried home and called his Paris number from the flat. They discussed more plans for the wedding and promised themselves a brief honeymoon afterwards. They decided that they would both start making definite arrangements for a month away in Goa, later on, nearer mid-November.

Paul slept until just before his alarm clock sounded. He did not make breakfast, but as soon as he was ready, he stuck a notebook into the small bag designed for his laptop computer and picked up his overnight bag, remembering as he did so that his father had had one, brown leather, which he had called a grip. As he left to catch the metro to the Gare de Lyon, he was wondering whatever had happened to the old man's grip.

He was early and so had time for a *café au lait* and a *pain aux raisins* in a station brasserie before finding his reserved seat on the train. He settled down and looked at the people searching for the right carriage. They were thinning out now on the platform. He recognized someone a little way down. Yes. It was Peter Brook, the stage director. Paul wondered if he were going to Avignon in connection with some forthcoming production at the festival. Perhaps. He then set up the laptop and got down to work.

***

Dr. Mary Rao walked into her surgery by the usual back door from her parking place. She was a little earlier than usual this morning. Liz had just arrived and was sorting out the first appointments for the morning.

"Liz, I'm getting married!"

Liz looked up, put down the files she was holding, and grinned. She got up and hugged Mary.

"That's great news. Brilliant! Who is it? Anyone I know? Let me guess . . . it's that tall man with wavy hair, the man who lives in Paris?"

"Yes, Paul. That's his name."

"I gathered that! Cool! Am I invited?"

"Liz, of course. But it'll be just a small, quiet affair. Informal. No toppers and morning dress."

"English rather than Indian?"

"God, yes. Indian would go on for days. What a circus that would be. But I'll wear a special sari."

"Would it be okay for me to have a sari, too?"

"Why not, Liz? Would your boyfriend approve?"

"He'll have to approve, whoever he might turn out to be! Brilliant. Can I have a red dot as well?"

"Why not?"

"Terrific! I shall feel very grand!"

There was a ring on the bell and the first patient, an elderly woman with a rattling smoker's cough, arrived in the surgery. Mary winked at Liz and left the reception area. Liz was still smiling. She looked up from a file and asked, "Mrs. Wilkinson, isn't it?"

"Yes," said the woman, tidying a stray wisp of greyish-orange hair from her forehead. She coughed again. Mary's green light was showing.

"You can go in to Dr. Rao. She's ready."

"Thanks, Liz love. Special day, is it?"

"Yes. How did you know?"

"I may be getting on, but I don't miss much, dear."

She opened the door to Mary's office and walked in.

CHAPTER THIRTY-ONE

Kim arrived by helicopter at an air force base where without formalities she was taken to a small jet. It took off almost immediately. There were three other passengers, all in battle dress. They had bulky nylon fabric bags containing their equipment.

"Bonjour," she said.

She had not worked with them before and did not know them. There was a chorus of *"Bonjours."* Then the chat was about the latest adventures of Les Bleus on the soccer field. They were soon disgorged on the airstrip of a military base flanked by forest and mountainous country near Montferrat. A very athletic and fit-looking colonel of the French Special Forces met them on the tarmac. The military people saluted.

"Bienvenue. Suivez moi," he said and got into a minibus next to the driver.

The four arrivals clambered aboard with their bags and were driven to an ordinary looking prefabricated building. Inside was a highly polished floor with a staircase leading underground from the exact centre of the room. Two soldiers with light machine guns saluted the colonel and checked each of his guest's IDs as they went down from the room. At the foot of the staircase, they appeared to be in a stainless steel box. The colonel stood in front of a control panel and then touched it with his fingertips. A door slid open to reveal a barred gate as in a prison. There were two guards with small, efficient machine pistols. The colonel again touched a panel and the barred gate slid into a cavity in the stone wall. The two guards put their pistols back at the salute position. The colonel ushered his party into an elevator that took them further underground. They emerged into a pleasant, wood-paneled room with a large screen that was in fact almost an entire wall. Kalitza preferred French for briefings—the language seemed to make them precise yet elegant, like good moves in chess.

"Welcome to our swimming pool," said the colonel. "It's leak proof. No recording. No bugs. We play water polo with our ideas and planning. We alone know what we do here. And we play to win."

He then briefed them on two very dangerous and unpleasant men who controlled a group dealing with drugs and fearsome military weapons. There was a political dimension to their criminal activities. In Paris, a decision had been made. Special Forces had to control this operation. Their criminal opponents had a villa in the mountains not far from the coast. It had splendid views of the roads through the mountains. But the necessary intelligence had been gathered. A series of "submarines" (electronic surveillance vans), cyclists, and hikers, not to mention an undercover man, had done a very good job. A top terrorist from Spain was visiting the mountain hideaway the next day. All necessary evidence for arrests had been gathered. Now it was time for action. The colonel paused.

"Kim, you will be sent in from an agency the gang uses and trusts as being absolutely discreet. Your role is expensive bed mate for the terrorist from Spain. By the way, do not speak any other language but French. You are called Zita on the agency list. Prick up your ears to any Arabic or Spanish."

Kim nodded. "*Entendu, mon colonel*," she said.

"*Bien*. You are to arrive in time for dinner and will be backed up if necessary by the infiltrator, who is one of the trusted domestic staff. He's the smallest of the male domestics you will see. In fact, he's the toughest of all three male staff bodyguards."

They all grinned.

"You three gentlemen from Paris will cycle into the mountains the same day with backpacks and a picnic. You belong to a cycling club. You use the paragliders you'll find in the shepherds' hut. After dark, you land on the roof of the villa."

The colonel pressed a button in his handheld wand and the screen lit up with a large map of the mountain road leading to the col. He pointed with a red dot at the road as it wound its way up towards the col. The red dot rested on a small oblong.

"That's your shepherds' hut. You jump from here." The dot indicated a small contour line with a drop of fifty-two meters. "That's the cliff edge where you jump. You glide to the villa down here to the right of the road. You'll find it by the light in an upstairs window. Our man will have forgotten to close the curtains all the way."

"Will we be able to see the light before we jump?" asked one of the crew from Paris.

"That's the idea, but we must be prepared for something going amiss. If there is no light, don't worry. You'll be going with compass and wind indications and night goggles.

"We shall bring in a large military helicopter due to arrive within a precise given time after your signal. You send the signal as soon as you land on the roof of the villa. This would be about the time the dinner is coming to an end and everyone's relaxed and we hope a bit tipsy. The Paris team will enter the house, neutralize, and handcuff every one of the "suspects," including the undercover man, if he has not had to break cover. Kim and you three will recognize him, because he's the smallest," the colonel smiled, "and he's the only black man employed up at the house. Kim will neutralize the Spanish terrorist hoping to get into bed with her. Kim, you can put him to sleep if you want."

There was a chorus of chuckles.

"All mobile phones will be jammed by equipment in the helicopter and be collected ASAP in a special evidence bag. All other forms of communication, including computers, must be de-activated as quickly as possible and collected as evidence by the helicopter specialists. The first Special Forces men to enter the garden will deal with guards and animals patrolling there. They will do this silently at the precise time that you jump. Any gang members trying to get back into the house after a night out will be neutralized by the Special Forces' people inside the garden. Any questions?"

There were no questions. The colonel flashed a large detailed plan of the villa onto the screen.

"Learn this from the copy I'll now hand out. It will be shredded before you leave this room."

He explained the layout and circled the dining room with the red dot. He pointed out the three staircases leading from the attic floor landing down into the second, first, and ground floor.

"We think there will be nobody in bed at this time. Guests and hosts will be in the dining room. Kitchen now: a female cook and two waiters. We think there will be just two guards and two dogs. The lower level gang members, living in neighbouring villages or towns, will be arrested by local police. These arrests will be made according to last minute instructions and coordinated precisely with the raid on the house, in such a way as to make it impossible for anyone in either target group to leak a warning about the operation. Questions?"

"If we attract any attention from the garden when we land on the roof, do we use our silencers?"

"Yes, if the Special Forces have not managed to find every person on garden patrol duty. But I understand that there are usually only two armed men and two nasty dogs. But as you know, criminals' routines sometimes vary. If someone is on the loose and sees you, shoot to kill without noise. We prefer them alive to interrogate them. Questions?

"No? Good. The helicopter will take the terrorist and the gang's equipment to a special military investigation centre. A second chopper will arrive for the others to take them and their guards to a separate prison block."

"Colonel, how do we get back to camp?"

"Oh, you can all relax by walking back across country! Only kidding. Two ambulances will arrive to whisk you away for debriefing."

The wall panel lit up again revealing the large-scale relief map and the position of the villa. Then came once more the detailed plan of the villa itself. Then came the plan of the garden. There were photographs of all the people who would be dining in the villa and another of the visiting terrorist. A relief map showing all roads was also projected. There would be roadblocks mounted out of sight of the villa just as the raid got under way to catch any stray fish. The colonel then went over the plan again in detail, asking for questions and dealing with points of clarification.

Kim asked three more questions. "Colonel, how many people know of this plan apart from you?"

"Glad you asked, Kim. I know the plan and now everyone in this room knows it. Others will know only what they need to know for their part of the operation. And only when it's necessary to get the required action."

"How and when do I go to the escort agency?"

"You'll be in your digs in town and you will be collected, when the agency sends you up to the villa by taxi."

Kim in her role as Zita had to be ready for action by seven p.m. the following day and would carry no weapons, but her beauty, sex appeal, and sharp intelligence. She would sleep in the afternoon before the operation like the rest of the team. They would be alert, fresh, and energetic for the night's work, whereas the people in the villa and their underlings would all be tired, and as the night progressed, less cautious.

Kim's third question followed. "Why do you need me? I wouldn't want to be just a passenger."

"Passenger? Absolutely not," was the colonel's response. "The terrorist mastermind has asked for a Frenchwoman of North African origin to entertain him." The colonel added, "You fit the bill superbly. Everything has to appear normal. In fact, your extraordinary, unarmed combat techniques and speed of reaction are just what we need for the after dinner arrests. We want this bit of trash alive. We couldn't extradite him, and now he thinks he has slipped in unnoticed. You will ensure his capture."

The colonel smiled. She appreciated his smile, and the hard glint in his eyes. *He's seen a lot of action*, she thought. *And she bet he had usually won.*

Everyone left the room knowing exactly what they thought lay ahead and all had their ways of dealing with the unexpected. In fact, they all expected the unexpected. In fact, the colonel won this time as well.

***

The only unexpected event was that before the attack on the villa came, the Spanish terrorist, a middle-aged man running rapidly to seed, announced that he had finished dining and would retire with his charming companion, Mademoiselle Zita. They rose from the table and Zita followed her target from the dining room and upstairs to his suite. Two guards sat on chairs outside near the door. They jumped up as the boss and his lady approached.

"Good night!" said the terrorist, opening the door.

Once inside the room with Kim, the terrorist shot a small, stainless steel bolt on the door.

"Follow me, Zita. Let's have some fun!"

Kim followed him across the sitting room into a bedroom. There was a king-size bed with a mirrored wall alongside and another behind the headboard.

"This should be very good fun," said Zita, shedding her shoes and dropping her clutch handbag on the bed.

"Shower first to start the fun," said the mastermind, leading the way into the en suite bathroom. He unknotted his colorful silk neck scarf and then put it on a counter near the sink.

He started to undo his shirt buttons. Kim moved close to him and brushed his hands before unclipping his suspenders and opening the top of his trousers at the waistband.

"Ah, you have plans," he said as his trousers fell around his ankles. She brushed with her fingers the man's stiffening penis.

"Yes, I do. Unzip my dress, please." She turned her back to him.

Her dress fell to the floor. Zita turned and pulled his jacket down a little over his arms and then reached again inside his boxer shorts. "Someone's having fun already!"

"Oh, Zita, Zita!"

Kim rapidly snatched the silk scarf, put it around the man's neck, and from behind him, pulled it tight to throttle him. His feet and arms were moving, but were hampered by his clothes. Kim tightened the grip even more and felt his body go limp. As his knees buckled, she tipped him across the edge of the bath, banging his head against the tiled wall. She pushed him face down into the bath and then used the scarf to tie his hands behind him at the wrists. Running into the bedroom, she returned with a small lamp with its longish length of cord. She bound his feet and tied his wrists again. A shirttail made a useful gag. Putting on her dress, she glanced at a bedside clock, 2310 hours.

She would have to wait for the beginning of operation *Tapenade. Enough time now*, she thought, *to search the place*. She looked in the bathroom cupboards. There was an array of soaps and toiletries and a first aid pack. Some adhesive plaster kept the shirt material in his mouth. He was breathing and had a pulse. *Good.* She put on her shoes and began her search. Under the pillows on the bed, she found a wicked hunting knife and a pistol. It was loaded. *Thoughtful guy*, she grinned. She checked the cupboards, and in a suitcase she ripped apart with the knife, she found a Kraft-type envelope containing two DVDs. The search finished in the bedroom, she went to the sitting room. She found nothing, but porno magazines and some hard-core porn movies, if the titles and lurid covers were anything to go by. They could, of course, have some documents and plans among them. These would all be checked later.

There was a faint sound of laughter outside the door. She placed an ear to it.

"I can imagine him with that great escort girl!"

"They're at it right now!"

"Think so?"

"You bet. Hey!"

A shot had been fired somewhere upstairs. It was 2328 hours by Kim's lady's watch. *Tapenade* had begun. Holding the pistol, Kim slid back the bolt and opened the door. One of the guards was facing her and standing a few feet away. The other was about three yards away along the corridor looking at the stairs. Kim shot the knee of the man in front of her and then shot the second man, again in the knee. She ran to pick up their weapons and then dodged back into the room and turned the bolt again. She took the big knife from the bed. In the bathtub her would-be sex partner was awake and struggling. Kim turned his head and smiled at him, before showing him the hunting knife. He stopped struggling. She patted the large bald patch on the top of his head.

She heard a few more shots and then, after a silence and some muffled shouted orders, there was a banging at the door to the suite. She called out that Zita was safe and well. The officer outside asked if Mr. Big was alive. Kim opened the door. Mission accomplished.

The colonel's shock team and the four from Paris spent the next few hours, after ambulances took them from the action in the villa, by warming down, relaxing, and debriefing. Kim recalled in detail the terrorist's conversation, flirtatious, coy, and aimed to impress an uneducated, young woman. But he had also said that he was looking forward to the next shipment of material promised for the end of the month. There was a little problem. It seemed the British had been too much in evidence. What were they up to? The big white chief of the arms smuggling operation at the end of the table had replied that there was no need to worry; all was under control. Merchandise would be there, as long as it had been paid for.

The others complimented the colonel on his weather forecasters, equipment, and planning, giving blow by blow accounts of landing, entry, and arrests with those of jumpy defenders the only shots fired. Some of the prisoners had a few bruises and abrasions. Since this was mainly a military operation, the colonel expected a good deal of useful information to surface by various means, including interrogation. There had been no leakage of plans to either the target group or to the press. Kim aka Zita was sure that the *Direction Générale* of Interior Security would be very pleased with the results. The colonel remarked that not a government shot had been fired, so that the paymasters would be pleased that they had saved some ammunition money. They all laughed and applauded. Kim had used the terrorist's gun so these shots had cost the authorities nothing. More importantly, the press could not show pictures of wounded suspects nor imply or complain that civil rights were ignored by a government bent on creating a police state, because the wounded defenders were in an interrogation center with its own hospital. The colonel thought that civil rights campaigners would keep a low profile over this one when the trial approached and hit the press. The chief terrorist was a ruthless man whom everyone who valued a free and open society would be glad to see brought to trial and imprisoned. The devastated families of his numerous victims would be pleased. Cooperation by different elements in the government forces and serious international cooperation, he reminded them, were absolutely necessary for the containment and arrest of terrorists. But the larger the spread of cooperation, the more chances there were of the one leak that could kill an operation and some, if not all, of its agents. Macho rivalries and clever Dick arguments between units had to become a thing of the past. *Vigipirate,* as the French call it, was a given of today's society.

The danger from leaks or double agents, though, was always part of the world in shadow. This being the case, Kim always had an abort and escape plan for each time she was active. She had quickly realized that she loved the job; it was like driving a very high-powered car under tricky and unpredictable conditions. And the job would change as conditions changed and as she herself changed and aged. At the same time, she disliked parts of her job; the continuous need to be like a jungle beast alert for predators; the waiting time in which nothing happened. One error could tumble her into the grave. Perhaps it was time to find another incarnation.

Thirty-six hours later, she was in Trouville, resting, walking, and eating freshly caught seafood. She avoided the casino.

CHAPTER THIRTY-TWO

Paul was pleased to be in Avignon again. The train was on time, the sun was shining, the temperature warm, not hot, fresh and breezy, but not cold, and he assumed the old bridge had not been finished. His phone rang as he stepped onto the platform in the TGV station some way outside Avignon's town walls. Mme. de Crevennes wondered if he might arrive that morning instead of in the afternoon. Absolutely. Paul made for a taxi, giving the driver the address. The house turned out to be about five kilometres into the countryside. It was an imposing private manor house standing in a large garden surrounded by a stone wall. The taxi dropped Paul at the gates, through which he could see a gravel path leading in a straight line between the lawns to a large and rather elegant porch and front door. On the stone gatepost, there was a code panel with a speaker grill. Paul pressed a button in the shape of a small, chrome-plated bell. There was a crackle and then a male voice: "*Allô?*"

Paul gave his name and said he had a meeting with Mme. de Crevennes. There was a buzz and Paul pushed open the gate. He strolled up the path with his two bags. The front door was now open. A strikingly handsome woman of about fifty with immaculate streaked brown and blonde hair swept back into a short ponytail greeted him.

"Mr. Wills, Paul Wills, I think? I'm Anne de Crevennes. How was the trip?" She was an elegant lady indeed.

"How do you do, Mme. de Crevennes. It's a pleasure to meet you. The train was on time and very comfortable."

She held her right hand in front of her. Paul took her hand and bent his head towards it, but did not actually plant a kiss on her fingers.

"Madame, the pleasure is mine. It's my privilege that you receive me.

"I see you have brought your bags. You came straight from the station? How thoughtful and lucky. You see, we have to go to Antibes."

"Now?" She nodded and smiled, showing regular and very white teeth.

"Yes. Don't worry Mr. Wills, we can talk on the way and we can change your ticket easily to get you back to Paris. Any extra may be charged to me. We can do it in Antibes. Did you book a hotel for tonight?"

"Yes. The Ibis in Avignon."

"That is no problem. Michel will call them now and cancel. Come in for a moment and then we'll go."

He followed her into a sitting room furnished with a comfortable modern settee and armchairs in a dusky-rose colored fabric. Tables and other items of furniture were antique, highly polished and elegant. *Eighteenth century*, Paul realized. *Real, not copies*, he guessed.

"I will not be long," she said, motioning him to the settee.

Paul watched her walk away into the hall. Her floral pattern silk dress looked very chic. Three gold buttons glinted at the cuffs of her long sleeves. He listened to her high heels as she walked along the flagstones in the hall. There was a hint of her expensive perfume still in the air. *Mitsouko? No.* He decided he could not place it. In the elegant antique mirror on the wall above the ample fireplace, Paul saw a man go to the front door carrying two suitcases. Paul sank into the cushions and looked from the settee towards a window with a view of the front garden. A pigeon alighted on the branch of an old, gnarled tree.

"Shall we go?" Paul got up and turned to see her smiling in the doorway. "Roger (she pronounced it the French way) will bring your bags to the car." Paul handed the two bags to Roger and followed him to the car, a sturdy, dark-blue Mercedes 320S. They were soon en route for Antibes, Paul and Mme. de Crevennes comfortably ensconced on the luxurious light-blue leather seats in the back of the car. The smoked glass windows kept out the glare of the sun and any inquisitive looks from other people. Roger was separated from them by a glass panel. Roger took the N7 to Aix-en-Provence, because Mme. de Crevennes disliked the less interesting auto route driving, where, as she said, one went through magnificent countryside like a bolting horse, oblivious of everything beyond hedges, screens of trees, and the occasional walls.

She pointed out local beauty spots to Paul for a few miles and then, turning to face him, asked, "Will you do the interview now, Paul? May I call you that? And do call me Anne, by the way. Roger will not, in fact, hear anything of what we say."

"Yes. Fine, Anne. You don't mind if I tape record the interview?"

"Oh, I don't think that's a very good idea. Take as many notes as you wish, Paul, but I would not enjoy a recording of my voice to be mislaid or taken by some unauthorized person, because one never knows what use could be made of it."

"I understand. I'll take notes. I am naturally very careful to protect my sources, you know. I shall scrupulously preserve your anonymity."

She laughed and looked at him with a sudden twinkle in her very intelligent, hazel eyes.

"That sounds truly as if you were a chaperone, my dear young man!"

Paul laughed too and then got down to business.

"Men of all classes, it seems, beat their wives, and the practice seems to span the history of humanity. *Battered wives* is a phrase we now find in books, newspapers, magazine articles, on the radio, and in television discussion programs. In fact, domestic violence seems to affect a hefty proportion of the population in so-called advanced societies. As a battered wife yourself, Anne, do you have any explanation for this syndrome?"

"My God, you sound like an article already! No, but seriously, I think circumstances make the cases a little different. There are many motives. They live in the hearts of men and women. Men are more prone to physical violence towards other adults than women are. But both can be violent. And both can be very cruel to children, even their own. Look into the heart of mankind and you see the devil as well as angels."

"May we talk about your own case a little?"

"That's why you're here. Go ahead. Ask me whatever you wish. I'll answer or perhaps not, according to the question."

"When did it start—I mean violence—in your relationship?"

"Do you mean marriage or a love affair?"

"Well, when did a man first beat you?"

"I was seventeen. I thought I was in love with someone. He was a student activist of the Maoist variety. He thought the world should be changed and could be changed. I found all this very romantic, but I affected a sort of gloomy bitterness about life. I was a Beckettian without the humour. It was fashionable at the time. Left Bank stuff. My young Maoist thought there would be revolution in France and he and his like would rapidly rise to the top. One day, the endless revolutionary talk was in full swing, when I suddenly thought of my family and what they had lost during the Revolution and the Terror. I suddenly saw the arrogance of all power—of kings, of governments, of criminals. I told him. Everything he said I countered. But I was more fluent and articulate. I was passionate. The Soviets had lost credibility by persecution of their own people and by making a pact with Hitler. Only intellectuals were still taken in by them. He told me the Communists were the only resistance fighters against the Nazis in France. I told him the Communists resisted only when Hitler broke the pact with Moscow. De Gaulle, though, had resisted from the beginning—as had many others, bourgeois, workers, aristocrats—and de Gaulle had been sentenced to death by the Vichy government for it. I told him that the Soviets and their followers could not take Western Europe. America, Britain, and France were too strong. The French were too individualistic in the end to accept left bank student Kommissars. He couldn't win, so he slapped me very hard across the face to shut me up."

"Were you living with him?"

"Good heavens no. We were close, as people say, but I had a very chic studio near the Panthéon. He would visit me in the evenings. After he slapped me, I ordered him to leave. Fortunately, he did, without further violence. But he crawled back, ringing the bell at all hours. I decided enough was enough. I never let him cross my doorstep again. He was soon living with a girl, also dressed all in black with huge, black eye make-up and a corpse-white face."

"When did you marry?"

"In 1976. That was the first marriage—and the last. I married an aristocrat who shall remain nameless."

"Did you have political arguments with him?"

"No. We both disliked the politicians. We never liked Mitterrand, for instance, and we never understood him!"

"Not many people did. Maybe the Socialist P.M. Jospin did . . . perhaps the rising Chirac on his way to becoming president?"

"I honestly wouldn't know, Paul. We, my ex and I, that is, thought M. Mitterrand was too self-important for words. France is small, and in any case is only a part of Europe, even if some of the politicians think that it can lead all the other European states. This is for some of us the French Dream. And it's just that. A shallow dream. But at least he didn't capitulate to the Soviets in the end. In fact, he gave some good intelligence on them to the Americans."

"When did your husband start beating you?"

"He didn't. He was violent, though, about six years after we married. Our relationship had become just a routine. We were occupied, busy, doing many things, seeing friends, but we were bored with one another, I think. At least I was bored with him. I like flirting a little. Being witty, when I can. But I am very loyal. I was never unfaithful. But my Monsieur de Ex began to be jealous of one of our friends. I became pregnant. It was my husband's child. I was never unfaithful. One night he accused me of trying to deceive him, palming off another man's child as the true heir of an ancient name and fortune. I was outraged. I told him I had an ancient name myself and this child was our child, his and mine. He didn't believe me. He kicked me and I fell against the arm of a heavy chair. I lost the child. When I got out of hospital, I never went back to that man. I left him to his own remorse, if he had any. He sent flowers and letters of apology. I have a sense of honour, too. It was the end."

"I'm so sorry," said Paul. "How miserable."

"It was. But it was a long time ago. I have learned how to live for myself. I enjoy life despite its horrors. I try to give pleasure to others. Friends. *I don't suffer fools gladly* as you English say. I don't argue with people and get heated. I rarely am guilty of intemperate speech."

"Why do our contemporaries still think domestic violence is a kind of right?"

"I don't know. Men are traditionally supposed to be the protectors of women and should theoretically be prepared to fight other men if the woman is compromised or in danger. Men are mostly afraid to fight each other, I think. But I've found that they are not so frightened of women, so they hit them. Perhaps it makes them feel strong? Traditional attitudes to marriage or to any sexual relationships seem to prevail for a long time, even when inevitable change has taken root and is spreading. Perhaps that's part of it. Homosexual couples also have their fights and even murders. Eve, we have learned, was the origin of wickedness. I think Adam was the real culprit. The myth has an element of truth, though, because many a woman finds the bad guy tempting, while steady, good guys seem boring! Our very own Baudelaire, of course, has diatribes against women *as such,* while Nietzsche philosophically advises men to take a whip to a woman. I think people respond in anger to many things and the damage is easily done."

"A lot of women never press charges for domestic violence. They don't even leave a marriage, as you did."

"They are sentimental or just stupid. But I should think violence between couples of whatever sex is really assault."

"In England, we'd call it assault and battery, I suppose."

"I think the state should prosecute all cases that come to be known, even if no victim complains. Penalties should depend on the gravity of the injuries and on any recidivism. Divorce should be seen as an honourable way out of marriage."

"Anne, may I ask you a very personal question?"

"Go ahead, Paul. I might not answer it, though."

"Do you have any paying work besides the history you publish or do you just live on your royalties and personal money?"

Anne laughed. She slipped her arm through Paul's and closed his notebook.

"I make more money breeding horses than from writing history," she said. "I talk to the horses, you know. And they don't answer back!" She released his arm. "I try to do only things I enjoy doing. Now I'm ready for lunch. How about you?"

"Yes. Do we stop somewhere near here? I'll pay," Paul offered.

"No. You're my guest. I took you out of your way by my change of plans. Roger will take us to my favourite village *auberge*."

It was a charming old inn standing a little back from the narrow road that led from the main road and ran right through the village. Over lunch, Paul tried to sound out his hostess on some of the statistics, issues, and ideas he had read in articles and books dealing with domestic violence. She preferred to talk about all that when they resumed their journey. She warned him she was not theoretical. She was realistic and practical, pragmatic. She preferred action to talk. *But she's French enough*, Paul thought, *to concentrate on the food.* They had a glass of wine each as an aperitif and also a bottle of Badoit water with the meal. The starter they both had was scallops, lightly fried in a cream sauce with Girolle mushrooms. They then both had duck breast with a wonderful dark gravy. It was served with poached pear and very crisp, thinly sliced roast potato. They skipped dessert and went straight on to the coffee, served with macaroons.

After they were on the road again, Paul tried to turn the discussion with Anne towards the various more abstract issues he would be writing about. She answered a little, but in an offhand way. Paul asked questions about the history of domestic violence in the nineteenth century. Anne then became animated as she developed her answers while they journeyed on through the afternoon. He asked if the women's movement would be able to stop all domestic violence in France.

She was silent for a while. Suddenly she turned and said, "I'm a woman and I stick up for women who have been wronged, but I'm no militant feminist. Violence can never be eradicated. It is too human. Too animal. Perhaps, over centuries, people change a little. Cultures change a lot. But I think feminism is simply one factor making for cultural change. Some of the attitudes of militants seem to me tiresome, even harmful. I do not think being obese is good, or that repellent ugliness is as good to be born with as refined beauty. I do not, however, demean unattractive people! I do not wear rape-proof clothing. I do not, when all is said, privilege ugliness. I do not scorn the rag trade or the cosmetics industry. I like elegance in dress and manners. I read the more intelligent glossy magazines dealing with antiques, horses, country life, and expensive houses and gardens. I am not a socialist. I'm not a conservative. No politician is going to dictate to me the way I think or vote. I vote for *people* who make a good impression on me or I don't vote at all. The only power I want is power over my own affairs. This naturally depends on an advanced society with various essential freedoms. I try to move around the mess the politicians often make of certain aspects of life. Call me stupid. Call me selfish. I don't mind. I like myself. I like my way of life. And lo and behold, we've arrived. I like it here!"

As well she might, thought Paul, as he contemplated a curving drive and plentiful trees.

The car turned into the private driveway, where an iron gate was swinging slowly open. Roger stopped the car inside the gate and waited for it to close completely, before he drove the next little way to reach the villa. He parked the car and opened his employer's door. She got out. Paul, following from his side of the car, noticed that in the late afternoon sun Anne's hair was shining like a very fine mesh of precious metals. They were standing on the gravel drive curving away from the gate, so that the house could not be seen from the road. The air was clear and clean. There was bird song from the trees and shrubs. Paul could see through the trees a stretch of glinting blue sea. She led the way into a modern, architect-designed house. In a spacious hall with an attractive slate floor, marble facing here and there, and wood and flowers and light everywhere, she stopped and turned. She took Paul's hands in hers, then kissed him on both cheeks, laughing at his look of surprise.

"Oh, you English! Welcome to Eden Roc."

CHAPTER THIRTY-THREE

Paul looked out of his window from the bedroom he had been given for the night. The sea was now a dark line in the distance. There were lights here and there, white and orange, showing through the deepened shadows of the trees. He turned and began to unpack the few things he had brought with him. He was always traveling. *Well,* he reflected, *everyone's life, whether traveler or stay-at-home, was a quest. There were always encounters with something new or unexpected. Now, though, he had a wonderful sense of security with Mary. He now had a real base. He would travel less in future.*

His guest bedroom was spacious, with a massive dark-oak beam running across the clean apricot of the ceiling, rather nearer the window than the door that opened onto the landing. *The wallpaper in classic stripes of dark red and light cream, gave the effect,* he thought, *of an old country inn of superior standing.* This was at odds with the modernity of the house. The queen-size bed was covered with a large handwoven bedspread in a rough, textured, tribal rug stripe of reds and browns and black. The paint on skirting boards, window frames, and cupboard doors was a light-cream lacquer. Ochre-colored curtains hung on their brass rings from a gleaming, solid-looking, though certainly hollow, brass curtain rod. There were some occasional tables, a dressing table, two easy chairs, and a wardrobe in solid oak. All the furniture had benefited from a deep polish that had brought out the beautiful natural effect of the grain. But it was more *olde worlde* than modern. *Odd,* he thought.

He was delighted, though, that he was spending the night here in this house among the trees. It was generous, and he felt privileged and grateful. All the same, he reflected, had he been able to do the interview in Avignon, he would have been on the spot to go to Orange to see the Roman theatre again. Perhaps he would have time to stop there on the way back next day. That, in fact, would be just as convenient.

This evening, he had been advised, there would be dinner, after Anne's business appointment in Antibes. Roger would drive him to the restaurant for about 7:45 p.m., where, over dinner, he would ask Anne for more information on French domestic violence and the policies that had over the years been advised in efforts to curb it. They could continue to talk of these matters, if necessary, back at the house.

There was a knock at the door. A young maid, small and neat, probably a local girl, asked which train he had to catch the next day. The staff would rearrange his trip if he gave her his return ticket. Paul did so, thanked her, and asked that the departure should be mid-morning with a stop at Orange. If he needed to continue to wind up his work with Mme. de Crevennes in the morning, could the ticket be altered yet again? There was no problem, the girl assured him. She smiled. Her oval face lit up suddenly with the whiteness of her teeth. Paul noticed that her dark eyebrows almost met in the middle. Her hair was very black. She looked Spanish or Italian. Her accent, though, was of the region, rather than foreign.

Paul had time to write up the day's notes on his laptop and take a shower, shave, and then don a dress shirt and tie with his light-grey slacks for the dinner date. He worked quickly, got spruced up, and went down for a stroll around the garden before the drive with Roger to Antibes. Business with Anne was, it seemed, to be mixed with pleasure. In the garden, he called Mary on his portable phone. Again, he caught her just after she had finished with patients for the evening.

"Mary, darling, I'm calling from Eden Roc."

"Eden Rock? Sounds Australian. I thought you were going to Avignon?"

"Yes, it does sound Australian, but it's near Juan les Pins and not far from Antibes. My interviewee wanted to change venue because of some other business. She brought me here to her other house."

"Lucky you. How many houses has she got?"

"No idea. But all expenses for changing the venue, et cetera are paid by her. No problems with budget-anxious editors."

Mary could envisage him, the phone in one hand, the other resting on the mouse attached to his laptop.

"I expect you are writing up notes one-handed?"

"Not a bit of it. I'm having a stroll in the sub-tropical garden. There are exotic plants, cacti, and palms. I should be finished tomorrow morning and back in Paris tomorrow evening."

"Good . . . because I have a surprise for you."

Roger, Paul noticed, was waving to him from the door to the terrace. Paul talked as he walked.

"You angel! Oh, here's the driver to take me to the restaurant."

"Wonderful. You are very Ritzy down there with another woman."

"Yes, but don't worry. She's an historian. What's the surprise?"

"Tell you later. What's history got to do with it?"

"Or what's love got to do with it, as Tina Turner might say to the bishop! You're wearing orange today? Sorry, I'm sounding like an adolescent again! I feel like one. Got to run. Love you."

"No, it's Marks and Sparks white floral lace. You're sweet. Love you, bye."

Paul heard the disconnect tone and then closed the phone and climbed the shallow stone steps to the paved terrace, where Roger was waiting.

"Ready, sir?"

"Yes. We're on our way then."

I am sweet, am I? Am I? Paul wondered.

CHAPTER THIRTY-FOUR

The following morning Liz called Mary, but she had already left her flat. Liz had then called the police. By the time Mary arrived, there was a policeman taking down Liz's statement, while another was wandering around the premises with a police dog, and yet another was dusting for fingerprints.

"Doctor's here now," said Liz as Mary walked in.

A sergeant spoke into a mobile phone attached to his tunic. An officer in plainclothes walked in within a couple of minutes.

"You are Dr. Rao, madam?" he asked.

"That's right. An incident of some sort, I suppose? What a nuisance. I have patients arriving any minute." Mary looked around, but nothing much seemed out of place in the reception area.

"There's been a burglary, in fact. I'm Detective Sergeant Wilkes. We should have a working space and the examination cubicle vacated in a minute, Doctor Rao. You can see patients then. Meanwhile, I have a few questions, if you don't mind?"

"Go ahead." Mary saw that he was fit, dark, and handsome in a rugged way.

"Do you keep any drugs in here overnight?"

"In that locked steel cabinet Liz can tell you about. No large quantities of anything really worth stealing. Painkillers, some dressings and disinfectants, surgical soap, some basic instruments, sterilizing equipment, boxes of surgical gloves. Liz here keeps the inventory up-to-date."

"I see. Have you had previous break-ins?"

"Once. About five years ago. That was sheer nastiness. Vandalism. Racist slogans. Urine, excrement, all over the place."

"Very regrettable. I'll check the records. This seems unrelated. Someone was looking for something. Apart from the broken locks, there's no wanton damage. Cash on the premises?"

"No. I can't think why anyone would bother," Mary said. "They haven't even taken the computers, it seems. Were they after drugs?"

"The radio and compact disc player's still okay," Liz said.

"Perhaps Liz can check things with me, then you'll be free when the patients arrive," the detective said, adding, "If there's any more work and papers to push around, perhaps we can clear that up at the end of the day?" He smiled.

He was tall, had a darkish brush cut, not too short, and his light-brown eyes were alert, intelligent.

"Yes, all right. About five forty-five p.m.," said Mary, thinking again that he was fit as well as good-looking, this policeman. He was also polite.

"Thank you, madam. We'll leave you to it then."

Mary's day turned out to be as crowded with demands as usual, with a visit to the hospital at the end of the afternoon. She was driving straight home, when she remembered she had had a burglary and was to be back at the surgery for the detective. *Amazing I could forget, or suppress, that,* she thought. She turned back towards her surgery and arrived at about ten minutes before 6:00 p.m. In fact, there was little to be done. Liz had reported that certain files on patients had been rifled and probably read. One was obviously out of alphabetical order. Another had been replaced correctly, but papers in this file were now in the wrong order. Liz had also checked the inventory. Nothing was missing, though the lock on the steel filing cabinet had been forced.

"Can you think why these patients' files have been looked at, doctor?" Detective Sergeant Wilkes asked.

She looked at the files. Mary knew at once that two of the files that had been looked at and replaced in a hurry belonged to patients who were drug addicts and had been referred to a special treatment centre. She hesitated.

Wilkes passed over the two files to her and continued, "These men are known to us. They are addicts. We keep an eye on them. Sutton's a small enough place, so we can act with a, shall we say, personal touch. We take an interest in following up on these people if and when they commit some offence or other. We want to keep them out of real trouble."

"I can't think of any reason why they or their files should be of interest to the burglar," said Mary.

"Or burglars . . . Would they want to see their own files?" asked Wilkes, rubbing the top of his brush cut.

"Not likely. They know what's in them. It's strange. Quite strange," said Mary. Liz nodded.

"By the way, is this your earring, Dr. Rao?" Wilkes opened his hand to reveal a small plastic bag containing a tiny crescent moon of diamond chips on a gold mount and clip.

"Not guilty!" said Mary. Wilkes smiled. "It seems that this could be evidence that the burglar, or one of them, was a woman."

"Or a man," said Liz.

"Men who wear earrings generally have pierced ears," Wilkes replied. "Besides, apart from the question of the clasp, this design seems more of a female type of look."

"How would you know, sergeant?" asked Liz with feigned innocence. The policeman smiled at her.

"Oh, we get to know these things in the force, Miss."

Mary turned to Liz as she remarked, "I know what you're thinking, doctor, but it's not from one of yesterday's patients."

"It was found just under the filing cabinet behind one of the legs. We think it fell and bounced into a place where whoever lost it couldn't see it," offered Wilkes and added, "They probably either didn't notice it was gone or they left in a hurry and couldn't stay to look for it."

"So, it's probably a clue then?"

"You bet," said Wilkes, "unless it was dropped five years ago in the last break-in."

Liz lightly touched his arm and he grinned.

"Do you two know each other?" asked Mary.

"We do now," said Liz.

Wilkes smiled. "Just cast a beady over these statements and, if they are in order, maybe you'd sign and then I'll be off," said Wilkes.

As Mary was reading and signing, Liz said, "The lock people came and we're all back to normal."

"Wonderful, Liz, you're a treasure." Mary looked at Wilkes.

"Do you hear that, David, I'm a treasure," Liz said.

"Well, then, you deserve a bite to eat. Coming? Good evening to you, Dr. Rao," said Detective Sergeant David Wilkes.

"Here are the new keys. A set for you, doctor."

"Thanks Liz. I'm off. You lock up, will you?"

"Sure. Good night."

***

Half an hour later, after a brief pause at some shops, Mary was at home. She made a cup of tea and then, feeling relieved that her flat had not been burgled, too, picked up the telephone. When he answered, she discovered that Paul was on the TGV after spending a bit of time in Orange. He was nearing Paris. The interview had gone very well. He sounded pleased.

"What's the surprise you have up your sari sleeve?" he asked.

"Later. First, the bad news. I've been burgled."

"Oh no! When?"

"Sometime last night. Luckily it was the surgery not the flat. Strangely, nothing was stolen. Somebody had looked through our files."

"Very strange. I suppose the police have nothing to report yet?"

"Nothing, except that Liz has a new boyfriend I think. A detective!"

"Every cloud has a silver lining! That's an English proverb."

"I know, you nignog."

"Glad I'm not a twit. I think nignogs are better than twits."

"You may choose whatever level in the hierarchy of idiocy you wish, my dear man. In any case, I've decided I need a break. I need to be with you. Can you be in Honfleur on Sunday early or late Saturday? I think I can be there late on Saturday evening and will leave late on Sunday."

"You're on, you wonder woman! That's the good news! But why Honfleur?"

"That's part of the surprise! You remember my pilot friend in Scotland, Jack Moffat? He is flying to Le Havre for a meeting. He says I could hitch a ride to France, returning next day, late."

"Perfect. I'll meet you in Honfleur in the bar of the Hôtel Baudelaire, on Saturday evening. I'll book us a room. It's central. You'll easily find it."

"Brilliant. I could perhaps be there about eight. I'm excited!"

"I'm not only a nignog, but I'm a lecherous nignog!"

"There's someone at the door. I'll see you the day after tomorrow then!"

"Perfect, perfect, perfect. Bye."

When Mary opened the door, Liz was standing there.

"Sorry to bother you at home, Mary, but I was worried about you being alone after the burglary and all."

"Not to worry. Come in. Cuppa?"

Mary led her to the kitchen and poured her a cup of Darjeeling tea, no milk, no sugar, and not too strong.

"You remember how I like it!"

"I do. But what about this dinner with the detective?"

Liz grinned. "He's a real juicy morsel, but he's trapped at the station 'til eight. Hey, that sounds like a song! Country Western stuff, you know?"

Liz strummed an imaginary guitar and sang in best country western manner, "He's a reeel juicy morsel, ma maine, but he's down at the stayshun 'til eight! Downtown at the stayshun 'til eight!"

"Liz, your Americanization is coming along just fine."

"Why don't you come out to dinner with us?" asked Liz.

"Oh, I couldn't. I'm not your chaperone. Not that you need one. Besides, he invited you, not me."

"It'd be a little test for him. I could see how he reacted to seeing the boss turn up as well."

"You're a witch, did you know that?"

"Actually I've been a witch for twenty years. Since I was three."

"You *are* a witch; you're at least twenty-six!"

"I know, but don't tell anyone!" They both laughed again. This was better than moping over the burglary. Mary liked Liz and her sense of humour. But going out on her receptionist's first date with a detective was not a good idea. She had a few articles to read and besides . . . besides, it just seemed odd.

The phone rang. It was David Wilkes.

"I'm at the station, Dr. Rao, but I shall be free for dinner at eight. I was wondering if you would care to join me and Liz?"

"Oh, that's kind of you, Sergeant Wilkes, but I don't think I want to play gooseberry."

Liz was nodding fervently and mouthing, "Say yes!"

"You know, after a burglary, even if it seems minor, it's still a bit of a shock. You might need to get a bit of a break and have some company."

"I know, after all . . . but, how do you know I'm alone?"

"Oh, when I was chatting earlier, Liz said you weren't married."

"I see. And what about Liz? Have you discussed this with her?"

"Er, no."

Liz wanted to speak to him. Mary handed her the phone. "Liz here, David. I'm with Dr. Rao at the moment." Liz listened to him for a moment and suddenly made herself go cross-eyed, so that Mary laughed.

"I think it's a great idea, if you do," Liz continued.

Mary suddenly thought, *why not?* She told Liz, "Okay, but we go Dutch."

"She'll come as well, David. But only if we agree to go Dutch."

"Fine. That's settled then. Will the Forester suit?"

"The Forester will suit us, David."

"At, say eight-fifteen, at the Forester, then. See you." He rang off.

Liz turned to Mary. "He thinks the same as I do. Or maybe it's thought transference."

"You're on the same wavelength of thought impulses. Or maybe you put a spell on him or hypnotized him at the office."

"That must be it. Well, I'd better dash and tart myself up a bit. Shall we meet there?"

"Good idea. That man of yours, he's a reel juicy morsel— after eight!"

"That maine o' mine, he's a reel jewcy morsel— He'll be gettin' his rayshun after eight. Ah juss cain't wait!"

They laughed and then Liz waved and let herself out. Mary had a glass of water and read a couple of articles before freshening up as her American friends put it. She thought that she'd like to go back to New York and California for one of her holidays. Next year, maybe. With Paul! Paul! Her "maine." She'd soon be in Honfleur! She started to hum a tune from *Cats* as she changed her clothes and set out for the Forester, a fifteen minute drive away.

CHAPTER THIRTY-FIVE

Graham Curtis was looking at his diary. The PhD comprehensive examinations were in a few days' time. He was worried about one candidate who seemed to have real trouble concentrating on the reading list. He knew one period in great detail and sweet Fanny Adams about the rest. Most candidates tested in recent years were shaky on saying briefly and clearly what their responses were to a series of brief texts they had probably not seen before. Graham sighed. This test in practical criticism had been undergraduate and schoolboy stuff in his day. Now it was difficult for many a graduate student to read briskly with understanding and to demonstrate that understanding with intelligent, perceptive comments. This led to colleagues shaking their heads. Some wanted the test dropped as hopelessly outmoded in an age of high-powered theory. Others argued fiercely for its retention. How could students actually understand the jargon-clad philosophical acrobatics we call theory, they demanded, if they couldn't understand a passage from critics of the clarity of Matthew Arnold or Edmund Wilson, or a short poem by Wordsworth, or by a recent, lively, contemporary poet like Robyn Bolam? "Leave Wallace Stevens out of it," Graham muttered to himself. He looked at an old theatre poster for Shaw's *Caesar and Cleopatra* and remembered how he had asked people in a graduate seminar how many had seen a play in a theatre that year and there was not one of them who had any interest in even going to the theatre. It was too expensive. Yet they'd willingly help to fill Bill Gates' pockets by rushing off to shop for software they did not actually need. Their idea of drama was to watch a DVD of a movie. Was theatre now just a middle-class remnant of an older culture fast seeping away? *Probably*, he thought. *Discuss*.

Graham usually kept out of committee struggles on these issues. After all, weren't students as lazy or as hard-working as they had always been? He was probably being unfair to them and to colleagues enmeshed in theory. *The limits of theory. Discuss. Spend no more than three hours on this question. Double-space your answer. Credit will be given for signs of intelligence. Credit will be given for signs of life. Credit will be given for neat, legible handwriting.* Graham then looked ahead in the agenda and saw Paris scribbled down. *Easter. The time of suffering and resurrection. From tomb to sunlight. From Hades back to Mother Earth.*

***

He had arranged to see Samantha Gilmore for lunch again. He hoped they'd be able to firm up the Paris arrangement. His head of department always talked of firming up dates and arrangements for academic activities, as if these dates were reluctant male members having to be aroused for coitus. *Yes,* Graham thought, *I need to get away from papers, exams, department bitterness and wrangling, as if academics were politicians on the brink of another war.* In the end, their decisions didn't kill thousands of university students, but they came near to ruining their career prospects at times. To hell with it! The self-important *cowardice* of the academic bandwagon! He smiled a tight, bitter, little smile. *Paris! Samantha! Paul!* Why had he suddenly thought of her in Paris before Paul? After all, it was Paul he was really going there to see. He would read Paul's latest package when he got home. He looked at his watch. It was time to go to meet Samantha for lunch.

***

Samantha was looking very sleek and alert, like a tropical bird, although she had just done a morning's work. She had to be at the hospital at 8:30 a.m. each day of her working week.

"You're radiant! You look as if you are in Hawaii on holiday!"

Samantha laughed and suddenly kissed him on the cheek. "Thanks, Graham. You look good, too, you know."

He could not really believe that. He had not slept well, having had a vague dream that disturbed him, but was totally forgotten when he awoke. Yet, he certainly felt better than he had done at any time since Jacqueline had been killed. Was it the knowledge that he would soon be traveling? He could get away from the scenes of his marriage. He could put new experience and the attendant memories between his fresh present and that married past. He had been cruelly torn away from the first life he had had. Was another life possible in the future? It had to be, for self-pity was a dead end. Life had to be lived again and perhaps traveling was always a prelude to living? Or was it an eternal attempt to escape from someone or something? Perhaps: that scholar's word.

They were settled and waiting for their order to come to them, when Samantha asked, "Graham, do you really want me and Greg in Paris with you?"

"Yes. Are you doubtful about it?"

"I am doubtful. It's a trip you need and you have to see your friend—Paul, isn't it? Greg and I would really be in the way."

"Are you in two minds about it? I obviously don't want to foist a trip on you."

"That's not a problem. I love the idea. But we'd be in your way, you know? A teenager trailing around? You need time, Graham. You have a lot to work through. You need time to yourself and with Paul."

"I have plenty of time to myself. Yes, I can spend time with Paul, too, talking. And you and Greg will be able to explore Paris while I'm with Paul. And Paul might also show us some of the Paris locals know."

Samantha liked Graham and she was sure that she and Greg would have a good time if they took the trip. She didn't want, at this stage of her life, though, any more possible complications. Spurling had wanted a sexy mistress. She had got out of that one and she was not about to get involved romantically with a grieving widower. Graham was cute, if professors could be cute! She thought, *Yes, this one could be cute.* Greg probably would not think so. Paris with a professor wouldn't be Greg's idea of a holiday, cool to the power of *n*. If they went with Graham, there'd be no hanky-panky. She would pay her and Greg's fares and expenses. She and Greg would share a double room with twin beds and that would keep Graham out of her reach. *Did she mean that? Or did she mean that would keep her out of Graham's reach? Yes*, she thought, *that's what I meant.* Greg was a good buffer zone, at home or abroad. Life could quickly become too complicated. Just now, after Spurling, she wanted simplicity, even keel, no rocking the boat. Life after George S., the Demon Lover, had to be more than the monotonous round; a celibate trip to Paris, she figured, would fit the bill. Graham, after his awful disaster, needed a chum, not a complication.

"You look a bit wistful, Samantha."

Part of her was wistful. This guy was not only cute, he was acute, too.

"You'd enjoy the break. Greg would enjoy it, too. It's full of interesting-looking students and the kind of clothes teens like nowadays. He'll love the Eiffel Tower if he hasn't already seen it and gone up it." His voice was warm and persuasive.

"Frankly, I need the break and it would be fun with you, Greg, and Paul. I'll not be in any way a moper. I will not be a drag. I promise."

"I believe you. You don't need to make promises, you know."

The food arrived. They were both having a chicken salad wrap with Pellegrino sparkling water. No dessert, they had decided. Coffee would be just fine. By the end of the meal, Samantha had definitely agreed to go to Paris with Graham and she had given him the days she would be available for the holiday. He said he'd book the tickets and she said she'd reimburse him.

After lunch, Graham altered Paris in his diary to coincide with Sam's dates and then went off to a travel agent, but not to the one he had always used for his conference trips and holidays. That agency would have brought back too many memories. He tried another one he had heard about as being very efficient. It was fast, and nothing was too much trouble. Graham made the booking and paid for the tickets straightaway with one of his credit cards. They would be in Paris on the ninth of April and would fly back on the eighteenth of the month. He phoned Samantha to let her know it was arranged.

***

That's it, then, she thought.

Later that evening, Greg was very excited by the idea of going to Paris over Easter. Samantha didn't tell him that Graham was a professor. That could wait awhile. Samantha wrote a check to cover the air fares for herself and Greg. She could mail it to Graham in the morning. Graham rang Paul and got the answering machine. He sent him a chatty e-mail giving the date of arrival, and telling him he was bringing a friend and her teenage son. Could Paul find Samantha and Greg a twin-bedded room in a nearby hotel? Could he kip down in Paul's flat? If not, a single room in the hotel would be okay. He signed off with, "Luv, Graham."

CHAPTER THIRTY-SIX

The sea was rippling its muscles and slapping the little
fishing boats and pleasure yachts in the old harbour. The
sunset had been unspectacular, but early evening was full
of charm: cafés, restaurants, and the hotels were all lit up
and beginning to attract their customers. The church of St.
Catherine stood quietly, like an upturned boat in dry dock.
Paul walked from the freshness of the evening, with a bit of
rain in the offing, into the Hôtel Baudelaire. He had booked
in earlier. All he had to do was wait in the bar for Mary to
arrive. The shadows of evening thickened. The bar was cosy.
Calvados? Scotch? Calvados, he decided. He sat at a table
with a view of the bar and the entry to the softly lit little
room. He decided on a Calvados, *eighteen years old, his
teenager-in-love mental age*, he thought, *or near enough!*
But now he had the experience of early middle age. This
was, he reflected, much better than being eighteen again,
with all those uncertainties and the university examinations
still to face. He called across to the barman and soon had the
precious liquid within reach in an elegant glass. There was
only one other person in the bar, perched near the barman
on a high bar stool. He was a beefy man with a weathered
face, a nose like pumice stone, and thick, bedraggled, grey
hair falling towards his open collar. The shirt was navy blue,
tucked loosely into old blue jeans. He wore navy canvas
yachting shoes with rope soles. No socks, Paul noticed. *A
professional fisherman, or a would-be one, or a retiree,
killing himself slowly with alcohol?* Mary was earlier than
he had expected. She walked into the bar and looked around.

The barman gave her a sprightly, "*Bonsoir, madame.*"

Paul was on his feet smiling broadly, while the old soak of
a yachting man looked balefully at her, eyes red-rimmed like
those of an elderly bloodhound. Paul nodded to the barman
after he had hugged Mary. The lovers laughed with glee. The

barman arrived. Soon Mary's champagne arrived. Over their drinks, Mary explained that they had had perfect conditions and then hit a patch of rain over the channel before it became clear again. There had been a light tailwind. Mary had then taken a taxi to arrive as quickly as possible.

Paul told her, "I've got a good little fish restaurant in mind for dinner. Will that suit you?"

"Yes, please."

They talked again about the wedding. Then Mary told Paul about Liz and the delectable detective. When they had finished their drinks, Paul paid the barman. He picked up Mary's bag and they walked from the bar hand in hand.

The old salt had gone to the gents. He took a cell phone out of his capacious pocket and dialed a number. Suddenly, he spoke in English, "She's clean; he's clean. But still monitoring until she returns to the United Kingdom."

Meanwhile, Paul and Mary found their seafood restaurant and booked their table for later.

"The hotel room," she said, "It's comfortable?"

"It's charming."

It was on the fifth floor, a non-smoking floor, and it was chintzy without being *twee*, luxurious without being over-the-top, and was further blessed with the charm of a harbour view.

"Perfect," said Mary as she looked at the bed and the bathroom. She began to unbutton his shirt. They made love hungrily and fiercely. There was a moment of poignant tenderness afterwards. Mary said suddenly, "Even at its sweetest or most intimate moments, when we can forget everything but the moment, life is always fragile, you know."

"It is, and your job is to bring it into the world and hang onto it as long as possible, isn't it?" He remembered seeing her in action as a doctor intent on saving a man's very fragile life.

"That's true. Life has mysteries, too. Where does it come from? Why in a universe of inert matter, does matter become life-supporting and flesh become mind- supporting?"

A sudden gust of wind outside bent some boughs, making twigs with leaves brush across the window. The watcher slouched in a doorway across the street from their hotel window.

Mary decided to tease Paul. "Back in the twentieth century, people wondered about the nature of thought. What is thought? Not the process of thinking, but thought itself."

"Well," said Paul, "I think . . . I mean, well . . . Yes, I think thought is a sort of energy we use when we think!"

"That's news to me," she said and then disappeared into the bathroom, where she bathed and made up.

Paul rested in the huge brass bed, thinking over his article and possible further interviews. Suddenly his thoughts were interrupted by a memory of Thomas Hardy's verse again, "Scarce consciously, /The eternal question of what Life was, /And why we were there . . ." The rest escaped him.

On the wall there was a very good original oil painting of a fishing boat in heavy seas. The painter, whose name Paul didn't recognize, had signed and dated the picture, 1881, he found, when he walked from the bed to examine the picture more closely. The painter had obviously been to sea, perhaps many times, and knew his fishermen and their gestures as they worked. Mary had soon finished with the bathroom and then Paul showered, shaved, and donned casual clothes for the evening.

They went into L'Ascot on the Quai Sainte-Catherine and ordered a tasty fish soup and then a seafood platter for two. A bottle of very acceptable Muscadet sur lie from the Grand Fief de l'Audigère kept them happy, while they manoeuvred and winkled out their shellfish from the circular bed of crushed ice. Paul wondered if Baudelaire, visiting his old mum in Honfleur during the nineteenth century, had enjoyed fish restaurants on the quayside. Or was it then a jumble of fishing boats and nets and sails? Baudelaire in Honfleur might be a saleable piece. Clouds had cleared and the moon made a guest appearance among the stars. Life was so good, Paul mused, if one had a reasonable, if modest income, in

Europe, North America, and parts of Asia. Africa was an extraordinary mixture of dark and light, as was the Arab world. And both were dangerous. Very dangerous.

"We're very lucky and privileged."

"Yes," said Mary. "But it depends too on choices, decisions. Thought. Delayed gratification. Planning. Getting a decent education. Getting a job."

"Absolutely. I was thinking more in terms of a civil society, democratic and humane values and the rule of law. A level playing field? At the turn of the nineteenth century, there were plenty of anarchists around, but anarchy isn't a good idea."

"I'm very pleased to hear that, Paul." Mary laughed and he laughed.

"Yes. You don't need lectures, do you?"

"No. I'll add this, though, to your dose of thinking about society: with the vast population groups we now have in almost every country, when order breaks down, the state of anarchy becomes terrifying very quickly. Mobs in the streets, in villages, in neighbourhoods, looters in race riots and tribal hooligans let loose are horrifying; with modern weapons and cell phones they are far more destructive than they were in the past. The way of life in the developed world has to be protected all the time."

They both fell silent. And then she added, "Yes. We need the police, armies, intelligence services, superior technology—otherwise all could fall into chaos and petty dictatorships. If civil society can hang on entrenched in the countries that enjoy it now, it has a chance to spread."

"I've seen states that once were vital and go-ahead fall into the ruinous round of corruption and disintegration," said Paul. He mused a little and then added, "When it happens, now, it happens fast. The weapons, as you say, are so effective." They reached out and held hands. "Why are we here? What's humanity for?"

"We're small and insignificant," Mary said, "But we can still love each other. Let's drink to that."

They had finished the meal and their mood of happiness reasserted itself. Their smiles and warmth for one another made them seem conspiratorial. They were conspirators for happiness, that ephemeral and fragile pursuit. They realized they had to enjoy their well-being while they had it, while it lasted. *Carpe diem!*

"What endures in the memory counts for a lot," Mary remarked. It counted for more and more, the older one became.

"Then we must fill our lives with good memories," said Paul. *There is no censorship or tax*, he thought, *on such memories. No government could steal them, though governments could certainly mess you up.*

"Governments can be worse than Mum and Dad."

"I know, Paul. They can be terribly strict and pernickety and stifle you with paperwork. So, let's get a great evening under way again!"

After leaving the restaurant, they walked around the little old town, enjoying the night air and the picturesque buildings of the port from which explorers, and Mary thought, notably Cabot, once sailed. They then made tracks for their hotel. They had the next day for doing nothing, but enjoying themselves. *How long can this last?* Mary asked herself the question and then put it aside. *Live. Improve the world and enjoy it as much as possible. Don't commit yourself to constant worry about all the agony in every crisis. That way led to depression or even madness. Work at helping people. Work and live.* "Live, but don't live selfishly," she said to herself, and then repeated it aloud. Paul heard the remark and thought about it.

"I agree," he said. After a pause he spoke again, "Try to improve things a bit in yourself and in the community and enjoy life as much as you can. Try to make a bit of cash, but don't be greedy."

"Yes, I think a lot of people live like that, even if they don't think about it much or talk about it," Mary added.

"It's simple enough," said Paul, "but somehow things all get complicated. Why?"

"Ah, that's where you have me. I haven't a clue. But it's hard to keep things simple. Anyway, that's your territory as a journalist."

There was a pause in their conversation as they walked along. They went up a street that led to a large house, its bulk dark against the sky. There was a light in an upstairs window, whereas most of the other houses were lit at ground floor windows.

"I like to speculate about the many different lives all being lived out in various houses. The people in their rooms all have a family network. And then there's the network of friends. Then of colleagues. The network of shopkeepers and assistants they all know."

"Talking of friends, what are you planning for Graham?"

"I don't really know yet, beyond just letting him talk if he wants to do that. How about driving into the countryside and exploring a little, before I take you back to the airfield tomorrow?"

"Yes. Where can we hire a car?"

"There's a place I spotted when I was wandering around earlier. I'll telephone."

It turned out that Paul could book the car immediately, collect it early next morning, and deliver it back the following morning, when the office would, in fact, be closed. All he had to do was park, lock the car, and then push the keys into a special box. And so it was arranged.

Paul was worried about the burglary, although Mary did not seem very much concerned. He felt that he should go to Sutton and make sure of her security in the flat by moving in earlier than planned. Over breakfast the following day, he proposed that he move in with her and begin to house hunt immediately. Mary was doubtful. She thought it unlikely that she'd be burgled twice within a few weeks.

"Forget the law of averages, Mary. Read the papers. There are many stories of the same premises being burgled again and again. Burglars seem to be creatures of habit!"

"Then why would they burgle my flat? They'd go to the surgery again."

"But they went there and perhaps were unable to find what they wanted. They might think you keep other files at home."

"Actually, I do. I see what you mean. But if you move in when I'm really busy, you'll see me at my worst!"

"I'm marrying you, remember? For better or for worse. I'll see you at your worst—it'll be better than many a woman's best! Really!" He sounded a bit indignant at her laughter.

"Why not *all* other women's best?"

"Precisely what I meant, angelic Mary."

"Okay, you win. When do I expect you?"

"Some day later in the week. I could probably arrive on Wednesday."

"Gosh, that's quick."

"I mean, if that's okay?"

"Well . . ."

"Mary, I have a sort of instinct about this. Let's do it."

"I think that will be fine. In fact, I can't wait for you to bear my worst."

"I've bared your best, I've bared your breast, and now I'll bear your worst."

"Ah, yes, I'll bare your wurst as well!"

And so it was settled.

CHAPTER THIRTY-SEVEN

Next day in the car, they visited ruined castles and a priory and lunched in a quaint country inn not far from a major training centre for race horses. Frequented by people with money to spend on good food, the inn was a real delight for lovers of traditional Norman cuisine. On the way back to Honfleur, they stopped in Cabourg for afternoon tea. They sipped Earl Grey in the somewhat faded glory of the ground floor lobby, in the Grand, once the spacious and elegant setting for the holiday makers of la Belle Epoque. Their genteel enjoyment of that fragrant infusion was watched by a large photograph of the novelist, Marcel Proust, who seemed to glance with faint amusement from his place on a wall quite near their table.

"We're youngish people in our second flowering," Paul remarked.

"Second? When was our first flowering?"

"Oh, I expect yours was in the fifth form."

"I think it was in first year of medicine," Mary said. "And yours?"

"I first flowered during my military service. At least, I think I did."

"You were too young for National Service. Come clean, Paul."

"I didn't mean National Service. I meant my short service commission in the Horse Guards."

"When were you in the Horse Guards? I never knew that about you."

"There are many things you don't know about me, Mary," he teased. "It was many moons ago. Before university in fact."

"You didn't talk about it in those days."

"I certainly didn't. Universities were full of part-time politicos who would not approve of Horse Guards. They probably still don't approve of Horse Guards. Tourists do, but I keep that military card close to my chest."

"So you ride?"

"A little. When I have the time and the opportunity."

"You're full of tricks!"

"For my next trick, I propose the Hôtel Baudelaire and a session on top of the sheets before I deliver you back to Le Havre."

"Yes let's," she said.

***

Back in Paris the following day, Paul listened to his messages. His next two interviews in France could be done on Monday. Graham was giving his dates for the Paris trip and sending an e-mail message. Paul had not completely overlooked the fact that Graham was coming to Paris for Easter. He had time to think out some practicalities. He rang his interviewees and fixed one for that afternoon and the other for the following morning. Then he would write it all up on Tuesday. He could get more material in England and finish "Family Matters" in good time to relax with Mary over Easter and work out what they would arrange for Graham. He got down to work. Before he went out to do the interview, Mary telephoned. It was her lunch hour. She sounded so British on the phone. He loved the warm quality of her voice.

"You were right," she said. "Do get over here on Wednesday if you are able to."

"I will, darling. Don't worry. I'll also be in touch with Graham about Easter."

"We should be together at Easter, perhaps all of us. New life can bury the old."

"Absolutely. We'll not resurrect old flames."

"I've not much that could rekindle. My upbringing and then medical studies and houseman overtime and GP overwork for the NHS didn't leave me much dillying and dallying time!"

"I thought medical students were notorious lechers, Mary?"

"That was the men. All those nurses were too much for them. But now I dream of Horse Guards!"

"I believe you."

They chatted a little more, exchanged sweet nothings, and then reluctantly went back to their work.

***

Kim felt a vibration to the left of her navel. She fished the mobile phone from a little pouch strapped around her waist. There was a message. She went into the lavatory marked LADIES and locked herself in a cubicle. She clicked a sequence of numbers to decode the message. *Blast it*, she thought. Putting the phone back, the message erased, she opened the door of the cubicle and applied some lipstick. She looked at herself closely in the mirror. *Do I really want to be a mum?* she asked herself. *How much longer*, she thought, *do I rush around from hotels to safe houses to secret classroom refresher courses to weapons ranges, to rendezvous with political villains, going to the gym to sharpen up muscles, reflexes, and unarmed combat skills, having sexual adventures in different countries for the good of the Republic, and adopting different identities, and never living a normal life and always protecting, while being unseen and unthanked?* That was the territory she was in. Perhaps she would retire gracefully soon and marry a rare, sweet man. "St. James Infirmary Blues" began to run through her head. She walked out into the hotel's lobby. She checked out and within an hour and a half a small jet was touching down. She was in an ordinary looking flat in Cannes before she had decided whether or not to plead her case for retirement, while she was still marriageable and capable of having children.

Kim read the paper on the desk in a corner of the cozy little sitting room. It was a photocopied newspaper clipping about two middle-aged women who had been found floating in the sea near the Fort Carré in the Baie des Anges. They were believed to have perhaps committed suicide. They had been identified from papers in their hotel room as an Englishwoman and a Frenchwoman. Someone had run a magic marker pen along the sentence explaining that one of the women had her shoes on the wrong feet. Another paper gave an extract from the police autopsy report. This stated that there was fresh water in their lungs. They had been drowned somewhere in fresh water and then thrown in the sea. Kim thought they could have been drowned in a bathroom anywhere in thousands of flats or hotel rooms along the coast. Any of the pleasure boats in the area could have taken them out to sea. *The bay had been visited by the angel of death*, she mused, *yet they had eaten their last meal in McDonalds*. They had also had a good dose of Scotch. Forensic science had investigated many a last meal eaten at the fast food chain, but was understandably reluctant to attribute the Scotch to McDonalds. In fact, they had not identified the brand of Scotch. Kim hoped they had enjoyed it, whatever the brand. When in doubt, go to McDonald's. *It wasn't as bad*, she thought, *as some food snobs made out*. One of the women had had a perm and color. Ash blonde. The products used were sold in the trade only to very select, up-market hair and beauty salons. The other woman had been content with just the color auburn. This could be a promising lead.

Kim had been given new identity papers for the assignment. She learned the new identity rapidly. It was an aspect of the job she liked. She came to life as a different person. The papers were made out to one Rosalind Kenyon. Rosalind, she learned, was an English woman of North African extraction, living in Spain near Barcelona. She grinned. *Nomenklatura* to use a Russian version, strikes again!

She started by viewing the bodies and then followed up with the beauty salons. In the third one, a boutique in the marina at La Baie des Anges, the manager remembered the two women. They had hung around for a few minutes after their hair was finished until a large white Mercedes picked them up. He didn't know the driver or the car. It was not, he thought, somebody who lived in the marina complexes of luxury flats. The two women had seemed excited, as if they were going on a date, the manager surmised. *How wrong he was*, she thought. *Some date!* Traces of a chemical used in bomb making had been found on their clothing, where air pockets had kept areas of the cloth from being fully submerged. Unlikely terrorists they had seemed, when she had looked at their faces. Perhaps they had come to know the wrong people by chance? Kim next checked the security video tapes from the quick food drive-ins for the day of the deaths of the unfortunate "tourists," as the newspaper called them.

The local cops were very pleased to cooperate with this colored English Rosalind. They plied her with coffee. A detective wanted to buy her dinner in a little place he knew in Cannes. Kim was, however, more interested in the videotapes. She found a large white Mercedes with a clear picture of the two women and the driver. There was someone else in the car, but it was impossible to see this person properly. The driver, though, was identifiable. He had been arrested in her last operation just a few days ago. Now he could be tied to a double murder, probably also to bomb making. The interrogators would find this useful. They had thought this man was a fairly small fish, when he was rounded up by the local police. Now it seemed he was a more important member of the group. La Baie des Anges had its fair share of demons, too, it seemed. The unidentifiable person in the car would soon be in their hands, if he were not already imprisoned. Actually, the interrogators discovered that the unidentifiable passenger was a Muslim woman, not a man. She had slipped away, the driver didn't know where, straight after the executions. She had spoken with an English accent. Her escape was a disappointment they would have to live with.

Kim made the necessary arrangements for her report to go directly to her controller. At the end she added, maintaining her codebook best practice, "P.S. I am now on holiday again. The lion roars tonight!" *That dates Control*, she thought, *I hope he gets the message.* She was free for dinner after all.

"What time will you pick me up?" she said, as the detective put his head into her screening office yet again.

"Nineteen hundred hours okay?"

"Absolutely. I look forward to it."

The detective, she decided, was good as a casual companion, but she would not be spending the night with him. After she had showered and got into a dressy pant suit in orange with some green costume jewelry, she packed her bag ready to take the TGV back to Paris after dinner. She would insist on going Dutch. No hard feelings; no great expectations. The detective arrived on time and resigned himself, with middle-aged wisdom, to enjoying a beautiful companion for fine dining, brisk conversation, and some glances full of longing, like a golden Labrador contemplating juicy forbidden morsels from a vantage point near the table.

Kim left on the train as she had planned, after a dinner of avocado, excellent bouillabaisse, and a pear sorbet splashed with vodka. She had shared a bottle of Côtes du Rhône blanc Viognier 2000 from Château du Trignon. She had drunk just two glasses. It was light-gold, fresh on the tongue, and reminded her of ripe apricots. She wondered, as the train flashed through the night, if she'd be able to find it in London. She alighted before Paris and stayed in Lyon, checking into one of her preferred hotels as Rosalind Kenyon.

Next day, she was on a flight to England as Doris Black. She alighted from her taxi at 71 Pall Mall and checked into the United Oxford and Cambridge Club as Alissa Partridge, Newnham, club number P7736, and then took the lift to her room on the third floor. The room's familiar clubbiness made her smile. It had a Victorian print of Pembroke College Oxford above the bed head. The dressing table had the club's stationery in its leather folders. The bedside table had its retractable shelf for the morning tea tray. She had ordered tea and *The Guardian* and *The Independent* for 7:30 a.m. next morning. Now she needed a bath and a siesta. Pembroke Oxford . . . Samuel Johnson had studied there she remembered. She was relaxed and relatively carefree. Nobody, not even Control, could find her here. She thought it was fun that she was in bed a stone's throw away from St. James's Palace. She drifted off to sleep thinking Prince Charles was probably in the palace sighing over the five years of official engagements awaiting him and from which there was little chance of escape. *Yes*, she thought, *I'll escape, I'll retire; I'll look for a prince . . . of my own.*

CHAPTER THIRTY-EIGHT

Another packet lay on the table in Graham's study, opened, and ready to read.

EVENTS AT NEUILLY

My most recent encounter with this dark phantom—as I now thought of her—was just a few months ago in Neuilly, to the west, just outside Paris. I was staying in a friend's pied-à-terre on a quiet street leading straight to the main road that borders the Seine. I was interviewing three different celebrities from the film and TV worlds. I needed to be on the spot, because they chopped and changed at a moment's notice and I had to conform to their schedules, even though they always appreciated extra publicity, especially when it became reading matter in quality journals for smart readers. Besides, I was juggling three different personalities within precarious time limits.

I was taking a morning walk to the Ile de la Jatte, where I could admire the converted barges and houseboats bedecked with satellite TV dishes. I planned to wander across the island and return by the busy main bridge.

That particular day, I set out on a wonderfully fresh November morning. The sky was that pale Parisian blue, and cloudless, as if it were a silken sail or perhaps a tent stretched tight above the busy world. There were not, at that hour, many people in the elegant, tree-lined streets of Neuilly. Suddenly a tall, dark woman in a beige trouser suit came from another street ahead of me and walked in the direction I was heading towards the island. My heart raced. It was her walk! It was Kalitza! I quickened my pace, for I was convinced I could reach out and touch her again—alive! She also seemed to fit the image that has stayed with me for so long of a naked angelic woman in Malvern walking towards a hospital stretcher bed before lying down to die. The effortless stride was the same. This woman, though, was in modern clothes and her arms were not feathered. She was the image of the woman I had encountered in Hong Kong. I felt the strange, exalted joy of that first encounter in Malvern as well as the tingling desire of the encounter in Hong Kong. As I caught up with her, my feelings intensified. I was being drawn to her, as if I were being reeled in on an angler's line! Her dark, now braided hair gleamed in the morning sunlight. I noticed the perfume of roses—was it Joy? I was beside her and looked at her fine-boned, perfectly elegant profile, the curl of her smiling lips, the dark brows and lashes. She turned towards me, and I felt a surge of delight with sheer wonder at her beauty and that she was indeed alive. I exulted in the recognition that this was Kalitza. The word *alive* kept ringing in my head like a perfect temple bell. She was the same young woman. And yes, I had found her again, as in Hong Kong. Incredibly, she looked not a day older than when I had first seen her at the ancient heart of Britain, though my own features had coarsened, and in my hair, alas, there was a touch of grey near the temples. Under what illusion was I living, fitting different strangers into the same mould, making of them a winged goddess? Yet, I was certain that there were no certainties, and that this creature escaped all certainties.

"Where are you going?" she asked in her low, pleasant voice. Speaking French, she had used the *tu* form, and I felt a flush of pleasure. Then it crossed my mind she used it as one would use it to a child or an underling.

"To the island. Will you come there, too?"

She smiled again and quickened her pace.

She was soon ahead of me, striding along so rapidly I could not keep up, unless I started to run. I felt that if I ran it would seem that I was a white man chasing a young, colored woman. I contented myself with walking as fast as I could and keeping her in sight. An elderly Neuilly resident came out of her front gate with a brace of black Scottish terriers.

As I swept past, they yapped and growled at me. The old lady was muttering something to herself about the trouble with daughters. As I reached the main road, I could see the figure in the trouser suit standing on a small pedestrian bridge. I was fifty yards away, waiting for a gap in the now heavy traffic that was rushing towards the traffic lights before they changed. I would cross the road and join her on the bridge.

I could hardly believe what I next saw. She kicked off her sandals. She had started to undress. She discarded her jacket, pants, and a short, dark-red slip. She wore no other underclothes. Now the traffic lights had changed. I ran across the road as she dived into the Seine. There was no direct way down to the bank, because of the high fence around the moorings and the houseboats. I had to get to the bridge.

As I started to tear off my jacket, I scanned the river, but could see no sign of her in either direction. She had been sucked under! I was on the bridge, pulling off my own shoes, when two young men grabbed my arms.

"Let me go," I shouted, "I must try to save her!"

"What's happening?" One of them, stocky with short, fair hair, quietly asked.

"A woman went into the river. I must save her," I yelled.

"Calm yourself, sir; we are off-duty police. You cannot follow her. The water's too cold. You'll die. You can't save her. It's impossible."

The other man, wiry, taller, and older, was now talking softly into a mobile phone with a short aerial. His thinning black hair was swept straight back and his vivid black side-whiskers, which were real, although they looked at first glance like make-up, seemed almost like straps hanging from the black cap of his hair. He closed the phone and put it in his jacket pocket. He reminded me of the man who had given me his ticket to the Egyptian exhibition in Vancouver. He was, though, not emaciated and his face was not skull-like. This man was obviously some sort of French police official.

"A team is on its way. Are these her clothes?"

"Yes." I knelt and buried my face in them.

"Oh, don't touch them. Calm yourself, sir. You knew her?"

"Yes, I've . . . uh . . . met her before."

"What's her name and address?"

"Oh, I don't know. I didn't even know she was in Paris." I did not miss a look exchanged between them. One gave a brief smile, which he then controlled. They seemed pleased, I felt.

"I saw her by chance this morning and followed her," I continued. "She was ahead of me, and I could not catch up with her before she threw off her clothes and dived in."

"Where did you see her before she came to Paris?"

"I saw her in Hong Kong."

"Ah, she was Chinese?"

"She's a dark-skinned woman with long, black hair. Not fully Indian. Not fully African. Not fully anything, as far as I know."

The men exchanged looks again. The older, black-cap man produced a folded plastic sack and then put Kalitza's discarded garments into it.

I was scanning the brown swirling waters of the Seine, hoping to see her head above the surface. Then I realized that these men could be like those whom Merrick had caught in Hong Kong and whom I had not been able to identify, because I had never seen them before.

The man with the phone took out a notebook.

"Your name and address, sir, please. You will have to make a statement describing the incident exactly as you saw it happen, and the time, as nearly as you can pinpoint it."

I nodded and gave him a false name and address.

"Your identity . . . or badge? I assume you are policemen?" The men both produced City of Paris police cards. The woman with the black Scotties went past and then stopped to take in the proceedings, while the dogs preoccupied themselves with the base of a tree trunk. It never occurred to me to appeal to her as another possible witness. The man with the notebook spoke to her briefly, noting her name and address, I think, and then she went on her way, following her little busybody dogs.

"Since you knew her, you might remember something useful." Before he could say more, the team arrived in a selection of wailing and hooting vehicles. Police, firemen, divers. So these men were not rival agents. They were genuine police. Nevertheless, I was a foreigner here, and it suited me that I could preserve a bit of privacy. I did not suddenly remember my true address.

"She went in about ten minutes ago. I was about three to four minutes reaching the bridge after she went in. You got to me as I was preparing to rescue her. That must be five minutes ago. All in all, I'd say ten minutes."

The dark man with the phone nodded. He seemed the senior of the two. They put me in a car and drove me to a *Commissariat de Police*, where I made a statement and completed all the bureaucratic formalities. The policeman who took my statement wanted to see a piece of identification. I gave him my French *carte de séjour* that had my true address. I doubted whether they would check and find I had first given a spurious one. They promised to keep me informed and to let me know if they found the body.

I never saw the policemen again. Nobody contacted me. I had begun to think they suspected me of having killed her and having dumped the body into the Seine in broad daylight. No, that was too silly a scenario. But they seem to have accepted the fact of the clothes. Why would I have them there with me? Unless, of course, I wanted it to look like a suicide! They could think what they liked. I would not be volunteering anything, even if they found me at my real address. Needless to say, no account appeared in the Parisian press of a body found naked in the Seine.

The words, the words came again: 'You cleave the river's flood with grain breasts seal-smooth . . . Slide, little swimmer, slide like a splinter through my soul.'

I know that one day I will meet her again. How could I not, after these events over the crucial years of my life, in Malvern, in Vancouver, in Hong Kong, and now in Paris? That day came sooner than I anticipated. I was walking along the platform at Louvre-Rivoli Metro station when I glanced into one of the display cases in the wall. The cases contained copies of objects selected from the Louvre's vast collection. I stopped, my attention drawn to an ancient wooden spoon, about the size of a seven or eight inch Celtic wedding spoon, yet austere in its carving. The handle was a girl swimming, her arms and legs stretched out straight, cleaving the imagined water like a blade. She was my little swimmer, but larger, much larger, not a splinter, but a complete object on a bigger scale. I was pleased to have seen this wooden spoon and resolved to see the original very soon. I had other business, though, with two different editors that day. I emerged to street level and walked towards the river.

My walk along the quays brought me to that splendid bridge guarded by sentinel angels with golden wings. I leaned against a wall and took in the splendour of the bridge. This was a far cry from the little bridge at Neuilly. The massive blonde Paris stones were blackened lower down, wet with the swirling waters, where the bridge's supports emerged from the Seine. The two angels disported themselves in heroic poses, and, on the apex of the arch, the rich cluster of black female forms with their full-breasted ripeness struck me as wild and wonderfully improbable. A *bateau-mouche* slipped along with its passengers and went under the bridge. I walked onto the bridge and looked down at the wash of the retreating boat gliding on its way.

There was a sudden commotion around me. People were looking at a little crowd gathered on the opposite pavement. Someone shouted, "That woman, that woman! She jumped!" There was a tall man wearing a long black overcoat or a "dryasabone." I was not sure which. He was looking at the dark sky as if sensing rain. He was emaciated, his face a skull with skin stretched across it. I pushed nearer, through the crowd, and crossed the road. I now saw the man's hair was cropped short, or else growing again, as if after a course of chemotherapy. The skin had an extraordinary pallor on face and scalp. He turned abruptly and in a trice was standing, ready to jump. Some people were watching, fascinated, while others hurried by, unwilling to be involved. The ghastly man on the wall looked straight at me over his shoulder, eyes wide and like those of a hare. His facial muscles seemed to be strung from the cheekbones and tensed under the skin so as to be prominent. His face was like an anatomical drawing in a medical textbook. It might be that he had walked out of some hospital, where he was in the grip of an implacable disease and was waiting to die.

"She has gone before me this year," he shouted.

"Kalitza, where is she? Tell me!" I yelled at him over the heads of people in the crowd. He was the man in Vancouver, I was now sure! Yet, now he was older and racked by some illness. Had he observed the events in Neuilly from the shadows, without my knowing?

"You love her dearly? You should know, you fool, she always comes back to me, smiling, yes, it always happens." He grinned, his teeth bared in a sort of grimace. It was derisive, a mockery of a smile. "And always, always, my tears, her tears, they are turned to ice."

He kicked himself free of a man who was trying to restrain him by holding his ankles. Then he jumped. I watched the body hit the water, the black coat spreading out like a skirt on the brown surface of the river. The gaunt man seemed to be no longer in it. It floated away, a pocket of air under it making a slight bulge. People rushed to the other side of the bridge to watch its progress. I walked onto the left bank. It started to rain. I knew that this was not the end. This was surely the man who had given me his ticket to the Egyptian exhibition in Vancouver.

CHAPTER THIRTY-NINE

Graham sighed. *Things like this are going on in Paris and tourists see these things from time to time. Paul thinks they are significantly connected to his psyche, his soul, his dream Why? People are strange and everybody is different, but equal before the law.* Graham settled again to continue reading his friend's saga.

HONG KONG AGAIN

I must now confess that I returned briefly to Hong Kong for a visit. To be precise, I was there in May, not long after the jumping fiascos. Chronology now seems important to me only in my journalism. To her, it is a matter of little importance. I was walking towards the underground at the Kowloon railway station, near the opening of the tunnel that leads towards the Festival Walk shopping mall with its supermarket, restaurants, smart boutiques, cinemas, and indoor ice skating rink. Queenie, a young woman who had been a summer helper on the newspaper, ran grinning towards me from the crowd of commuters.

"I'm Queenie, do you remember me?" She was grinning and bowing.

"Of course I remember you, Queenie! What are you doing now? Where are you going?"

"I'm going to City U. I'm still studying journalism."

"Good for you," I said and then added, "But isn't it a bit dangerous, or restrictive, being a journalist now in Hong Kong?"

"No, not really, because there's still a lot of freedom of speech and we cover news from all over the world for our readers, to keep them as fully informed of foreign countries as possible. Anyway, I shall specialize in reporting on the arts rather than politics in the People's Republic. Oh, it's so good to see you. I thought you had left Hong Kong forever!"

"Well, I'm just back on a visit. How lucky to run into each other like this by chance."

"Isn't it! But I have to run or I'll be unacceptably late for class. But let's exchange e-mails." She dug a scrap of paper out of her bag and scribbled down an e-mail address. I gave her my card.

"Bye-bye, Queenie, we'll keep in touch!"

Off she went along the tunnel with a surge of students all heading for class. I turned and walked on my way, going down a level to the underground or MTR as they call it there. The train for Mong Kok came rushing in almost immediately. It was packed. I managed to wedge myself in and stood facing an old woman sitting seemingly asleep on the stainless steel bench. As I looked up and down the train, mainly above the heads of other passengers, since I am taller than most, I thought again how lucky I had been to meet Queenie out of all the thousands of people who throng and thread their different paths through the Kowloon Tong station. I would keep in touch. It would be fascinating to hear from a resident journalist about the latest developments along the dynamic South China coast and the rapid modernization of China.

As the train swayed along, I noticed that the old woman was looking at me closely. Her face was a shiny mask stretched over her skull. Her age was registered in the wrinkles at the outer edges of her eyes and the little seams around her lips, the brown splashes on her face and hands, the arthritic finger joints. Still fixing me with her gaze from brown eyes with small, milky flecks on the eyeballs, she raised one hand. A jade bangle hung on her wrist. She made a sign of exactly the same type that Kalitza had made, when she saw me at the corner of Nathan Road. I looked at the old lady with frank astonishment. She held my gaze and repeated the strange salute. She smiled, revealing many front teeth capped with gold. Then she beckoned me to come closer. She got to her feet and motioned to me to take her seat. I shook my head, refusing, feeling ashamed that an old lady should offer her seat to me. Her bent fingers were surprisingly strong when she gripped my arm and pulled at me to take her seat before someone else took it. The train was slowing down. I smiled and took her seat, realizing she must be getting out at the next stop.

"Thank you, thank you," I said in Cantonese.

"You go on plane, Chek Lap Kok," she stated, in English.

"In a few days."

"Where you go? Rome?"

"Paris." She cackled as if I had amused her. I was surprised that this old girl in a cotton pyjama suit, hair pinned back, like hordes of retired old servants in Mong Kok, would even know there was a Rome, let alone mention it.

"You go Rome," she cackled again. "My daughters go Rome, London, New Yorkee."

Opening her battered carrier bag, she took out an oblong piece of red glossy paper on which were printed two black Chinese characters. She thrust it into my hand and turned to get off the train with a few other passengers. When she had opened her bag, I thought she was going to give me her daughter's address in Rome. Obviously not! I waved after her as the train started again, but she was not looking back. A tall, slim woman with long, black hair and dressed in a light-tan trouser suit had her back to me, and had taken hold of the old woman's arm. And then I was in the tunnel, looking at the reflections in the blackened window. Was that one of her daughters I had seen with her on the platform? I looked at the paper she had given me. A young man with a briefcase was standing near me.

"Excuse me," I said, "can you read this for me?"

"Of course. It says, 'Helpful man.'"

"I see. Well, thanks. This is my stop. Please take my seat."

I stood up, and he took my place as I nudged my way towards the door as the train prepared to stop. I put the paper in my wallet.

I thought no more of the incident, until I was preparing for bed that evening. Then the whole scene replayed itself in my memory so vividly that I could almost hear the train and feel the air conditioning. As I read in bed, the encounter with the old woman came back into my thoughts and I had to reread several paragraphs. Unable to sleep, I got up and went to the window. I altered the Venetian blinds so that I could look out over the view of the sea. There was a fisherman's sampan or maybe a junk out there in the blackness with a single light. Did the old girl on the train know about Zhang Ji's poem? I expect she did. I remembered some of it:

Over the maple-lined river
Heavy with sorrow
And the sleepless night
Spent staring at the boatman's light.
Han Shan Temple outside town
And the ringing of the midnight bell
Reaching us where we moored our boat.

A few days later, I boarded the flight for Paris. Over the Mediterranean, we developed a mechanical problem and the pilot announced that we were cleared to land in Rome. I thought immediately of the old girl on the underground in Hong Kong. Had she known all along that I was going to Rome? I dismissed the thought, but her face came back to me, grinning broadly, flashing gold teeth.

CHAPTER FORTY

For Graham, Rome was a city that he had to visit at least three times if possible. *He had been once, Paul gets around,* he thought. *Well, back to Paul and his ability to make everything he does some sort of romantic intrigue!*

EVENTS IN ROME

We landed safely in Rome. I decided I should break my journey before continuing to Paris. I had only once visited Rome and just for two days. The prospect of being there for a day or two more was an opportunity not to be missed. Besides, it was fated that I should come here, I persuaded myself, for had not an old Chinese granny in a tunnel under the earth told me I should go to Rome? I went to a modest, but comfortable hotel not far along a street above the Keats-Shelley house, now a museum. My first morning in Rome, I spent wandering the narrow streets and found a continual delight in arriving at some small piazza. Each was a personal discovery. In the afternoon, I visited the rooms where Keats and Shelley had stayed and where Lord Byron had visited. I saw no ghosts, but I shall not forget the exquisite sketch by a friend of Keats. It was done when the poet was near to death. The dying Keats, his fine features bathed in sweat! Later on, I wandered back into the streets and was duly impressed by the ruins of classical Rome. Quickly, I learned to love the layers of history in the architecture of this city, once the greatest in the western world, and still, of course, one of the greatest cities on earth. I was attuned to its atmosphere, but I was not expecting the artistic splendour of Nero's house, or what was left of it. A later emperor had filled much of it with rubble and made it the foundation of a splendid and enormous Roman baths. This in turn was in ruins. Ironically, the work of the archaeologists now revealed to the public enough of

Nero's passages and frescoed rooms to show, despite the gloom of the half-light, the skill and taste of the design, the masonry, the mosaics, and the crumbling, faded decor. I was lagging behind my little group of sightseers when I turned a corner to find a floodlit statue carved in white marble.

It was a young woman of delicate beauty wearing a simple, diaphanous dress wonderfully rendered in that medium of hard, white stone with a skill totally appropriate to its place in the Golden House of Nero. *Domus Aurea*. But the statue was mutilated. Had it been vandals? Or drunken Roman revelers? Had the face, now vanished, been that of a notorious and hated woman whom the mob would have liked to murder? What destructive forces had found pleasure in mutilating such art? The savagery of the vandalism seemed deliberate rather than the haphazard action of the centuries' weathering. One of her legs was sliced away down from the knee. Her other knee had been cut to remove a wedge of marble, like a piece of cheese. Her musician's arms and hands were gone. She had been almost decapitated and her face carved away from that noble head. For all this desecration, the beauty remained; a simple testimony to the artist and the inspiration that began it all. The navel on her stomach remained perfect under the diaphanous robe. She had been born of perception, of memory, of the sensitive skill of an artist's hands, eyes, and brain, all working in a delicate and precise fashioning. Stone, too, had given birth. She was vulnerable, fecund, and magnificent in her way, not majestic, as the Victory of Samothrace, not commanding as the Venus herself, but almost unconscious of her own vulnerable beauty. Yes, still, after the desecration, she celebrated life.

Reluctantly, I turned to rejoin the group, to follow the guide. The calm, white Grecian marble, it seemed, had embodied one of the Muses. One of the sisters, daughters of memory, she, it was, alone in this archaeological site, whom I knew as another guide. I had been led to her across cultures and across time, not by chance, but by some mystery I could not, for the moment, question. The gaunt, death-pale man on the Parisian bridge came stubbornly into my mind. God, if I met him again, I would match myself against him, struggle to get her free of him. Of course, I would lose. The real world is as full of illusions as the ephemeral domain of spirits.

Outside in the Roman sun-shower weather of that weekend, I walked the little streets and big squares until I found a haven of good cheer: a restaurant with a terrace covered by canvas awnings and dotted with fairy lights. It was just what I was looking for. *It must be animated and colorful in the evenings*, I thought. It was nearly sunset. I decided to have a drink or two, or three, and then stay there for dinner with a modest half bottle or carafe of light red wine. Ensconced at a small table on the terrace, I had a wonderful view across the square to an elegant church with a not overly decorative facade. I was sipping my martini and watching people sauntering across the square in haphazard patterns before disappearing down narrow streets. *This is Rome*, I thought, *and here I am with bread, salt, olive oil, a few olives, a perfect drink, and nothing to do but enjoy it all. Life is not all suffering and gloom. Leaders should and could be working hard at a country's problems in order to make the quality of life bearable, pleasant even, for their people. No bribes and unearned money squirreled away in Swiss banks!* Then I smiled at the irony of these thoughts passing through my mind as I sat in one of the most decadent cities in the world. The history of Rome! What grandeur, what beauty married to what treacherous and ingenious brutality.

I glanced across at the church, marveling at the way the ripened sun had lit up a golden mosaic in a semicircular pattern above the great stone porch. A few people were going into the building. A woman I instantly recognized was running up the steps to the porch. Of course, it was Kalitza. So, it had been fated that after all I would see her again, after her "suicide" in the Seine. I sprang up, looked wildly about me like a startled horse, and shouted to my waiter in Italian, French, and English, "*Torno? Torna? Torna!* Don't worry. *Je reviens.* I'm coming back!"

Dashing across the square, I entered the dark interior of the church. My voice, calling her name, echoed around the church, disturbing one or two people at prayer. I looked around. She was nowhere. As my eyes became accustomed to the dim interior, I noticed some stairs to one side. Kalitza, holding a large flower in one hand, and lifting her long tresses with the other, as if to hear the better, was just beginning to go up the stairs. I had to buy a ticket, of course. By the time I got to the viewing platform overlooking the square, I was dreading what I might find. *She will be poised, ready to jump. I can't face finding her and losing her again like that.* I looked hastily around, but she was nowhere to be seen. I looked everywhere she could have been. I found no sign of her. Looking down over the stone and metal, I scanned the square. Sure enough, she was at the edge to the left, near the restaurant. She walked past it and entered one of the little side streets. I rushed back down to the restaurant and looked in vain down the side street before going to my table. The waiter was pleased to see me. I ordered a hearty meal and a bottle of Valpolicella. It was hopeless, I realized, trying to pursue her. With a sudden feeling of self-disgust mixed with anger directed at her, I muttered to myself, "She's leading me by the nose. She's teasing me. She's playing games." Then I calmed down and had another idea. It was I who was to blame. I happened to see her, and then I rushed to confront her, to hold her, to possess. Possession was not on her agenda. *I must let her come to me. She will find me when it suits her. I must not force myself upon her. She comes sudden as the spring and then she vanishes and I mourn her passing. Nobody keeps her all the time. Yet she always returns.* Carlo Toselli's lines came into my head, "The nenuphar/ like a lantern/ to light the way . . ."

Carlo Toselli had his Terracotta Maiden, the voice of his verse speaking three languages, Italian, French, and English.

My cell phone wobbled in my pocket. I had a message. There was e-mail waiting for me. It could wait a while. Back in the hotel after dinner, I opened the laptop to which I had treated myself. I was soon reading a bunch of messages. And replying. There was one from Queenie. She politely apologized for her imperfect command of English. Actually, I think her English is very good. Do we have a perfect command of anything, even our own lives? Life itself is a language, imperfectly understood, never mastered.

Anyway, Queenie said that a tall, dark woman had left me a message. She had just come up to her when Queenie was studying at her desk in the City University library and said to please give a message to Paul Wills. The message was simple: "Do not forget Heather at Haworth."

This intrigued me, because I don't know anyone called Heather. How on earth, then, could I forget her? I did remember Haworth. As memories came back to me, I understood the message.

EVENTS AT HAWORTH

When did these fragments of experience start in my life? Where on earth did they come from? They have clustered themselves in various localities, but I have carried them away with me around the world. The localities are specific and real enough, but the origin of the events remains obscure. Perhaps memory itself is part of the fog. Now that I remember Haworth, I can say that the fragments of experience started for me when I was a small child there in that small Yorkshire village. The significance of paranormal experiences there became clearer when I returned to the village as an adult.

My earliest memories are, in fact, of people and events in the district around Haworth. I remember tramping with the grown-ups and sometimes being carried across the moors to a place with a rocky outcrop. Here we stopped and a check green and white tablecloth was laid out on a flat place with short, springy grass. It was for a picnic. I hadn't heard this word before, but I liked it and kept repeating it as we unpacked sandwiches and little homemade buns. I soon started climbing the nearby rocks. An older cousin noticed me, scooped me up, and sat me on a large, level stone.

The little devil's on the Brontës' seat!" remarked one of the grown-ups.

I'm on a bontyseat! I'm on a bontyseat!" I shouted. Everyone laughed, so I laughed.

It was only at school, several years later, that I read and came to appreciate those Brontë girls, as my grandfather and the rest of the family called them. I also remember a "sweet shop" in the precipitous main street. There was a slot for coins in the old wooden counter, and golden scales for weighing out sweets in their pans, the sweets in one pan and little golden weights in the other. The upstairs bedroom windows opened to give the only access to the back garden. All the houses going up the hill were built like that, I was told. The winters were cold even inside our cottage, and a dripping tap froze into an elaborate cavern of icicles which gleamed rainbow colors, when the sun shone in through the kitchen window. I remember the day my grandfather was still in bed after breakfast, and no matter how I tugged at his pyjama sleeve, he would not wake up for breakfast, nor ever again.

I left soon after and did not visit Haworth again until years later, when I had completed my university studies. I was being interviewed for a job with *The Ripon Rover*. It seemed only natural for me to drive across country via Haworth. I would revisit the place where my earliest memories had been accumulated.

As it turned out, I recognized very little. And that little was indeed little in size, although in my child's mind, it had all seemed big. The main street that climbed steeply up from Keighley was, though, just as wonderfully steep. One winter evening, I remember, we were on the bus when everybody but the driver had to get out to push the vehicle up the icy hill. At the top, we all got in again and rumbled on our way. As my small, second-hand car laboured up the hill, I realized that my childhood memory was quite accurate in some respects, but the scales and weights in the sweet shop had not, I think, been gold.

I had no previous memory of the parsonage, but when I saw it, I was delighted. The neat, friendly museum was enchanting. I was charmed by the little hall, where a lady's bonnet, gloves, and a sprig of heather were placed on a chair, just as if one of the Brontë sisters had come in from a walk on the moor. I loved the polished wood, the period furniture, and the proportions of the rooms, by no means big, but not poky. It was a house I could live in with a good deal of pleasure. How it could have housed that troubled family and afforded enough calm for the works of genius the sisters produced was beyond my ken. *They were though, better off*, I thought, *than the Wordsworths had been, when they lived in tiny Dove Cottage.* The notebooks and manuscripts on display intrigued me, yet I remember nothing of what I read. I imagined the sisters peering at their papers, pale fingers bent sometimes around their pens, perhaps simple schoolroom wooden pens with steel nibs, and always the ink of the words they wrote gleaming in the lamp light. As I left, I touched one of the Victorian gloves on the chair in the hall. I touched the sprig of heather. It was real, not plastic. Good!

They had lived hard by the village graveyard. Beyond the low wall stretched the wild moor. As a teenager, I had started reading Emily's poetry, mainly because her poems are short and fiction is long. In the sixth form, I read *Wuthering Heights* for general interest outside the set texts of Jane Austen and Charles Dickens. For a while, I was obsessed by Emily Brontë, to the extent of wandering with my dog over windswept, grimy suburban fields, crying "Heathcliff!" into the polluted air, much to the surprise of dads and boys trying to fly model aeroplanes. *Heathcliff,* I thought, *as demon lover, must be derived from the Romantic poets and was later on a part of the sexual equipment of D.H. Lawrence's fiction.* This was my adolescent version of the Great Tradition. Reading the novel later, as an adult, I realized it was as much about education as it was about passion.

It was with some reluctance that I left the little parsonage. I had to be getting back on the road soon, if I were to reach the hotel before dinner time. I was tempted to browse in the nearby antique shop, but decided instead to walk a little down the hill to revisit the little sweet shop owned by a cousin of my mother. I was delighted to discover that the shop was still there, still a sweet shop, and still had my mother's cousin's name as proprietor painted in faint white letters above the weathered door frame. To the infant me, the shop had seemed like an Aladdin's cave of delights. I remembered cone-shaped paper bags, huge glass jars of boiled sweets, and again a countertop with a slit cut into it for depositing coins. There was at the time no cash register. Now the shop window was dusty with neglect. A wrinkled piece of plastic formed a base for anything placed in the window. There was only a faded and curling cardboard display for Mars bars. To one side of this, a couple of flies and a wasp lay legs up, long dead.

I knocked on the wooden door. The shop was closed, although it was mid-afternoon. Getting no answer, I knocked again, rather more loudly. A stubby little woman with a ruddy complexion, wearing a fawn woolen overcoat and a chiffon headscarf bulging with half-concealed hair curlers, waddled down the hill with her black plastic shopping bag packed with bulky articles. I knocked again and stood back off the pavement to look at the upstairs windows. I detected a slight movement of dingy lace curtains. As the woman passed me on her way down the hill with her loaded bag, she rattled off a sentence in the local accent, "Thou'lt get nowt out of 'er, lad!"

As I watched her retreat down the hill with her self-satisfied assumption that I was a young man somehow on the make, I realized again that I had better be on my way. My intention had been to make myself known, ask after my relative's health, and give her news of our side of the family. I would have stayed just a few minutes, saying I was "just passing through, like." The house was still silent. I trudged uphill. A thickish fog was rolling in off the moors as I reached the car. It was just as well that the old recluse in the sweet shop had ignored my attempts to rouse her.

I drove away from Haworth on the narrow road towards Stanbury. The fog thickened and the temperature suddenly dropped. I turned up the heater. It was not very effective. I felt a powerful urge to turn around, to look in the back of the little car. I felt that somebody was behind me. The hair on the back of my neck stood up. Cold fingers would suddenly cover my eyes unless I turned to glance over my shoulder. I looked in the rear-view mirror, and then I turned my head. There was nobody in the back. I looked to the road ahead and found that I had veered off-course and was almost off the road. I was now crawling through the fog and sounding the horn at every bend in the road. All the time I was convinced some compelling presence was with me in the car, hoping that I would turn, and that it might materialize so that I could see it at last. My heater was at full blast, but I was horribly cold. Even so, I was not ready to die in a senseless accident. By a stubborn effort of will, I kept my eyes on the road ahead and peered through the swirling fog. Not even Emily Brontë could return from the dead. Yet, I was suddenly convinced she was on the rear seat, attempting to cover my eyes. Then I thought that even if Emily were able to return from the grave, why bother with me? John Fowles or Antonia Byatt or Martin Amis would surely be more appropriate as hauntees. I turned a corner and had to do an emergency stop. A few yards ahead, a bunch of about a dozen cows sauntered towards me, their great black and white faces nosing and waving from side to side through the fog. The cold suddenly went, leaving the heater's fan working overtime I turned it down and mopped my brow. I had traveled only about three miles, but it seemed as if I had been on the retreat from Moscow.

All was back to normal. The cows and a farm boy with a stick passed by, totally uninterested in me or my little car. I watched him behind the car, herding the cows ahead of him. It was when I was about to continue on my way that I looked over my shoulder, in a driver's reflex, and saw the lad looking back at the car, and pointing to the space above it, as if he saw something on its roof. He looked, his mouth open, and then he turned and ran, pushing his way through his little herd, with their swinging udders ready for milking. I put the car in gear and moved off. Had that lad seen a ghostly figure hovering still over my car? I was not about to investigate. I no longer felt a presence. That was good enough for me. I speculated, though, as I drove into and beyond the next village, on the possibility of spirit attempting to communicate in some way across that dimensionless space that stretches between the living and the dead.

Enough of this. Right, monkey! I thought, as I switched on the radio and drove on through the now thinning fog. A voice, an actor, was reading a chapter from a book. As the voice read, I recognized the account of Heathcliffe's wild grief at the grave of Cathy. I listened, fascinated by the words and the coincidence. I switched off only when I stopped at a little café. It was called The Bakewell and so named, I supposed, after the famous tart. I was nowhere near Bakewell itself.

The little café was crowded, even though the roads were empty. I was glad to be back in the land of the living. When the waitress gave me a choice of waiting for a table or joining another customer, I opted for sharing a table The waitress led me to one near an inside wall. A woman, fashionably dressed, already ensconced there with a pot of tea and some scones, smiled as I joined her. We exchanged polite pleasantries. She had a standard English received-pronunciation voice. The way she said with a lighthearted irony that it was 'a grand old day' made me think she was perhaps Anglo-Irish. I ordered tea and Bakewell tart. By way of conversation I explained that I had just visited the Brontë Museum. I then told her of my feeling a presence in the back of my car.

She smiled. "Do you believe in ghosts?" she asked.

"Only at times like then!" I replied. We both laughed. "No, but I have a theory," I continued, "that a sort of mental energy could be projected and picked up by the living and that when people die, a great rush of this energy gets into the places they lived in."

"Their haunts?" she said, smiling.

"Their stomping grounds turn into their haunts," I replied. We both laughed.

"Have you ever been to a séance?" she asked.

"No. Have you?"

"I AM the psychic," she said, getting up to go. We both laughed again.

"Look, I have to leave now. But you have a spirit guide. Write things down. I must go. Check the back of your car before you start out!"

We laughed yet again, and waving to me from the cash register, she paid and left. I finished my snack, paid, and went out to where I had parked the car. The fog had now cleared. I would make good time.

I unlocked the car, went to get in, and then dutifully tipped the seat forward to look in the back. I looked down inside near the back seat and again the hairs of my neck stood up. It was a small, but sharp shock. A little bunch of heather with a few root fibres, black soil still clinging to them, lay on the floor behind the front passenger seat. I picked up the heather, meaning to throw it as far away as possible. I changed my mind and decided to keep it. Wasn't heather a sign of good luck? I put it in the glove compartment. Superstition! The crumbling of reason and intellect! Yet, I could not deny the sequence of strange events. Had the medium opened the car with a bunch of skeleton keys she kept handy for such tricks and deposited the heather before locking the car and going? How could I know? How could she have known which was my car? Our table was nowhere near the window. Had the ghost of Emily Brontë, preposterous as it may seem, put the heather in my car? If so, had the medium left me a message?

Maybe the medium was the message! A message from the other world, was it? She had sensed that something had been left in the car, in any event. Or had she simply made a jocular reference to my story?

Such questions seem to me only details of the larger question: what order of experience have I been trying to describe in these clusters of events that cling to the life of an ordinary freelance journalist, doggedly pursuing people and events, not in the spirit world, but the real, rather messy world? The cumulative effect on me, as I look back on these curious moments, is to bring me to the point of saying that I have been in contact with some kind of angel, perhaps a spirit guide. If not, I have to believe in a fantastic chain of coincidences linked to defects in my own perception. Am I deluded? Am I, in effect, a little crazy? Or is there a sort of conspiracy of actors, presenting me with fantastic scenarios, none of them real? This I have to reject out of hand, because who would pay such actors and why? Actors, in my experience, would not perform unless for some kind of reward. Was I an unwitting stooge for a secret service training agents as cunning actors? Kalitza, it seemed to me, could certainly be a spy of some kind. The more I speculated, the more fantastic the speculations became. I cannot accept, either, that I am mad. I am too much attached to the real world.

All the mysterious events I have recalled are as real to me as a teapot or a coffeepot on the breakfast table. Furthermore, the events are unforgettable, whereas most of the reality I read in the morning paper I have forgotten by the end of the day. Far from removing me from life, the mysteries, as I now think of them, have taught me to appreciate keenly the richness and the stubborn worth of all the simplest of human experiences. They have rescued me! I am no adolescent intellectual standing haughtily apart to embrace abstractions. I do not arrogantly dismiss those who are content to live a life without books and diplomas. There is a thickly intermeshed tangle of experience, not all of which can be readily explained. After all, the art of Caribbean countries and the Americas allows to spirituality and mysticism a privileged space, as recent critics have shown. Why, even academic conferences are held to discuss such matters. No, I have been in touch with many people in my travels; I have also been in touch with thinking souls. In embracing them, I taste something of their liberating power. I have felt the excitement that comes from uncovering facts that people sometimes try to hide. I have felt the freedom given to those who recognize the mystery that belongs to facts themselves. All facts are a mystery. What is science, but the exploration of mysterious facts and events?

I cannot now abandon my sense of unknown dimensions to the inner life. The dark female has taught me patiently, again and again, revealing things I need, before I even know I need them.

I was nearing a military base with high fencing and some barbed wire. A Spitfire and an old trainer jet stood inside the main gates of an RAF base. I drove by and soon found my hotel in a village near Ripon. That night, I put the heather in a glass of water on my bedside table. I recall no dreams, waking or otherwise. The interview with the editor went well next day. I had a verbal agreement that I would supply a regular column, but could sell freelance work wherever I wished. Little did I know that when I returned home, I would find a letter from him putting in writing a fee for the regular monthly column that would be enough to keep me for a month, or if I splurged, it would cover three weeks' living costs. It was a lucky arrangement that I had not expected. It changed my life forever, giving me more confidence in my own work. The extra time it allowed me for working on substantial special assignments was invaluable. I still had the heather with me. I have planted it in my window box, hoping its remaining roots will take to the new soil.

When he had finished reading, Graham poured himself another drink.

Yes, he thought, *Paul is a lucky man. He's convinced he's guided by strange forces, and mostly by spirits in the shape of beautiful women. Some guys have all the luck!* It was a kind of buffer, though, wasn't it? He thought marriage and a family would enable him to dispense with the buffer, but buffer against what? Life itself? No. That wasn't it. A buffer against harm? Not really. There is no security. It was not a question of defences or buffers. It was courageous of Paul to admit to all of this and tell his close friends. It was indeed a puzzle. Graham was sure that his friend was now finding his true way, his impending marriage. That was it! After all, old Willie Yeats had been led by the spirit world. And his marriage to Georgie, not the mysterious Maud Gonne, had been the making of him as a "second wind" writer. Paul might be on a similar path, but as a mere journalist rather than as an extraordinarily dramatic writer of Yeats's stature. Graham tidied the papers together and filed them with the others he had received. He had cracked the Kalitza syndrome in Paul's imagination. This called for a glass of wine and a few olives.

CHAPTER FORTY-ONE

The burglary of a doctor's surgery was reported in the local Sutton Coldfield press and also picked up by *The Birmingham Mail*. There had been no arrests to date. It was now Wednesday and Mary was nevertheless pleased. Tomorrow Paul would arrive. Next morning, on the way to the hospital, Mary called in on Nelly Baxter to see how mother and new baby were getting along. The baby was thriving. No more hiccups. Shunting itself around in the playpen with cuddly toys and brightly colored beads, it waved its hands around and grasped the ears of a black and white rabbit. Nelly was in the midst of ironing. She looked very tired and owned up to being "down," whereas the baby was gurgling away and grinning with little red gums showing when it opened its mouth. Then the little man started wittling and seemed uncomfortable.

"Oh dear. I'd better change him," Nelly said, wrinkling her nose.

"I'll fold this blouse for you, Nelly."

"Oh, you shouldn't, doctor, this won't take a minute. Thank God for disposables!"

This was a rallying cry in her practice, it seemed. Babies often needed changing when she was visiting. Mary wondered whether she provoked the bowel movements. She folded the blouse, and the little crisis was over. Nelly had a bit of the postnatal blues, despite the fact that Ted was now working back in England.

"You're down, but I'll give you a tonic. You've been there before with your first baby. You know you'll be over it in a week or two. Try to get a rest over Easter."

"Actually, my hubby's mother says we can go over to her place near Shenstone and we can go out and around a bit, while she looks after the kiddies."

"Ideal. That's very good news. You deserve a bit of a break. And I bet Mrs. Baxter senior will enjoy fussing over the little Baxters. Have you agreed on a second name yet?"

"Yes, we have, doctor, it's John Howard, but we all call the little imp Howie."

"Oh, yes, I remember John. Is Howard a family name, too?"

"My husband's mad on ice hockey and there's a Howie Gordon or Gordon Howie over there in Canada, the Hall of Hockey Fame, I think. And my mother's father was a Howard. So that settled it."

"Well, who's a little Howie Wowie?" Mary tickled the baby's chest to get a gurgle of delight.

"Look," she added, taking out a pad and writing rapidly on it, "here's a prescription for that tonic. Do you need anything else?"

"Only a nice young man to do all my ironing!"

"Don't we all!" They laughed at the idea and Mary was on her way again, this time to see a couple of patients in hospital.

One of the patients had been admitted with an advanced case of stomach cancer. He had never complained of any medical problems until he had pain. He had come to see Mary on spec as he put it, when it was already too late. He had had an operation, but the cancer had spread. When Mary arrived to see him, he was asleep after a massive dose of painkiller. Old Mr. Holden would be dead in the next day or two, according to the surgeon. His wife and grown-up children would be at the hospital again later that morning.

The other patient was in for an appendectomy. He was a young man who had complained of being sick before the soccer matches in which he played for a local team of enthusiastic amateurs. After one recent game, he had collapsed. Mary had rushed to the soccer ground and immediately sent him to the hospital, suspecting appendicitis. He was lucky. The young surgeon said if they had left the condition to worsen, he would have had peritonitis and might well be dead. He was sitting up with a bowl of fruit at his bedside. His mother, a brunette with a frizzy perm, was warning him not to swallow the pips in the grapes, when Mary arrived.

"Hello, Mrs. Tanner. Hello, Brian. And how are you feeling today?"

"Foine, doctor," said Brian.

"'E wants to go kickin' that football around again, Doctor Rao, ee's football mad, this one."

"Well, we'll have to see what your surgeon thinks. There's no point in opening that wound by playing too soon. You want to be sure it's all okay. We wouldn't want any infection. But not to worry. You'll be playing again very soon and better than ever, because you won't feel sick, and you won't even have an appendix!" said Mary.

They chatted briefly about Villa, Birmingham City, and Albion, and the Wanderers. Then Mary looked at her watch.

"I have to go," she announced. She shook hands with Mrs. Tanner and put her hand on Brian's shoulder, giving him a little squeeze.

"I hear he's going home tomorrow. When I say it's fine to do so, you'll be playing again, very soon, but not before my say so, Brian," she said, as she left the ward.

"Orl roight," Brian replied, resignedly.

Paul arrived at the surgery at about five in the afternoon. He walked up to Liz at the reception counter.

"Liz! How are you? I don't have an appointment, but I'm here!"

Liz looked at him, did an eyes heavenward expression, and grinned. "Mr. Wills! Dr. Rao said she was expecting you to arrive today."

"Call me Paul. Even my enemies call me Paul."

"On the premises we're formal. After hours, I'll call you Paul. Now you go and get a seat in the waiting room, if you can find one. It's busy, busy, busy, today."

Paul put his head into the waiting room. There were two free seats. Should he look at the *National Geographic* or *Home Chat* or *The Countryman* or a *Rupert* annual, or *The*

Boys' Wonder Book. Actually, he was tempted by *The Girls' Wonder Book.* A man sneezed noisily. A mother told a small boy to stop grizzling, and an old woman coughed with a lung-rattling smoker's throatiness, which she tried in vain to keep under control. Her frail shoulders shook every time she coughed. Paul closed the door. He decided he would stroll down to the public library instead.

"I'll just go for a stroll, Liz. The public library seems like a good idea. Can I dump my bags behind the counter? I'll be back in an hour? That sound right?"

"Right. See you soon. I'll tell Dr. Rao you've arrived."

"You're a gem, did you know that?"

"I was thinking along those lines myself, Mr. Wills. See you."

Paul walked rapidly down the road to the library, a quaint Victorian red brick building that looked as if it had once been some sort of neo-Gothic chapel. He was surprised to see that the library had acquired some computers with a catalogue system showing the holdings in this particular branch. Some books that obviously had some demand, but were not in this particular library were noted as being in another of the libraries in the district. *That's handy*, thought Paul. He looked at his watch and then searched the catalogue for books on family violence. The library had about three up-to-date titles, and then some from the late 1970s. The Birmingham Central Reference Library was where he would be doing much of his research. Writing it up, he could do here or in Mary's flat. So, he was moving in! He was surprised at himself, in a way, and at her. He still thought of both of them as singles, yet here they were, about to be married in May.

It seemed to have all started with the strange, but beautiful Kalitza. *She was a phantom of delight.* He muttered the phrase to himself. Phantom! Was she a phantom? She now seemed like some figment of imagination, yet he had met her, slept with her, seen her dead, seen her alive again. Or was it just another woman? No, she was real. But she was now an intellectual problem if anything, not a woman commanding him; he was no longer in her thrall. Nor was he alone or palely loitering. Kalitza was not an emotional problem. Mary was his woman and he was Mary's man. Mary was close, was everything. Kalitza was remote. Kalitza was a sort of theorem. She was enticing as a problem; nothing more. He half hoped that he would not see her again. But that was going too far. Mary had suggested, hadn't she, that Kalitza represented a creative force unleashed or unblocked in his psyche. In a way, she was part of him. If he met her again, could he look at her dispassionately, as an editor might look at something Paul had written? Yes. He would see her with the kind of admiration one gave to lovely women in a picture in an exhibition, as one passed by.

He looked at his watch. It was just after five-thirty. He'd glance through the newspapers on those huge wooden rods. *The Times* perhaps.

"We close in twenty minutes." It was a statement addressed to all and sundry. The voice had a clarity, a volume, and an authority that astonished Paul and made him jump involuntarily. He looked round to see a small and neat woman librarian surveying the all and sundry in question from behind her desk. She had a brisk and determined look on her thin, heavily made-up face. She looked at a large wall clock behind her. The big hand lurched forward another minute.

She's ready to go home, or maybe ready to meet the man in her life, thought Paul. Before he turned back to the newspaper, he noticed that she had a brownish rubber thimble on one of her fingers.

He sank into a chair and sighed as he looked at depressing headlines. He got up and replaced the paper. He then took up a copy of *The New Statesman* and started glancing quickly through an article on the Channel tunnel. The shareholders had lost a packet on that one. The tunnel was a great idea. Eurostar was a boon. Paul hoped the massive debt could eventually be paid off. *What do you do with a tunnel under the sea if nobody can afford it? You could not sell this to an American or a Japanese company to reassemble it back home as a tourist park.* He went back to *The Times*, turned a page in the newspaper, and saw an item picked up from a news agency. The corpses of two middle-aged women had been found floating in La Baie des Anges. Apparently they were suicides, but there were some doubts. It must have been around the time he had been interviewing Mme. de Crevennes or just before. Were they driven to suicide by some marital unhappiness or a disaster of another kind, or male violence? Were they stockholders who had lost everything in the channel tunnel company or some other thing, like the NASDAQ crash? Was suicide the coward's way out? But Romans had not thought that. Disgraced or defeated Japanese samurai were not cowards. Was the prime motive some ineradicable shame? Paul wondered if he might write on suicide. No. It was too depressing. He did not relish spending some of his newfound happiness in life by researching and writing just now about suicide. He looked at his watch. It was time to go back to the surgery. Before he left, he filled in a form, so that he could get a library ticket. He would use this quiet retreat as a writing and research office when he needed it.

Back at the surgery, Liz was tidying up her reception area.

"She's just finished her last consultation. You can go in now. She'll be writing up a few notes or just packing up, too."

"Thanks, Liz. You're . . ."

"A gem!"

"That's the word." Paul knocked on Mary's door.

"You're here early! Liz tells me you popped into the library. Wonderful. Let's go home!"

CHAPTER FORTY-TWO

Kim put down the phone. Her old supervisor from student days, Grimly Grimble, as she was known to her students, had remembered her, and suggested she get in touch with Miss Barbara Mason, head of a good girls' boarding school in Cumberland.

"You may mention my name for what it's worth. We were in touch only a week ago, and she told me she was looking for a language assistant. Try her, Alissa, and do it now. Take down this number."

Kim was smiling to herself, as she thought back over her conversation with Dr. Grimble, not long retired from her university teaching post, but still associated with Newnham. She picked up the phone again and tapped in the number. The ringing tone repeated five or six times before someone answered.

"Tomkyn Bridge School . . . Can I be of help?" The speaker was a little out of breath.

"Yes," said Kim, "I'd like to speak to the head, Miss Mason. I'm calling from the Oxford and Cambridge Club."

"Your name, please."

"I'm Alissa Partridge. Dr. Grimble told me to contact Miss Mason."

"I see. The head is available, as it happens. I'll put you through. What is it about, if I may ask?"

"Oh, tell her I've been in touch with Dr. Grimble. She'll know."

"Right. Hold the line please." There was a click and silence. Kim thought she had been disconnected in error, but a voice, very clear and very precise in articulation, suddenly spoke.

"This is Barbara Mason on the line. To whom am I speaking?"

"I'm Alissa Partridge. Dr. Grimble was my supervisor at Newnham. She told me I should call you. I understand you need someone to teach languages?"

"That's correct. Which languages do you teach?"

"I'm fluent in French and Italian, with an almost equal command of Arabic."

"I see."

The rest of the conversation took place in French and the upshot was that Miss Alissa Partridge would report to Tomkyn Bridge School near St. Bees next day for interview. Her expenses would be paid and she had the choice of a hotel in St. Bees for one, perhaps two nights, or accommodation in the school itself. Kim opted for staying in the school.

"Good, Miss Partridge, that's a wise decision. You will get an idea of the premises and our way of life here. Take a connection that will get you in here around five p.m. I'll send a car to meet you at St. Bee's station. You will see the driver holding a notice bearing the name of our school."

"Thank you, Miss Mason. I look forward to meeting you and to seeing something of the school."

"Until tomorrow then. Good-bye."

Kim hung up and rolled on her bed laughing with glee. Control would never expect or anticipate this. *Nomenklatura* would soon have to scrap the code name, Kim. Still smiling to herself, Kim made up and sprayed a little perfume on her neck and then dabbed some behind her ears. She went to the club's library. It was very comfortable, well-stocked with newspapers, weeklies, and an extensive range of books, some still catalogued with index cards in little wooden drawers. The catalogue was now mostly on the computer. The library was deserted. A CIA man had once told her that this library was far better than the Harvard Club's library in New York. She settled down with *The Economist* after looking up Tomkyn Bridge School in *The Public Schools' Yearbook*.

The door opened and a man, seriously overweight, announced himself with a fit of sneezing into a capacious red handkerchief. He sank into a leather armchair with a sigh of profound satisfaction, tucking the handkerchief up his left sleeve. Kim stood up. This intruder's florid face suggested a blood pressure problem. As she walked past him, she noticed his watery blue eyes seemed huge behind the lenses of his glasses. He smiled with purplish lips, revealing a perfect set of teeth. Kim smiled. They were, after all, fellow club members. *One should not judge people on casual observation*, she thought, fixing the man's image in her memory as she went out. The old-fashioned elevator creaked her down to the ground floor, where she found the Squash Bar. Two young men were playing in one of the courts. A poker-faced barman with thinning black hair parted to one side was polishing glasses. He put down the tea towel.

"Good evening, madam. Do you want a drink or are you waiting for the gentlemen?"

"I never wait for gentlemen," said Kim. "They wait for me."

"I'm sure they do." The barman smiled and waited with raised eyebrows.

In fact, Kim always arrived at a rendezvous in time to find an inconspicuous way of surveying the place for hints of a trap. "Give me a club claret and a few nibbles."

She took her claret and a little bowl of potato crisps to a table. The claret was as drinkable as it was affordable and as affordable as it was welcome just then.

"Are you in town for the marathon, Miss?" asked the barman, smoothing his hair. Out in the corridor someone sneezed.

"The marathon! No, as a matter of fact, I have to be in Exeter tomorrow," said Kim, thinking, *that'll fox anyone who might be trying to trace me.*

"Never been there myself, but I've heard it's a good holiday area."

"I think that's right. Devon and Cornwall are interesting counties."

"So I've heard. I'm not much of a holiday man myself. Do a bit of fishing sometimes at the weekend, if I'm not on duty."

"Trout?"

"Sometimes. I've taken a pike or two and eels in my time. Salmon, if I get lucky. In Scotland, I caught a salmon once."

They chatted a little about changes and renovations in the club premises. Kim looked at her watch. She downed the rest of her claret.

"Goodness. I must be off. I'll be about eight minutes late for him."

"Eight's fine. He'll be eager to see you without being too vexed . . . er . . . impatient. He won't mind a bit, if I might say so!"

"You might and you have. Bye-bye for now."

As she walked out and up the stairs, she knew the barman was watching her every move.

She hailed a taxi outside the club and went to buy her rail ticket for next morning. She timed the trip to the station. At the station, she stayed in the taxi and asked for a nearby travel agent she knew, where she could buy her train ticket voucher. She paid for taxi and train with cash as usual. She was wise to have bought the ticket. Sure enough, there was a route getting her to St. Bees at 5:03 p.m. the next day, but it would mean an early train from London to make her connections. What with breakfast, checking out, and morning traffic jams, she felt it was an extra saving of time, a little insurance that she could catch the train without mishaps. If one of the connections were to be delayed, the journey would take longer. In that event, she would telephone the school secretary to let them know. She walked from the travel agency to a busy main road, where she took a bus going to Leicester Square. In a small street just beyond the brightly-lit square, she got off the bus and walked along a quiet side road where she knew a good Chinese restaurant.

She had some boiled rice, a small, freshly steamed fish with ginger sauce, plump steamed prawns in a crab sauce, *bok choy*, and red bean dessert soup. With this fairly substantial, yet light, but very tasty meal, she drank several cups of very weak jasmine tea. Each time the waiter appeared to pour tea or hot water she glanced round the room. Nothing unusual; no watchers.

"Where you from, lady?" asked the waiter when she was looking at her bill.

"Singapore."

She left a modest tip, big enough to satisfy and small enough not to elicit gossip. The road was empty of pedestrians. She walked back to Pall Mall by quiet streets behind the National Gallery. Nobody was following her.

***

The train journey next day was long, but comfortable. She traveled second class and reread a novel by Julien Gracq, *Le Rivage des Syrtes*. She also leafed through some of his *Lettrines*. When she was younger, she had read Gracq's novel with subdued, controlled excitement. It was a prose poem, but with a hint that France might play the big power game again. This time she was still impressed by the quality of Gracq's prose. She liked the love scene best. Yet, France had now missed her chance for *le grand jeu*. France, in fact, though a lovely country, was in Kim's opinion, and that of many other French citizens, a bit of a mess. It needed a government with the will to reform, to get things moving, and with politicians big enough to face down the people who thought the street must rule, whenever a vote went the wrong way. France needed charismatic statesmen who could define the direction of the Republic amid the vast and rapid changes in Asia that were leaving France and other European countries behind. Yet, the threats from terrorists were growing. Control and his British, German, and American partners needed the best agents they could find and train. Politicians posturing in Europe, cuddling the Germans, ignoring some aspects of significant foreign news, and marginalizing England in the media, were not good enough. The most enterprising French people knew this, but outrageous policies over the last decades had left France trailing behind the dynamism of North America, post-Thatcher Britain, and the Asian tigers. *France,* she thought, *was fast becoming a leftist museum.* It still had an active Communist party with trade union clout! *The Czechs have a museum of Communism in Prague.* Kim thought that it would take another three years for two of the current politicians to gain the necessary clout and stature—if they ever did. But would it then be too late? And would the new "giants" work together for the good of the country or would they try to destroy each other? If they did that, France would become a kind of Portugal. *How did I get here from Gracq's book?* she asked herself as she closed it. Ah yes, *le grand jeu.* Agents often thought they were privileged participants in that game. Kim was not deceived about that. She knew she was a cog in a machine in place mainly to knock out limited menaces to French interests before they became too big to handle quietly. She was now hoping she could play her last hand and retire with some modest winnings. *Let others protect the anonymous families and her family-to-be among them.* She wanted to move out of the shadows.

Kim noticed that her train had arrived at 1705. She walked the small platform, trailing her little case on wheels. Outside there was a car park and she immediately saw a neatly dressed woman holding a sign: TOMKYN BRIDGE SCHOOL. Kim walked up to her and smiled.

"Miss Partridge?"

"That's right."

"I'm Mrs. Holroyd. I'll drive you to the school. Miss Mason's expecting you."

They shook hands.

"Here, let me take that." Mrs. Holroyd wheeled Kim's bag to a red minibus that bore a discreet little crest in gold paint on the driver's door. The crest depicted a hump-backed bridge surmounted by a bishop's miter. Kim walked to the front passenger door, while Mrs. Holroyd put the bag into the van. There was a crest on the passenger door as well. She recognized it from the yearbook entry she had read. She climbed in and Mrs. Holroyd lost no time in getting out of the car park and onto the road. She was a slim woman of about sixty, with a complexion roughened and lined by the weather. Her rosy cheeks and pepper and salt hair, done up in a knot, gave her a homely, yet efficient air. Her eyes had a merry glint suggesting a certain understanding of people and sympathy for them, even, perhaps especially, adolescent girls.

"I expect you are tired. You've come from London, haven't you?"

"Yes. And I was excited to be coming for an interview. I was up at six!"

"Oh, my husband and I are up most days at six. He's the school gardener and handyman, you know. He's the only man permanently on the premises. But he's over sixty. Fit as a fiddle, mind. Holroyd's a good man. Knows gardens. He gets on with the job. I sometimes tell him he's like a sultan with all these women and him the only man. He just grins, but once he said I should be careful. What if he was the eunuch, not the sultan! It was unexpected coming from a man. We had a good laugh over that one. I told him not to worry."

"Are there other married women on the staff?"

"Oh my, yes. But the marrieds live off the premises. Some of those young husbands are better in their own homes in St. Bees, so far as the school is concerned! Holroyd and me, we're the only marrieds at the school. We're in a flat above the old stables. And we hope it stays like that. They've made us very comfortable there. Done us proud. It's where the stable lads were before it was a school."

"What was it before the school took over the premises?"

"It was Bishop Tomkyn's house; Palace, they called it, but it wasn't for royals. At least, I never heard of it as a real palace."

They were now on narrow country roads and had just passed through a village when Mrs. Holroyd turned into a gateway with a sign on a white board. A red rectangle was the backing for the school crest and in black lettering at the top of the white border was the name of the school. At the bottom of the board, again in black lettering, was written: PRIVATE. AUTHORIZED VISITORS ONLY. The same information appeared again on another board about ten yards further along the drive. The drive curved gently and was flanked by grass, bordered in turn by trees and bushes. Kim noted and counted five mole hills. After about another sixty yards, they were in front of a sizeable country mansion, mainly seventeenth century by the look of it. The drive swept around a rich lawn in front of the house and widened into a rectangular area wide enough for vehicles to turn and to park if necessary. The drive led from the other side of this area to a fork, one branch of which rejoined the drive beyond the lawn, while the other curved along the side of the house and perhaps led to other buildings at the rear.

Mrs. Holroyd stopped the minibus near the flagstone steps that led in a shallow flight up to the heavy oak door. Kim noticed the ecclesiastical Gothic design of the windows. There was a balustrade of elegant stone along the first floor level in front of the windows.

"Where are the students? It seems peaceful for a school."

"Oh, they'll be in their study rooms doing prep. *O* Levels and *A* Levels are not so far away now. They have to 'swot.' In between the hockey and swimming and all that.

"I'll take you up to your room and introduce you to matron. Then you can rest before coming down to meet the head at six thirty p.m. She'll take you in for dinner at the staff table."

"Excellent. I'll follow you, then."

The front door opened into a large reception hall with a solid-looking parquet floor. A double staircase led up to a landing area with oak handrails, so that, once on the landing, one could look down into the hall. Kim followed

Mrs. Holroyd along a blue carpeted corridor to the left. A little way down there was a heavy mahogany door with a brass plate etched with the words GUEST SUITE. Below this was a small brass frame into which a pristine white card bearing the red and gold school logo had been inserted. The card proclaimed in bold black print: MISS ALISSA PARTRIDGE.

"Miss Partridge, I presume?" Kim turned round and smiled. A squat, comfortable-looking woman in a plain grey suit and wearing a cameo brooch on a light-apricot blouse was coming along the corridor from another part of the house.

"I'm Miss Partridge," smiled Kim.

"I'm Mrs. Hickson, or matron. I trust you've had a good journey. Mrs. Holroyd has got you here in very good time. Oh, Nancy, I'll see you on that other matter before the dinner gong does its thing!"

"Right. I'll be there. Make yourself comfortable, Miss Partridge."

"Thank you, I will, Mrs. Holroyd."

Mrs. Hickson opened the door and ushered Kim into the guest suite. "You may want to write up notes or letters or watch television in the sitting room. That door near the window leads into your bedroom and there's a bathroom en suite. If you want a bath, take it now or after eleven p.m. The girls use a lot of hot water, and after they have done their washing and bathing and showering, it takes time for the boilers to get the water hot again. Showers are fine any time because they work off an individual heater in your bathroom."

"Wonderful. Thanks for the tip about the bath. I have an appointment with Miss Mason at six thirty p.m. . . . ."

"Yes. She'll send a prefect from the sixth form to take you down to her rooms. She'll knock just before six thirty p.m."

"You are wonderfully efficient at Tomkyn Bridge School."

"We do our best to please. I'll be seeing you at dinner. You settle in. Bye."

Kim took her luggage and crossed to one of the two windows. The view was of extensive lawn and then the trees. She could not see the main gate or the little lodge next to it. The windows opened and were not barred. She opened one and looked out. The air was clear and unpolluted. The air is like wine she had once heard someone say at a coastal resort. The minivan was now moving around to the side of the house. It was 1800. Just outside, there was the stone balustrade she had noticed on arrival. It would be possible to hang at arms' length from it and drop into a flower bed. In the room, a comfortable-looking sofa and two armchairs were covered in floral chintz. The curtains matched the furniture. A writing desk stood between the windows. There was a bookcase with a lamp and an easy chair beside it. The bedroom was papered with a powdery kingfisher-blue with a subdued pale-olive foliage design. It was superb and old, though still in good condition. *That's William Morris, I'll bet*, thought Kim. The bathroom was all modern plumbing with excellent chunky fittings. There was a small heater in a rectangular casing near the showerhead. Kim decided to have a quick shower. When she had put on the pale yellow dress she had brought with her for the evening, she decided not to use any make-up. She put on a little perfume. Mitsouko. That was it. She checked her handbag and put away her case. She would not unpack now. Slipping on a pair of simple, not quite flat-heeled black leather shoes, she looked at the books on the shelves in the sitting room.

CHAPTER FORTY-THREE

There was a knock at the door.

"Come in." The door opened and a tall girl with blonde hair in a ponytail and wearing a school uniform of dark-green cloth with a white blouse came into the room.

"The head asked me to collect you."

Kim got up and walked over to the door. The girl had a badge of dark red enamel with the word "Prefect" picked out in gold lettering.

"We'll go down then. My name's Miss Partridge."

"I'm Clara Greatrex. Welcome to the school, Miss Partridge."

On the ground floor, they stopped at a large mahogany door near the school office and reception area. Clara knocked and they heard a female voice say, "Enter." Kim opened the door and walked in. A woman with silver hair plaited into two coils pinned on either side of her head stood up, smiling, and held out her hand above a large, Victorian, leather-topped oak desk.

"Miss Partridge? I'm Barbara Mason. Welcome to our school." The two women shook hands.

"Thank you, Clara. You may go now. It's almost time for the dinner gong. You no doubt want to give your friends your impression of Miss Partridge!"

The head and Kim sat down.

"You had a comfortable journey, I hope?" continued the head.

"Yes, thank you. I was able to catch up on some reading. And the guest suite is wonderful. Thank you for putting me up in the school."

"Would you care for a sherry or a Perrier before we go in for dinner?"

"A Perrier would be very good after that journey."

Miss Mason went to a cabinet with a discreet little oak-clad fridge. Miss Mason came over with a small bottle of cold Perrier and a cut glass tumbler. She went back for a tulip glass of cold Fino sherry and then settled on the sofa beside Kim. Miss Mason had a slight limp. She wore a pale blue twin set with a double string of pearls. She had discreet make-up, a rose lipstick and a little powder. Her manicured nails were painted with clear nail varnish.

"Now we are comfortable, tell me about Dr. Grimble. How is she? Did you see her in Cambridge?"

"No, I was in the Oxbridge Club in London when I was in touch with her and with you. It must be about three years since I last saw her. She seems to be just as active as ever."

"Yes, I think retirement holds no terrors for her. After all, she's still working on that 'hobby book' as she calls it."

"Is that her projected edition of Rimbaud's lost North African manuscripts?"

"That's the one. It's a delicious idea. She's written about a hundred and fifty pages of fake Rimbaud prose poetry about Berbers, in French, of course, but with some Arab phrases such as Rimbaud could have picked up," Miss Mason said, laughing cheerily.

"Yes, and she told me she had started the introduction," added Kim. "She's writing a Lacanian spoof analysis of Rimbaud, the life and the work. But I understand she still has to add the mock scholarly notes." They both laughed and sipped their drinks.

"She told me why she is writing it," offered Miss Mason.

"Really? Does she learn more about Rimbaud this way?"

"She said she's doing it for fun, first of all, and then to see whether she can do a convincing pastiche, and thirdly because in doing it, she learns about Rimbaud in a way that uncovers things a more orthodox approach does not necessarily reveal."

"How interesting."

"Yes, it is," said Miss Mason. "And now she's convinced that Rimbaud had plenty to write about in North Africa."

"I expect," added Kim, "that she thinks there really might be a lost briefcase under the dunes that a sandstorm could one day uncover. And in it, there would be perfectly preserved manuscripts."

"Then in that case, the Pleiade edition would have to be revised and expanded. What fun!"

"Yes, and Rimbaud of the desert could be compared with the fake Rimbaud," added Kim.

"Yes, and then they would turn out to be identical!"

"And perhaps the *Times Literary Supplement* would publish a long article about it."

"Perhaps some scholars would accuse her of having found the briefcase earlier and copied the manuscripts for her own book!"

"But we could testify that she had been working on the forgery long before the literary sandstorm," said Kim. *We're both on the same wavelength, having literary fun*, she thought. At that moment, a gong sounded briskly, almost impatiently, and echoed throughout Big School.

"Ah, dinner. I can see we shall get along just fine, my dear. Follow me," said Miss Mason, as she touched Kim gently on the arm. Then she got up and walked with her slight limp towards the door.

The dining hall had a ceiling with Italian plasterwork from the eighteenth century. The oak paneled walls seemed to be seventeenth century, but could be nineteenth century renovations, Kim speculated. There were portraits of various Heads and on the wall behind the staff table at the end of the hall was a well-lit portrait of Bishop Tomkyn. The dinner was good, honest, institutional food; there was consommé followed by steamed cod and mashed potatoes with young spinach that did not taste of earth, nor was it leaking a flood of green water. The table was supplied with crisp salad and crusty bread rolls in dishes placed at intervals. Dessert was an apple crumble with thick, but not lumpy custard available, if desired, from silver sauce boats. There was water or homemade lemonade. Bottles, carafes, or glasses of wine could be bought by staff members at their own extra expense. The meal started after the diners had risen to say grace. After the main course, a senior girl had the privilege of reading aloud from a heavy lectern a passage she had chosen either from the Bible or literature. This meant that the girls listened each term to an anthology of passages reflecting the taste and interests of the seniors.

Conversation at the staff table began with Miss Mason introducing Kim as Miss Partridge who might be helping with languages.

Kim realized that the interview had in effect begun from the moment she had arrived. Her clubability or congeniality was being tested. *Rightly so*, she thought, *if I'm to live and work with these people day in and day out.*

The conversation was energetic and wide-ranging— travel, sport, languages, politics, school activities. Miss Mason was anxious to know if she liked hiking and could survive if lost on Exmoor or in the Cumberland hills. Kim, a hardened survivor, said the thought of being lost in the hills was a bit alarming, but she had been a senior girl guide in her time and had camped and played the wide game in the Welsh hills. Exmoor could be a real danger, and in any case, going out on hikes alone was, in fact, a stupid thing to do in rugged country. She thought she would be prepared and cautious and have to get to know the Cumberland hill country. During the dinner conversation, there was much genteel rather than raucous laughter, and when they all went to the senior common room for coffee, tea, or herbal infusions, the atmosphere was very convivial.

Kim was relaxed. She thought she had already been accepted by most of the staff. The exception was a thin woman of about fifty who had a receding jaw and an overbite that should have been corrected in the days when British dentistry either scorned such things or did not know enough to succeed. This woman could barely conceal her dislike for the beautiful and milk chocolate colored Alissa Partridge. Her attitudes in conversation had revealed a sort of dogged political correctness. Kim was amused to see reflected in Miss Tew's every facial expression an internal struggle between right-thinking approval of a half-caste or *métis* colleague and that visceral hatred for a beautiful and younger woman. Miss Tew looked out of a baleful pair of eyes. Miss Tew was predatory in her passive way. *I'm a predator, too*, thought Kim, *and I'm well equipped to win.* Being liked by colleagues was important for Kim, but it was clear to her that she could not be liked by everyone. *Hell*, she asked herself, *how many people do I really like?*

CHAPTER FORTY-FOUR

Blah, blah, blah, thought Graham as he scanned the technical heading of the e-mail, before reading the message:
Dear Graham,

> You ring the concierge's bell: code 7615 ;pl bell
> sign. She'll be up and about by the time you arrive
> from Chas. de Gaulle airport. She's Mme. Goudier
> and she has the keys to my flat and a little corner of
> my heart! She'll let you in and explain workings of
> doors and keys to you. There's a clean little hotel
> for your friends a few minutes away, Hotel Mimo-
> sa. You have their tel. & fax and e-mail from some
> time ago. You make the reservation or I will if you
> give me the exact dates. If you need me, you can
> phone me (mobile).
> Cheers, Paul.

Graham had written to Paul:

> Dear Paul
> Got the packet. You've found your true way. We'll
> stay in Paris as you suggest. Don't bother to come
> over because my friends want to see London too
> and they are intrigued by the name Sutton Coldfield.
> We all assume we must bring winter woollies and
> macs, if not wellies, though certainly brollies. How
> do I get the key to your flat? We arrive about 7:30
> a.m. on Good Friday. Best, Graham.

Paul's previous mail had started this chain:

> Dear Graham,
> This mail is to ask about your Easter visit. I'm now
> in Sutton Coldfield and have moved in with Mary.

The holiday in Paris could be arranged like this if
you think it is good: you arrive whenever you like
and occupy my flat in the rue de la Collégiale. Your
friends can be in a nearby hotel from whenever they
arrive. When Mary can get away, we can nip over
to Paris for a couple of days, when we shall be in
my big bed and you, my dear chap, will be on the
canapé or on the hearth rug. Alternatively, you can
nip over to United Kingdom whenever you like
from Paris—either all three or just you, according to
your wishes. How's about it? Reply quickly so we
all know what we're a-doing! Did you get my latest
and last packet? Cheers, Paul

***

Breakfast in the dining hall of Big School was porridge
or cereal followed by eggs, grilled sausages or bacon with
mushroom and tomato, followed by brown or white toast
and a selection of jam, marmalade, honey, and golden syrup.
Tea or coffee was served with the meal. After breakfast,
there was an assembly in the chapel with prayers, hymn
singing, and the reading of a passage from the Bible (the
King James version). The choir had sung the Introit "Lead
me Lord." Announcements about activities of school teams
and clubs were then made before the students were dismissed
to proceed to classes. The head said she would be free for
the formal interview in her study a half an hour after the
assembly.

When Kim arrived for the interview, Miss Mason
introduced two other members of staff who constituted with
her the interview committee.

"Miss Partridge, I'd like you to meet Miss Hillbourne,
Deputy Head, and Mrs. Chapman, our Head of Languages."

"How do you do?" Kim smiled and shook hands with the
two women.

"You didn't meet them at dinner because both were out of Big School on other business yesterday. Now let's all sit down and make ourselves comfortable."

Miss Hillbourne was a tall, fit-looking woman with a swathe of dark hair gathered in a French pleat. She wore a light-green suit with a pin stripe over a dark-blue silk blouse. She had gold, circular earrings. Clip-on. Rose-bleu lipstick. She was discreetly using make-up to emphasize her good cheekbones. She smiled and looked alertly at the interviewee with intelligent, hazel eyes. Mrs. Chapman had short, blonde hair in an urchin cut that had been done in an expensive salon. She wore a pale, rose-pink dress and matching court shoes. She had discreet make-up as well, nothing in any way vulgar.

"I've looked over your file, Miss Partridge, and find that you were taught by Dr. Grimble. The school has been fortunate in having her support over the years, and we have every confidence in her recommendations. You taught for a short time after graduation, but then moved into research in the Cultural Affairs Department of the French civil service. Are you really interested in teaching again? What can you offer us in language teaching and extracurricular activities?" demanded Miss Hillbourne.

"Yes. After all the bureaucracy, I really would like to teach again. I can teach French and Italian and, if anyone were interested, Arabic too. And I would enjoy helping with extracurricular things."

"Good. Mrs. Chapman can discuss the language side in detail. You see, we do teach other things besides the game of bridge here."

Kim laughed and said, "Yes, that name is ambiguous."

"I'm glad you like my stock joke, Miss Partridge. I find it serves to break the ice. But what about helping with clubs and activities?"

"I assume you have a house system, unless it's been changed since the last edition of the year book."

"Yes, we have six houses, and you would be assigned to one of them. Would you look after a house team—let's say swimming or net ball?"

"I could certainly do that. Even the bridge team!" The others smiled. "What about skiing? Do any girls need instruction in that?"

Here Miss Mason responded to Kim's query, "We do have skiers and skaters, but students who take up these sports need a parental waiver of school responsibility for any accidents. Of course, we have insurance. Now, Mrs. Chapman may want to ask you about your approach to language teaching."

"Thank you, head. Miss Partridge, how do you approach language teaching?"

"I take a multi-pronged approach, Mrs. Chapman. I believe communication is a great motivation factor, so I favour direct method, simple conversation, and directly useful vocabulary and idiom. I believe in a programmed learning approach to grammar. And I feel that as soon as we can begin reading in a foreign language, we should use extracts from texts likely to interest students at each stage of their school life. Writing follows with attention to dictation."

"Dictation! You still believe in it then?"

"Yes, I do. Am I terribly old-fashioned?"

"Not at all. We believe in it too and we used to arrange every year to tape the French national dictation contest. Pity that's been scrapped. We, however, still use our tapes. We involve the students, and we have a similar contest at school every year."

Kim was pleased by this.

"That involves students in listening to genuine, educated speech in French, in awareness of a number of oddities and exceptions in usage, in spelling, and also the fun of it with the winners of their own age in the junior section serving perhaps as role models. I think some advanced students would benefit from watching tapes of *Questions pour un Champion*, the quiz show where there is very rapid speech for certain parts of the game. Yes," and as if thinking aloud, she added, "Unfortunately, the televised national *Dictée* as you say has finished. Everyone retires."

"Yes. In a nutshell, and yes! Now, do you think that you can teach a foreign language without needing to go into the literary side of things?"

"No, I do not. Native speakers grow up with nursery rhymes, songs, fables, children's stories, and proverbs, et cetera. I think foreigners learning the language should do the same. In my experience, a language involves a culture and its best literary works, classic and popular. It makes sense to introduce songs and adages, and literary texts for reading aloud and translation and comment."

"But when we were at school, don't you think we had to do difficult texts too early?"

"Yes, that was so. I would hope to introduce literary texts appropriate for age groups and doctored so that useless vocabulary doesn't block the very useful words and synonyms that are current and necessary. Complete texts can be left until students have enough mastery of the language to read with enjoyment."

"Do you use translations of English texts into French ever?"

"That depends. If students are obsessed with Harry Potter, for example, I think a French class or Italian or any other language class could use sections of the translation and compare it with the original."

"An exciting idea, Miss Partridge. I have no other questions."

"As head, I am also interested in your fitting into the daily life of the school, Miss Partridge. I have a few personal questions for you, if you don't mind. You do not have to answer, though, if you don't want to do so."

"I understand, Miss Mason."

"Are you engaged to be married or are you thinking of marrying in the near future?"

"No, is the answer to both questions. I am still seeking the right man. I would like a family sooner or later. I take it that married members of staff live off the premises?"

"Correct."

"If I were to marry someone with a career centered on, let's say Glasgow, Aberdeen, London, or Birmingham, and I decided to keep on teaching here, if appointed, could I commute in the holidays and certain weekends, but still live in school?"

"I think such an arrangement would be suitable for us, but would it be best for you?"

"I think it would be easier to find a good husband in those big cities than in the local village. So yes, it would suit me." They all laughed.

"Yesterday, you mentioned hiking. Do you ride?"

"I've done pony trekking and even a bit of hunting."

"Could you supervise girls obsessed with horses—as well as Harry Potter?"

"Yes. I have some rosettes for dressage and show jumping. I know the discipline involved and the likely causes of accidents."

"Accidents are a problem. We insist that girls doing riding here are paid for as an extra by parents and that they be privately insured, too. Do we have any other questions for Miss Partridge?" Miss Mason looked at the others, who shook their heads. "Are you a member of a church or a political party?"

"I am a member of the Church of England, but I have no political affiliations. I feel that governments nowadays face specific problems and should come up with answers that work, rather than try to divide everyone by ideological struggle."

The interviewers sighed and shook their heads. Miss Mason spoke again. "If only our politicians thought like that! Perhaps you have questions for us, Miss Partridge?"

"Yes. If appointed, would I be on a contract for a certain number of years, renewable?"

"You would sign a contract that would be open-ended. We could give you one term's notice to leave or you could give us one term's notice if you wanted to leave."

"And are there prospects for promotion?"

"If appointed, you would already be second to Mrs. Chapman in the languages section. However, in terms of the house system, you might be eligible eventually for the post of House Mistress, too, but this involves you in extra administrative duties and counseling and the like."

"Living in school involves having my own rooms and taking meals in school, I suppose. How much is deducted from my salary to cover these things?"

"We do it on 3 percent of salary. That's very advantageous. It means many members of staff can afford mortgages, if necessary, on a house that could be suitable for retirement or simply as an investment."

"That's a generous perquisite. It puts salaries in effect a little ahead of the state salaries, although at first glance, they seem a little behind."

"You've hit the nail on the head. Other questions?"

"No. Thank you for the information."

"I have a final question for you—do you really want this job, teaching all girls in a rural, shall we say, retreat?"

"I would very much like the job."

"Thank you, Miss Partridge. We shall call you back in here for our decision."

Kim had taken half a cup of Earl Grey tea in the empty room with its large central table and rows of pigeonholes, when there was a knock at the door. A senior girl appeared to take her back to Miss Mason's study.

The three interviewers were all standing and beaming at their Alissa Partridge.

"Congratulations, Miss Partridge. We think you'll be a very good addition to our staff here. You are able to start work here after the Easter holiday?"

I am the resurrection and the life, thought Kim. She smiled. "Yes, certainly. Thank you so much. I am sure I shall enjoy working with you all. When should I report for duty?"

"Come back here about two days before we start. Let's say April twentieth. As for making your way back to London, there is a train before lunch, or you may stay for lunch and catch the one forty-five p.m. Or you could stay another night and leave by the early train tomorrow."

"I'd love to stay for lunch. I should get a train back today, but thank you for offering me another night in that beautiful suite. Tell me, it *is* William Morris?"

Yes. I'm pleased you noticed that. It's one of our treasures."

"I loved being in the school and I am sure I shall enjoy working here. I have a number of things to arrange now that I shall be coming here to teach. So, I'll leave after lunch."

"Good. Mrs. Chapman can show you our language lab. And the books we use and explain how she runs the language section, before we meet again for lunch."

CHAPTER FORTY-FIVE

Kim was back in her section HQ. She had a meeting with Control in a few minutes. At the appointed time, she pressed her fingers and palms left and right in turn against a panel that appeared to be made of glass. A red light above her head flicked off. A green light shone in its stead and the door slid to one side.

"Come in, come in, *ma belle*. Sit down here on the sofa. Tea? Coffee? San Pellegrino? Or some other water of yet another spa, or how about Canada Dry? Let's be comfortable. You are *ravissante* as always. And I must congratulate you yet again. Wonderful."

She sat on the sofa, resting one arm along its brown leather back and Control hovered by the Louis XV table on which an array of drinks had been placed on an enormous silver tray. He was a solidly built man of about forty-five with a rugged Jean Gabin face, though he was taller than the famous actor. He could have been sired by Gabin on some tall and slender leading lady from Hollywood—but he was not. His father, in fact, had been a French career diplomat, his mother the daughter of a specialist maker of sports cars who had sold out to one of the automobile giants in the late 1950s. His mother, until she was eighty, enjoyed driving fast cars. She had had exceptionally fast reflexes. Control had inherited these.

Control's genial good humour was genuine, but also served as an effective mask. He was meticulously professional. His calculations were as accurate as those of the computer he regularly used, and, when necessary, as heartless. They were informed, however, by an understanding and an instinct that computers do not yet possess. Control understood human beings in all their moods and had an instinct for anticipating the likely actions of those he was asked to defeat. He had had more successes than failures. He had lost very few agents to enemy action or simple betrayal. This was one of his best rewards, since most of their and his activities remained undisclosed to the press. When he retired, that event would be marked by the discreet award of a medal and a comfortable pension. His agents, of course, knew nothing of his private life—if, indeed, he had any.

"Canada Dry, please. No ice, no liquor."

"Good. I'll have the same."

Control crossed the white and gilt room, traversing the splendid Persian carpet. Butler-like, he carried the drinks on a small silver tray, which he set down on the antique lacquered table in front of the sofa. *Eighteenth century Japonaiserie,* thought Kim. She always liked this table on the rare occasions she was in this room. This was, in effect, only the third time she had been with Control in his sanctum since she was assigned to section.

"What's all this about early retirement, Kate?"

Control was using the name she had been recruited under, Kate Corbet. She was supposedly the daughter of a Frenchman, now passed away, who had worked in Alexandria and had married a local beauty, half Egyptian and half English. Kate knew her own beauty as a problem but she also knew how to use it. When she was using her great-great grandmother's name Kalitza in Hong Kong, that inherited beauty had provided a solution to a tricky situation. She turned too many heads. She used disguises, of course. Control had removed her from one or two troublesome situations by having her killed under assumed identities. This procedure sometimes involved fake archive material. It was easy enough to plant and to retrieve, if necessary. It amused him to think of archival researchers finding such material years later and treating it as fact.

Kate smiled at his use of her genuine name instead of her *Nomenklatura* codename, Kim. In fact, Robert Corbet, her mother had confided once, was not her father except in name. Her father had been a Scot, but her mother would not reveal which of the men in her Alexandrian entourage at the time had been the culprit as she had put it, chuckling to herself. Kate took a sip of her Canada Dry.

"I know you respect my work, Monsieur Martin, but I feel I am getting a little blurred at the edge, like a blade that needs resharpening. And, I am no longer a young woman ready to risk all for the Republic."

Control was amused by her tit for tat use of his real name instead of Control.

"It would be regrettable, very disappointing, if we were to lose you at this stage. You are ready to join me in planning, you know, and there'll be a vacancy there in about a year's time. And you are by no means long in the tooth, Kate."

"Am I a planner, though, Monsieur Martin? Am I farsighted and subtle enough? Am I cold enough?"

"You've just summed up some of the qualities I look for in that aspect of our work."

"Yes, but have I *enough* of those qualities?"

"Look, you have another operation, because of those famous earrings we've matched up. You'll have to have a little refresher in waterworks, starting tomorrow. You can whet your edge with that! You'll have to work over Easter I'm afraid. But after this operation you can take off for a couple of months. Have a good rest and go to a gym every day as well! Then we'll talk again."

"I really do want to retire."

"Out of the question, Kim. Oh. We'll see. Don't tell me you've met a handsome civilian?"

"No, sir, but one day I shall."

"Is that a promise or a threat, Kim?"

"I would never threaten you, *Patron*. It's a promise to myself."

"Let it remain a promise, Kate, my dear, for a while to come. You deserve only the very best of mortals. I expect you know you're a goddess?"

"Flattery will get you into my good books, Control, but I still want to retire."

He finished his drink and waved her request letter and file at her. "We'll talk again, when you come back from your mission, if I'm free. If not, it can wait until you get back from the leave I've promised you."

"You'll really give me that long leave? You won't go back on it, sir?"

He stood up and looked at her with a how-can-you-suggest-such-a-thing expression on his rugged face. He did not speak though, until she was near the door.

"Good luck. Come back safe and sound and successful, Kim. As usual."

Control pressed a concealed button and his door slid open. The interview was over.

***

Kim walked to the operations room to examine the orders for her mission. Her first job was to report to River Police in Paris. Water again. Then fly to Antibes and to England, if necessary, for the real thing.

Who was that British woman who evoked life as a frog? Shapcott. Yes. The lines swam around in her consciousness. Kim closed her eyes. *Mm. Yes, Jo Shapcott. That was it.*

CHAPTER FORTY-SIX

River Police had a secret divers' complex, small, but highly effective as a suitable base, under the land surrounding Notre Dame. Divers could emerge from the tunnels beneath water level and swim along the Seine well below the river traffic. The new wet suit she had tested with Bruno was ultra-thin, very tough, a second skin, and yet warm as a duvet on a cold night. It came in various colors according to need for specific jobs. Kim was issued with a dark suit perfectly matching the color of the Seine on a spring day. The fabric was capable of stopping small arms fire and leaving very sore bruises. Her helmet, looking like a sleek wig, had sound-link equipment in slim and concealed headphones that also countered pressure changes. The air supply equipment was no bigger than a half bottle of Scotch, but was good for two hours under the surface. Goggles slipped down from inside the wig or could slip up inside it. A pair of sunglasses could also be attached to the wig and worn on top of the head until needed. They were specially designed for night vision and murky water. The diver's watch was issued with a small capsule that, once detached, could slip under the tongue. This gave out enriched air in small amounts automatically every three seconds. It could be used in emergencies. It lasted only a few minutes; 195 seconds to be precise.

The officer in charge of "refreshers" and known to her as Yves was satisfied with her performance after a day of exercises. She was ready to go on mission.

"When you go swimming, Kim," he said, "you might be wearing that nude look suit again, or something less spectacular, but don't forget your watch or your flippers!"

"Thanks a lot. I'll remember that good advice, Yves. When I get back, we'll celebrate with a plate of frogs legs at L'Escargot."

"You're on. Good luck, safe journey."

And that was it. She was off to Antibes and to whatever awaited her there. She was amused to think that if she survived this one, she would be back in England very soon. As it turned out, she was sent over to England—and much sooner than she expected. By the time she arrived in Antibes, there had been further rapid developments. An earring of crescent moon design had been matched positively with one found in a doctor's surgery in Sutton Coldfield. It seemed to be connected with a burglary in which files had been disturbed, probably copied, and nothing had been stolen.

"You can't look at the two corpses again, but study these pix. Good, aren't they, Rosalind?" She was known to the people down here on this mission as Rosalind Kenyon still.

"Handle this earring. The Anglo-Saxons have the other. They let our guy examine it. They might let you see it, but you might not need to do so. It's just a link and neither of those women is wearing these particular earrings again."

"Who were those women? Do I need to know?"

"You don't need to know. Let's say they were a bit careless and someone nasty got hold of them. The Anglo-Saxons have a lead to a mosque. Black Country, they said. You will work with an agent they have. He knows which mosque. Call him Momo. He'll meet you at Birmingham." He showed Kim another photograph.

"Handsome brute, isn't he? Memorize this remark he'll make as you walk past him, 'I saw you in Poughkeepsie,' pronounced 'pukipsy.'"

"Will he say 'pronounced pukipsy' or only the first five words?"

"Hi, hi, hi! *Très drôle*, or as they say over there, ha bloody ha! First five only. He'll get you out of the airport without any formalities. He'll give you any arms you need."

"What about my waterworks equipment, I won't need it now?" She sounded disappointed.

"If you do, get a message to us through Momo, or to Loire Valley if Momo is unavailable. Give the color needed for the suit, et cetera. Greyish brown is in demand in England. We'll get it to you in less than three hours, if it's fairly urgent. If not, give us a day."

"Is Momo one of ours? Working for us, or the Brits? Or both?"

"Don't know. Only thing is, he can be trusted. He's kosher, if I might use the expression."

***

Paul and Mary were in Mary's bed, soundly asleep at 6:00 a.m. as only contented young couples, or even youngish couples can be, when the phone rang. Mary yawned and reached for the bedside phone that was sitting up on its base like a dog on a rug and begging to be answered.

"Is that Mary?"

"Yes. Who's this?"

"It's Graham, Paul's friend. He gave me your number when I called him earlier on his mobile."

"Do you know what time it is here?"

"Oh God, I woke you. It's, my God, it's just after six."

"Yep. It doesn't matter. Here's Paul."

"Graham. You oaf. No, stop apologizing. It's okay. We'll get up and have some brekkie, while we think up a punishment for you. Why are you ringing?"

"We were diverted because of some terrorist alert. We landed in Shannon! Then we managed to get on a plane to Birmingham. We arrived so late that we stayed in an airport hotel. Didn't want to disturb you in the early hours. Zonked out. Woke up and rang. I guess I'm disoriented about the time."

Mary gestured to Paul and he gave her the phone.

"Graham, it's Mary. Where are you staying? Aha. I know that extraordinary place! Actually, the breakfast is okay. Included? Well, I suggest we drive over and pick you up. We'll have breakfast here, you have it there, and then we'll meet you in the hotel lobby."

"That's great. But how long a drive is it? We don't want to give you a hassle."

"We'll live with it. Here's Paul." Mary handed Paul the phone and said it would take about forty-five minutes, what with traffic, to get to their airport hotel.

"Graham, Paul again. We'll see you in the lobby at eight forty-five a.m. or nine a.m. Sounds good. No, of course not. We can chat on the way to Sutton. It's cool."

"See ya!" He heard Graham's voice with a rush of pleasure. Paul handed the phone back to Mary.

"Well, we're off to an early start," she said. "You've probably a lot of catching up to do. And I want to see this Samantha woman."

"Yes. So do I. He says some people call her Sam."

"Sam, Sam . . ." said Mary, imitating a Music Hall turn.

"Pick up thy musket," said Paul.

Mary got hold of his penis and started to tug him to get him out of bed. "No musket drill. Breakfast!" she said.

CHAPTER FORTY-SEVEN

Kim walked past an Indian man who sat near the entry to the building where the small plane had come to a standstill. He had said the five magic words. She walked to a door marked LADIES above which was a silhouette of a woman in what appeared to be a crinoline dress. The man followed her inside after a few seconds.

"Call me Momo."

"Momo, how good to meet you. I'm Rosalind to you and to strangers."

"Well, I'll be blowed," he said. "Follow me."

Momo went into a cubicle, which turned out to be simply a sort of vestibule. There was a door where the lavatory should have been. They went through the door into an anonymous plasterboard corridor. This turned a few corners and stopped at another door. Momo opened the door and then opened the rear door of a car parked just outside. He got in, followed by Kim as Rosalind. It was comfortable and private, having dark, tinted windows. The driver was separated from them as in a taxi. In fact, when they emerged onto the roads, Kim realized the car was a taxi. She kept her bag on her lap.

"You, Rosalind, are one of my wives, visiting me and then going off to Morocco to stay with a couple of retired relatives on my mother's side."

"Excellent. But no monkey business."

"How could you suggest such a thing to a man of honour?" Momo grinned. He had a lovely smile with a glimpse of good teeth, not the irregular and stained variety. "I'll introduce you to people at the mosque. You will wear Arab dress and keep your face and hair covered most of the time."

"Good. My obedience might keep me safe from prying eyes. Tell me what you know about the earrings."

"Ah yes, those. We had an English woman, a convert to Islam. She attended the mosque and she wore the earrings on occasion. She was, in fact, an agent working for us. She and another woman, I think French, also working for us, looked up some files in a doctor's office. They were medical files on a number of men suspected of being in a terrorist, criminal network. I am not privy to the reason for this minor operation! Probably the operative was angry that an earring was lost."

"They were valuable?"

"If they were genuine, they would be. She told me they were diamonds set in a white gold crescent. The largest stones in the centre and flanked on each side by three smaller stones, making seven in each or fourteen in total for the pair. The biggest stones were one carat each."

"Really?"

"She wasn't just angry, she was hopping mad when she lost one!"

"I'll bet. She didn't break in again to try to find it?"

"No. A Cambridge Arabist, another convert, who attends the mosque when not in Cambridge, told her the police had it."

"How did he know?"

"He's one of ours, also."

"Well, I'll be blowed!" said Kim. "Two converts, two agents. One Brit down, one of ours down, and two Brits to go and one Frenchy to go, if you count me in."

"The two ladies I call the angels. There were positive identifications of the corpses you have over there. They disappeared one day when shopping in Handsworth."

"Yes. Then they turn up dead off the French coast in La Baie des Anges. How did they get to France? Do we know?"

"Our Cambridge Arab I call Porky Pig, but don't tell him that, says they told him they were following a lead. Something to do with a file they had seen in a doctor's office. They had to be away for a day or two. Porky is known at the mosque and to us as Dr. Westlake."

Kalitza laughed. Then she had a sudden image of the library in the club. *I wonder*, she thought. "Will I be meeting him?"

"If he attends the mosque this vacation, you might."

The car stopped at the back of a nondescript house in a terrace of identical houses with depressing back gardens. They were next to a garage door. They slipped out of the taxi and then into the garage, where an unremarkable Toyota Corolla was parked. The taxi moved off. Kim and Momo walked from the garage to the house along a pathway covered with a curved plastic roof held aloft on sturdy poles. This was ostensibly to guard against rain and snow, but it also made it difficult for prying eyes to see who was coming and going.

"This is one of our safe houses. Get to here if you have to. Otherwise, keep clear. We'll operate, in fact, from where I live."

Momo then briefed Kim on their mission, with the aid of large format maps of Birmingham, Dudley, and Wolverhampton. He had photographs of three young males and two females who were most probably part of a network of terrorists. One of them, the older of the two women, certainly was a terrorist in Momo's opinion.

Momo had been supplied with some listening and tracking devices. They came in pairs. There were thin strips that self-adhered to the inner edge of the heel of a shoe under the instep. These could be stuck to the shoes the worshippers took off when entering the mosque or on other occasions. It was difficult to detect them. Each strip worked in a link with a central monitoring base. The other sophisticated component adhered to a garment, under a lapel, or somewhere near the neck of the target, or on a sleeve or near a hem. These devices looked like a small cotton thread and were supplied in several colors. Matches could be made up for specific garments and then might go undetected for days or weeks. They survived movements, but might be brushed off or lost in dry cleaning, washing, and drying. Ironing would probably not destroy them, according to Momo, unless the iron was very hot. These threads, too, were monitored, being audible in special listening vehicles. A very useful feature of both devices was that the listeners knew where the targets were whenever they spoke. Conversations were recorded automatically and their positions clicked on map coordinates as people moved about. Another advantage was that they went with the target and so one did not have to break and enter a place to plant a bug that was useful only when someone was at home.

"Nanotechnology is a wonderful thing, Momo, *n'est ce pas?*"

Momo rubbed his hands together with glee and wriggled his fingers, as if he were Fagin about to demonstrate how to pick a pocket for the young Mr. Twist.

CHAPTER FORTY-EIGHT

Mary and Paul met their guests as arranged. In the car on the way back to Sutton, they all got better acquainted. Greg was amazed by the number of small houses and shops and the rarity of countryside. For him, England was kinda clustered and huddled. Towns were so big they seemed to go on forever. Paul agreed, but added there was still a good deal of wonderful countryside. Very little of it was nature's countryside, rugged and wild. Most of it, he explained, had been rearranged by mankind over centuries. Mary and Samantha soon arrived at exchanging notes on the quirks of surgeons they knew and Graham kept touching Paul on the shoulders in an affectionate way, as if he needed simple human contact in his desperate loneliness.

Lunch at Mary's was a happy affair of homemade chicken tikka, beef and vegetable curry, with patna rice and an array of side dishes, mango chutney, poppadums and nan bread. The meal and the talk stretched through the afternoon. They all went to a nearby Post House for a drink in the evening and a bite to eat in the coffee shop before the visitors went early to bed. Paul and Mary drove home. The plan was for them all to go to Lichfield the next day to explore the town and attend a service with the Cathedral School choir. That night Samantha and Greg had another early night while Paul and Graham talked over beers in the bar. Mary stayed in and caught up on some of the medical reading she needed to do.

"It's really good to see you again, Graham, after everything that's happened."

"You, too. What do you think of Samantha?"

"She's a very capable person and attractive. Distinct sex appeal."

"Yes. I'm not involved with her, though. Greg's her buffer zone! It's better that way. I am still living with a woman I loved who was stupidly murdered by rotten bastards. Samantha's getting over a thing she had going that turned sour. But, we get on and like the companionship we can offer each other every so often. It's a comfort for us both."

"Do you need to move around, travel? Is that why you're here?"

"That's true. I needed to talk to you, just be with you, you know? You don't have to offer words of wisdom or anything."

"Yeah, I know. It just helps to be with some old friends sometimes."

Paul, you are one of my oldest friends. And dearest."

"Aw shucks, fella!"

"It's true."

"I know. I value our being pals for so long. It's a rare thing nowadays. A year seems long to some people. Friends are instant and instantly forgettable with some people. Friends shouldn't have 'use by' dates stamped on them. Speech over." They drank some more beer.

"Are you coming over in the summer, Graham?"

"Maybe. It all depends on how I feel. I'm supposed to be working on an academic book about autobiographies. But I'll probably need to go somewhere totally different."

"Cuba?"

"Actually, I was thinking of Africa. One of those safari packages, Paul—that could be something very special. It's expensive, though. And then renting a place in a quiet town with no distractions. Or are you and Mary interested in a trip to Corsica? We could go there together."

"Hmm. Are you just trying to run away from yourself?"

"Maybe. I don't know. I was stupid enough, lousy enough, to think Jacqueline was pregnant by another man. She *was* pregnant. It was certainly our child."

"Christ. That double murder seems even more senseless."

A cocktail waitress asked them if they wanted another round.

"Yes, please," said Paul.

Graham's eyes had filled with tears. He wiped them with a clean handkerchief. "That girl's manner reminded me of Jacqueline. Don't know why. I'm sorry."

"Don't be. You have to talk about her and let grief loose. It's natural."

"Words are fine. But they don't bring people back, do they?"

"No."

"They fill a void for a moment. Break a silence."

"Comforting at times. They offer a comfort, Graham. Like a log crackling in a fire."

"Do you think I'm unfaithful, bringing Samantha here, even under these strictly proper conditions?"

"Unfaithful? Do you mean disloyal?"

"I think that's it: disloyal."

"No, I don't. Oh, Graham, no, it's a sign of healing. You're beginning to heal. You are too alive to lose interest in life and the world and other people."

The waitress brought their drinks and this time Graham's eyes did not swim with tears.

"I hope you're right," he said.

"I think I am, but just now Mary and I must seem insufferably smug to you."

"Yes, you rotters."

"Now that's what I like to hear. You're bouncing back again, even if you sound like a schoolboy in a comic book."

"Now what about this Kalitza—is she still a . . . an obsession?"

"No. I think you and Mary are right. She represents something in me that I was projecting and, maybe, protecting. But I am very much conscious that something in me unblocked and now I can truly . . . well, marry Mary! If I saw Kalitza again, I would not follow or try to accost her."

"Good. You've crossed a sort of crisis line. You've come to terms with something in you, yes?"

"I'm sure of it. I feel free. I think Kalitza was an unforeseen help of some kind, whoever she is."

" 'Who will grieve for this woman? . . . In my heart I never will deny her . . .'"

There was a silence. The words were there, binding them for a moment, invisibly. Paul and Graham both knew they were the language of genius. Paul broke the silence.

"Who said that?"

"Anna Akhmatova."

"Ah . . . when the chips are down, we need poetry, even if we don't value it most of the time."

"The best thing about my teaching is contact with talented young adults. It's the knowledge that, despite TV news, the world is not just crime, terror, and misery. The young people in the schools and universities give me hope for the future. The next is that I'm paid to read books I'd read anyway."

"Well, that's good, Graham. Enjoy it. I bet you're good at your job."

"I try."

"You don't boast a lot, do you, Graham?"

"I try not to."

"We're all pretty insignificant in most ways, like Akhmatova's woman, but we still matter—at least, to each other."

***

Kim as Rosalind, in Arab dress with a burkha covering her face, also wearing a thread device that could be tracked by an Anglo-French unit called *Val de Loire*, went with Momo to the mosque. If she got into any difficulties, her own people would hear her immediate remarks or those around her, and would know where she was. With a bit of luck, they could extract her. Rosalind wore the thread inside the waist of her panties, snug against her hip. After prayers, she followed respectfully behind Momo to a group outside, chatting before going off in their various directions. One of them was the suspect woman, known to him as Jasmin Habibi. There was a sneeze behind Momo and then another. They all turned to greet Dr. Westlake. He spoke rapidly in Arabic about the weather and a tiring journey he had had from Cambridge driving on crowded roads to get a few days' peace at home. He had no trace of a British accent. He sounded Moroccan more than anything. It so turned out that Porky Pig *was* the club library sneezer. Rosalind was pleased that he could not see her face.

Momo and Rosalind had entered the mosque just after Jasmin, their chief suspect. Momo had placed his own shoes next to hers. It had been a simple matter to put the device on the heel of one of her sturdy walking shoes. After the prayers, when they were all talking in a little group outside the mosque, a man had approached selling roses. Momo bought one for his suspect and another for Kim. He pinned one on Kim's coat.

"This is my wife, visiting from back home," he said to the little group.

The suspect, Jasmin, was holding her rose and started to pin it on her coat.

"Can I help?" Momo pressed her lapel between finger and thumb.

"No, I can manage."

"Good enough," replied Momo.

"Do you always allow your husband to buy roses for other women as well?" Jasmin asked.

Rosalind looked down modestly. Only her eyelids were now visible. "My husband is a man of honour and gallantry," she said, thinking at the same time, and if truth were told, he's a bit of an Egyptian conjuror. He's done it.

Jasmin cut across the chat to ask, "Why are you called by this very English name, Rosalind?"

"My father liked it above all other names. He had once met a woman with that name in Alexandria."

"How strange!" said Jasmin, shrugging.

Rosalind listened to the chatter. It was pretty standard. The Mullah was a good, moderate man. He was not like those stirring up racist as well as religious hatred of westerners and their democratic societies. As they were leaving the mosque later on, Jasmin said she had to run because of an appointment. Westlake asked if he could give her a lift anywhere. She thanked him and declined gracefully. They all split up and Rosalind followed Momo respectfully, a few paces behind him. She felt very odd doing this. But she was glad she was almost totally shrouded from prying eyes. It was an excellent cover.

Back in their marital home, she took off her veils and deactivated the personnel bug she was wearing.

"Why have I been sent over here, I wonder? You seem to have it all under control, Momo. That Porky Westlake is an amazing Arab linguist."

"Dr. Westlake is a phenomenon all right. Actually, I've no idea why you're here, but I am very pleased you are. You make an excellent wife. Ours not to wonder why. The world of Special Branch is a mighty maze, but not without a plan!"

"I'd have drunk to that before I became your fourth wife."

There was a ring at the front doorbell. It was a man from the gas company.

"Problems with the cooker, love?" he said, when Kim opened the door.

"Yes," said Momo from behind her in the hall.

"Well, I'd better have a look at it, sweetheart," the man declared with a wink, as Kim closed the door behind him.

"Rosalind, let me present Pike. He's a wonder man." They shook hands.

"Momo, I've been sent directly to brief you and show you some toy maps and things. People are moving earlier than expected. Everything has to move fast. There was a message almost immediately after prayers from the purposeful Jasmin. She rang from a public box to Dr. Westlake's mobile phone. We know its number, of course, but we haven't had luck on the mobile phone front recently. We were not listening in on him, anyway."

"Right."

"Jasmin spoke of an operation planned for two days hence. New Street Station is a target. Kamikazes were mentioned and a depot where they have a cache of explosives," Pike informed them.

"Did the serene Jasmin tell us its address by any chance?"

"No such luck. But the old Porker replied. It was him all right. No mistake."

"Did Dr. Porker Westlake ring you to tell you the glad tidings?"

"No. Not yet. I have a funny feeling he's been turned and gone double."

"The bastard!" exclaimed Momo and added, "I didn't think a man that big could go double!"

Pike grinned and his small, sharp teeth suddenly made sense of his code name. "Good one, Momo. But he did give us a clue. He asked how long it would take them to *walk* from the explosives dump to the New Street station mall."

"Huh."

"Twelve minutes. And then she said, 'but the others will take a little over fifteen minutes by boat to target'!"

"So, it's two-pronged. Have you sent the transcript anywhere yet?"

"No. I left the others in place with orders not to reveal anything yet. In view of the Porker, I thought I'd come straight to you."

"Give that man a kiss, Rosalind, I think we'll have roast pork tonight, whatever the dietary restrictions."

"If things are moving this fast, let's look at one of our toys." Pike took a large format map from his tool kit and spread it out on the table.

"Here's New Street station. Now a circle of ten minutes to fifteen walking time."

"Look. A canal," said Kim.

"Rosalind has hit the nail on the head," said Momo.

"It's about five minutes from the coffee stalls and wine bar barges near the Arts Centre. Oh God, there's usually a crowd of kids around there. Or further along the canal, there's another busy place," added Pike.

"Any likely buildings along that stretch of the canal between the centre and this place?" asked Kim, placing a slender forefinger on the map.

"It's mainly Victorian warehouses. A shambles of light industry. Ideal," replied Pike.

"I think they'll bring a barge up the canal as well," observed Kim.

"If they've got explosives dumped there, why bother with a barge? It's slow. Just get your bombs from the dump and walk into the crowds." As he spoke, Pike looked sceptically at Kim.

"You could be right," she murmured, "but what important buildings are there around the area?"

"Apart from the arts complex, there are the wine bar barges and offices for business and civic affairs. Full of files. If they go up, there'll be administrative chaos. A barge bomb in the middle of all that . . . Bugger me, I think you're right, darling."

"I suggest we have some people take a discreet walk from the station through streets small and narrow that will take them to points where buildings back onto the canal. I'll go along, too," suggested Momo.

"Why don't you and Rosalind do this alone? We've already got a possible leak. We can involve the Special Branch when we need them, say last thing tonight after a recce. That will leave just the three of us needing to know as long as possible," Pike said.

"Can we mobilize enough firepower at the last minute to make the arrests?" asked Kim.

"No sweat, Ros darling," smiled Pike, adding, "You two go for a walk and I'll get back to analyze what else has come up from the air waves."

"Agreed," said Momo. "I'll call your number when we have the gen from our walk."

Pike left and Kim told Momo she would be ready in a few minutes. She went up to her room and into the en suite bathroom. She went to the toilet and tapped a three digit number on her mobile phone.

"*Val de Loire, parfumerie*," said a female voice.

"Rosalind. One set of waterworks equipment needed. Deliver to Proctor's Private Bank in Birmingham city centre tomorrow before seven a.m."

"*Difficile.*"

"Can do? No can do?"

"Can do. But we can sometimes hear your tummy rumbling!"

"Well, live with it. I do!" Kim cut the line and flushed the toilet. She washed her hands and put on her veil. Less than twenty minutes later, she was following Momo from New Street station along the roads they had earmarked on the map. About ten minutes later, they were in a street that was narrow enough to be Victorian and was a messy mixture of buildings. They passed a run-down looking pub with a grimy sign saying, The Bargee's Arms. Next door was a place with windows made of dark reflecting glass, one door, and a small sign in brass with one word engraved on it, Tamco. Next door but one to Tamco was a red brick factory with a large sign saying that Britpak, a construction firm, was going to develop the space into convenient modern offices for lease.

"That's a likely customer," said Momo.

They walked further and five minutes later emerged into a windy crossroads with a traffic island. They crossed the road and sat on a metal bench in a vandalized bus shelter further disfigured by graffiti. Momo took out a Welcome to Birmingham tourist map.

"That development site is about here," he said, placing a stubby forefinger on the map.

"Tamco might also serve their purposes," said Kim.

Momo nodded assent and folded the map. A bus was approaching. They got on it and got off again when it was in a busy street. They stood in a doorway and Momo spoke into a mobile phone.

"Momo," Pike replied with his one word code name.

"Anything fishy going on?" asked Momo.

"The fat's sizzling. We go tomorrow!" There was a click and Momo put the phone back in a pocket.

"Rosalind, let's go to the fish and chip shop," said Momo.

They were not far from the parking lot at the old Snow Hill station site. Momo found the car he kept parked there, courtesy of the British government. It was a battered old Rover to look at, but was modified under its bonnet and on the chassis; it could, in fact, outperform many a sleek seduction model, if Momo needed to outrun someone. He rarely needed to break the speed limit, however, for he knew how to look after himself. He anticipated. He planned carefully. The "submarine," or "Fish and Chip shop" as Momo called it, was parked in Lambourne Road, on a stretch bounded by high walls. Momo drove past and turned a little further along the road. There were no people in the street. Momo and Rosalind got out and walked to Pike's Ford Transit van. A side door slid open and Momo climbed inside the van followed by Rosalind.

Pike and his assistant were wearing ear pieces. Everything they heard was recorded and also entered automatically into a computer. There was, if they needed it, instant print out. If the voice was in a language and then suddenly switched to another language, it was possible to get the automatic transcript printed out in both languages.

"Madam ringleader says they have to be at the factory at five p.m. in order to get maximum damage in the crowds and make the nine p.m. news."

"Tomorrow?" asked Momo.

"She isn't saying in so many words. But traffic intensity suggests it. There's a big festival with hordes of people in the station and canal areas tomorrow. It'll be happy hour in the wine bars and pubs. She'll tell them at the last minute, I think. Maybe tomorrow morning."

"Do we know how many?" asked Rosalind.

"Four. Madam herself will give them the word and be heroically watching out at home in Handsworth. That's what she told Westlake. She's going to pray for them."

"Terrific boss. Very thoughtful," added Momo.

"Hang on. She's talking to Porky again. I'll be hanged if he's not getting ready to catch a train. She's saying a pity you couldn't stay another day or two. He says he's got to be in Cambridge tomorrow. She's wishing him a good trip. Try to watch the news tomorrow, she says. Gotcha madam."

Pike turned to them with a grimace of triumph. His row of small teeth, with two pointed canines showing like sentinels, gleamed between his dark-red, rather shiny lips.

Not a pretty smile, thought Kim.

"So, it's tomorrow. But she hasn't told the others yet. And we don't know where the factory is. Westlake is not offering us anything?" asked Momo.

"No. He's turned, I fear. He's supposed to be intelligent, poor sod. No luck today as to whereabouts?" asked Pike.

"Not yet confirmed, but we have likely premises near The Bargee's Arms."

"Nothing coming through now."

"Okay, Pikelet, we'll continue our search," Momo said.

"Okay you two, all clear, off you go."

They slid open the door, got out of the van, and walked to the car they had left some way into another road.

"What now?" asked Rosalind.

"I think, Rosalind, we'll have to see a man about a dog."

A couple of skinheads were rapidly coming towards them. They wore huge boots and studded gear. As they approached, they grinned.

"A couple of saintly Pakis."

"Shall we do 'em?"

"Why not?" said the first, pulling a knife out of his pocket.

"It's a fucking black ghetto here. Let it go."

The knife man lunged at Momo. The other jumped at Kim, landing in front of her with his arms and legs akimbo.

"Booh!" he shouted.

Momo grabbed the knife man's wrist, pulling him even further forward, and rapped his other fist hard and fast into the man's neck. He coughed and choked. Momo kicked the knife man's knee cap. One down. The other glanced to see what was going on. Kim moved in fast, threw him to the ground, and stamped on his neck. Kim and Momo looked at each other. It had taken less than ten seconds.

"Heads?" asked Kim. Momo nodded and they both banged the shaven heads on the pavement until they drew blood. They walked to the car and drove away. Pike was chuckling as he monitored it all in the van.

"They must have been color blind or something," said Momo. Kim smiled.

CHAPTER FORTY-NINE

Paul crept into the flat, but Mary had not yet gone to bed. "Graham is still pretty fragile. He wept again," said Paul.

"I think Samantha is a good thing just at the moment. Greg keeps him thinking in the present, too."

"That's a point," Paul responded.

"Do you feel like a walk around the block and back?" asked Mary.

"Yes, let's."

They walked and talked for about twenty minutes. It was a mild night with no wind and not a hint of rain. Mary had decided that Samantha was a very competent and healthy woman. *We could be friends*, she thought, *if they are to become regular visitors to the United Kingdom and if she and Paul went to Vancouver from time to time.* It was agreeable to meet new people with different lives. She thought Samantha an excellent example of a single mother. She was dynamic, not a ditherer. She was firm with Greg, but clearly showed her love for him. The happy result, perhaps, was that Greg was turning into a very decent young man. Or else he was just decent and coped with the family rift quietly in his own way. *Do we ever really fathom another human being? Everyone has a shadow or shadows, and even if we live examined lives, do we understand ourselves? We can deliver surprises, even to ourselves*, she mused. *Other people delivered surprises quite regularly. That's the nature of life. Especially when we reach a fork in the road. Graham and Paul, on their different paths, had reached forks. Paul had made a choice. What would Graham do?*

"Graham has changed so much since I was vaguely aware of him, when you two were students knocking about together," Mary observed.

"Yes. This has been a bitter and terrible thing. I think he needs a complete change. He's thinking of taking off to Africa or Corsica. Anywhere."

"Is that running away from himself?" asked Mary.

"I thought that. I don't really know. He suggested we might go to Corsica with him."

"That's not a good idea. I'm too busy. I bet you are, too."

"Yes. You can say that again. He forgets I don't get four months of pay with no classes in the summer!"

"That's a pretty good deal. Four months!" exclaimed Mary.

"I think I'll suggest he apply for a sabbatical for next September and go away to Portugal or somewhere quiet to think and to meet a Fado singer and write an academic book."

"If he met a Fado singer, he'd not write the book," laughed Mary.

"Maybe he just needs to plunge into a really absorbing academic project, or become a head or a dean. Then his time would be filled with worries of other people, budgets, and all that. A new direction for him."

"He's at a fork in the road. Maybe he needs to meet your Kalitza!"

"She'd lead him a merry dance."

"Would you be jealous, Paul?"

"Jealous? No. Not a bit."

"Not a teeny weeny bit?"

"Not a teeny weeny bit."

He put his arm around Mary. He could feel her warmth. They smiled and headed for home.

"No," he resumed, "not a jot. Kalitza's a very lovely woman, but she's a sort of experience of force and release. I needed her. I needed those strange experiences and appearances and maybe the disappearances, just when they occurred. Now I don't. I need you, Mary, I need you."

She turned to him. She put a hand on his shoulder, saying, "I need you, too."

They left it at that. It was enough.

***

The street running parallel to a canal in Birmingham was deserted except for an Indian man with his wife following respectfully behind him, and, a little ahead of them, a comfortable middle-aged married couple walking their dog. The dog started pulling on its lead and growling as if it smelled a rat.

"He's smelt a rat," said the woman.

"Yes. Tamco. Look at the way he's scratching that door. Well, we must be on our way," said the man, giving the dog something in his left hand, and then pulling the dog with him to a nearby fire hydrant. The dog gave it a brief doggy squirt.

"Good boy! Well, my dear, we'll walk Prince home and have a nice cuppa."

"Good idea," said his wife.

To any observer there was nothing unusual in the scene. They reached the red brick building and the dog made for the doors. If it had not been on a leash, it might have leapt at the doors. The man pulled it on and made for a lamp post several yards further along.

"And that one."

"I say," said Kim to herself and to Pike, who was listening now that she was 'turned on.'

"I say, I say. Capital. Top hole," she continued as she reached Tamco and stopped to take a tissue from her bag. She dabbed at her nose.

"Site one." She resumed her walk and then stopped to examine a notice board advertising office premises to be let. The board covered a window of the red brick building.

"Site two," she said.

The couple with the dog and the Indian couple following them continued up the road in an unhurried way. Pike noted

Rosalind's position on his map and pinpointed the two buildings.

***

The next morning in Sutton Coldfield, Mary and Paul awakened to a perfect spring day. The friends all met for breakfast at Mary's flat. They would take a picnic lunch to Lichfield, since the weather was so lovely. After exploring the town and the area around there, they would have tea in the Beaux Stratagem Hotel and then go to the cathedral for a magnificent evensong. After that, it would be fun to have dinner in a country restaurant on spec or by reservation if they found a decent place in a village during the afternoon jaunt. Graham, Samantha, and Greg would do most of their packing before going to bed, so as to be ready to fly to Paris next day. While the adults, sitting around the kitchen table, were discussing these plans, they heard from the sitting room a ravishing sound. It was a moody piano piece by Chopin, played with a lingering, caressing touch.

"Listen everyone," demanded Paul. And they listened.

"That's so clear. The radio or a disc?" asked Graham.

Samantha smiled and said, with no little measure of mother's pride, "It's Mary's piano. Greg's trying it out!"

"He's wonderful!" exclaimed Mary. "I just cannot make it sound like that."

"Does he have lessons?" asked Paul.

"Yes. Twice, sometimes three times a week. He practices at home for an hour or two every day."

"You don't push him to do it though, do you?" Graham asked.

"No. He started thumping the piano when he was two and he has always liked music. I started him on lessons when he was interested enough to take them. He can pick out things and play by ear as well. I love to hear him settle down to play after he's finished his homework. Sometimes, I just sit with a book, not reading but thinking, with the music flooding around me." Samantha stopped suddenly. Then she sighed, "I don't want it to stop; one day, though, he'll leave home."

"You sound very happy," said Mary.

"Oh, I am. We do well, even with no dad around."

"More coffee or tea anyone?" asked Paul brightly.

***

"I'm Pike. I'm Pike. Solihull, do you read me?"

"Solihull here. I read you, Pike."

"Good. All five weasels can be bagged today, repeat today, after fourteen thirty and before fifteen hundred hours."

"Understood. Details as agreed."

"All have big eyes and ears?"

"Yes. As usual."

"Great. Out."

Pike needed to call Momo and Rosalind. He would check with his big white chief, Solihull, as required. In fact, at that moment Momo and his wife were leaving their house to drive to Pike's submarine.

Momo dialed a number on his special mobile phone.

"Pike."

"Momo with Rosalind. Have you had the removal men?"

"Yes. We're in Wood Lane, near the vet's surgery."

"I know the place. It's nice to have a change of scene. We'll be over to see you in a few minutes. Bye!"

Pike and Solihull, the Boss Man for this operation, would arrange for the rapid capture of the two premises on the canal bank. A few minutes later, Momo banged on the side of the van and they both climbed in to consult with Pike. Two anonymous aides were now there as "big ears" listening for traffic on their headsets.

"Have you been able to arrange already for two separate teams, one for each building?" asked Momo.

"They can both be ready by 1300 hours," Pike responded.

"Truly wonderful! How did you manage it?" queried Rosalind.

"Quite simple nowadays, Ros," Pike grinned, "The PM is not worried about our budget—if we get results. Frankly, the authorities are so pissed off with these killers that they work hard to do what we ask. Luckily, we've been getting results lately."

"Let's hope our luck holds then," added Momo. "What time," he continued, "should we take over the bomb factories?"

"We can coordinate it with the arrests," said Pike. "If there are people in there waiting to kit out the kamikaze kids, and I think there must be, acting also as guards to keep nosy Parkers out, then they will be expecting to hear from our suspects. We'll blot out communication when we move into their premises. If possible, the separate groups of terrorists will all be isolated and kept that way. During and after arrests, no detainees can even touch a mobile phone or other means of communication. Any questions, Rosalind?"

"Do you think they'll bring up a barge as we thought earlier?"

"I think it's ninety percent sure. Solihull says we cover all doors and windows giving onto the towpath. We'll need you two to go in after the assault teams. You'll be equipped to hear what people are saying or shouting inside the building, and you can relay instructions to the men as they are working the buildings, if they need help of that kind."

"We'll need one of us on land and another on the water side. I can work from that canal," offered Rosalind.

"Can we get you the necessary equipment?" Momo asked, looking from Pike to Rosalind.

"Yes, we can, if you take me to Proctor's Private Bank in good time. Equipment should already be there."

"Proctor's Private Bank!" exclaimed Pike. "Why?"

"We French have a soft spot for Proctor's Private Bank. It's Scottish. Mary Queen of Scots and all that."

"Rosalind, you didn't tell me. Why?" said Momo.

"You've had a leak, a double, and two deaths of agents. Something's going on!" Her voice was not loud, but slow and emphatic. She smiled.

"Agreed. What time do you want us at the rendezvous for the factories?"

"You'll need to be kitted out with the sound and voice equipment and be briefed by the Boss Man on the spot. Rendezvous is The Bargee's Arms, and be there at eleven forty-five hours. This op is code-named *Basilisk*. From now we refer to Basilisk." Pike looked at them.

"It's all happening. But be ready to improvise, if it can save lives. Anything can happen unexpectedly. I don't need to tell you to be ready for the unexpected, but I will anyway."

"Thank you, Mr. Pike. We'll contact you as usual on your secure line every half hour until Boss Man starts Basilisk," said Momo.

"I was about to suggest it myself. Of course, ring me whenever you need, as usual, but if I don't get the half-hourly, I'll worry. I'll think you've been nobbled."

"See you, Pike."

They left and drove to Proctor's, which was in a Victorian red brick Gothic structure like a gnome's castle. It was in a side street off Cathedral Square.

CHAPTER FIFTY

Paul was driving Mary's car with Graham sitting next to him. Mary and Samantha sat in the back with Greg between them. They had seen Dr. Samuel Johnson's house and Greg asked, as if imagining Johnson as a boy, "Graham, did Dr. Johnson when he was a boy know other boys of his age?"

"Oh yes," said Graham, "Johnson went to Lichfield Grammar School before he went to Oxford."

They were now heading for a Roman site beyond Lichfield in the countryside. They planned to picnic there.

"Mary, what's scrofula?" asked Greg.

"Ah, you are thinking of poor Dr. Johnson. It's a disease, also called struma, where swellings erupt in the skin. Lymphatic glands are diseased. In Johnson's day, it was also called the King's Evil; people thought that if the monarch touched a person suffering from the disease, he or she could be cured."

"In the museum it said he had scrofula and was taken to be touched. I don't suppose it worked?"

"He was touched, I think, by Queen Anne," said Graham. "It didn't cure him, though, Greg."

"Did Queen Anne catch the scrofula when she touched him?" asked Greg.

"Not that we know. She probably wore gloves or touched people with a special rod!" added Paul.

"Interesting. I wonder if it was a real laying on of hands?" chipped in Graham.

"Poor man," said Samantha.

"He wrote a novel in two weeks," said Graham.

"That's amazing," said Paul.

"Well, most was translation really. He was desperately poor and had to do it fast to pay for his mother's funeral," explained Graham.

"Don't worry, Greg," said Samantha, "I've already put a special account aside for when anything happens to me."

"Don't say that, Mom."

Samantha could have bitten her tongue. She squeezed Greg's hand. She was also thinking of Graham and his own recent loss. "I'm sorry, darling," Samantha said.

"Johnson wrote a wonderful collection of brief biographies: *Lives of the English Poets*. It has a fascinating life of a poet called Savage." Graham's voice betrayed nothing of his feelings, beyond admiration for Johnson as a writer.

"Wait a minute," said Paul, "Isn't there a book called *Dr. Johnson and Mr. Savage*? I was in W.H. Smith's on the rue de Rivoli a few weeks ago. I saw it there."

"It's a very intriguing study of the relationship between Johnson and Savage. They were great friends for a time. They were so poor they walked the streets, all night sometimes, because they couldn't afford lodgings!" Graham informed them.

"I'll check the Sutton Coldfield library for it," Paul said.

"Read it after you've read *The Life of Savage*. You'll be intrigued and you won't be able to stop reading them once you start. Give yourself a weekend off to read them," Graham enthused.

"Did you know that Johnson was in some great salon in a nobleman's estate and a visitor, another Samuel, Samuel Richardson, was amazed to see a big booby jumping and shaking and behaving erratically in a corner. He assumed it was a demented member of the family, kept at home to be cared for instead of being sent away to Bedlam. The booby jumped and hopped towards the group and then launched into learned conversation and axiomatic remarks. It turned out to be Dr. Johnson!"

"Amazing!" said Samantha.

"Another amazing thing is that King George III had a large library next to his bedroom. The Queen's bedroom was as far away as possible at the other end of Buckingham Palace. The king obviously loved his library! Yet, amazingly, he allowed any person who wanted to use his library to come to the palace, go through his bedroom, and read in the library! It is said that one day he went in and found the scrofulous Dr. Johnson in the library. Johnson conversed with George and realized that he was a cultivated and widely read man." Even though in full flight, Graham stopped his mini-lecture as he looked out of the window.

"We've arrived. See that sign?" demanded Paul. He stopped the car on the grassy verge beside the road.

"I'm hungry," Greg stated.

"Same here!" they all said in a spontaneous chorus.

"Graham, what's Bedlam? You made it sound like a place."

"It was. A hospital for the mentally unbalanced and mad people. It was called Bethlehem and gradually became known as Bedlam."

"So that's why people say it was bedlam!"

"Exactly. Want a sandwich? Ham, tuna, or chicken?"

CHAPTER FIFTY-ONE

Proctor's Birmingham branch, closed for the weekend, had a large brass bell push, shining in the morning light. Kim rang the bell at the side door of the building. From a small grill above the bell push a voice asked, "Who's there?" and then added, "We're closed."

"I'm Rosalind from the Val de Loire."

The door opened and a black sports bag was handed to her by a tall man with a waxed moustache. He wore a navy-blue track suit like an athlete. The man closed the door.

"They're obviously closed!" said Kim. "I'll check this out in the car."

"I was hoping they'd opted for bank holiday opening," said Momo as he carried the bag back to the car. As they were driving along, Kim checked the contents. Everything she needed was there.

***

"Look here, Jasmin, this sudden change of plans is a bit of a nuisance. I'm supposed to be in Cambridge," said Alex Westlake petulantly. He let a sigh escape from his small mouth nestled above the ample chin and throat.

"That's too bad," she said.

They sipped more of the sweet mint tea she had served. Dr. Westlake suddenly leaned forward, his eyes having closed, and almost fell from his chair. Jasmin sprang up and, with her hands against his chest, pushed him back into the seat. She was wearing a dark green track suit and sneakers under her dark-blue robe. She took a length of clothesline from a locker and tied Westlake's hands securely and then his feet. She lowered over his head and shoulders something resembling a life jacket. In fact, it was filled with high explosives. She then attached the firing device. She could trigger the life jacket and other explosives packed into the barge they sat in simply by tapping in a number on her mobile phone. Jasmin looked at Westlake. He was clever. He had been useful in exposing the two women agents. Yet, she was unsure as to whether he was still prepared to betray their operation to his British masters at the last minute. This operation must succeed. Afterwards, she would move on to plan something in another of these decadent western countries. Westlake could have been a fine figure of a man. Instead, he had turned into a decadent wreck. If they could identify him later, they would learn what fate awaited their agents. She looked at her watch. It had been relatively difficult to slip the tail Westlake had obviously put on them as a precaution. It was time for the barge to move and destroy the people milling around in the arts complex area. She nodded to a silent young man at the helm, her mute volunteer for glory. He started the engine and the barge moved slowly and innocently towards the centre of Birmingham. She would stay for the ride until they reached her jumping off point. Her young volunteer would take the mobile phone and tap in the numbers when he was sure of a good kill. His yellow life jacket was snugly fitted around him with its Velcro fasteners. Should she mutilate Westlake? She thought a moment. It was tempting, but she didn't want his blood splashing her clothes. No. Let him be blown into shreds.

***

The Bargee's Arms, the dilapidated pub near their target buildings, had a discreet room in the cellar beyond the casks of beer. It was ideal, as a mustering point, for the team went in at different intervals as if they were customers. The equipment they needed was all there, delivered earlier by a big brewer's truck. The team was silent and well briefed for Operation Basilisk. The rooftop people were already crouched, waiting near the roof angles of their target buildings. Kim was in her special diving gear. She had tested her sound system. Momo said a few words of Arabic and she immediately spoke its equivalent to Boss Man Solihull in English. All watches had been synchronized. Momo again checked his watch. She checked hers and also the handy air supply device. She gave a thumbs up to Momo. He and the Boss Man repeated the gesture.

She slipped out of the back of the building and crossed a small yard close to the wall. A wooden door opened onto the narrow cinder towpath. She saw nothing on the canal in either direction. The Bargee's Arms itself behind her seemed quietly normal for this time of day. A few gusts of laughter could be heard from time to time. It was good. She lowered herself into the water and submerged. In a few seconds, she was at the shelf-like edge of the other side of the canal. *The water was murky. Good.* She let her head come up for a few seconds and then swam to a position where, at surface level, she would have a clear view. Her head was near the brick edge of the canal. A rat slithered past her, making a small ripple with its nose.

"I'm Rosalind. I need a viewing."

"Solihull. There's a big fish slowly coming our way. You won't see it for a few minutes. Prepare for interpretation if you hear the lingo. Move now."

"I'm angling. Out."

Kim swam underwater, her wet suit making her invisible from the surface. The mud at the bottom cushioned a few objects dumped since the city's last clean-up. She reached a position she had chosen between the two target buildings and across from the back of The Bargee's Arms. She let her head come out of the water near the towpath.

There was a sudden crash of splintering glass. The assault had begun. She heard more crashing of glass. Kalitza was waiting for an explosion. Nothing yet. They could all be dead or injured in the next minute or so. Nothing. Suddenly a man flung himself out of the back yard of Tamco and plunged into the canal. One of the assault team had his gun pointed at the water.

"Hold your hooks! Rosalind sees one little fish. I'm after him. I'll play him."

She was on her way and, through the murky grey-brown of the water to her left, she could see a man swimming under water away from her. She was after him like a shark. His clothes were impeding his progress and large air bubbles were tending to bring him near the surface. She swam deeper and faster and then caught his thrashing ankles from behind and swam to the deepest centre of the canal taking him down with her. He had taken in mouthfuls of water. She let go of his legs and then pushed herself quickly up to the surface with the powerful flippers. She pushed the retching and spluttering man underwater again by the shoulders and clung to his back. He stopped struggling. Kim swam back to the armed man at the rear of Tamco and beckoned. He said something into his mouth mike and then immediately dragged the man out of the water and got him into the yard.

"Ros here. Solihull's looking great. Basilisk ahoy, Out."

The little gate closed. Kim went underwater and swam back to her observation point.

"Solihull. Thanks. He can be wrung out and canned. Clouds on horizon. One of ours may be theirs, too. Coming your way. Someone ended up chasing his own tail."

"Understood. Oink, oink."

"Lady with a load of fireworks. Go and land a big fish."

"Angling it is."

"Wait. Take along this gift."

Kim looked across the canal. A man emerged from the red brick factory's yard and threw two coils of rope into the canal. Each rope had some metal hooks attached.

"I'm going for it."

As she swam, under the surface and right across the middle of the canal, the voice in her headphones spoke again.

"One is to catch the big fish. It should stop all progress along the canal. Use the other to get onto a whale's back if you need it."

"Understood."

The coiled ropes were tied with a plastic tie twisted on itself. *Easy to undo. Thanks, Boss Man!* A three-pronged metal hook like a miniature anchor was attached to each coiled rope. Kalitza retrieved them as they slowly sank towards an old tin trunk that was half-submerged in the mud at the bottom of the canal. She swam fast under the water. Soon she could hear a steady throb. It was the barge. It seemed like an enormous black whale coming towards her. It was slowing down. Kalitza, still under the surface, squeezed between the sides of the barge and the wall of the canal. She was afraid that on the shallow water shelf she might be seen. Then she was behind the barge and down into the deeper water. She surfaced her eyes at water level about fifteen yards astern and was amazed to see Jasmin leap from the barge and fall and roll on the towpath. She got up and set off as a casual walker up the dead-end lane leading to the canal. A man wearing a windjammer with a hood concealing most of his face was at the helm. The barge began to pick up its former pace. Kim spoke rapidly, her head just out of the water.

"Rosalind. Jasmin jumped ship, wearing dark green track suit and runners. Is walking along the lane from the canal. She doesn't seem to be a walking bomb."

"Solihull. Understood. Hook the whale blubber."

Kim didn't reply, but was swimming under water. She could catch up in about a minute. She was untying the two coils as she swam. Now she had one on each arm, hooked over her shoulder on each side. She was level with the lumbering barge. The screw was not huge, as she had thought it might be. She put one coil over her flipper and brought it up around her left leg above her knee. She unwound the other coil and let the rope tangle around the screw and its stem, then she put the three-pronged hook onto the screw. There was a squealing and a grinding and the metal began to bend. Kim didn't stay to watch. She was off, going ahead and away from the screw, afraid that vicious bits of metal would start flying in all directions. The barge was gliding on its own momentum now and was slowing. The engine had not been turned off. She wriggled the second coil from her leg and undid some of it and got a few feet free with the hook on the end. On the surface, she could see the man with the hood looking astern. She threw the hook up and over the prow. First time lucky! She hauled herself silently aboard, climbing the rope and then up a metal frame hanging on the bow. A mop and a shirt were hanging there to dry. She was now on the deck, the quiet torn still by the squealing and clanking of the barge. The man was leaning over the stern, still wondering what was happening. She could see his bulky life jacket on his back. *My God, he's wired*, she thought. And any second he would turn and see her. Kim made her choice. She shot him in the back of the neck. It was not a lucky shot. It was exactly what she had aimed for. He slumped forward, half hanging over the stern.

CHAPTER FIFTY-TWO

The barge began to nudge the edge of the canal bank. There was a horrible grating crunch each time. Kim took off the flippers and raced forward in bare feet. She had to find out if there were other crew members aboard. If there were, they'd be on deck in seconds. She looked cautiously down the hatch to below deck and saw Westlake tied up, wearing a life jacket. He was either dead or fast asleep. There was no movement. The space below seemed full of parcels. She saw a bunch of keys hanging from the ignition switch. She switched off the engine. The screeching stopped. Now there was just the scraping of barge on brickwork. She listened. Nothing. No moves. Westlake was breathing.

"Rosalind. I hooked a big one!"

"Solihull is sunny today!"

"It's one for Guy Fawkes night. Get the Bang-Bang men down here quick."

"Okay. No sign of Jasmin. If you see anything like a phone, remember not to play with it!"

"Okay. Out."

Kim spotted the little silver lozenge of the phone on the helmsman's curved seat astern of the wheel. He had probably put it down when he looked over the stern. Lucky! She opened a locker full of old ropes and a bucket. Should she throw the trigger, as she thought of the phone, into the canal? She put the phone in the bucket in the locker. Jasmin, on the loose, could be doubling back, or simply preparing to explode Westlake's or the dead man's jacket from another cell phone. Get them both off the barge! She tipped the helmsman into the water. Kim watched the hooded corpse drifting a little way away. Not far enough. There was no sign of Jasmin. Scanning the towing path leading back to the warehouses, Kim saw three men in black fatigues and masked with balaclavas. They were running, carrying their equipment. They wore police arm bands. *Thank you, Boss Man.*

"Solihull, I'm at Solihull. Three men for you. Okay?"

Okay. No sign here of Jasmin."

"We have her. No sweat for us, plenty for Jasmin."

"I'll welcome the boys."

"Her cell phone's immobilized. Out."

"She should have a bigger cell. Bars on it. Out."

Kim held out a hand to each bomb expert as he climbed aboard.

"Don't untie the fat man. Get rid of his life jacket, though." She motioned to the corpse floating nearby.

"That one needs removing, too. A probable trigger phone's in that locker. I'll push the corpse to the bank for you to deal with him."

"Right, Frog Lady. We're onto it," said one of them. And they were.

CHAPTER FIFTY-THREE

The Roman villa had been excavated to reveal a rather fine mosaic floor and bits of wall. A notice board depicted an architect's drawing of the reconstruction of the villa and its grounds. There were only a handful of other people there. When Paul and Mary's group saw the mosaic, they stood and looked closely at the work, still in surprisingly good condition. There were patches that had been destroyed. There was a board depicting an idea of what the original might have been. A pattern of foliage made a border between parallel lines. Within the large oblong, one could clearly make out a boy playing some kind of horn. A smiling man with a garland around his head was perhaps dancing. His legs suggested as much. His arms were incomplete. Two hands, left and right hands, from a missing figure were, it seemed, clacking together two metallic discs. A double flute protruded from the lips of a head on a ragged torso. It was as if a moment of Roman colonial life, nostalgic for the centre of the world, had been clinging here to this now English land. A female head with one large eye intact, the other missing, was isolated from a portion of a delicately fashioned robe. It was poignant for being incomplete. It was as if a bomb had blown the revelers into pieces. The villa had been blown away by the explosions of successive histories.

"I expect the Romans who lived here had locals as slaves," said Graham.

"They might also have brought slaves from Rome or Gaul with them, when they built the villa here," Mary hazarded.

"Do you think it could have been a holiday home?" asked Greg.

"Could have been. More likely, though, it was a place of some colonial boss doing his Roman duty or maybe he was in exile. He was stuck here and longing to get back to Rome again. Or even Pompeii or Herculaneum. He was sick of the climate and Bolshy Brit gardeners and farmers on the estate. His effort to impose Roman law on the true blue Brits of the period was not a total success," suggested Paul.

"Don't forget, though," said Graham, "that Roman law has had a lasting influence on bits of common law and quite a lot of French civil code."

"You've got it all worked out pat," laughed Samantha.

"I still think it was a holiday villa, like in ads nowadays," said Greg.

"You may be right, Greg," said Mary.

"Can I have another sandwich now?" demanded Greg.

They all thought it was a good idea and started looking for a suitable place to spread out a blanket, a cloth, and other food they had brought with them.

***

Operation Basilisk was over, except for the warm down activities and debriefings. Dr. Westlake's interrogation had begun as soon as he was conscious. He was clever and had an excellent pedagogic reputation in university circles. The interrogators were clever also and had some excellent information they could keep up their sleeves until their subject had led himself into an impasse. One of them was nicknamed the Knight, not because he had a title, but because he was a master of sudden knight's moves and the discovered check in his interrogations. When he played, it was always checkmate, never stalemate. There was a ripple of amused surprise, when it was found that Jasmin was really a man. Her interrogators could and would make use of this. There was a troublesome factor. Although a man had been pulled from the water and resuscitated, again another interrogation suspect, Rosalind had killed a youth, almost without hesitation. Could she not have crept along the barge's deck and stunned the youth? Her defence was that he was wearing an explosive device. But what if she had not hit him, but the explosive device? But what if as she went to stun him, he had turned and set off the explosives in the barge himself? But he would have had to reach for the cell phone and tap in a sequence of numbers. But Rosalind did not know the phone was on the bench seat and had to have numbers tapped to set off the bomb. She had had to act rapidly and effectively to bring a loaded barge into a safe condition. She had succeeded. Solihull was prepared to defend her all the way if there were some enquiry. Kim was allowed to warm down.

The warm down was in a large building near Barr Beacon. Here the teams involved in Basilisk could work out and reduce the tensions built up by the operation. It was good for their health. Besides, for people on an operational high to go onto the streets right away was risky, because a sudden, random noise, or some petty altercation could lead to lightning reflex actions endangering the public. The Boss Man's teams had to be peaceful, ordinary folk when off duty and lethally effective when duty called. Kim, and a couple of men she had not met before, finished the warm down with a jog around Barr Beacon. After her shower, she put on her robes and veil with her preferred sunglasses. When wearing them, she was protected from glare and UV rays, but also from people following her. A portion of each of the lenses was designed to reflect the street behind her.

Momo spotted her carrying her black waterworks bag. He was relaxing with a non-alcoholic drink, a diablo, in the common room.

"Ros! A drink? Can I drive you anywhere?"

"I don't need a drink. I've had a bottle of Evian. But let's go to Proctor's and then get my other clothes. Then a drink somewhere else?"

"You're on." Momo quickly finished his diablo. Later on, when they rang at the side door, it was opened by a different man, though he also sported a waxed moustache.

"Why does Proctor's personnel department have a penchant for the waxed moustache?" asked Momo, when they were back in the car.

"It not only grows on them, but it grows on me, too!" laughed Kim. "Maybe they all worship the old Regimental Sergeant Major Brittain, the terror of Aldershot!"

Momo lifted her veil. "That must be it," he murmured. "You don't have a waxed moustache!"

"Not yet. Give me time, give me time."

"Are you staying in the United Kingdom a few days or do you have to be back in France?" asked Momo as they were driving back to the safe house.

"Actually, I have to be in London today, and I could be off to some as yet undisclosed destination next week," said Kim.

"Why don't we go to bed together?" asked Momo.

"I don't want to. That sociable drink's what we need. Besides, I have to be in London."

"I'll come to London."

"That won't make a scrap of difference. You're not on my list."

"Pity. Can we take a rain check?"

"Perhaps. Lists can be added to."

CHAPTER FIFTY-FOUR

When she had collected her things, Kim appeared in her traveling clothes and a veil, but kept the Arab robe and other veils in a plastic bag inside her travel bag. She had returned her sound and direction kit at the debriefing. Solihull had not thought it wise for her to take some of his equipment back to France, just as her waterworks had had to be taken back to the bank in person. One had to be punctilious about these things. Inventories were inventories. The list is essential for good administration, as all good civil servants know.

Momo offered to drive her to the station or wherever she was going, or even to London, if she so wished. He explained that he now had a spot of leave.

"This arrant persistence has just lost you a sociable drink. Take me to Birmingham airport, James," she commanded.

Momo drove to the nearby motorway and followed it before cutting off to the airport. He said she was a hard woman. They were followed by thousands of vehicles, but by no one in particular. At the airport, Momo agreed not to come inside to see her off. She would drop off at the departure point. They hoped to see one another again, said their farewells, and Kim kissed him on each cheek. Then he was gone. Once inside the airport, Kim surveyed the departure boards. There was a flight to Malaga just about to start boarding. She went to a ticket counter for the airline and asked if there were seats available. There were. She could catch the flight if she hurried. She caught the flight.

At Malaga, she went into the ladies and left her plastic bag with the Muslim outfit and all her veils in a cubicle. Selecting a different credit card, she bought a ticket for Madrid and stayed there overnight in a large, central hotel with enough stars to match any American general. She relaxed in the luxurious bathroom by taking a bubble bath and started to read a novel by Deirdre Madden. She had dinner by room service and watched *Questions pour un Champion* on television and then the news on CNN and also Sky News. She watched the Spanish news and bits of a bullfight. She then read more of Deirdre Madden and eventually drifted into a deep and refreshing sleep.

***

They emerged from the Beaux Stratagem Hotel and strolled to Lichfield Cathedral, admiring its splendid exterior as they approached. Before going inside to take their places in the congregation, they walked around the outside, impressed by the ancient stonework and more recent renovation work. Once inside, they walked along beside the Stations of the Cross and the side chapels, rejoicing in the colors and craft of the stained glass windows, and intrigued by ancient sepulchres and tombstones with their worn, semi-legible Latin inscriptions.

"Samuel Johnson prayed here and walked over these very stones," said Paul, as they found seats.

It was an obvious enough remark, but it struck a chord with the little group of friends.

The choir was superb. The trebles gave the impression of flights of angels. One small boy with very big ears sticking out either side of his rosy cheeks sang, it seemed, with his entire body. He was a vehicle for the purest, sublime descant. Mary noticed with particular interest that there were several colored people in the choir. *One day, when she had more free evenings*, she thought *she might join a choir*. She knew Paul supposed that Lichfield would be a good place to live, if they could find the right house. *Didn't Keith Aldritt, a critic and novelist, live here? He might be an amiable person to chat with over a beer.*

The rest of the evening went very well. They piled into the car and found a wonderful old coaching inn on the way to Stafford. Here they had a substantial dinner, with green pea soup followed by fish for the adults, but a steak for

Greg. The new potatoes were a delight. Greg was equally delighted with his French fries or chips as these Brits called them. There was a dessert trolley groaning with goodies. The adults had shared an excellent bottle of Sancerre Blanc, while Greg sampled the house homemade lemonade.

Their Portuguese waitress supplied Greg, at his request, with a piece of paper and a pen. He then wrote a note to the chef declaring that the meal had been just great, but the chocolate mousse and lemonade were, as he put it, works of art. He added a P.S., "Tomorrow my mom is taking me to Paris, but I doubt if I'll find anything better over there! Yours, Greg."

Reading this over Greg's shoulder as he wrote, Graham said that Greg should seriously think of applying for the Canadian diplomatic service after his studies at university.

Back home in Mary's flat after dropping the others at their hotel, Paul switched on the TV and they settled down to watch the late news. There was nothing very dramatic. There had been an accident on the M1 in a patch of fog, but nobody had been killed, amazingly enough. Then on *Breaking News*, there was excitement; an arms and explosives stock had been found in Birmingham. Some suspected terrorists were in custody.

"Well, thank God for that," said Mary. "In fact, although these things seem remote from our little lives, I'm very glad someone is looking out for us."

"You're right. Sutton Coldfield's right next to Brum," said Paul. "Tired?"

"I was just thinking we might turn in and make love."

"Great idea! Why didn't I think of that!"

"Liar! I bet you did."

"I did."

CHAPTER FIFTY-FIVE

Easter arrived and vanished, except for chocolate eggs as big as rugby balls, as well as hordes of rabbits, and hens, complete with their chicks and tiny eggs, all on sale at jumbo savings and giant reductions in the supermarkets. Graham, Samantha, and Greg were off to Canada after enjoying a Parisian spring. The window boxes were ablaze with red and pink geraniums, the chestnut trees had suddenly acquired conical candles of either white or pink blossom, and one could not see clearly across the Place des Vosges, because there was a mass of foliage. The cafés were doing brisk business, and some of the *bouquinistes* along the quays were now open most days, sitting on their stools near their opened steel boxes, displaying leaves from ancient books, all manner of engravings and prints, postcards, posters, classic books, and more dubious publications.

At the moment that Graham, Samantha, and Greg sat in their jet, awaiting take off from Charles de Gaulle airport, Kim was in Control's office. He had studied in detail the debriefing tapes featuring Kim, courtesy of the Boss Man, Solihull.

"This is an excellent example of Anglo-French cooperation, Kate. Solihull was impressed by your initiative with your waterworks equipment and the way in which you stopped that barge."

"I had to shoot a man."

"We can overlook that, Kate, because you managed to clear British jurisdiction very neatly and rapidly. There could have been an inquiry over there, you know, with all kinds of tangles, if you had stayed around. If the gutter press had got hold of 'FROGGIE SLAUGHTERS DEAF MUTE BRITISH BOY' what then? But if that young man had killed you first and reached his target to create havoc and carnage, we'd have had to put up with 'FROG AGENT FAILS TO

HALT CANAL CARNAGE IN CITY CENTRE.' Don't let
guilt get to you, Kate. And I don't need to remind you that
if he'd seen you and blown himself up and the barge with
him, you would be very dead. And you would all have been
in little pieces like Osiris or Dionysus or whatever. And so
would a host of innocent people in the buildings near the
canal. More seriously, what if the barge had reached the
explosives dumps and he had set them off as well! What a
mess. How many lives would have been lost then?"

"I can still see the hood he wore and the explosive jacket."

"Of course. That's natural." Control sipped his tea. "I
admire also the way that you brought out the Proctor's Bank
connection at the last minute, in case of further leaks."

"Thank you, Patron. I felt it could be a matter of success
or failure."

"How right you were."

"I don't want any more. I'm good at deception, but I hate
it."

"I understand completely." Martin looked at her, holding
his cup in mid-air, poised above the saucer he held in his
other hand; he deliberately left a pause before he continued,
"That's why I want you in planning."

Kate admired the fine bone china with its orange Japanese
blossom-on-a-twig pattern. *English Crown Derby? Antique?
Control's logic was right, of course.* She would have liked
a set of four such cups and saucers with a matching teapot,
milk jug, and sugar bowl. Perhaps Control had the rest of the
set in one of his cupboards.

"Have you thought any more about that?"

"To be frank, I have not. I really do need that leave."

"Of course. You're free until twenty July. From today,
that is. How's that for generosity?"

"Wonderful. I really appreciate your negotiating
bureaucratic tangles in order to get that approved." Kim
smiled.

Control finished his tea, placed cup and saucer on the
elegant walnut occasional table near his chair, and stood up.
The interview was almost over.

"You're at a fork in the highway, Kate. It's your decision."

She walked over to him and kissed him on both cheeks. Twice. This meant she considered him not just a boss, but a friend, almost family. He held her with arms outstretched, but certainly not at arms' length. He looked into her dark, lustrous eyes with their brilliant white. He found no hint of their being bloodshot. His eyes were always alert, calculating. Then he hugged her. As his arms went around her, he felt the silky swathe of black hair hanging below her shoulders. She hugged him, too, but then made a slight effort to detach herself. He let his arms drop to his sides. They were face-to-face. Close.

"I want you in planning. I hope you'll decide to join me. Let me know your decision as soon as possible, even from wherever you are for your leave. After all, I have to plan the planning!"

Kim joined him in smiling at his own joke. She felt his pressure, his needs, and his demands. She smelled the tea on his breath. She did not want to be his close associate and mistress, or even wife. Just his associate, a key member of his team. Perhaps she could expose for him the agent who had a fake background and could be intent on bringing down the whole outfit. But she had her own agenda, too.

"Yes, Patron, I'll be in touch."

"Take care, my dear, and Kate, don't do anything I wouldn't do! That gives you scope! *Au revoir!*"

"Au revoir, et merci plein, patron." As she left his secure and soundproof room, the office, Kim thought, *I bet he wouldn't teach in a girls' school, even to save his life.* And then she thought, *but maybe he would, especially to save his life. On his life depended so many others in the French Republic. Control was an enigma. Just as well*, she said to herself.

CHAPTER FIFTY-SIX

The flight was full. Greg was in a window seat, Samantha next to him, and across the aisle from them was Graham. He was thinking of Anne de Crevennes. She had appeared at Paul's flat one morning just as Graham was about to go to Samantha's hotel. She had explained that she was trying to contact Mr. Paul Wills to give him some more historical details and sources. Graham and she had chatted about history. She was interested in the fact that he was a professor and author. They arranged to meet later that day for aperitifs. Graham had enjoyed his encounter with Anne, so much so that he had rung Samantha to say he would not be available for dinner. The aperitifs had led to dinner in a restaurant near the Palais Royal and dinner had almost, perhaps, led to bed— in Anne's luxurious apartment near the Place Vendôme. Anne had asked him about his marriage and he had asked about her past. They had talked intimately and searchingly, but then a moment when their eyes met had passed. In that moment, something had happened between them. It was a complicity that promised a further relationship. To make love had been in both their minds, fleetingly, and then the mood passed. *To hell with Africa*, Graham said to himself. *I'll be back in France come May first and then I'll try to build on this beginning to a relationship with Anne.* He had said he would phone her as soon as he got home. Her reticence he knew was partly because she was older than he; partly also because he was a recent widower. Anne realized, of course, that a friendship that might develop and deepen was helpful. Any disloyalty to his murdered wife would become intolerable for him, if he were to have sexual relations with any woman just now.

"You seem to have made a hit with Anne," Samantha remarked as she leant across to him. She was smiling.

"Do you think so? She's a handsome woman and she knows her nineteenth century history all right."

"Well, in that case, she's not all bad! She seems very capable. I think she's rich, too. Did you notice her jewelry?"

"Now you mention it, yes. She seemed to sparkle, in more ways than one."

"Do you think she'll visit?"

"I wonder. I never asked!"

"I think she'd enjoy a visit. She seemed sad to see you going off home."

"Really? You really think so?

They lapsed into silence as a flight attendant brushed past with a trolley hard behind him. The attendant following him with the trolley stopped a little way beyond them and, with one practised flick of her foot, depressed a small brake for its wheels. The flight attendants then started serving drinks with small packets of salted nuts. There was another eight or nine hours to go, depending on the direction and strength of winds, before they would be home. Graham had a Scotch and soda and started to read Danièle Sallenave's, *Le Don des Morts*. Paul had lent it to him.

That's one way of looking at the literary heritage, Graham thought, *it's the gift of dead writers to living readers. In fact, dead writers, if they have said something in a way that is permanent, not perishable, are still alive in the minds of their readers.* It was that question that used to turn up on examination papers: 'All great writers are contemporary—Discuss.' Now, though, "great" was in some circles a word to avoid, just as "genius" was a false category. Some educators argued that Mozart was simply a product of a father with musical talent and the ready accessibility of music and musical instruments for the growing lad. Graham knew that, in fact, there were hundreds of pushy parents with houses full of every musical chance available for their children. There were hundreds of these privileged children who progressed little further than "Chopsticks." Now Greg, though no Mozart, had some real talent. He would help him along his path, whatever that might be. That would be his gift to Greg's gift or talent. *Le Don des Morts*. What was

Jacqueline's gift to her husband, now that she was . . . dead?
The memories he had of her? Yes. Something else, too—the
effect she had had on him as a result of his having known
her. He knew he had grown because of her. He felt that he
had experienced what it is to love, genuinely.

CHAPTER FIFTY-SEVEN

"You lost your way, Dr. Westlake, didn't you?" asked the chief interrogator for this session. "Didn't you?"

"Yes, I did. But they were onto me. They'd have beheaded me if I hadn't given them information."

"Yes, but you betrayed two very useful and agreeable women agents. We hate disloyalty, Westlake."

"You don't understand. I . . ."

"You university types, I know, you think that everything is complex and only you and your friends really understand complex issues. You're wrong. In fact, the people who keep countries afloat by their work are not all stupid. That's why our political bosses hate to have a referendum."

"No. It isn't like that."

"Isn't it? What is it like? Saving your own copious skin? You know that your friends have experts in flaying people during interrogation? I'll tell you this for nothing. When bullies start making trouble, they have to be stopped. Simplistic rubbish? Go back to school, Porky, and look at the little beasts in playgrounds. They will persecute their so-called friends and even the teachers, if they can get away with it. We don't like bullies, and we don't want them to get away with blowing up innocent people. We don't like them trying to destroy our hard-won freedoms. Do you? I suppose you don't care for freedom. You think you're one of the chosen who can tell everyone else what to do—or else? And we have only contempt for people who double-cross us."

"You'll destroy me in court. And my father . . . Thank God my mother's dead."

"I'll have to wipe away my tears. We've read your boring file, Porky. No, I'll tell you what, we'll spare you the court jig. I think we'll put you down near one of their training bases. They'll be convinced you nobbled Jasmin's lot. I think they'll give you a reception you won't enjoy. And if they try to sell you back to us for a ransom, so they can finance more terror, we won't pay. We won't pay. We don't negotiate with terrorists."

***

Kim was on her way to London. Soon Ms. Alissa Partridge would flash her membership card and go to a comfortable room in the Oxford and Cambridge Club. In fact, Kim made good time and was able to settle down with sparkling spring water kissed with lemon zest in the bar. She wondered where Dr. Westlake was sweating it out under the lamps of the interrogators. He'd be well and truly cooked. Neither she nor Cambridge would see him for many, many years, if ever again. She would be truly grateful if more terrorists were rounded up from information he had. Before eating, she wandered into the library. Of course, the public schools' year book had been put back on the shelves. They always reshelved books left out on tables.

Her first day in London had not been uneventful. She had been making for a bijou hotel and noticed that she was being followed by a small man in casual clothes, black jeans and a wind-breaker jacket urging everyone to buy diesel. He was probably from North Africa. She would lose him. Once inside the hotel, she was shown to a table where she ordered tea and brown toast. She then went to the Ladies' powder room. There were three other women in there at the mirrors and wash basins. The door opened again behind her as soon as she was inside. She heard something clattering. It was a hand grenade. Kim shouted, "Get behind a door!" She kicked the grenade towards the threshold, dashed into a cubicle, jumped on the toilet bowl, and locked the door. There was a crack like a steam hammer pounding the tiled floor when the grenade exploded, followed immediately by a deafening roar. Bits of hot metal hit the walls and doors. Mirrors shattered. Some of the fragments flew horizontally into empty stalls and others under the doors. Kim, balanced precariously, her feet astride the toilet bowl could smell the acrid smoke of the explosion as it thickened the air in the enclosed space. Her door was at a crazy angle, but had shielded her. She could hear nothing. She stepped clumsily between a woman lying on her back in her neat Coco Chanel suit, now just blood-soaked rags. One of her legs was blackened, the other missing. She was open-mouthed, as if screaming. Two other women were inert. There was smoke everywhere, and water tinged with blood ran all over the floor. Had someone photographed her? Not in Birmingham. She had been veiled. Westlake? In the club? Her book? Had he seen what she had been consulting that first time? Possible. But not the particular pages. There was a great commotion. She was still deaf. She staggered out, past the women on the floor and debris of wood and broken marble. One of the hotel staff, white-faced with shock, led her to a place where she could sit down. There was great confusion. People were coming and going, their mouths opening and closing. Kim got up and moved silently, but shakily among the people until she could get clear of the hotel. As she walked away, a police car raced through the clogged street towards the hotel. A pedestrian crossing was in her favour, so she crossed the main street and took a side road. *Walk quickly.* She looked back. Nobody was following her. She turned into another street and stopped. It was a crossroads. Nobody was following her. There was a bus stop ahead. She waited in a doorway nearby. She would take the next bus that came. She got off the bus in a neighbourhood full of undistinguished bed and breakfast houses in a terrace near Paddington station. She could hear the street sounds as if they came from some way away. Good. She booked into one of them for a couple of nights, paying one night cash in advance. This she achieved with gestures, the waving of cash in her hand, a few words in a loud voice that was hers, together with written commands and her signature on a form produced by the receptionist. Kim stayed in her room with the evening papers. Her hearing was coming back to normal, now, eardrums undamaged.

Next morning, the papers were full of the grenade attack. She went out and found a ladies' hairdresser, where she had her long hair cut until she had a short, urchin style. In an optician's, she chose a pair of designer sunglasses as well as some frames with plain glass which did not interfere with her twenty/twenty vision. The evening papers reported that an unusually gaunt, emaciated man had been seen walking into Claridges just before the explosion. They were calling him the angel of death. Her last morning, she read over breakfast that the angel of death had been found by Special Branch officers trying to board the Eurostar bound for Paris. He was now helping them with their enquiries. Kim paid her bill and then walked the streets thinking about Bruno. Had he been trying to protect her? Had he been tracking the little North African? Or were they accomplices? Was Bruno the agent who's real identity Nomenklatura had never possessed? Or was Nomenklatura the traitor? That was not a possibility. If Nomenklatura was the traitor, why suggest the false identity clue? It made no sense. Only Nomenklatura and Control had everybody's profile. She found herself at the noble church of St. Martin in the Fields. Inside, she sat listening to a bit of organ practice. She turned these events and suspicions over as she regained her normal state of mind. She realized she had been very lucky. Her speed had been just enough to save her from serious injury or death. She had just beaten the grenade's three-second delay. After about half an hour, she walked out and then found a taxi to go to a car rental agency near the Victoria and Albert Museum. She then drove to Manchester. From Manchester, she drove towards Birmingham, stopping at a Little Chef near the motorway. There she ate a salad and a chicken sandwich. *Mineral water to go with it will be good*, she decided. After going to the toilet, after much hesitation, and this time without incident, she went to the car. She sat and watched other people, cars coming and going. There was no one on her tail. *Was she stupid?* Birmingham was where she might be recognized and taken in for an enquiry. But the attempt on her life was a direct result of her activities there. At least she suspected as much. She convinced herself she had to go there and perhaps trap a hornet in its nest. The two agents had been rifling through the files in a doctor's office. Maybe she should check out that doctor.

In the Birmingham central reference library, she found the information she needed. Dr. Mary Rao had a surgery in Sutton Coldfield. She would check to see what might be obvious to her, but not to another investigator. Kim went to Great Barr and then checked into a large hotel next to the motorway. From there she could get to the doctor's surgery quite easily and quickly. She parked some way away from the surgery, walked a deserted bit of a Sutton Coldfield street, turned a corner, and located the surgery. No one was on watch, no police presence. It was 2232! *Hey*, she thought. She found a side gate in the tall wooden fence. It was a simple lock, but the gate was bolted on the inside. She looked around and then leapt and clambered over the fence. *That was a bit noisy*, she thought, as she landed on a paved path on the other side. She unbolted the two bolts top and bottom. There was a Yale lock knob this side and she could make a quick getaway if necessary. There was a breeze and the clouds were scudding across the sky. A row of three plastic rubbish bins loomed near the gate. She lifted the lid of one marked paper. *Old wrapping paper. Nothing like files. The police would have them, no doubt.* Kim pushed some wrapping paper aside and suddenly saw peeping from under it a torn piece of a file folder. She picked it out and found it was part of a folder's tab. She saw written in ink: Dr. P. West. The rest was missing but it was enough for Kim. She opened the gate quietly. No one about. She walked back to her car, keeping to the hedges of the small front gardens. After driving back to the hotel, she slept until 7:30 a.m. *Perhaps the mosque should be stirred into a bit of wispiness?*

Room service brought her a continental breakfast and a national newspaper together with a local one. As she read, Kim smiled. This was her lucky day. The British police wanted Mr. Norman Quarry and Mr. A. S. Nandin to come forward to help with enquiries. Their photographs made Kim laugh aloud. Nandin she had seen at the mosque and Quarry was the little man who followed her before the grenade attack in a London hotel. Since there had been a connection with people in France who had murdered the two British women and dumped their bodies in the Baie des Anges, it was possible that Quarry and Nandin had already skipped to the French side of the channel. If the angel of death was Bruno, perhaps he had been with them, and all three were now back in France. Or perhaps Bruno had tracked them as part of an operation in which he was involved. *Was Bruno still in custody*, she wondered. Suddenly the urgency she had felt for finding her would-be assassin evaporated. The authorities knew who these people were and would be right now trying to trap them. *I am on holiday*, she thought, *and the authorities can deal with it. I'll go to the art gallery to see the pre-Raphaelite collection.* She would also step into the cathedral to see the stained glass windows.

CHAPTER FIFTY-EIGHT

Mrs. Holroyd met Miss Partridge with the red minivan and a gasp of surprise followed by a big smile.

"Welcome back and, by the way, it suits you!" she greeted her, beaming, "I'm so glad, Miss Partridge, that you got the job."

"Same here," said Kim, climbing into the van beside her. "So, the hair is a success? I'm looking forward to the beginning of term. I expect everyone's very busy now up at the school?"

"That's right."

Mrs. Holroyd started off on the short journey to the school. "Yes, it's all go, as they say. But we've had a bit of a setback. Miss Tew has resigned."

"Oh dear, so now they have to look for a replacement."

"Worse. She took off without working this term. Of course, the head's really annoyed. There are some of her classes preparing *O* and *A* levels. These senior classes have to be covered, of course, as best we can."

"I expect the search is already underway for a new teacher. But who'll be able to come for the summer term at this stage?"

"That's exactly it, Miss Partridge. The head's planning for this year is all messed up and the plans for next academic year will have to be modified."

"I should think so," Kim replied. *Planning!* she thought. *Maybe she'd be roped in for it here! That would be rich.* At the same time, she felt a warm glow of pleasure at the thought of not having to cross swords with the sour Miss Tew.

"By the way, you can call me Alissa. It's not term yet and we're off duty."

"Thanks, Alissa. Call me Nancy. Well, your new hairstyle will distract them from the Miss Tew problem!"

"Good. But what a nuisance that she took off so suddenly, Nancy."

Nancy Holroyd laughed, and her eyes shone brightly above her rosy cheeks.

"Yes, but I've not heard many moans about missing her."

Approaching Tomkyn Bridge School again through the splendid grounds, Kim was once more impressed by the great house itself and the calm, English quality of it all. *Lucky students, lucky me*, she thought.

She soon unpacked and settled into her rooms in Big School. She had a sitting room *cum* study with two casement windows looking over the grounds behind the house. There was a cobbled yard, some stables and outhouses, a walled garden, a large greenhouse with a smaller, newer one near to it. There were also some glass-topped frames she could see in the walled garden. *Cucumber beds, perhaps?* She had a bedroom beyond her sitting room, complete with en suite bathroom. The bathroom had a pinkish marble tile floor with white tiles on the wall. There was a tub with a glass door and a detachable showerhead at the end of the tub where there were the hot and cold taps. The shower had the Tomkyn Bridge regulation water heater. She would have a quick shower before dinner. Her bedroom had a single bed that would accommodate two at a pinch, but it was not a real double bed. It had a deep apricot-yellow bedspread. There were very pale apricot walls with white paint on doors and window frames and sills. The fitted carpet was apple-green and in almost new condition. She wondered who had occupied these rooms before her. Miss Tew? A window, opposite the bed head wall, again looked over the back of the building. There was a fire escape from a small platform near this window. A curious little gothic pointed door in the wall gave onto the metal platform. In case of fire, it was an easy matter to go from her window to the fire escape. There was another window on the far side of the fire escape. *Another teacher's rooms*, she surmised.

Kim's sitting room had the same apple-green carpet and the same paint work. The furniture was solid, comfortable.

She had two armchairs, a sofa for two adults or three girls on best behaviour, sitting up, not lolling. There was a bentwood chair near to one side of an oak kneehole desk between the two windows. The desk, probably Victorian, was topped with a rectangle of green leather. It was also equipped with a four-tier, in-out tray set. The chair in matching green leather was an old-fashioned swivel chair. Each arm ended with the carved head of a lion. It was obviously for someone working at the desk. There were bookshelves lining most of one wall and one bookcase with glass doors. To one side of the room, near the door leading to the bedroom, there were two louvered wooden doors that slid open by folding. Behind them was a counter. At the end that backed onto her bathroom was a small sink with hot and cold water. There was a cooking device with two rings, a kettle, an automatic drip-feed coffeepot, and a toaster. Above the counter were cupboards containing four cups and saucers, four soup or cereal bowls, four side plates, four larger plates, four tumblers, and four wineglasses. Under the counter were cupboards with cooking utensils, and cleaning equipment such as sponges, cat's tongue scourers, washing up liquid, and Vim. A drawer contained knives, forks, spoons; a second drawer contained a plastic spatula for cooking, a can opener, two corkscrews, and some nut crackers.

"Gee, what a lucky girl am I!" exclaimed Kim aloud. She was already thinking of how she could make the place cosier and give it a little more character.

There was a knock on the door.

"Come in!"

A tall, weather-beaten man entered. "I'm Holroyd," he announced. "I believe you've met my better half."

"Yes, indeed Mr. Holroyd."

"Well, I've got some heavy parcels on the dolly. I'll unload, shall I?"

He spoke with the local accent, Kim guessed.

"Fine. Put them over there, would you, by the bookshelves. That's kind of you."

"Just doing my job, miss," he grunted as he unloaded two of the parcels.

"Well, I appreciate it." Kim smiled and he smiled briefly, then looked away quickly to turn to other parcels waiting to be manhandled. He seemed a little embarrassed.

"Well, I'll be off then." He looked at her hair rather than into her eyes and then trundled the dolly back along the corridor.

Kim closed and locked her door and went to the bedroom, locking that door. It was time for her shower. She undressed and walked into the bathroom. Looking at herself critically in the long mirror, she had to admit that she looked good and different from her usual self. The new look pleased her. Control no doubt would agree. So would Momo. Perhaps Mr. Holroyd had been made shy by her new good looks.

***

Dinner was a more relaxed occasion this time. People shook hands and said they were pleased she was joining the team. Miss Mason said she liked the new hairstyle and was pleased her books had arrived safely. Tomorrow, she could meet with her HOD (Head of Department) to study the plans for the summer term. Kim smiled to herself about the similar use of initials as in the civil services. Miss Mason also wanted to see her at 10:30 a.m. to talk about extracurricular activities. Could she coach girls on a pistol range? Kim said she thought it a good idea as she had once done some shooting herself. Safety was very important, of course.

As she went to bed that night, having arranged her books, Kim thought again of the hooded young terrorist dying on a barge turned into a bomb. And all for some fanatical old men? Some religion challenged by a modernity that had arrived so rapidly? For a patriarch sacrificing young men and women and then some matriarchs wailing over bits of their corpses? This was history. And history was a long and cruel narrative. Control was right. Choices had to be made.

She now felt certain she had made the right, the only choice, back there on that barge gliding towards a huge explosion. Someone had made the choice to assassinate her. The other women in the toilet, the dead and the wounded, had had no choice. They had to be victims, though they were not the target. She was certain of that. Was she making the right choice now? Time would tell. She had a new identity, a new job, a new term in which to discover whether she would stay in the open world or move back into the shadows. And what about love? Control wanted her. But was he capable of love and was she capable of making him love her? Was *she* capable of love? If the man appeared who could unlock her heart, love would be released. She was sure of it. Yes, she could love as fiercely as she could fight. She was suddenly almost asleep. Milton's lines came to disturb her briefly:

And now the sun had stretch'd out all the hills,
And now was dropt into the Western bay;
At last he rose, and twitch'd his Mantle blew:
Tomorrow to fresh Woods, and Pastures new.
Tomorrow.

Who had betrayed her? How had they managed to find her? *We move on, we move on*, she thought—and drifted into sleep, into that other country, where we dream.

Kim was in a stone cottage she had not seen before. She moved across a living room to a narrow staircase leading to the rooms above. She paused at the foot of the stairs. Bruno was speaking.

"I shall now kill you if you don't tell me where she is." A man's voice, scarcely audible, and one she did not know, replied.

"I have told you. I have never seen this woman. I don't know her."

There was a gurgling noise and a thump on the floor above. Then someone was coming down the stairs. Bruno's voice was muttering something.

"You silly bastard. Choke on your own blood. I'll find her. I shall peel the skin from her face before I kill her."

Kim was ready. As he reached the bottom step, she grabbed the ankle that came into view, pushing it vertically upwards. He was on his back. His head hit the stairs with a satisfying crack, before he could even let out a cry. His knife clattered to the floor. Kim broke both his ankles. His eyes were fluttering. She blinded him with her fingers, as she'd been taught. Why bother with his knife, except to slit his veins.

"You listen to me, you swine. I'm slitting your veins. Now, one and now the other. With your own knife. You're dying, Bruno. You're dying. I'm not!"

Kim woke up. She was safe in bed in her rooms in Tomkyn Bridge School. *Thank God. Good-bye, world of shadows.* She got up and made a cup of tea. She planned some French lessons before going once more to sleep before another dawn.

CHAPTER FIFTY-NINE

Graham dreamed that he was walking through a forest of silver birch trees stretching from the foothills of the Rocky Mountains east of Jasper for two hundred kilometres towards the city of Edmonton. It was, it seemed, late spring. There was no sound, but that of his and Anne's progress as they walked hand in hand along a trail in the forest.

"Whatever happens, Graham, we shall survive. You'll see."

He felt that yes, all would be well, all manner of things would work out for the best. Then he woke up. It was 2:00 a.m. by his bedside alarm. He got out of bed and went to the telephone. It would already be day time back in France.

"Hello, Anne?"

"Non, monsieur, stay please. I go for *madame. Je vais la chercher."*

"Allô? Anne de Crevennes. C'est M. Wills?"

"No, Anne. Graham Curtis here. I just wanted to speak to you again."

"How charming. But you already phoned when you got back to Canada."

"Yes and now I'm phoning again. Can you spare a minute?"

"For you, of course. But what time is it there?"

"Er two five a.m. But . . ."

"Ce n'est pas vrai! You should be asleep at home."

"I was dreaming and I awoke. We were in a vast forest of silver birch trees in Alberta. I think we were lost."

"Oh, *mon dieu,* did bears run after us?"

"No. It was very quiet. Only our tramping on twigs could be heard. But I was somehow uneasy."

"Were we scared?"

"I don't know. Not exactly. But you said something very clearly and I recognized your voice. You were with me and we were holding hands.

"In that case, whatever happens we'll be okay. We will survive in this dream. You'll see."

"My God, it's uncanny. Anne, that's what you said a few minutes ago in my dream!"

"Really? Well, that's very strange. But it's what I think. You will be okay, Graham."

"Anne, I am truly astounded. Look, I can be in France early in May. Can I see you then and we can do some things together?"

"Of course. Why not?"

"Everything will be all right. I know it will."

"Yes. I think so, too. I am glad I feature in your dreams! Now get some sleep. We'll talk again another time. But now, dream of me again!"

"I'm sure I will! Good. Good night, Anne."

"Good night, Graham, my dear, dear man."

***

They were both working against the clock because they were also fixing last minute details for the wedding. They had decided to marry in the local church Mary sometimes attended. Not a really regular churchgoer, Mary, however, knew the clergyman, the Reverend John Batchelor. It amused them to be married by a Batchelor, himself a married man. Mary liked the way he sang in services and intoned *Grant peace in our time, O Lord*. The church was called St. Mark's, but bore no resemblance whatsoever to St. Mark's in Venice. This did not worry them one little bit. Mary's mother would give her away. Graham was to be best man. He had asked when he rang them from Anne de Crevennes' place in Eden Roc whether she could attend with him. Paul and Mary had no objection to her swelling their small numbers a little. In fact, Paul was very impressed that Graham was obviously getting along just fine with Mme. la Marquise. Perhaps, he said, they should try to get married in Lichfield Cathedral. He then said no, and Mary said no. No. St. Marks it would be, as in their recent plans. Afterwards, there would be a small, but expensive reception in a country house hotel that stood in its own grounds.

The day before the wedding, Paul stayed in a comfortable local hotel. Mrs. Rao, his mother-in-law to be, had arrived by train to stay with Mary. Paul and Mary had driven to Birmingham New Street to meet her. They embraced and chatted comfortably and without any stiffness, even though Paul and Mrs. Rao did not really know one another very well, having met before only a couple of times. Nina Rao was a slim woman of middling height with a strikingly handsome bone structure with fairly high cheekbones. Her eyes were still large and expressive, despite the age that showed so clearly in her skin. She wore a smart woolen suit in chestnut brown for traveling, with brown leather brogues and a matching leather handbag. The wrinkles and lines of her neck were partly hidden by a Hermes scarf in white, brown, and green with touches of orange. In her late sixties, she was still a handsome and active woman.

"I don't need to tell you this, Paul, but I will. Mary's a very fine person. And I know you very little, but I feel instinctively that you are right for her. I like you very much from what I know about you. I've read a good deal of your writing, you know."

"Really? I'm very glad, Nina. Flattered, in fact."

"Flattery isn't it, Paul, I just wanted to know what my Mary is getting into! I'm a mum after all."

"Oh Mother!" said Mary, who was driving and concentrating on the road and other drivers.

"You're a very conscientious one at that. I'm proud to be marrying your daughter and having found you as my mother-in-law."

Mrs. Rao put her hand briefly on his shoulder. They were almost at Mary's. Paul unloaded her luggage at Mary's flat and lingered awhile just to see Mary a little longer and to see if he could help in any way. Mary had spoken by phone to her locum; she had five free days. When Nina Rao caught sight of Mary's engagement ring, she admired it just as much as Paul had done when he had found it in Paris. It was now a familiar part of Mary's being, her presence. Liz, too, had been enthralled by its beauty on Mary's slim hand. Paul told Nina how they had found it in a small jeweler's just off the Place Vendôme. Mary was really delighted by its classic beauty, but mainly because it brought back their time together in Paris, and the day on which they had found the little shop just off the famous square.

Leaving Mary's car for her and her mother if they needed it, Paul walked back to the hotel, ten minutes away on foot. He ordered a coffee and checked everything once more. The license was taken care of; the wedding ring reposed in a dark-blue box lined with white silk in the little safe in his hotel room; his passport was beside it; there was a packet of bank notes there, too; his suit and other clothes for the wedding were together, hanging ready in the wardrobe for tomorrow. His bag for going away was almost packed. He had to check with the photographer and the florist. Two more phone calls ensured that all would be well the next day. The cars were next on his list. He checked with the rental firm. All was confirmed. His cell phone rang.

"Paul? Graham here. How's it going?"

"Just fine. It's only a matter of getting the best man here on time!"

"We're on our way. Anne and I will arrive later this afternoon. We've rented a car."

"Great. You can drive straight to the hotel; it's not far from Lichfield."

"We've confirmed and pinpointed them on the map. We are booked for tonight and tomorrow night."

"Perfect, Graham. How's Anne?"

"Wonderful! She's looking forward to meeting you again and to meeting Mary."

"They'll get along famously. I'll see you at the Marlborough Hotel's restaurant in Sutton Coldfield, when you are ready. We three can have dinner together and go over things for tomorrow. Is that okay"

"Sounds perfect. What time shall we present ourselves for your inspection at the Marlborough?"

"Whenever you like. Tell me when you'll be ready to come."

"About six p.m. to six fifteen p.m.?"

"That sounds about right. Okay. Wonderful. See you soon."

Paul ate a light salad lunch with a bottle of Perrier water, not champagne. The mobile rang again.

"Jack Moffat here. Is that Paul?"

"Yes, it is. Hello, Jack, how are you?"

"Fine. It's just to let you know I'll be flying in tomorrow. All details are confirmed."

"Excellent. You can drive to Sutton Coldfield, or do you need transport from the airport?"

"No. I've a car lined up. I should get to Sutton in the forenoon or maybe about noon."

"Good. Come to the Marlborough Hotel. They serve a decent lunch. We can lunch together. We've booked you in at the White House, not far from Lichfield, for that night, along with the rest of us."

"Great. One thing. Do you mind if I wear the kilt?"

"Good Lord, no! It's *de rigueur*. We'd be annoyed if you didn't."

"I'm not bringing the pipes."

"Do you play?"

"Wish I did. I was just setting your mind at rest."

"Get on with you. The 'Pibroch of Donnal Dhu' is one of my all-time favourites. You could say it's a golden oldie! Mind you, not quite the song for a wedding with its, 'Leave the bride at the altar.'"

"Great Scott! Well, best of luck and all that. Mary's an ace. See you tomorrow."

"You bet. And thanks so much for the postnuptial arrangements."

"Looking forward to it. Bye now."

After lunch, Paul spent nearly an hour swimming in the pool. He was in good shape and wanted to keep it that way. He then went up to his room and telephoned some editors he knew quite well to see what was brewing. One wanted an article on the pedophile Internet market, another on the arms used by criminal gangs in Britain, and another on the *Entente Cordiale*, the anniversary of which had come and gone without making waves. He chose to tackle the latter first. The article could bring up the whole question of Anglo-French relations and the noticeable attempts in the French press to marginalize Britain, as if the awkward little place didn't exist, except for ludicrous customs like tiddlywinks championships or else disasters like mad cow disease. On the British side, he deplored the gutter press version of Froggies and Frogland. The deadline was light years away by his freelancer's reckoning and it allowed for some interesting historical research. The editor who suggested the project noted that Lord Lansdowne, as well as King Edward VII, should get plenty of space as well as the French side of the equation. The more he pondered this, after putting down the phone, the more Paul liked the project. Its Anglo-French topicality was something he could address very well and very astutely. He might be able to interview the current Lord Salisbury and the Marquis de Breteuil whose grandfathers had signed the original accord. What with the wedding, the friends coming to the wedding, and this new project, Paul was feeling that life was full of rewards as well as horrors. He must not forget that. People needed the good times.

He decided to buy a small gift to welcome Graham and Anne. He was walking away from a bookstore with a copy of *The Piano Shop on the Left Bank* when the phone rang.

"Paul? Graham here."

"Yes, how's it going?"

"We've settled into the White House. Love it. We thought we'd drive over now and see you at the Marlborough. Or is it too early for you?"

"That's just the ticket. I'll be in my room. It'll take about thirty-five minutes."

"Okay. See you."

Things are warming up, thought Paul, as he turned into the street leading to the Marlborough. Back in his room, he checked the safe. Everything was there as it should have been. *No burglars here, thank heavens.* Why was he fussing? *Relax*, he said to himself. He lay on the bed thinking of what his life had been so far. Family, such as was left of it, since the early deaths of his parents. School and school friends, sport, studies, university, more study, more friends, a number of girlfriends from about the age of eleven onwards, his first jobs as a news reporter, his articles, his travels, and then Kalitza. He had made love to her once, entered the blood heat of her body, felt her passion, known his own lust and passion, and then the misery and loneliness, when he had thought she was dead. She had changed his life. His obsession with her had been at first a kind of madness. His obsession with the mystery of her actions, her relationship with that frighteningly skeletal man, these now seemed a strange aberration, unconnected with the reality of his own life. He had left behind his frustration and vexation. The reality of his own life! He remembered the exquisite anticipation and excitement of Kalitza's making love with him in the Mody Road area of Kowloon. But then he had turned to Mary, had taken up again with Mary. And this was his most precious reality. Mary was no mirage, no angelic being, appearing and disappearing at will. He thought over this wonderful time, when they were wooing each other, time that traced a path, quite short and straight, in fact, to today, tomorrow, a significant future, for them both. Did his heart say to him that he must duck out? He must run? He must find Kalitza again, wherever she might be? The answer was no. Did he feel good treading the path leading to Mary? Yes. Did he feel excited to be marrying Mary? Yes. After such a short time of intimacy with her, everything had fallen into place. It felt completely and satisfyingly *right*. He was in touch now with his true feelings. Was he in love? Yes. Did he love Mary? Yes. Did he want children? Yes! He knew, at last, where he was going. It was, after all, a path human beings had followed for a long time!

Graham and Anne arrived at about 5:30 p.m. The front desk alerted Paul, who combed his hair, put on a jacket and his shoes, and went down to meet them in the lobby lounge.

"Ah Paul, *c'est un vrai plaisir!*" Anne seemed sparkling and younger and energetic in her light-blue linen pant suit and jangly bracelets, her shining costume jewelry. They kissed on both cheeks.

"Welcome to Britain, Anne, even if it's only the Midlands. There's a more exotic England that awaits you another time! But we are very happy that you could come over for the wedding. Graham, you darling man, thanks for coming such a long way and for being best man!" The friends hugged.

"Paul, I have to ask you a leading question, before we do anything else. Do you have the ring?"

"Yes, I do."

"That's what you have to say tomorrow."

"Oh, that's droll," laughed Anne.

"You see, Paul, Anne laughs at my jokes, even if you don't."

"Come on, let's sit down and laugh our way through a pot of tea or coffee. Tea cakes? Scones anyone?"

"Tea with a slice of lemon will be good," said Anne.

They ordered. Paul's cell phone rang.

"Paul Wills."

"Darling, I wondered when you'd be able to get a moment. Has anyone arrived?"

"Yes. I'm with Anne and Graham. They arrived a few minutes ago."

"Maggie Yeung?"

"Not yet. Don't worry. Hang on. There's a fabulous Chinese woman in the lobby here—she's just walked in and gone to reception. It's not the quiet and self-effacing Maggie we knew as students."

"Well, she's a specialist now!"

"Ah. Well, she's looking good. Hang on. Excuse me a moment. I'm going to reception. Hello, I'm Paul. Do you remember me? Maggie? Yes?"

"I'm Maggie Yeung. You're Paul Wills, the one we used to call 'Scruff'!"

"'Fraid so. Look, have a word with Mary."

Paul handed Maggie the phone and went back to join his other friends.

"It's another guest?" asked Anne.

"Yes. And she remembered that I was called 'Scruff' when I was a student!"

"How naughty of her," said Graham.

They could see Maggie laughing and talking at the desk. Then she closed the phone and walked over to them. She was an elegant woman, tall for a Cantonese. But her grandfather had been from the North. Her long, black hair was tied in a ponytail that fell below her shoulders. She wore a close-fitting yellow coat with matching casual, low-heeled shoes. Over her shoulder was slung the gilt chain of a Chanel black leather handbag. The men stood up.

"Graham! You were a graduate student, wasn't it?" They shook hands.

"Guilty!"

"Maggie was a student with us years ago, though I hasten to add that Maggie looks about three weeks older than when we knew her," said Paul, touching her lightly on her arm.

"Good one, Paul," said Maggie.

"In any case, Maggie Yeung, this is Anne de Crevennes, from France. Graham is over here for the summer and they have arrived from France today. We're all booked into the White House, a hotel not far away and we'll make our way over there after dinner. Is that okay?"

"Perfect. How do you do, Anne?" said Maggie. The two women shook hands.

"But Mary's invited me over to have dinner. Mary, Mrs. Rao, and I are all having our hair done together early tomorrow morning! That's why I booked in here and not at the White House for tonight."

"That's all fine then," said Paul. "Do you know how to get to Mary's from here?"

"Yes. Don't worry. I'm usually bored at the hairdressers, but this will be fun. I'll go up and get ready for the evening."

"Fine. We'll probably be gone for dinner ourselves soon. If we don't see you again tonight Maggie, see you tomorrow," said Paul.

***

Light began to strengthen and leak in at the edges of the curtains in Paul's room the next morning. He was relieved that he was no longer a young lad among the other young lads, relieved that he had not been made hopelessly drunk, relieved that he had not been driven to the middle of a forest miles away and left to make his way back to his own wedding, and relieved that a gaggle of grinning young men had not forced him into the arms of a half-naked call girl to help him say farewell to his life as a bachelor.

Paul had invited Graham to take room service breakfast with him. Anne had been considerate and discreet, having the previous night placed an order for breakfast in her room the next morning.

It was when the two friends were at breakfast that Paul gave Graham the ring.

"Paul, what a lovely ring! You are absolutely sure about this?"

"Hey, I'm not marrying you, you chump!" They both laughed.

"No," continued Paul, and then, "Absolutely sure. No second thoughts. Mary is a marvelous woman and will be a wonderful wife for me. We are both very much in love. I feel very lucky."

"That's great. I think she's superb, an ace, in fact, and I'm certain you'll be very, very happy together. You seem exactly right for one another. I'm glad for you both," said Graham."Someone else called her an ace. She's the ace of hearts, Graham."

"Sure is."

Paul and Graham arrived at St. Mark's ten minutes early with Anne, who was in a lime-green dress and matching coat with a navy trim. Her elegance and poise made Graham wish he could see her more often. Then he felt a sharp stab of guilt. Her hat was a cluster of exotic feathers, her gloves where a soft white, matching her high-heeled shoes. Her French look seemed emphatic, dramatic, and sophisticated. Graham wore a tan summer suit with a bright-blue shirt and a designer silk tie with large poppies on a yellow and green background. Paul was in a light-grey suit of French design with a tie in silk from Lyon. It was hand painted with a design copied from a pair of gentleman's stockings of the eighteenth century. He had found the tie in a small boutique in the arcades of the Palais Royal in Paris. His black shoes were impeccable. A few minutes later, Liz and Dave turned up, Liz in a dashing, off-the-shoulder silk outfit in blue with gloves and shoes to match, a light piece of veiling, navy blue, with a matching velvet bow serving instead of a hat. She had changed her mind about a sari; it could seem a pretentious upstaging of the bride! Dave was in a light-cream linen suit, pink shirt, with a kingfisher-blue silk tie covered in tiny red elephants. Jack came close on their heels wearing the complete Scottish outfit, including a dirk in his sock, and grinning from his brightly shining face.

"Sorry I'm a bit later than I should have been," he announced, "but at the car park, I was stopped by an old sailor who insisted on telling me a long rigmarole about a sea voyage!"

"Ce n'est pas vrai!" exclaimed Anne.

"It certainly isn't," laughed Graham, "He's referring to Coleridge's poem, 'The Rime of the Ancient Mariner.'"

"Graham will give us a lecture on it later on at dinner," said Paul.

At this point the organist started to play the music they had chosen. The Reverend Batchelor appeared in his soutane, covered with a wonderful lace "pinny" as Liz referred to it later.

Paul had to stand facing the altar with Graham to his right. The Rev. Batchelor suddenly beamed, and Paul turned to see the object of his evident pleasure. The music was louder and triumphal as Mary entered wearing the dress Paul had not been allowed to see before. It was a shimmering silk in very pale-yellow that clung to her figure, but behind and at her sides a huge wave of white was the train which Maggie held for her. Mary's veil had a spume-like train, also, which contrasted with the glossy dark coils of her elaborately pinned up hair and the serpentine tendrils that coiled down the sides of her face from her temples. On her head, above the veil, she wore a coronal of small yellow roses. She carried a bouquet of streaked red and yellow roses, just opened from bud into flower. Although Mary's mother was giving her away, Jack Moffat was looking suitably avuncular and beaming.

Nina Rao was in a biscuit-colored suit with matching shoes in a rough linen texture. She wore a cameo at the neck of her cream silk blouse. She carried a similar bouquet to that of her daughter. Maggie was a wonderfully sleek bridesmaid in her simple, sleeveless dress of classic cut. It was in orange Thai silk, with Chinese collar and a cheongsam-type slit up one seam rather than both, and this revealed the shapely lines of her right leg as far as mid-thigh. Her matching shoes were emphasized by the very light brown of her legs in gossamer hose. On her shining, highlighted, urchin cut she wore a coronal of red and yellow roses.

The ceremony was a simplified Church of England one. They had kept, "With this ring, I thee wed," and "With my body, I thee worship," as well as "to honour," but they had dropped "obey." Neither would obey the other and so they would live in honourable chaos. The vows and exchange of rings went off without a hitch. Neither of the rings was dropped to roll out of sight and fall through a black metal grating into the crypt or a tomb, or to any other un-get-at-able place. So they got hitched, as Jack said afterwards, without a hitch. When they signed the register, Mrs. Rao and Graham were witnesses. Nor did anyone shout out objections to the marriage from the small congregation. There was no attic in a mansion owned by Paul with a mad first wife languishing there. Apart from the wedding party, there was a cub reporter in attendance from a local paper, one from a Birmingham paper, and an old lady who was one of St. Mark's regulars. She was there every day, rain or shine, as she put it. Weddings were one of her treats.

The bride and groom, Mrs. Rao, and Maggie, with Graham holding her hand, emerged from the church to be strewn with rice and confetti by Liz, Dave, Anne, and Jack, all in splendid form. The professional photographer went into action again. He had been discreet in the church, getting digital shots of crucial moments in the ceremony. This time he was using an elaborate 35 mm Canon, with an Olympus as back up, in case of any glitches with the Canon. He was delighted that Jack Moffat was in his Scottish dress. It added a very fine image always to the "pix"—the photographer kept using this word as he got them ready for his shoot. Jack had to hold hands with Maggie for a number of pix and she didn't mind, even though Jack was a relative stranger.

Later, when they were all at the White House Country Hotel, there was much frivolity when they had more pix as they drank an elegant Bruno Paillard champagne and wandered about the formal garden in front of the old manor house. After all the photographs had been taken in the garden, the photographer gave Graham a few disposable cameras for use at the dinner by anyone who might want to take pictures themselves. Graham could mail them to him in the special envelope he provided, and the results would be sent with the official pix to the bride and groom. Jack and Maggie found themselves standing together on a diamond-shaped lawn.

"Well, it's a perfect day for it."

"Yes. Jack, isn't it?" Maggie replied.

"That's right, I am Jack Moffat, by the way. And Maggie, what's your surname?"

"Yeung. I'm Maggie Yeung."

"Young. Are there a lot of Chinese with that surname?"

"Millions, I should think," she laughed, "but it's not 'young' as in 'We are just the young ones'! It's more Yi-ung."

"Yi-ung," repeated Jack.

"Now say it again, quickly, and repeat it quickly, quickly."

Jack followed her instructions until she told him he had it perfectly.

"Are you a teacher?" he asked.

"No, I'm a doctor. Mary and I were medical students together. We're old friends. How do you know Mary, or is it Paul?"

"Oh, I met Paul a couple of times, but I know Mary from when she was about seventeen, and she wanted parachute jumping lessons."

"I didn't know she did that for a sport."

"She doesn't. In fact, her mother didn't want her to do it, because it's dangerous, and Mary's her only child. Mary came to tell me she could not continue."

"I expect she was disappointed. When she sets her mind on something . . ."

"I know. But I gave her a ride in a glider as a consolation prize. We've kept in touch ever since."

"Where did you learn to fly?"

"Oh, instead of paying for lessons, I joined the RAF and got into pilot training."

"Wah! Was it dangerous, Jack?"

"Only when you're a beginner and only when there's a war on!"

"Are you still in the RAF?"

"No. I got out after five years, Maggie."

"So, what do you do now?"

"I have a small company in Scotland and give people short trips around the country for pleasure or business."

"Fabulous. So you give joy rides. Would you give me a joy ride?"

Jack looked straight into her brilliant jet eyes. Her perfectly made-up face was a beautiful mask. There was no hint of humour. It was a perfectly straight remark, or was it?

"Come to Scotland. I'd give you a joy ride any time, Maggie."

She suddenly burst out laughing. Jack laughed as well.

"Jack, I'll give you a joy ride, too!"

"Now that's an offer I can't refuse."

"Well, that's settled then."

"You two! Do you want to play croquet?"

It was Dave, wearing the cream linen suit with pink shirt, now a bit rumpled. He looked like a TV celebrity. Liz was grinning and swinging a croquet mallet. She looked attractive and relaxed in her silk wedding outfit. She had taken off her shoes to play barefooted on the grass, unaware as yet of the dangers of croquet.

"Okay. If you show me how to play," said Maggie. As she turned to join the others, she said to Jack, "I'll see you in Scotland."

But he followed her so that Maggie and Jack soon found themselves playing croquet with Dave and Liz.

After their drinks in the garden, those who were staying the night found their respective rooms, bathed or showered, and dressed for dinner. None of them was a vegetarian, but since Mary had planned the menu, there were plenty of vegetables, an excellent salad, and dishes of fresh fruit. They started with lobster bisque. Then they had langoustines. Salad was served with an appetizing balsamic vinegar dressing. There was then a choice of coq au vin, turbot, sirloin of beef, or leg of lamb, accompanied by new potatoes, braised leeks, cauliflower, broccoli, and green peas. There was a board of English cheeses from selected farms rather than the nearest supermarket. The Stilton was creamy, yet firm and inimitable. The cheddar was nothing like plastic or whitish rubber. It had a pleasing bite to it. The Lancashire was agreeably crumbly with a delicious delicacy. The Caerphilly, from a farm near Carmarthen, was delicate and yet, insistent. Dessert was either lime sorbet with vodka or a soup of red fruit. There was wonderfully nut-laden, homemade brown bread and, of course, bowls of fresh fruit. The wedding cake, a modest three tiers, stood in the middle of the table with a huge silver knife nearby. Not surprisingly, as Graham remarked, all of them were good trenchermen and trencherwomen, added Dave.

"Can we have trencherpersons?" asked Liz.

"We could," said Dave, "but why not trencherfolk?"

"Trencherfolk," said Graham as he tapped his glass with a silver fork. He stood up and raised his glass of Sancerre, served after the bisque.

"Trencherfolk, I give you the bride and groom."

The little band of well-wishers stood and drank a toast.

"Paul, a few words, please," said Graham.

Paul stood up. He looked around the table at his friends and his wife. Wife!

"Friends," he said, "I've just realized I'm married and I have a wife!"

"I'm glad that's sunk in," said Graham. They all laughed.

"An excellent woman. And I have a wonderful mother-in-law. I have also a marvelous group of friends. Thank you all for being here. Especially Mary! I don't know what we'd have done without her! No, but what is love? As the Bard said, ''Tis not hereafter.' It's not in the afterlife, this human thing, it's in the here and now. And if you can find it, you have to have it, and hang on to it. This is the happiest day I have ever had. I hope that I can give Mary as much happiness as she gives me. I want also to say a special word to my mother-in-law. In the short time I have known her, I realize how lucky I am that she got married and had Mary! I've also realized what a fine woman she is—she has helped us unstintingly without telling us what we should do or what we should have done. That's a big temptation for some parents. Another thing I have realized is that behind every reasonably competent man, there's a greater woman! Let's drink a toast to Mary."

There was a chorus of "To Mary."

"And now," Paul continued, "let's drink to Mrs. Rao."

There was a chorus of "Mrs. Rao."

Paul sat down and kissed Mary and Mrs. Rao. There was a round of applause. Before the chatter resumed, Graham stood and tapped his glass again.

"I'm now going to say a few words. I'm going to reveal all. Paul will never be the same again at the end of this speech!"

Loud laughter and cries of, "Tell us! Tell us!"

"On second thoughts," said Graham, "there's not a lot to tell. Paul was born, grew up, went to university, became a journalist, traveled about a bit, and then, goodness knows how he did it, married Mary. Oh, and made a name for himself in the United States by calling Jimmy Carter the greatest president since Abe Lincoln."

"Not true!" said Paul.

"Actually, Paul is a really true friend. Over the years I've known him, that's what I have discovered. Oh, and another thing. He has a medal for bravery. That's true as well. He rescued a woman who was on fire in a lodging house he was in, when he was a young man of twenty-four."

Paul looked embarrassed as the little group of friends applauded.

"There are different kinds of love," Graham continued. He stopped suddenly. There was an expectant hush. Graham then went on in a voice only slightly distorted by the emotion he was feeling, "My mother-in-law, and I, and Anne, and Mrs. Rao, all know about married love . . ."

"Call me Nina, please," said Mrs. Rao.

"Nina . . . Nina, she also knows about a mother's love. Friendship, if it's honest, and true, and generous, is also a kind of love. I think everyone here knows about it."

Cries of, "Here, here!"

"A toast, then, to friendship and to love."

"I just want to say something," said Mary, standing up. "Paul's parents have both passed away and sadly cannot be with us today. I, too, am grateful that they produced this man of mine!" There were cheers. "For all my medical knowledge, it's still a mystery to me how our parents ever manage to have children. I cannot imagine how! Why did I say that, Mummy?"

The guests laughed, especially when Nina Rao spoke up, "It's a bit late now for me to instruct you in the facts of life. You'll just have to find out for yourself, dear."

After the main course was over and the cheese was being passed around with vintage port, Anne de Crevennes tapped her glass and stood up. The little group of friends looked at her expectantly.

"I will just say a little word. I see the happiness and pleasure of this couple. I have known Graham now for a short while. But I see he has humour and warmth. I saw Paul only briefly. He was working on an article. He interviewed me. But I am very touched by the way I have been accepted into this small group and been given the privilege of joining you. As an historian, I can say that marriage has a very long history, and despite its different forms in different cultures and its obvious difficulties, people have never abandoned it. Even nowadays, people keep getting married. Today proves it! And now gays want to get married and are married. So, it has some mysterious power. And history teaches something else. As we've already been reminded, behind every great man there's an equally great woman. I know Paul said something similar and know he will be pleased that I emphasize that remark. But behind every great woman, there's also a great man! You see, he's grinning. To two greats: Paul and Mary!"

They all toasted the bride and groom again.

"Just a word," said Jack, and they all groaned.

"To the big cheeses! I mean, of course, Stilton and cheddar!"

And they started on the cheese with gusto.

***

That night Jack knocked on Maggie's door.
"Who is it?"
"It's Jack. Can we talk?"
She opened the door a little and looked round it.
"In Scotland!" she said and gently closed the door.
Jack fished in his wallet, took out a visiting card, and slipped it under Maggie's door. He went back to his own room. Maggie, near her bed, saw the card come under the door. She went over and picked it up. *Yes*, she thought. When she had a space of a few days of free time coming up, she would phone him, and go to see him and probably make love with him. He needed a wife. But not tonight.

***

The next morning, the small group had a friendly, relaxed breakfast, a bit sad that they were all going their different ways. Jack, though, was flying Paul, Mary, Graham, and Anne to France, before he flew back to Scotland. *And there*, he thought, *if I can make it happen, I'll get Maggie to visit me*. He thought she was a gem of a woman. He liked her very much. He wanted her in bed. Now, he realized, she had been right not to allow him into her room the night before. He had something to look forward to, with a longing he had not experienced since he was about twenty! What was happening to him? Not that, surely? Not falling in love? As he did the checks before they took off for France, Jack was humming to himself, "Falling in love again. Never wanted to. Don't know what to do. Can't help it!" As he hummed, Marlene Dietrich's smoky voice haunted his mind's ear.

This wedding was an old and new adventure beginning, as weddings always were, and still are. There was so much hope, so much passion, so much adventure, and so much promise in life. Anne was thinking, too, that life's wonder was all so fragile, her hand in Graham's, as the little aircraft passed into French air space.

CHAPTER SIXTY

Near St. Bees, in a classroom in Big School, Kim, known to her students as Miss Partridge, or the Game Bird, was teaching French to a group in the lower sixth form. It was made up of fifteen- and sixteen-year-old girls. It was almost the end of the period. Before the bell went, Alissa Partridge asked if there were any questions or general points to be cleared up. A bright girl, with auburn hair done into a top knot, said she was puzzled by something she had read in another class.

"Can I ask about it now, Miss Partridge?"

"You may, Brenda."

"Well, it was that statement in Keats, 'Beauty is truth, truth beauty—that is all ye know on earth, and all ye need to know.' I still can't see what it really says, Miss Partridge."

"Brenda, lots of people are puzzled by it. But we could talk about it for an entire seminar if we had the time. In any case, this is French, not an English literature class. I think, though, you have to be clear as to whether it's the urn that's speaking. You might think about the problems of translating those lines into French. It's 'Ode on a Grecian Urn,' I think?"

"Yes, miss."

"Remember the urn is a decorative work of art, but, in fact, it also depicts scenes of love and dancing and music and of some pagan sacrifice. In fact, it shows human life going on. And yet, the people who looked at the vase over centuries of its existence, where are they?"

"Dead and gone, miss."

"Yes. But the poet is alive, in a sense, still, because he's looking at the vase and writing about it. Is it beautiful and is the poem beautiful?"

"I think the vase is beautiful, and I think the poem's just as beautiful."

"I agree, Brenda."

"And is Keats dead, Brenda?"

"Yes, miss, he died so young, and I can't bear it, miss, that he's dead."

There was a silence in the room, broken only by the cries of some girls outside on the hockey field.

"But now we have his vision of Greek beauty in the poem and our experience of the beauty of his poem, don't we?"

"Yes."

"Beauty, when we can recognize it, is undeniable. It's a form of truth. Like love. There are lovers in the poem."

"Yes, miss. But is love a form of truth, like beauty?" Another girl put up her hand to speak.

"But lovers deceive each other, miss. What about Madame Bovary?"

"Yes, Fiona, but lovers are not quite the same as love. I think when they deceive each other, they have lost real love, or they are not experiencing love any more. I think love is fragile."

"But is beauty truth?" Brenda persisted.

"I think he means when we experience beauty, we are in the presence of an undeniable truth. And that truth, if in the beauty of a work of art, is true for every generation. And I think when we experience real love, it is undeniable; it's like truth in that we *know it by experiencing it.* We have certain experiences and processes of thought that are true for us. When we have lived right through something, it can't be shrugged off as lies. We may not know what truth or beauty or love is, and we may not be able to define them, but when we have experienced them by living them, we know those truths and what they feel like."

"Have you ever been in love, miss?" piped up another girl. The bell went.

"Saved by the bell!" said the Game Bird.

The girls joined in her laughter and noisily picked up their books. In the now empty classroom, Kate or Kim or Alissa the Game Bird walked to the window and looked out towards the hockey field, where girls were walking back to the pavilion to change. Had she ever been in love? In another life, and using another name; it seemed long, long ago. She realized she was now in the process of changing. Again. She kept changing. Why? Did she really want this new life? She had the luxury of teaching this one term before the summer vacation. The breathing space would give her time to find her real self, if she had one—or then at least to see if she could fashion a new self, another life. Control had to have an answer. She trusted her own feelings and thought processes. She usually found a way through the maze. The answer to her future would come to her one day, maybe quite soon, like a bird suddenly alighting near her in a garden, or at night, like a voice in her sleep. Then she would know. And with that knowledge, which would arrive as unexpectedly as snow in summer, she would make her decision. Yes, she was the game bird. But there was a hunting season and game birds became the prey. She brushed the thought aside. She had been responsible with others for the security of her country. Now responsible for her students, for some part of their future lives and, maybe, for a few choices they might make when leaving school, she was content. She was a responsible woman. She knew also that she was the Game Bird.

THE END

CPSIA information can be obtained at www.ICGtesting.com
Printed in the USA
LVOW06s0504100614

389268LV00001B/36/P